The Empire Of Texas
And
The Star Of India

By Rodger Olsen

With Special Thanks

To Lt. Col. Dave Grossman
For His Help, Editing, And Advice

To Leo Frankowski
For encouragement, comments, and editing.

To Mike Hubble
For His Help, Editing, And Advice

To Chris Ciulla
For a great idea and a great cover.

And
To the dozens of people who helped with editing, critique, and
encouragement.

Hunley Graphic Artwork copyright Daniel Dowdey
and used with his permission.
See www.dowdey.com for his other work.

Cover by Chris Ciulla

Published by Great Authors Online – And Rodger Olsen
16440 Monterey St. Lake Elsinore, Ca 92530

The Code Of The West

1. Don't kill no one who don't need killing.

2. Don't steal unless your children are hungry.

3. A man don't lie unless he is fishing.

4. A man protects woman and children.

5 Your word is your measure. If it's bad, so are you.

6. Do not insult or injure others, and do not allow them to do it to you or yours.

7. A man don't ever pass up a good chance to shut up.

8 . A man don't pick on the little guy.

9. A man minds his own business.

10. A man don't complain and don't need to Explain.

11. A man's word is his law.

12. Blessed be Samuel Colt, for he made all men equal.

Chapter 1   A Walk in the Moonlight

Ranger recruit Burton Adams, future Emperor of Texas, someday to be King of Kansas, Duke Of Arkansas and NewMex, and protector of his people, turned 18 years old sitting on a pile of rubble in the roofless ruins of an abandoned gas station. It wasn't surprising, as all the emperors of Texas began their working lives as "Ranger Adams." Tonight, he scanned a moonlit panorama of rubble through the empty window frame. Abandoned for 400 years, most of the wooden buildings in Old Lubbock were just piles of grass covered termite food. Some of the concrete and brick buildings had done better and had recognizable walls and even a few roofs. On the horizon, a few short stubs of sky scrapers could be made out against the background of stars. More than buildings had been lost. Even with a sharp intellect and the best education in Texas, Recruit Adams had no idea what a gas station was or that the building he was sitting in had been one.

His friend and fellow recruit, Wilson, watched the shadows from a side window, resting his Winchester on the empty sill in front of him. They were in this town, this night, because bandits had been raiding the mining companies in this area. West Waco Mining was burrowing into an ancient skyscraper for it's steel frame and copper wiring. Two other nearby companies had been attacked by bandits who came after dark, overpowered the guards, and drove away with the ore wagons. It wasn't a fast way to get rich, but robbing a Texas bank was as close as a man could come to legal suicide, and ore rustling must have seemed safer. During the last raid, they had simplified their getaway by killing the guards, and that got the undivided attention of the local Rangers.

As with all night duty, the real problem was not fear, but fatigue. Adams fought to keep his eyes open and his mind on the shadows outside. There were several other two-man teams in the ruins around him and the lieutenant watched with four men on a surviving roof behind him. This was their second night of waiting and watching. It would be their last. Adams glanced around at Wilson and whispered, "Think they'll come tonight? "

Wilson's nodded slightly. "Unless that's a pack of the biggest and quietest dogs you ever seen." He gestured with his rifle. "Look over there."

In the bright moonlight, the bandits were moving down an overgrown and rubble-strewn street. The movement that Wilson had seen was the leader stepping over a fallen concrete lamp post. Behind him, five men were doing a bad job of crouching, tip toeing, sneaking and stumbling through the semi-darkness. Eventually they reached the point where they were spread out in a line in front of the troopers.

The Rangers watched the group as it drew close to their position. Wilson joined Adams at the front window, and after a moment, nudged his friend. "Something's wrong. Watch for some more of 'em."

Adams kept his eyes on the bandits. "I don't see any more out there."

Wilson scanned the darkness. "They took more than a dozen ore wagons on their last job, and they didn't do it with six stumblebums, so watch for the rest."

Their conversation was interrupted by the flares rising from the lieutenant's position and arcing down behind the bandits. When the flares hit the ground, the bandits were brightly back lit and the Lieutenant's voice rang out from the darkness, "Drop 'em or die with 'em".

Dazed by the light, the bandits froze momentarily, and then dove for cover and started shooting into the dark. The Rangers' plan was to wait out the first volley from the bandits, and then the Rangers at ground level would flank the intruders while the men on the roof kept the bandits' heads down. The plan lasted exactly as long as most battle plans do, until they met the enemy. With their backs to the front wall, both Adams and Wilson could see the rooftop their lieutenant was on, and suddenly realized that it was taking fire instead of providing it. Adams cocked his head first to one side and then the other, then pointed through the side window that Wilson had been at. "There. The shots are coming from there. They've flanked us and they watched where the flares came from."

Wilson, no longer bothering to whisper, shrugged, "Yep, but they don't know where we are. Time for a walk?"

They shifted their rifles to their left hands and, waiting for a loud burst of gunfire to cover the noise, vaulted out the window side by side. Then, crouched almost to the ground, Winchester in one hand and Colt in the other, future Emperor Adams went to earn his crown.

The ruined city provided enough cover to allow easy movement in the moonlight. Ahead of them, Adams sighted two men ahead moving in the same direction as himself and Wilson. One he recognized as Jack, the squad leader. He whistled "whippoorwill" twice to let them know he was behind them in the near darkness. Jack looked back and, after a moment, gestured to Adams and Wilson to catch up. When Adams got close, Jake whispered, "Going somewhere, Partner?"

Adams answered, "Moonlight stroll with Wilson. I don't think we have much time. Our guests aren't going to hang around when things get hot."

Jack looked at the luminous dial on his pocket watch and whispered, "That'll be in about nine minutes. We left Ted behind a wall with a pile of grenades and a lot of ammo. He's gonna open up loud when we get in place. I figure everyone else'll take the hint and join in."

Adams pointed toward two lamp posts still standing and just visible against the stars. "I figure they'll go out the way they came...about that direction. We need to be behind them, about where those two big post things are."

Jack looked quickly over the trash pile between them and the bandits. "O.K. You can see it better than me. You lead, I'll take up the rear. Everyone keep quiet from now on. Remember nine minutes, we need to be there."

They moved quickly but quietly, bearing always a little to the right, trying to circle around the bandits. Adams suddenly stopped and gestured at the men behind him. He could see a bandit over the next row of debris. The man was looking away from Adams, probably watching the rooftop where he thought the Rangers were. Adams quietly drew his Bowie knife and crept forward. After a moment, he slowly put his knife back in the sheath and reached down for a heavy stick on the ground. He got all the way to the bandit and knocked him out with a blow to the head before the man even knew he was there.

He was putting cuffs on the unconscious bandit when the other three rangers caught up. Before they could say anything, he glanced up and said, "Better find something tall to stand behind."

When they looked puzzled, he pointed south , "Listen to the shooting. The roof is that direction, and so are the bandits. This guy must've been the rear guard. When Ted opens up, he'll be shooting at us, and there's no such thing a friendly fire. The bad guys should be leaving right through here. Find something thick to stand behind and get 'em when they go by. "

The four Rangers each found a man-high section of block wall to stand behind and stood facing away from the bandits – and the Texans on the rooftop. Adams holstered his pistol and clutched his Winchester across his chest. Momentarily, he wished for a trip rope. Shoot to kill is a redundant phrase. If you shoot a man, you shoot to kill.

Wilson was hidden in the shadow of a wall fragment about 15 yards to his left, spaced out to his right, Jack and the other Ranger stood with their backs to their walls and waited for the shooting to start.

In less than a minute, the light of the first explosion barely beat the whoomp, whoomp of the first two grenades hitting behind them. Then explosions went on like a string of huge firecrackers. Ted must have thrown a half dozen grenades in the time it took the first fuse to burn down. The rest of the hidden Rangers behind them took the hint and opened up. Lead flew everywhere, hitting the wall Adams was pressed against and the ground in front of him. It didn't take long before the he heard the sound of men running. They ran by him without stopping. When he couldn't hear any more behind him, Adams stepped aside, out of the shadows and, in one motion, spun around to look behind him for more bandits, and, seeing none, continued his turn until he was crouched facing the fleeing bandits. He fired two quick shots just over the heads of the bandits and yelled "Drop or die. Now!" By now the other Rangers were each on one knee aiming at the dozen or so bandits near them. Five of the bandits immediately dropped to the ground, letting their weapons fly out of their hands. A moment later, the others were also on the ground, after the Rangers rapidly and methodically shot them. With the Rangers, there was never a second warning. No hurry, no problem, no armed survivors.

When all the bandits were down, the Rangers moved forward to handcuff the ones who surrendered, bandage the two others who were still breathing, and to check the dead. They could not see that the lieutenant, Ted, and the other Rangers had left their positions and were moving in on the six men Wilson had first seen on the street.

Burton Adams, future emperor of Texas turned over the first man he had ever killed, looked into the dead man's eyes, and wished he'd had that trip rope.

Texas was not always like this. At one time Texas was not an empire and there had never been an Emperor Adams. Then, about four hundred years before, the world had ended. The odd thing is that people were actually surprised. Every newsstand had books on global warming, the coming ice age, and the "Disease That Would Wipe Out Humanity". Bearded men wandered the streets carrying signs "The End Is Coming" and every Sunday, the evangelists warned their parishioners that the end was near.

People loved these stories. It gave them the same safe thrill as a roller coaster ride. Why were they so surprised when it happened? It even happened where everyone knew it would. The world ended where it began, in Africa.

Chapter 2 The End Begins

Democracy is the damnedest thing. It has never been proven that rule by popularity contest is particularly effective. It never takes long before the politicians start buying votes with other peoples' money. They call it entitlement programs, which means that they take money from people who have earned it and who are entitled to it, and give to people who are not entitled to it to buy their votes. When the electorate is wide enough, you begin to realize that half of the people have I.Q.s of under 100. They want to hear how good things are, they want simple solutions, and they don't care if the plan is as realistic as Disney World.

President Thomas was elected in that era. He was tall, thin, grey haired, and very fatherly looking. He had a soothing voice and a way of making you feel that he cared. He had been chosen as his party's standard bearer because he was electable, and so prudish that no one could find any hint of scandal in his past.

He was not unintelligent. Stupid men do not get elected president, but he had never spent a single day of his life in the 'private sector'. He had gone from Yale University to the Civil Rights Bureau, state service, the US Senate and then the presidency – without ever doing one single productive day's work.

He was listening to a briefing by the NASA director. The meeting was large one. All of the secretaries were there along with several NASA scientists. The faint smell of hot coffee and pastries filled the room. This was a review. The problem had been discussed by several committees before being presented to the larger group.

The director was standing in front of screen that showed an Antarctic scene on one side and several large graphs on the other.

"It's ironic that we spent so much time worrying about global warming – and now we find that cold will be our problem. Gentlemen, if you will open your folders, I will fill in the details of what we are facing. The first hint of a problem came four years earlier. A glaciologist at the Massachusetts Institute of Technology was running ice flow predictions on their new Sony Supercomputer. His data consisted of ice cores from Antarctica and weather information from other sources. Part of his test program was to go into the past and predict where the ice had been in previous centuries. At first, he thought he had made a mistake. The computer showed that Antarctica had been free of ice several times in the last one hundred thousand years, and that the last time was about twenty thousand years ago. It took him a year to verify the data and another year to explain it."

The director glanced meaningfully about the room, and then continued, "It turns out that there is a maximum amount of ice a glacier can carry. When it gets too heavy, the pressure of the top ice makes the ice on the bottom melt. That forms a lubricating layer that starts the glacier sliding toward the ocean. In a few years, the ocean levels can rise by twenty feet, inundating vast coastal areas. Knowing that the problem that we were investigating only happened once ever twenty or thirty millennia, we funded a trip by the glaciologist to Antarctica primarily as a public relations move. We thought that it would be good for an article in Scientific American, or at least Popular Science and a good news conference. We supplied the scientists with Global Positioning Service devices. They went out onto the ice shelf, drove tall stakes into the ice at several positions, and measured the glacial movement with extreme precision. The results were unexpectedly bad. It verified their worst fears. The ice will slide off of Antarctica within our life times and, in the worst case, during this administration."

Someone asked, "I am not certain that I understand. Is this a part of global warming?"

"No, just the opposite. This has nothing to do with global warming. It's just a matter of gravity. During cold periods, the ice on the Antarctic shelf gets thicker every year, and when it reaches a certain thickness, the weight of the ice on top melts the ice nearest the ground and the whole thing starts to slide off into the ocean. It doesn't melt. The thickness of the snow pack causes it to slide off into the ocean. Within a year or two, the ocean level can increase up to twenty feet. In addition, the world ends up warmer because there is less ice to reflect sunlight back into space and even more ice melts, raising the sea level more over the years."

President Thomas was a delegater. He spoke the "big picture", "laid out the expectations", and picked the (politically) correct people to do the detail work. He had spent the previous two weeks reading reports, speaking to visiting dignitaries, and deciding on a scapegoat should the current plans fail. He would only be satisfied when they figured out how to blame the other party for the disaster.

Steven June, the Secretary of Health and Welfare was in danger of dozing off. The cabinet seemed to want only to repeat excuses, lay blame, and delay decisions. He felt his eyes drooping when he was startled by a tap on his shoulder. Looking back, he saw that it was one of his staffers with a message. He quietly accepted the message and waved off the staffer. Cabinet members do not interrupt the Tuesday meeting to receive messages.

Holding it down near the table, he opened the message as little as possible and glanced at the contents. He saw that it was from the office of the Surgeon General. Reading on more openly, he came wide awake by the end of the message. It was the update that he had feared. He stood suddenly and addressed the President, interrupting a discussion of the GPS devices being used to track the Antarctic ice flows. "Mr. President, I have news that requires our immediate attention."

"Jesus, Steve, what can be more important than the fact that our coasts will be flooded in fifty years."

"I have just received a message from Dr. Cary, the Surgeon General. We have disturbing news from Africa. Ebola, or something very similar, has mutated. It is now airborne, and in the last seventy two hours, three villages in Zambia have been totally wiped out. Several patients were moved to the capital city for treatment yesterday. Today there are eight hundred new cases in the capitol. This thing spreads faster than anything in history. It also remains one hundred percent fatal in spite of the mutation."

The president stopped glowering. Looking concerned he asked, "Ok, Steve. What to you want to do? Do we send them drugs, naval doctors, food, hospital ships? What do they need.?"

"Need? Them? It's not them! They're all going to die, and we can't do a damned thing about that! We need to try to live. Us! This plague is going to make the Black Death look like a mild cold. Let me repeat – it is one hundred percent fatal, and nothing can be done to treat it. The first thing we have to do is to isolate Zambia. Stop all flights from Africa, send troops to seal their borders and keep the rest of our troops here to keep everyone out. If it comes, we die!"

"Steve, you can't be serious. I campaigned on the promise of human rights. We will not keep fleeing refugees out of this country. We simply cannot let people die because they can't leave their country. We have clear reciprocal visitation treaties with most African countries, and we will not be the first to break those treaties. In any case, our own laws, which I support, forbid discrimination based physical handicaps and health problems."

June was clenching his fists. A bad thing to do in front of the President. In a tightly controlled voice he said. "Perhaps you don't fully grasp the situation. This is not a political campaign. It's the lives of your children, and your family, and yourself. One hour after the first infected passenger gets off the first airplane, the disease will be out of control. Six weeks later half the people in the country will be infected, and in three months, we will all be dead. I remind you, our predecessors in these chairs faced a similar but milder problem. They could have treated AIDs as a communicable disease requiring quarantine, but instead, they treated is as a 'rights' problem – and one million six hundred thousand Americans died before we finally found a cure. This will be much worse. You won't have to do anything but breathe to get this one."

"Steven, " the president said in a reassuring voice, "Remember that this party supported those AIDs laws and that we are still proud of them. We will not let a virus change our values or our belief in human rights. Virtue always has a price."

It suddenly dawned on Steve that no one was listing. His father had always said, "The only thing worse than being a fool is arguing with one. They ain't equipped to listen."

He shook his head and spoke in a soft and sad voice. "Gentlemen, I will be leaving in a few hours. I have a remote cabin in Utah. My family and I will be there. We'll spend our last few months together, and maybe get a little more time if we stay on our mountain top and away from people. You may consider this to be my resignation." He didn't bother to pick up his briefcase, his cell phone, or the message. They were all now irrelevant.

He was wrong about a few details. It took more than six months, not three.

One of the first centers of contagion was Washington DC, brought in by a diplomat who got off the plane under his own power – and then convulsed on the way to the hotel. One of the first victims was President Thomas.

After his death there were serious attempts at containment which temporarily slowed the spread several times. Russia and Israel finally did what should have be done the day Steven got the message. They nuked Zambia. It slowed the contagion a little, but it was too late.

The good news was that it was not one hundred percent fatal. Around the world, almost one person in a thousand survived. And fifty percent of their children were immune.

Chapter 3   467 New Era. - Heresy Happens

The Luddites have always been with us. As certain as it is that millions of years ago, a man picked up a rock and shaped it to be the first human tool, it is also certain that someone in his tribe wanted to know why he couldn't just use the damned rock the way nature intended, round and blunt. They became famous in the eighteenth century when workers marched against, protested against, and even burned labor saving machines.

They didn't go away. The first generation of parents with televisions screamed at their children that television light was different than natural light and would ruin their eyes. Even though computer monitors were nothing but televisions without tuners, millions of people bought shields to protect themselves from "the harmful radiation." The same people spent money on radiation shields to protect their brains against the tumors that cell phones were supposed to cause.

It reached the height of silly when Luddite web sites used the high tech internet and email to rail against progress. The fear of the new seems to be fixed into the human genome. The Luddites were always with us. It's just that they never ruled before. No one had ever deliberately created a dark age before.

Fortunately, even the dark ages are never as dark as you expect. A mere four and a half centuries couldn't wipe out oral history. It was, after all, only six or seven human lifetimes. The memory of Atlantis lasted twenty five lifetimes before it was written down, and the battle for Troy lived in the memory and voice of man for fifteen lifetimes before the Greeks committed it to print.

Men still remembered curse words like "electricity", and "car" and "doctor" and knew that the world was once smaller – and better. Some remembered and wanted it back. Most desperately feared it might return.

To look for it was heresy, unless you were an archeologist seeking history, and booty for the fires of the righteous.

The wilds of Texas were always wild. Even in the last days before the New Era, much of the state was virtually empty scrub land. Now that the population was less than a tenth of what it had been, the empty spots were empty counties. The column had just passed through what had been the town of Mineral Wells, and there wasn't much to see. In Russia, China and parts of the middle east, houses had been made from stone, brick, and concrete. Many houses from Before the New Era, still stood with their two foot thick walls intact and some were even occupied. However, in what had been America, houses were generally made on a balloon frame of sticks, covered on the inside with a sheet of cardboard and gypsum and covered on the outside with aluminum over a panel of glued together sawdust. After 400 years, they were low mounds of grass in the forest. Not all was lost. In the major cities, the stubs of some skyscrapers were visible and an occasional building had been saved. One, and only one part of the American house had been designed to last forever. The ceramic toilet bowls would probably outlive mankind. Texas had not had to manufacture one yet. The old cities were mined for steel, copper and toilet bowls.

The only sign that Mineral Wells had ever existed was the wide lane that had once been the major road through town. Occasionally the way was marked by a melted lump of blacktop sticking up though the dirt.

Most of the men in the column were cowboys. Not one of them had anything to do with bovine production, but, in Texas, every man without another profession was considered a cowboy. They wore practical flat topped, wide brimmed hats and red bandanas. To a man, they were dressed in rolled up blue jeans, checked shirts, and leather vests. Since they expected to do manual labor, only two of the fifteen wore belt holsters. Most of them had their pistols latched down in chest or underarm holsters. They lead five pack horses with shovels, picks, bags of flower and lanterns peaking out from under the canvas.

At the head of the column, Sir Robert watched for a campsite. The sun was still low above the horizon, but horses don't come with headlights and they needed to be down from the trail before dark. He and his two companions stood apart from the rest of the column. At first they looked similar to the others, but they were dressed in tan clothing and their hats were soft felt rather than leather. Their vests were studded with pockets, and they wore their pearl handled revolvers in belt holsters strapped down above expensive boots. Even their bandannas showed the extra quality that money can buy.

He really should have had a lot of pockets in his pants and a whip on his belt, but the field of archeology had just been re-invented a few months before, and no one yet know what an archeologist looked like. It was not an accident that everyone looked like a cowboy. When the first Adams, later known as "The Founder", established the empire, he knew that you couldn't build a lasting nation by conquest. People need to have a common identity to be part of a country. Being a history buff, he knew of the tremendous appeal that the old cowboy legends had, so he borrowed shamelessly from Zane Grey, and John Wayne, and Sam Houston to build an image. He convinced everyone that they were Texans now, and always had been. The result was a world where every man was a cowboy and the only law was the Code of the West that had never been.

The man nearest to him leaned closer in his saddle and asked, "Do you think we're getting near?" Sir Robert took his pipe from his mouth and fumbled with a map and a faded and torn newspaper clipping, both of which he was trying to hold in his other hand. "We should be close, about there. Watch for a mound or a rise in the ground. It was a ground level steel door a few hundred years ago, so it ought to be a mound of dirt by now."

Greg, the other man dressed like an archeologist was a little younger than the other two. He had added red arm bands to his outfit and had made time for a haircut before hitting the trail "Well, I want to get there before dark. You guys can watch the map. I'm going to scout ahead to see if I can find it." With that he spurred his horse ahead with the impatience of youth.

About 15 minutes later, they rounded a curve in the road to see Greg sitting on top of a small hill with an exaggerated attitude of relaxation and a grin on his face. "Old guys, I think this is it. There's steel showing through a few places on the side." He jumped up and down twice and then said though a smile "and, look, it hasn't killed me yet."

Robert leaned forward in his saddle. "Sonny, maybe you just ain't close enough yet."

Chapter 4 The Road, Long, Long Ago.

A few hundred years ago, the road through Mineral Wells looked different. It was still empty, but it ran between ranch houses and tiny strip malls, all covered with overgrown brown grass and festooned with broken windows. Cars sat on the side of the road and in the abandoned driveways. Most of the doors were still on hinges and many of them swung and creaked in the summer breeze.

What is now a wide grassy lane in the woods, was then a flat ribbon of blacktop winding out into the countryside.

Colonel Chris Scylla had to dodge an occasional bicycle or trash can laying abandoned on the street as he rode his Gull Wing slowly through the town. Although the boot of his bike held enough contraband to get him killed if it were discovered, he showed no signs of nervousness. He wasn't likely to attract too much attention from the nuts even if they saw him. Even the back-to-nature crazies were still using what cars would still run. They ran them until they died, and then picked up another one. Doctors were for killing and scientists were for burning, but evil knowledge is any knowledge that you don't understand, and most people who lived in 2 N.E (New Era) thought that they understood cars and motorcycles. It was only televisions, computers, books with big words and other mysterious things that were evil.

Colonel Chris had been a flight surgeon. That could get him killed in a hurry, so, while he still wore his uniform, the patches were gone. Somehow he had not been able to discard the uniforms in the two years he had been wandering. They seemed to be his last link with a vanished world of order. Might not have done any good anyway. You can get rid of the uniform, but after 15 years in the service, the posture, walk, and clean shaven appearance forever marked him as a service man. He had been stationed on an aircraft carrier when the plague hit, on patrol in the middle east, bullying the locals, aggravating the bad guys, and generally proving that the U.S. Was the Bad Ass on the block.

Within a week of the first outbreak, they were recalled to the States. Because the navy had the best discipline in the world, the crew held together all the way back to the States. It held in spite of the fact that by the time they reached the midpoint of their trip home, home was no longer there to go to

Chris could almost share the crazies hatred of the internet. Communications links like the satellites and the internet held for weeks after most of their operators died. Thanks to instant communications and video links, he had been able to watch his wife die, with the body of their daughter bloody in her arms, and he was not alone in his grief.

By the time they reached the coast of Galveston, there was no way to dock the ship and no reason to do so. The tugs were gone and so were all of the people who gave the orders for the carrier to return. They rode at anchor a few miles off shore for two days while the crew fumed, discipline waned, and tempers rose. Then the captain addressed the crew. "We have been in communication with the other surviving members of the fleet. So far as we can determine, there is now no viable command structure functional in the United States. The ranking surviving officer seems to be Admiral Hubble of the Pacific Fleet. He has, therefore, assumed overall command of all surviving forces. He has issued the following communiqué."

There was a rustle of paper audible on the speakers as the captain prepared to read the statement.

"Of course, the first instinct for all of us is to rush home and try to help. However, all ships that have docked in population centers have ceased to communicate within a few days and are assumed to have succumbed to the plague. It is therefore ordered that all remaining ships shall remain at sea as long as possible. With luck, we may ride out the plague at sea and survive to help those still on land.

As these are extraordinary times, any man, not designated as essential by his commanding officer, and who wishes to leave his ship, is free to request immediate discharge at any time in the next three days. Commanders are ordered to make all practical efforts to land such discharged personnel in the nearest port. However, it is further ordered that no person who approaches within one mile of any shoreline will be allowed to return to any ship. There will be no exceptions to this order."

Less than a quarter of the men left the ship. There was, after all, nothing and no one to go home for. Discipline inevitably relaxed after several weeks. The men set up distilleries and drank and the officers soon joined them. The carrier stayed at anchor until she ran out of food and low on fuel for the generators and then, reluctantly, went into Galveston harbor. They beached the now useless carrier at dock side and climbed down into the smoldering city, hoping that the plague had run it's course by that time.

Maybe they were lucky. Maybe it had. Maybe that's why more than one in five were still alive a week after landfall, or maybe there just fewer disease carriers around in the now empty cities. Some of the crew lived, and Chris was one of them.

For a few weeks after landfall, many of them tried to maintain a sense of organization, but there was no one left to rescue, nothing left to do, and without purpose, they began to wander off to find their own fates. Chris learned early to avoid other people. Most of them had cracked under the strain and gone completely loony. They babbled, they cried, they glared, and they usually ran from other people. However, some were forming loony bands of destructive crazies. Those were dangerous. The city had been smoldering because wandering groups had burned all the libraries and bookstores and were now moving on to office buildings and warehouses. The only people really equipped to handle this world were the worst kind of fundamentalist street preachers. They had lived in a fantasy world of hate and retribution all of their lives and they were ready for this new world. The more charismatic of the surviving preachers were leading their shell shocked flocks on a rampage against all the "evil" in the old world. Finally, some one would believe them when they railed that video games and doctors and secular books and ANYTHING THAT QUESTIONS GOD! was the cause of all of their problems. "Burn, Burn The Evil.", rang out from voices screeching under fists raised to heaven holding the Holy Book. The only book a righteous man needed!

Like many of the almost sane survivors, he traveled a lot. Why not? There was plenty of free food in the stores and free gas in the automobiles. He came to prefer motorcycles because of their ability to carry him away from trouble in a hurry.

He wandered numb and without purpose until he got to Austin. As he rode through the downtown, he passed the clinic. Two of the surviving doctors had, apparently, tried to open a clinic for the other survivors. Their bodies now hung from the cross arms of a street light. By the time that he was close enough to read the sign, "Sinners, Be Warned!", that hung from the post, he could see that they had not died from the hanging. They had been beaten to death and then hung for display. It was the first tear he had shed since his wife died, and it opened the gates. He sat on the curb and sobbed for two hours, and when he stood up again, he had purpose. Someone had to save the world. Not this one, the one to come.

He rode slowly for hours, not seeing the road, not knowing which direction he went, living inside and thinking hard. "If no one does anything, this could last ten thousand years. We could have a hundred or a thousand generations of savages born into ignorance and living very short and very painful lives. I've got to do something." In spite of his anger and his determination, he breathed a sigh of relief. It was good to have a reason to live. He still looked on the wandering bands of crazies with hatred, but now it was hated with a purpose.

By the time he reached the city limits, he had a plan. He had realized that it would not take much to break the chain of ignorance. It might have taken ten thousands years to invent the stirrup, but it could be passed on in one moment with one picture. He looked down at his saddlebags. *I could hold a hundred paperbacks just in those bags. Hell, I could teach science with only one or two if I had the right books. You don't have to teach all the details. If we give them the basic laws and some practical knowledge about paper, steel, physiology, and a few other things, they can figure out the rest for themselves. If I can get the books that I need and hide them where they'll be found after this madness goes away, I might be able to give the future one Hell of a present.* He glanced back over his shoulder at the smoke rising from the skyline of Austin, *But I had better hurry,*

It took him six months to gather the right, exactly right, books from places missed by the crazies. He had to assume that the eventual discoverers of the books would not know English, might even be illiterate, and knew nothing about numbers higher than ten. He began with children's books and worked up to science. The libraries were already gone, but he found what he needed in private homes and in offices where the crazies never thought to look. It's easier to look smart when your opponents worship ignorance. It took another month to decide on the missile silo for a hiding place. He would put the books there, lock the bombproof hatches and bury the site with a bulldozer. By the time that mankind had the time and resources to open the silo, they would be ready for the books.

Today, he rode the path that Sir Robert would someday take.

Chapter 5 Back To The Future

The diagram they had was a line drawing from a four hundred year old newspaper miraculously preserved inside a metal tin. It was probably there as packing material. Translating the diagram into a useable map took the rest of the day.

The printed map was a line drawing titled "Typical Atlas Missile Silo" and printed in a long dead newspaper. With no more power for the printing presses, newspapers still existed but they were small and rarely printed daily.

The workers dug several test holes and what they found was matched to the drawing. By evening, they thought they knew where the personnel hatch would be.

In the evening camp, the archeologists sat apart from the workers. They talked earnestly while the others mostly bragged, gambled and lied about women, fights and whiskey. When the tin plates of stew were empty and the biscuits reduced to crumbs, they lit their pipes and, as men are prone to do, repeated conversations from past days.

Eric gestured at Sir Robert with his pipe. "You, know, Bob, I still don't know if we were smart to go looking for a missile thing on our first expedition. I mean, we don't know what the Hell it is, but we know that it held some pretty ferocious weapons. We could end up getting blown into Hell before the luddies can damn us into it."

Sir Robert nodded, "I know, Eric. But really, it has been four hundred years. I've never seen a piece of B.N.E. science that wasn't a rusted lump, and I can't believe there's much chance that any thing is still dangerous after that long. Anyway, You know why we're going for it. This thing was a complete self contained outpost designed to do everything for the Rangers in it. If it had a complete range of services, it must have a complete bunch of whatever they used. We could get everything we want on the first try. Maybe we'll even find out what a 'generator' is."

Eric blew smoke rings into the air and grinned. "I'll go along with that, but just remember that if you see me running tomorrow, try to keep up. I'm younger and faster than either of you and I'm not going to wait around if anything starts moving."

Even in the quiet of the empty hills, sleep came hard for all of them.

Morning came with the usual aches and soreness from sleeping on the ground. A saddle does NOT make a good pillow no matter what you've heard. Breakfast took a little longer than usual. This was going to be a long day and the men needed more than the usual bread, oil, and cheese. They waited while the cook heated up slices of ham and cooked them slices of beef to add protein to breakfast and stamina to the day.

Eric and Sir Robert had finished breakfast before most of the men awoke. Eric pointed to a section of the map, and said, "If this is correct, we'll find the personnel hatch about twenty yards north of where that test shaft is." Bob pointed to the place on the map where "Artists Conception" was printed. In fact, it took three tries to find the buried personnel hatch. The three archaeologists were patient. They expected their search to be a long one. Four hundred and fifty years of fanatical

Luddites had managed to burn almost every book and destroy every vestige of technological equipment.

It took an hour to remove the rotted concrete and dirt from around the door. The door was hard stainless steel, slightly warped, and jammed shut. It took a half day of prying with iron bars and soaking with oil to open it enough to enter. When it was finally open enough, they looked at it hoping for Tutankhamen and fearing Pandora. Sir Robert took the lead with an oil torch. It took only a moment for the disappointment to appear on his face. He said disgustedly, "Well, there goes the Tut hopes. She's been ransacked."

Robert and Eric crept slowly into the dark interior, torches held high and a little ahead of them as if the invaders might still be waiting. Smashed machinery was everywhere. The early anti-techs, still aware of the power of parts, had smashed and burned right down to the component level. They had probably returned for years for pieces for the Holy Fires. Near the entrance was a large room that had, apparently, been a mess hall. There was a large burned spot on the floor where all the paper, computer disks, books, and tapes had been burned.

In the debris was a partially burned skeleton. Eric pointed to the shoulder and said, "This one must have fought them hard." He kneeled by the skeleton and gestured at the bones. "Look, the left arm is separated and he had two, no, three fractured bones in addition to the skull fracture. I'll bet he was still alive when they threw him on the fire."

He stood and wiped the his hand on his pants. "Yep, They were doing the 'work of God.' The fanatics always seem to find particularly vicious gods to work for."

Chapter 6   The First Find

October 13, 0004 N.E.

Colonel Chris awakened to the sound of something heavy thudding against the door. By the time he shook the sleep from his eyes, he could hear the crazies outside.

He had gotten into the habit of talking to himself during the lonely months. *What the Hell kind of chant is " 'Killers, Killers, Techno Killers, Kill the Godless killers,"' They must have killed all the poets with the scientists. I'm going to die with 'Killers, Killers, Godless Techno Killers' ringing in my ears.*

That battering ram sounds pretty heavy. I don't That door is going to hold much longer.

He looked around the room stroking his chin, trying to breath slowly and normally, trying to convince his body that we was calm.

My own fault. I should have closed the outer door. They must have heard the bike when I rode in. I just thought this whole county was empty. This was a bad time to get careless. I think I just killed myself, and doomed all of the books. Something sure went wrong. I wonder if this qualifies as suicide or death by accident. Stupid thought. I must be getting nervous.

His eyes fell on a gray box about eight inches on a side and two inches thick. As long as he was talking to himself, the panic stayed in control..

Well, we've lost the books. They'll find them and burn them and brag to God about how holy they are. This thing is a long shot, but it's our last chance. Damndest thing is that I could put everything the future needs to know on a chip the size of my fingernail. Hell, I could put a whole library on the memory chip in my kids camera. He winced as he saw momentary picture of his daughter bleeding from the eyes and ears, quickly dieing. *Problem is, they won't have any idea what it was or what to do with it. We'll just have to hope that there are enough clues in the way it's made. It's self contained, with a built in screen, CD reader and controls. Somebody should be able to figure out what it does. Disk, something to hold a disk, reason out that the holder does something with the disk. Maybe they will still have record players. I just have to get it to the right people a hundred years from now. Problem is, how do I hide it from the morons and make sure it's found in hundred years or so"*

He tried to keep calm while his eyes scanned the mess hall. His eyes stopped at the tool box on the wall and he began to look grimly hopeful. *Ah, there it is. Fix cars! Mend your clothes! Ease childbirth with good old duct tape. I'll hide the player and the CD under something and hold up with tape. In a few decades it'll fall down when the tape fails and the next person here will see it.*

He loaded a CD into the player, "How Everything Works". One of the pretentious self help books published by the hundreds of thousands when CD's got cheaper than books. This one covered everything from batteries to nuclear power stations, bicycles to steam engines.

He reached for duct tape and dove under a heavy counter, he began to tape the player to the underside of the counter. *Damn*, he thought, *I left the batteries in. In a hundred years the player'll be ruined!* The battering at the door had taken on a different sound and his calm was evaporating. His hands shook as he hurriedly removed the batteries and re-taped the player. He taped the batteries into a second layer of duct tape to give the discoverers an example of what they needed to make the player work. *God, I hope they can figure out what batteries are for. Here you go, future guys. With a couple a a-cells you'll have the magicians spell book, the secrets of the ancients, and all the magic formulas you can use.*

In the next room, the door gave way and death flooded through the door. He had been right. The last thing he heard was that stupid chant as they threw him on the fire.

July 21, 459 N.E.

They were new at this, and re-learning the techniques as they worked. Like any generation of archeologists, they began with a plan. Science had died, but intelligence had not. The laborers camped outside for the rest of the day while the archeologists mapped out the site.

Despite the size of the underground structure, there were not many rooms - and none untouched. Eric drooped visibly when he saw that even the innermost door stood open. He had hoped that it would still be closed. Unfortunately, it must have been left open when the last plague survivors had headed for home. It was now full of debris about two feet high.

He could almost hear their voices. "Leave it open Sergeant. There's nothing left to protect. Damn." He thought, I was hoping that we would find out what a 'generator' looked like. The initial survey found nothing intact.

Greg and Eric each took a seven man team of laborers into the silo to clear the wreckage and look for anything useable. Sir Robert and the remaining man sat outside, sifting the rubbish as it came out.

Smaller teams would have been more efficient, but Greg and Eric had to keep a close watch on their workers. They were carefully drawn from the ranks of the atheists, non-believers, malcontents, and loners that most societies are blessed with. They were generally good men, but there was always the chance that one would be overzealous and try to gain glory with God by immediately smashing anything "evil". They were, after all, told that any finds would enhance the glory of Destruction Day.

They began with brooms and shovels, sifting any small finds and setting aside any larger pieces. It was hard to see clearly in the light of the torches and candle burning lamps, so even the most useless trash got hauled outside for examination. They found several intact but useless circuit boards, several gauges with broken glass that seemed that they might still work, and nothing of significance. There was no telling even what the gauges gauged, and no one knew what a "circuit board" was for. Everything but a few of the gauges would be turned over to various churches for the Destruction Day fires. That was what covered their work.

Two days later, they got to the mess hall. Eric had left it to last because it was obviously the center of activity for the marauding Luddites and the tomb of a man he did not know but mourned. There wasn't much chance that anything had survived. The room was relatively empty and eerie in the torchlight. Things brought here had been burned. He was peering into the gloom when he heard a call from Greg, standing at the upper door. "Light coming down!"

Greg had found several slabs of sheet metal that were still shiny. He had stationed a worker at the mouth of the tunnel leading from the door and two more at a corner, using the metal to reflect light into the mess hall.

The light streamed in over Eric's shoulder. Like a searchlight it fell on the surviving counter. He heard himself say, "Greg!! Get Robert in here, quick." When the others got there, Eric was standing a few feet from the bench with his arms outstretched as if he were holding back a crowd. "Bring something flat - about two feet each way. We have an unbroken find. It's about the size of a large jewel case, no, larger, and it's not smashed."

They gingerly moved the mechanism to another metal sheet and then carefully moved every scrap and rusted part near the mechanism onto the sheet in about the same relationship as they were on the floor.

As the four of them lifted the sheet, several workers joined in to guide it out of the silo without hitting anything.

The archeologists and the team leaders squatted around the mechanism peering but not daring to be poking. The rest of the workers stood as close as possible and stared at it. There was a clear window on the top of the thing and printing on the disk inside could be made out through the yellowing plastic. "How Everything Works".

Robert broke a long silence. "Looks like some kind of a book. I love that title! Looks like Bones has given us one hell of a present. Look at that gray cloth. It was under the bench when we found it. I think that's tape. He must figured the tape was going to hide it until the Luddites left." Eric grunted as he leaned over the thing. "Must have been a sharp man."

"Let's get this thing packed in cotton and get it back to Austin. I want a lab and a team before we tackle it. I don't know exactly what this thing does, but it looks real good."

At first light they had buried the skeleton outside the silo. Someone had made a wooden cross that read "A Good Man Lays Here". Eric leaned forward on his horse and looked down at the fresh grave. Below him the pack train was moving toward Austin.

"Thanks, Bones. If you did what I think you did, we'll be back to build you a tomb fit for a pharaoh."

Two days later they approached Austin. The restored blacktop road began to get crowded. Horse drawn busses plodded stolidly ahead while cyclists and their mini-trailers dodged and sped by. The lumbering wagons of cargo haulers blocked entire lanes. Occasionally a mail courier would pass, blowing his right-of-way horn, and often being ignored.

Sir Robert arranged his workers in one line of five horsemen on each side of Eric and Greg as they drove the surrey they had requisitioned to carry the chest with the artifact. He brought up the rear, watching nervously over their find.

Austin was visible about from about five miles away. Smoke from the foundry area blackened the sky as a hundred one and two man foundries and pottery shops fed their fires. The man powered cranes on the riverfront towered over the city walls as they got closer.

Near the city gates, he moved ahead to lead them into the fast lane for government people. In the cargo line a city inspector was fussing with a Rot and Fungus examination of a wagon of fruit. He would continue looking and fussing until the wagon owner figured out how to pass over a small bribe.

Sir Robert passed over his papers to the guard in the government lane. They were impressive three color printed papers that identified him as an Empire Of Texas Archeologist. The guard read the papers carefully and compared the tintype of Robert's face on the papers with his current face.

The guard said "Well, Sir Robert, you seem to be you and you can vouch for the rest of this crowd. But I need to look in that cargo hold to see what you're carrying."

"No can do. That is a bonafide state secret. No one examines it."

"Can't let you pass, Sir. I have my orders."

Robert gestured to the side of the road. "Tell you what, we'll park the column over there while you semaphore your headquarters. Give them the name 'Sir Bob' and the code 'FAC'. The semaphore vanes on the gate began to waggle as they parked the caravan.

The wait was a long one in the summer heat. The workers started a dice game, Eric tried to nap and Greg nervously watched the cargo.

Suddenly, a troop of guards appeared moving fast and nearly out of breath from double timing in full gear. They jangled as they jogged, loaded down with breastplate, Bowie knife, musket, caplock pistol, and decorative chains.

The sergeant shouted to the gate guard as they jogged past "Looking for Sir Robert". The gate guard pointed to Bob. Approaching Sir Robert, the heavily armed guard said – out of breath – "Sorry about the delay, Sir. Headquarters had to send a runner to the barracks and then we had to get out the combat gear. I've got orders to escort you straight to the Archeology Institute and let nothing happen to your cargo."

"If your cargo will fit on a palanquin, I would feel safer if the men carried it." The workers carefully lifted the wooden box from the surrey and placed it on a six man palanquin that looked like a stretcher with six handles. At the order, six guardsmen stepped smartly to the sides of palanquin and hoisted on command.

Robert turned to Greg. "You might as well send the teams home. We don't need them now, and they're probably anxious to get home. Tell them they can pick up their pay at the institute tomorrow."

Catching Bob's eye, the sergeant moved the palanquin and its protecting guards through the gate and into the city. They were in good shape, and even though the sergeant watched carefully for any obstructions or problems, the archeologists, who had left their government issue horses at the gate, had a hard time keeping up. They were grateful to see the Institute before they had to call for rest.

Sir Wilson, the director, was in the double doorway waiting for them. He stepped aside as the palanquin was carried in. He held back to let Eric catch up. "What in the Hell do you have that justifies a class one code."

Sir Robert waited until the guardsmen left and then said, "A unbroken device that looks something like a magic machine, which is housing a disk shaped object with the label 'How Everything Works'! I don't know yet how we're going to read whatever it is, but it was important enough for a dying scientist to preserve it just for us. And the title sounds too good to be true."

Greg and the workers had been paid off and given the usual warning of what horrible things would happen to them if they spilled government secrets. The warnings, as usual, were dire enough to guarantee that at least one worker would catch on to the fact that this knowledge was worth selling.

Back outside, an hour later, Bob pulled the chain to raise the Hack Flag on top of the building. He said to Sir Wilson, "Join me in a cab?"

"No, thanks, I want to walk off a little nervous energy. Thanks anyway. Tomorrow we start the real work"

Chapter 7   December 14, Year One B.N.E

For most people, it was a magic time. Anything not understood is magic. With so much magic in the world, religion flourished. Many could not really see the difference between a doctor with magic potions and machines and the preacher with magic healing powers. It was a time of alternative medicine, faith healing, copper bracelets, and crystals. If a computer could know all about you, why couldn't God? They were equally mysterious.

The most popular international show was Reverend Roberts. In religion, as in many human institutions, the participants range from the divine to the evil. On the divine side are the ministers who try to feed the poor, care for the sick and comfort the dying. On the other side are the preachers. The Reverend would stride back and forth in front of the studio audience, sweating in his two thousand dollar suit and weighted down by his two carat diamonds (purchased for the "Greater Glory of GOD") and extort his viewers to righteousness. His religion was of the branch "You send me money and God will make sure that you get rich!"

"Brothers and Sisters, the Lord has spoken! And you will heed his call.

You have let them transgress into Gods' arena. Every day they announce a new usurpation of Gods power. They fill the air with poisonous rays of EMF and microwaves. You know it's wrong. God has warned you! You have suffered from the headaches and fatigue and felt bad in your soul.

You have seen the wretchedness of the word. There are drugs, sex, and crime all about you. The Lord is angry. Soon the Lord will strike this civilization like he did Sodom before us!

Now the scientists claim they will make a soulless human in a test tube. IS THERE A GREATER EVIL? These men would take GOD'S place! You know what's wrong with the world. Our ancestors lived in more peaceful times. Children respected their parents. It was safe to walk the streets at night. Neighbor helped neighbor in a spirit of Christian fellowship. People went to church on Sunday and praised the Lord's name.

Now the world is a cesspool. The Lord watches as children go to video arcades to play games dripping with sex and violence. These children even attack their parents if they are not saved! God sees that every show has immoral, and some times unnatural sex acts and He is sickened by it!. You can't go out a night for fear some drug crazed Godless pervert with attack you.

Is it not easy to understand why the Lord has loosed the plague that is devastating mankind? Do you wonder why God has caused the waters to rise? Pestilence! Flood! Gods way of dealing with sinners!

The Lord said 'Thou Shalt Not Want' – and he meant it. Thou shalt not want video games and computers and cars and microwave towers and sinful entertainment. You must rid the world of the signs of evil and those 'scientists' who do the evil. The Lord has told you - you can live in a simpler and more holy life in God's way – or not live at all."

Have times been hard for you? Has the Lord not smiled on you recently. It may be because you are not supporting his works. To pledge support for the holy causes of the Lord, call 1-800......."

In the control room, the producer looked over at the technician beside him. "He sure puts on a Hell of show. Now every believer who has a headache will know that it's God's punishment for his evil ways."

"Yes." The tech answered, "And that a few bucks given to the Rev will get God to smile on you. But this moron is a television evangelist who just told people to hate science. Where is he going to be when they start smashing up their televisions and stop using the 800 numbers?"

"I said he was a good showman. I never said he was a bright showman."

Chapter 8 The Emperor Enters

Emperor Burton Adams was working his way through the stack of papers on his desk. He wore expensive work clothes - silk shirt, paisley pants, ritual 45 colt revolver, and, of course, the purple cloak of office that he had thrown back over one shoulder. His light weight working crown was on the desk in case he had a sudden meeting.

The muscular build under the silk shirt was the body of a man who lead troops in the field by sleeping where they slept, eating what they ate, and drinking dirty crick water if that is all his men had. No Adams had ever had to worry about the loyalty of the Rangers. He was young for a profession where most men took the job only on the death of their fathers. He could not have been past his early thirties. The family motto was engraved on a plaque that hung on the wall behind him.

I'm a pacifist.
There are only two kinds of pacifists.
Well Armed Pacifists
and Dead Pacifists.

"Jonathon," he said to his secretary, "This one is the worst of the day. Hell, worst of the month. Some jackass lawyer in New Houston wants me to pardon his client because the client was drunk and tanked up on Loco when he did the assault. When you send the standard refusal, add a quotation from my grandfather. 'The right to go to Hell in your own hand basket implies the right to pay your own the fare when the Devil comes.' Wait a minute, add a sentence telling him that if he can identify the men who forcibly held him down and poured whisky down his throat, we'll punish them instead."

Jonathon's assistant rapped on the open office door. "Your Majesty, the Director of the Archeological Institute is here for his appointment."

"All right, send him in."

Adams set the papers he had just picked up back on the growing inbox and reached for his crown. He called out to the assistant's retreating back, "And make sure we are not disturbed!"

The director was a man of about the same age as the Emperor and almost as muscular under his formal dress. He wore his bright red formal double breasted jacket over a paisley vest and white tubular slacks. He held his western hat in one hand and a leather folder in the other. As he bowed from the waist., a fashionable bulge showed where he carried his 38 caliber dress revolver under his left arm - even in the presence of the emperor. A Texan surrendered his firearms only in court, in church, and when he was laid in his coffin.

"Your Majesty, I respond to your summons." As the last servant left the room, he relaxed with the familiarity that could come only from being childhood friends, and said, "You don't have to wear that crown to impress me. I already know that you're the emperor."

The crown was a little askew where he had scratched the back of his neck. "The damned thing isn't very comfortable, but I try to keep up appearances. I have no idea what moron decided that kings should wear metal hats. I sent the messenger because I saw the code one alert on the daily reports. Anything I need to know?"

Actually, part of the reason he had sent for Wilson was to see someone besides his mother who could use his first name. Being the Emperor was a good job, but a lonely one.

"Eric, Greg, and Sir Robert found what may be a technical manual. This folder contains the complete report and photographs of the device. This thing may be more valuable than Merlin's spell book and the answer to all our dreams, or just the God's joke on us. It's some kind of old magic device. You know the old tales. It's said that the Ancients could record all of the knowledge of humanity on the head of a pin. This doesn't do you any good if you don't have anything that will read the head of a pin."

The emperor looked up from the folder. "Got any ideas on how to read it?"

"Just hope. It looks like a wax phonograph record, except that it's some kind of shiny plastic. It has to be encoded with something. It has to be magnetic, or physical or visible, and they weren't trying to hide it. We'll probably find the codes by the time we finish examining the disk. Once we know how they wrote on it, we'll have a lot harder problem learning to understand the writing."

"You lost me there."

Sir Wilson shook his hand in the air, "Look, I send you a letter. The first thing you have to know to read it is that we are doing visible encoding, that the pattern of ink on paper holds the message instead of say, the white parts or the creases in the paper. Finding out what kind of 'ink' they used is the first step. Going back to your letter, once you figure out that the black lines are the message, you have to figure out is that the thing that looks like a cross is the character that makes a 'T' sound. Then you have to figure out which way the encoding runs. This one probably runs around the disk like a record, but we don't know yet. Chinese is up and down the page, Latin languages are left to right, and some ancient languages run back and forth both ways. That's the hard part. That could take so long that we would be better to just invent everything all over again."

"I wish we had time."

"We could do it a lot faster than you expect. Once we get started, we have things that the first set of scientists would have sold their souls for." Wilson held up one hand and began to count out on his fingers. "We start with universal standards. An inch is an inch everywhere. We have standard threads, relatively accurate clocks, and we know about standard parts. Once we build better furnaces, we will have a wealth of raw materials in the old cities that doesn't even have to be mined. Most important, we know where we are going. They didn't. The first industrial revolution took three hundred years. If we can get it going good, ours will take thirty years."

Wilson's eyes focused far away and his voice dropped. "The problem is not the technology. It's the riots. You know that people are going to die doing this. Your idea for the Archeology Institute was brilliant. Archeology touches so many disciplines and still doesn't threaten the present. We even get the support of the churches because we pretend to turn over all "evil" finds to them. We have a nice core of thinking men there and we're safe for a while. But when we start this going, it's going to show. We know from a few surviving buildings that power plant is big and hard to hide even in a country as big as Texas."

The Emperors' eyes also focused back into the present. "Actually, I don't exactly how we're going to do it. But, Dad has offered to help and he was always brilliant with public relations. We'll find away sell this."

"That's good news. I thought your dad was the happiest retiree in New Houston. Last time I saw him he was playing golf all day and 'interviewing' servant girls all night."

"I guess he got bored. Besides, worrying about Texas gets to be a habit for the Adams family. We have been doing since the first Adams became the Founder. Actually, Dad's a long term thinker and I think he's a little more concerned than he lets on. He'll be at the archeology conference next week."

The weekly meeting of the Archeology Committee was held in a large but normal looking conference room. Walls in Texas tended to be thick concrete and the fact that these were a little thicker than usual and harbored sound proof windows and double doors was not obvious.

The old rules are the best rules. The best place to hide is in plain site. The budget of the committee was not even a "black item". The coffee and doughnuts for this meeting were right on the public budget.

However, few meetings began with a secrecy ritual. Wilson stood at the head of the table an intoned, "Know ye that we intend to conduct business both secret and desperate. Any man or woman in this room who cannot keep a secret is placing his or her life in danger by his presence past this moment." The "woman" referred to the empress sitting next to her husband at the head of the table. "Any man wishing to leave must do so now or accept the oath and responsibility."

Around the table each person responded in turn, "On my own head be it". Even the emperor and his wife intoned in turn.

It was a paneled boardroom. The stained glass windows on the outer wall looked decorative but kept secrets well. The paneling covered three foot thick concrete walls, and were pierced only with double glazed windows, each layer of a different thickness. The doors were double, thick, and soundproof. In addition to the Royal Family, the twenty foot table seated Eric, Bob, Wilson, and ten other of the most learned men in Texas. Men wise enough to know that the public knowledge of this matter could be deadly.

The mechanism sat in the middle of the table between the fifth and sixth pair of seats. The objects with it were arranged in about the same manner that they were found.

As president of the committee, Wilson spoke first. "It has been a remarkable two weeks. By now you all know that Eric and Bob have found what they believe to be a technical manual of unknown type, hidden in one of the abandoned silos around Mineral Springs. In those weeks, Mitch, Harold, and Greg Seale have examined the device carefully, while Steve and Milton have done the historical background work. I know that you have all helped with various pieces. During this meeting, we will summarize what we know and develop a plan to go forward. Mitch, why don't you tell us what the technical team learned."

Mitch was tall, thin, and a little nervous until he started to speak. He was highly intelligent, a person who cared what happened to others and that kind of nice guy that all women loudly proclaim there just aren't enough of, and was therefore generally dateless. He unrolled a three by five foot paper banner with several line drawings on it and attached it to head high hooks in side wall.

"We can thank Greg for the drawing. He has also put photographs of the object in the package in front of each of you."

The photographs were made from a dry print glass negative. Plastic film was still a forgotten art.

"Let's start with the brown lumpy stuff to the north of the object. That appears to be the remains of batteries. We haven't seen intact ones, but we know from our previous studies that such a power source uses acidic compounds and two different metals. The lump is acid, carbon, copper, and cadmium. If we assume that Bones knew what he was doing, he probably removed the batteries before hiding the object. The lack of tape associated with the batteries indicates that the hider knew that they would only last a few years and so he made no attempt to hide or preserve them. For those of you who haven't figured it out, Bones knew that if he left the batteries inside the object, they would eventually decay and release the acid. Then the device would eventually resemble a larger lump of that brown stuff."

Pointing to the first drawing on the left, he continued. "The object is about six by ten inches by two inches high. The measurements are not exact, so the originators may have been working in the metric system. It has seven buttons. The ones that we can make out are 'Play', 'Stop', 'Eject' and some that have only symbols. You can see the symbols more clearly on the chart than on the object itself."

He pointed to the drawing where symbols such as "<<I" and "II" were drawn. We have no idea yet what those signs signify, but Harold thinks that they may be volume controls. There is a flat panel five by eight inches above the keys. It's function is unknown, but it has a wide cable of wires attached to it, so its' function can be assumed to be complex. There is something else about it that tells a lot. Greg, would you take over for this section."

Seale was sitting near the device. He was a bright but somehow clumsy person and he looked like a scholar. His glasses made his shortsighted eyes look small behind his beard. It was no accident that his looks fit his profession. When the other kids wouldn't play with him, he sought solace in magic, old books, and finally education. Now he was smiling like the little boy who knows his card trick is going to work. He stood up and leaned across the table. "Gentlemen, if you will watch closely." He gently extended the index finger of this left hand and moved it toward a tab on the surface of the device. When he pushed the tab, the device opened.

"Most of the clues we have come from that opening."

Gingerly he lifted the disk out. He lifted it so that the others could see it and then gently placed it on a thick cloth.

"This is a two part device. If we follow the logic the fact that the disk can be removed, it hints at a device meant to process several disks, the way a record player works. Wind it up and play. Only this one doesn't have a handle and a spring motor, or even a sound trumpet."

Harold leaned forward in his seat. "Unfortunately, that ends our good news, and now it's time for the other news. I did manage to get a look inside. I rigged some small mirrors and magnifying glasses and managed to get a long exposure photograph. That is the second photograph in your folder. Even in black and white, you can see the obvious damage."

Wilson was barely the first to ask "What happened to it."

"Bones, as you call him, almost made it. It was good thinking. Unfortunately, that area has been flooded several times in the last hundred years. Perhaps the vents were open or maybe the door was ajar in some years. The fact is that the device has spent months, or maybe years under water. It didn't affect the plastic case, or the buttons, or the disk, but the works inside are rusted into lumps. It's not all bad. The disk itself must hold all of the information we want. It's like a music record. We don't have a record player, but we have a good record. We won't be able to use the device, but we might be able to figure out how the disk is encoded. I don't want to offer false hope. It might be as hard to read as hieroglyphs were. They took several years to decode even after the Rosetta stone was available."

The emperor interrupted. "What will you need for the task? Personnel, resources, time?"

Harold was prepared for question. "Nothing special. This is mainly brain work. We will need the best microscope in the Empire and the best brains. However those are all already in this building. We will use the large lab in the subbasement and can call on help as we need it. The time is this year, next year, or during the reign of your son. If we get lucky, we will unlock the wisdom of the ages this year. If not, at least we have solid hope for the first time."

Chapter 9   Solomon White Feather

November 20, 0462 New Era

It's a shame that Destruction Day has gotten so commercial. People just don't respect tradition anymore.

When I was a kid, my mother would fix us a special breakfast and we'd all have to eat very carefully because we were wearing our best clothes. I remember that mother had a blue silk babushka that she only wore to Destruction.

Mother and all the other women would fix up the best dinner they could make and we'd all pack into the wagon for the trip to town. I can still remember the smell of the fresh pie and the creaky sound of the wagon wheels.

When we got to town everyone was there. People you never saw any other day. And there were peddlers and candy sellers and street entertainers and in the middle of the town square, the Holy Bonfire.

About noon the ceremony would start and we'd each bring up the evil pieces that we had found that year - a light bulb, a chip, a piece of newspaper or book, anything that looked like evil and we'd throw the stuff into the bonfire while the Preacher blessed and thanked each of us. One year I even won the prize for a small radio that I found in a buried trash heap.

We would wait and watch that fire. There was a block long table behind us, but we couldn't eat a bite until the evil began to melt. The older boys would feed logs to the fire while everyone else watched and waited for the melt to start. When the fire got hot, we'd begin to chant and stare at the fire. I remember actually blowing at the fire when I was about five years old. I was so impatient for it to go. Then something would start to melt and there would be a big cheer and a great day.

Boy, I miss those traditions.

The room he was in would have been called an "examination room" by American doctors, but they would not have furnished it with hay seats, chairs roughed out from tree branches, dried branches on the walls and a fire pit between the Shaman's chair and the patient. The wooden shutters were closed and the dim light of a fire pit enhanced the Indian-like look of the man seated on a tree stump. He wore a white feather in his hair, a necklace of beads and bear claws on his neck, and a red bandana with his otherwise normal Texan clothes. He was prematurely gray and had the lean look of a man who sometimes simply forgot to eat.

Shaman Solomon White Feather was explaining to the anxious mother, "Rub this poultice on the cut. Then you must soak the hand in a mixture of hot water and this powder every day until the evil leaves her hand. You can see the evil leave as the hand returns to it's normal color."

The grateful mother cradled the five year old in her lap. She had seen what happened to other children who began to be red around deep cuts and who died with high fevers and delirium in the arms of helpless parents. She was still nervous and scared for her child and herself.

"Shaman, how can I do what you say when my man will be in the house. He'd kill me if he knew I was here. He is a very good man."

"Don't worry. These are not evil medications, they are natural gifts from God. This powder is a substance found on the ground in desert areas. The poultice is a mixture of tree bark and river mud. There is nothing of man or evil in either one. He need not know that you got them from me and you need not fear that you are using anything evil. You must also say the prayer of lost souls three times a day while she is recovering, for only God will determine the outcome. I'm certain that your husband would help with that."

The mother's emotions fought a hefty battle between fear and love. Love won. She took the powder and the poultice and left hurriedly .

Shaman Solomon removed his feather, bandana, and beads as he entered his private rooms. He knew the crisis would come soon. He had been curing small numbers of people for several months. Doctors died quickly, usually by the first available hand. Everyone knew that doctors were the main reason for the plague because they had tried to usurp God's place and that the entire world had suffered as a result. Even those who were not superstitious knew that it was the meddling of doctors that had loosed the plague.

He hoped that a Healer with religion intertwined with the cures might survive. It had worked so far, but this last patient was not the silent type. The mother was fearful and would probably "confess" to seeing the Shaman as soon as the child was out of danger. Someone would yell "witch craft" or worse yet "Doctor" and someone he had helped would say "Healer". He had helped enough people to get quite a following and he had to hope that they wouldn't be too quiet. Normally the loudest yeller led the mob.

Having thought that, he left the consultation room for his more modern quarters in the rest of the house. The nervous types don't try to make their fortunes by breaking the rules and Solomon was soon lost in his search for a better antibiotic than he had.

When the day came, he was almost surprised. Two men appeared at his door unexpectedly. They were tall, obviously healthy, and were wearing well made cloaks to hold back the rain. He invited them into the meeting room in response to a polite knock on the door, "Gentlemen, please be seated."

Out of the rain, the men unhooked the front of their cloaks. They were both wearing imperial breastplates and very well armed. *Shit, she told the Imperials! Well, I won't go easy!* Solomon thought fast, but the unexpectedness of the crisis made him miss his last chance to bolt from his captors. He was as well armed as any free Texan but he had left his guns in the lab because they made his robes lumpy. *Damn,* he thought, *I'm going to die for fashion!*

The lead officer was at Solomon's side. "I'm sorry, but you can understand our need to move smartly. We won't have time to chat or even to sit Where do you keep your tools and books?"

Solomon knew when he was beaten and was too intelligent to waste a moment on futile protest. The material they wanted was in this house and they would find it with or without his help. "My lab is beyond that door. I have hidden the books under the floorboards in the kitchen. My lab manuals are in the lab with the other equipment." He felt a perverse pride in laying out what he was doing. If he couldn't take a few with him, he could still show the guardsmen that he was Texan.

The officer turned to his assistant. "Call in the rest of the squad. Take everything in the room behind that door. Pack up the kitchen and the Shamans' personal effects. Tell them that they will find the materials under the floorboards in the kitchen." Turning to Solomon, he asked "Is there anything else that they need to take?"

"No that's all of it. Take it and be damned."

The officer looked puzzled but continued. "Then you and I should be going. We have a long journey and an angry crowd to beat." He handed Solomon the cloak from a peg near the door, "After you, sir."

Solomon thought, *He's a damned polite and sarcastic executioner,* but he refused to show his fear.

There were several wagons and two surreys in front of the cabin. The officer approached the nearest surrey and motioned for Solomon to get in the far side. Realizing that the surrey would be between him and the guard, and that the rain would give him some cover, Solomon thought about making a break. Realizing that the guardsman could kill him from four hundred paces, he decided to get into the surrey. They took the double rutted path toward the town.

When they got within sight of the town, the officer stopped the surrey. He reached under his cloak and brought out a pair of hand manacles. "We had better put these on before we get to town."

"That's not necessary. I won't run."

"Oh, I know that. But we may meet some of your angry neighbors and I want to assure them that you are in good hands. By the way, my name is Fallon, Lieutenant Fallon. I'll be escorting you as far as the Eastern River."

With a very calm voice, Solomon asked, "What happens to me then?"

"I'm afraid that they don't share long term plans with lieutenants. I only know that I am to deliver you to the military packet at a plantation dock on the river. The material from your home will follow as soon as we can find another craft to carry it."

Sure, Solomon thought. *You'll need the evidence for the trial.*

The captain of the packet had been told that he would have a special passenger for a fast run to Austin. The orders said nothing of the status of the passenger but he did see Fallon removing the hand manacles as the surrey approached the dock. He decided the safe thing to do was to treat the man with courtesy, but post a guard at his side.

The boat was under way moments after Solomon came on board. Twenty polers shoved ten poles on each side into the soft river bottom. The winds were favorable and they were able to run up the sail before they reached the deepest part of the river. The polers rested at their stations over the water ready to help with turns or to take over if the wind failed.

Solomon was escorted to one of the two cabins at the stern. The first officer entered the cabin with Solomon, a very tight fit and said, "If you haven't eaten yet, I will have the cook bring you a schooner."

The mention of food was a sudden gut wrenching reminder that he had not eaten for almost twenty-four hours. His fear and determination had been masking the hunger. "I'd be grateful for a meal. This was obviously not a trip that I expected to take."

It seemed that the first officer was gone only a few minutes before the cook's helper showed up. The young boy brought a hearty meal of typical hearty field rations, a half loaf of bread hollowed out to hold a beef and vegetable stew with tortillas for silverware and flat beer to wash it down with.

Solomon waited until he judged the night was almost past and then, about three a.m., he decided it was time to cancel the rest of this trip. He opened the door a crack and peeped out. The polers were asleep and only a helmsman and sail trimmer seemed to be awake up near the bow. He silently slipped from the room.

"I wouldn't do that, sir. The deck is full of gear and dangerous enough in the day time, let alone at night." The guard had been sitting behind the door. "Is there something I can get for you?"

"No", Solomon said, "I was just getting a little fresh air. I guess I'll go back to sleep."

"Well, sir, this is a good place to practice sleeping. It's quiet, cool, and your old lady can't find you. Good night, Sir."

It's almost impossible to get sea sick on a riverboat, but Solomon had a record of doing hard things. By the time the captain's invitation to breakfast arrived, he was not only too ill to accept, he was almost too sick to answer. He spent the next two days in his room eating plain bread and beer when he felt up to chewing and swallowing. The third day he felt well enough to venture out on deck again.

The same guard was sitting by his door. "It's good to see you back in the land of the living. It's a good time to be up. We should put in at Austin in a few hours." The guard smiled wryly. "Take a deep breath and you'll see how close we are."

Solomon leaned on the railing and took a deep sniff. The smell of cooking fires, smelters, horses and humanity was slight but definitely in the air. Solomon, well aware that this might be his last chance ever to see the world, stood by the railing for over an hour hungrily taking in every sight, trying to commit to memory everything he saw and relishing every breath.

The boat docked at the Austin military pier. They were waiting for him when he disembarked. Two guardsmen escorted him to a waiting carriage. The ride was in silence. The guard was known for their western hero type chattiness. On duty, words were spent as if they were gold plated.

Solomon watched out the window and was happy to have the time to himself. This was his first, and probably last time in Austin. Everyone on the streets seemed to be in a hurry. The traffic was terrible even for the imperial service coach, it's right of way being more theoretical than real.

He was amazed at the sheer number of people. He had heard that Austin had almost three hundred thousand inhabitants, but the number was just too big to imagine. Most of the buildings were two story brick or poured concrete structures with tile roofs. On the main streets, the buildings had small shops and restaurants on the ground floor and apartments above. Down the side streets, he could see the occasional three or four story apartment building. There were even a few buildings left from before the New Era. They looked odd with their low roofs and lack of decoration.

The people all seemed to be in a hurry to be somewhere and dressed nicely for wherever that was. The men seemed to all wear low city boots and brightly colored clothes. The small white Stetson was in style again. The women were dressed as women always are, in bright dresses with long sleeves and a bonnet to protect their pale skin from the sun. He was surprised to see that only a third of the men and virtually none of the women were visibly armed. He could understand the women going unarmed. They had as protectors every man in earshot. The average Texan would punch you in the face if you said he was chivalrous, but he'd kill you if you harmed a woman or a child. The men, though, looked strange without side arms.

One street they took was filled with mansions. Most were large three story buildings with vast green lawns, iron fences, and wide driveways leading to private stables. The deep purples and bright reds showed clean and new. Most even had clear glass windows under the shutters. He had been enjoying the view but suddenly turned bitter. *Christ. He* thought, *I'm going to be dead or tortured and you'll still be partying in your damned mansion. Screw you.*

A few moments later, the carriage pulled up in front of the Imperial offices. One of his escorts presented a form to the receptionist. She passed it back to the guard behind her. He glanced at it and said "The emperor has been informed of your arrival but will not be available for about an hour. Perhaps you would like to wait in our 'Ambassadorial Suite'.

The servant brought fruit and tea – and, when his nose informed him that Solomon had been on the road for three days, a change of clothes.

"The servants will deliver a tub and toiletries so that you can freshen up before your appearance with His Majesty."

Solomon thought, *Yep, no one wants the condemned man to look pitiful. But, damn it, I'll look the best I can and I'll stand on both feet.*

The bath tub was delivered in few minutes. A servant girl stayed to help him scrub and shave. The toiletries included toothbrush, mouthwash, pomade, a razor, and after shave. The clothes were more fashionable than what he normally wore.

They consisted of a white bloused shirt, dark blue tunic and matching trousers. The tunic had a leather front and cuffs. The slacks had a leather stripe down the side, but had white fringe on the cuffs. A yellow neck scarf and low boots finished off the ensemble. He did look sharp for a condemned man.

He had only a few minutes to admire himself in the mirror before a guard entered the room.

"His Majesty will see you now."

Solomon suddenly realized that this was going much too fast. He expected to die but only after being jailed and questioned and publicly charged with heresy. In his mind, he saw his medicines and books being added to the Holy Fire next Destruction Day and then, perhaps, himself tossed in to celebrate the Melt.

He wasn't ready for this. He was too lost in reverie to notice that they had passed the Throne Room, but was still surprised when he was escorted into the royal working office. The Emperor himself sat at the desk wearing his working crown and smoking a pipe. He had apparently been in conversation with the three men seated around the room. Two were military officers and the other was, unbeknown to him, Sir Robert Wilson. As he entered, the man in the chair directly in front of the emperor moved to a seat on the right.

The emperor waved him to the chair in front of the desk. "Please be seated. I hope that your trip was not too arduous. I'm sorry we have to move you on so fast, but this matter requires fast action."

The emperor looked at Solomon. "Most of your equipment was sent upriver on a trimaran row ship. Major Samuels was just filling me in on the contents. It's a very impressive list."

Oh, great, thought Solomon, *I even get a sarcastic emperor!*

"Major, please continue your report."

"Sire, Mr. Solomon had several texts hidden under the floor. They were wrapped in oil cloth and seem to be originals. The men have handled them very carefully due to their age. There were twelve books in all . They included texts titled 'Grey's' Anatomy". 'Natural Cures', and 'Biochemistry Book 1" There were seven books on medicine, two on pharmacology, two an horticulture and, strangely, one book on geology."

The emperor looked at Solomon, who answered the unspoken question, "The better to find Epson Salts with."

The major continued, "Mr. Solomon had a well equipped lab. Wilson's people have identified a microscope and something Mitchell Seales described as 'a simple but effective centrifuge'. It's all under guard here and ready to be sent to the farm."

The emperor again turned his attention to Solomon. "This is the most impressive stock of material that we have ever uncovered. Frankly, it is more then we ever hoped for. Unfortunately, Shaman Solomon White Feather has to die today."

No man hears his death sentence without the pit of his stomach experiencing weightlessness. Solomon managed to keep his composure but could not for a few moments hear what the emperor was saying.

The emperor continued, "The major tells me that we just got you out before your neighbors arrived with the traditional pitch forks and torches. A woman whose child you had saved betrayed you to her less than intelligent husband. Our men only got your equipment out by telling the crowd that they would be given credit when it all went into the Holy Fire. We promised them special blessings from the priests. Well, Mr. White Feather, you have a choice that few living men get. Have you any preference about what we ascribe your death too. Shall it be drowning in an escape attempt, a brave fight with the guard, or a river fever? You want it heroic or mundane?"

Solomon was beginning to hear again. "Sire, Is it not cruel to ask the condemned man to select his own death."

"What condemned man?" The emperor noticed the ashen look on Solomon's face. "What do you think in going on here?"

"It's obvious. I have been arrested for Heresy, my equipment dragged here for evidence, and now I will die. I don't object to the sentence as I knew what I was doing and a man pays his own bills. But asking a man to pick his own death seems unusually cruel!"

The emperor literally did not know whether to laugh at the situation or cry for the pain that Solomon had obviously gone through. "Jesus, this is not a trial. It's a job interview! Relax and get your pulse back." After a bit, he continued, "We heard that there was a healer in East County that was better than most. When our local people heard that you used a powder that reversed the infection after you set that boy's compound fracture, we figured that you might have some knowledge from the old era. It took us a few weeks to set up the pickup. Then the major tells me we had to jump early because of the ungrateful parent. Apparently you were not informed because the guard came early. Major, this man seems to have gotten all the way here thinking that he is a prisoner."

The Major cleared his throat. Covering your arse was not acceptable behavior in the service. You could be fired faster for an excuse than a failure. "We never considered the possibility. Only the advance man and the initial moving team knew of his status. For obvious reasons, no one else is told. If he missed the advance man and misunderstood the guards at his door, there was no one to inform him. Mr. White Feather, you have my most profound apologies. I assure you that we will takes steps to make sure this never happens to anyone else."

Sir Wilson stirred from Solomon's other side. "I am the one who arranged your pickup. You have my apologies also. Let me clarify why we brought you in. As His Majesty explained, we were fairly certain that you had old texts or at least copies of B.N.E. information. However, what impressed us was the Shaman act. The blending of religion and medicine to come up with the 'healer' was brilliant. And it almost worked. I personally think that it would have worked if you had started in Austin or New Houston. People there are less adamant about superstition and are more likely to let themselves be fooled for a good cause, the best cause being their own skin. That village you were in was not the best place to try this."

Sir Wilson turned to the emperor. "Your Majesty, may I inform this man of his situation and ours?... Thank you. Solomon, we have a little ranch about two hours north of here. You passed it on your trip down river. We want you to join us there. We will copy your books to safeguard them. Then we'll work on a plan to reintroduce healing without reintroducing lynching. We have a group of men there that I think you will like and enough good work to last us the rest of our lives. We would, of course, value your contribution regarding the healing arts, but we will also need a man of imagination to help with the planning and a man of courage to carry out the first public steps. On the down side, Solomon White Feather has to die now. No kin or friend will hear from him in this lifetime. We cannot have the emperor suffering an evil tech to live."

Solomon's color was returning. In a shaky voice he said through the smile that he couldn't control, "That's alright. I've got no kin. My birth name was Samuel White. I'll be grateful to go back to it."

Lead by the emperor, the men in the room rose from their chairs.

Sir Wilson extended his hand, "Welcome to Imperial Employment, Mr. White."

Chapter 10   The Visitor

He stood just off the street in the alley nearest the Imperial Pavilion. Dressed in his tight pants, blouson shirt, leather vest and bill cap and carrying his tool sack over his shoulder, Bishop Artemis looked every bit the prosperous tradesman in the prime of his life. But he was a long three thousand miles way from home.

He had traveled into the lion's den by papal coach, wagon train, tinker's wagon, stagecoach, freight wagon, river boat and shanks mare. Once, he had crawled two miles on his belly to avoid a guard post. If he lived, he would describe it later as "an interesting trip".

Well, he said to himself, *live or die, now's the time to know.* Dropping the tool sack, he removed a bright red monks robe, donned it, and pulled the hood over his head. He stooped again to retrieve a flat package wrapped in velour and an envelope with the red papal seal visible on it. Without hesitating, he rounded the corner and started up the steps to the imperial office building.

The resemblance to the Pantheon was not accidental. The huge room had tiled floors, a domed ceiling, western frescos and statue niches on the wall. Like the Pantheon, except that here, the niches held guardsmen, live, breathing and holding vicious, four hundred year old AK47s. They looked almost festive in their striped pants and colored vests, holding the multicolored Ak47s, steel where the original parts were and brass where replacement parts had been hand crafted and fitted.

The room was almost empty and he glided across the floor to within a few feet of the receptionist. Before the guards began to react. They could be forgiven for a slightly slow start. None of them had ever seen a Papal monk. There hadn't been one in Texas since the Emperor's' grandfather had evicted them during the Papal War of '37.

He hooked his thumbs under his hood and threw it back.

"I am Bishop Artimus, an envoy from his Papal Majesty to the Sovereign Empire of Texas. These are my credentials."

This was like Borman parachuting into England during WWII as a representative of Nazi Germany. Borman never again saw a day outside of his cell, and jails now were less common than cheaper and more permanent solutions.

A guardsman stepped out from behind the receptionist and bowed slightly. "Uh, welcome …Bishop. I am Lieutenant Adams. Let me call the OD to verify your credentials. It will not take long. Perhaps you would like to wait in our ambassadorial suite"

Artimus handed him the envelope and said, "Thank you", but noticed from the corner of his eyes that two additional guards now stood before the doors the Imperial Office and two guards had slipped closer to the front door.

The "Ambassadorial Suite" was a small room with comfortable overstuffed furniture, elegant carpeting and a hand carved desk. Tapestries lined the walls and felt curtains hid the fact that the windows were narrow slits in the wall. A servant had brought tea and fruit shortly after Artimus settled on one of the couches. It was comfortable as cells went, and he decided not to see the peep holes in the ceiling and walls. He balanced the velour package on his knee as he waited while the servant poured tea. The package had not been more than a few inches from him for two thousand miles.

As the servant set fruit on the table, the chamberlain was already in front of the Emperor. "Your majesty, there is a monk here claiming to be an ambassador of the Pope!"

The emperor sat quietly thinking for several seconds while the chamberlain fidgeted. "I don't know who you have out there, but I doubt that he's an ambassador. We are technically at war, but Pope Jones must know that he could have had an ambassador present his credentials at the border and we would have provided an "honor guard" to bring him here.

"Send a messenger for the chief of intelligence. Tell him who this guy claims to be and tell him to come with some way to check this man out. Have the servants inform the visitor that I am not in the building but that I am expected in a few hours. Meantime we check him out."

It was less than an hour before the chief of intelligence was in the emperor's office with his brief pouch and a very young and timid looking assistant. He was almost too excited to wait for the emperor to give him the nod to speak. Intelligence was an over-rated job. This was the first time that he had actually seen anything real.

"He's real, Sire. In fact he's more than real. Jedson is head of our pope squad. Jedson, would you show his majesty what you found out."

Jedson handed the emperor a drawing of a handsome man with a spade beard and a hand written fact sheet.

Jedson was smiling big enough to make his face break and having a hard time keeping his voice calm. "Sire, I observed the subject though the peep holes and compared him with the drawings sent by our agents in Albany. Not only is the face identical, but those two small moles near his left ear make the identification positive. He obviously shaved off his beard to look more Texan, but his personal movements are also as described by our agent. They say he never makes nervous moves, but you can see him close his eyes and control his breathing as he does a relaxation exercise. He is Bishop Artimus, but that is not his full name. It's even better. He is Bishop Artimus Jones! Son of and heir apparent to the Pope."

Jedson sat there with his hands spread out and a silly smile on his face, as he realized that he didn't know what to say next.

The emperor saved him. "What do we know of his personality, if he is Artimus Jones?"

"Well, sire, he is a graduate of the seminary at Annapolis. He's been working for the theocracy since he graduated. His father has given him a variety of assignments over the last twelve years and he seems to have done well in all of them. He led a company against the Virginia rebels. Rumor is that his men loved him and that the establishment hated him. Oh, on his personality. Well, he graduated with honors but had demerits for several practical jokes. It was suspected, but never proven, that he was the one who removed a sign from the Chapel and hung it over the local bank. The sign said "Jesus Saves"! He's married and as of our last report, about a year old, he has a four year old son."

The emperor sat back in his chair. "Then I guess I'll have to see him."

Seeing the confused looks on the faces around him, he added, "Pope Jones isn't going to send his eldest son to commit an assassination, and the way the Jones feel about family, Artimus will do his duty, but he won't orphan his son unnecessarily. I'm perfectly safe and dying to know what was important to bring here this way. There's no point in getting a gaggle of people involved. I suspect that he came this way because neither of us is going to want anyone to know he was here. While I talk to Artimus, you two start figuring out who knows about him and what we'll have to do to keep it quiet. As you leave, tell the chamberlain to inform the ambassador of my return and have the gentleman escorted to this office."

Artimus was not impressed with the chamber. The papal court ran to ostentatious ness and all of the bishops had larger and more gilded offices than this one. Emperor Adams chose quality but functional pieces for his office and never saw sense in working in cavernous surroundings.

Artimus stood while the chamberlain sat a silver tray holding the papal envelope on the desk. Taking up the envelope, the Emperor said to the chamberlain, "The guards may leave us. We will not need them for this initial meeting."

The guards left the room, and then immediately joined the rest of their squad at peep holes in the false walls of the office.

Looking at the now open letter, he addressed Artimus, "Let's get the formalities out of the way first. You are hereby accredited as a legitimate ambassador from a foreign, if not friendly, country. As such, you have our personal assurances that you will not be questioned, interrogated, tortured, killed, unreasonably impaired in your movements, or detained here against your will. You may be seated."

"Thank you, your majesty. I come with a message from my master. You may wish to read it in private. Before I present it to you, I must emphasize that we do not intend in any way to insult your beliefs. If our analysis is correct, this will be of much interest to you. If we are in error, you have our and my sincerest apologies."

As he unwrapped the felt covered package, the emperor indicated the chamberlain, "Chamberlain Smith is cleared for all state secrets." He did not add that the fifty-ish Chamberlain was also an old battle companion and trusted advisor. As he opened the bound cover of the message, a look of surprise came over his face. "I see what you mean. Chamberlain Smith, please leave us. Send in the captain of the guard."

The captain was in the room almost before the door closed. Like all good guard captains, he had a permanent steel rod in his back and was capable of a glare harder and more dangerous than a steel blade.

"Captain, you are to remain with us, but I want all other guards away from this room."

It took a few seconds, but the faint rustling in the walls indicated that the order was being followed.

"Bishop Artimus, you have our apologies. I agree with you but cannot leave myself totally without security. The captain of the guard will have to stay."

He looked down into his hands. It was a book. It was painfully hand made copy of the original. The artist had even duplicated the red bands that were on the cover of the original. "Cleveland Institute of Electronics" was in white ink on one red band and "Lesson 1 of 20" on the other. Possession of it was worth a crucifixion anywhere in the civilized world. The fact that Artimus not only had it, but carried it though thousands of miles of Texas was astounding.

He was still leafing through it, when Artimus spoke again. "This is more a token of good faith than just a simple message. I am instructed to tell you that we have seventeen of the nineteen additional volumes. My master wishes to make you a present of them."

"What does your master want in return?"

At the question, Artimus relaxed almost visibly. The greatest danger had passed. "Only to be allowed to present them to you in person and in secret. These books are, of course, heresy. I am not privy to all of his plans and am not at liberty to discuss all that I know. I can assure you that his goals are honorable and there is no treachery in the wind. I am to await your answer or your pleasure."

Emperor Adams was still looking at the book. "Whatever analysis you did, you are correct. This is of interest to us. It will, however, take some time to consider your proposal. You understand that you may be with us for a considerable time. Captain, ask the chamberlain to arrange for suitable quarters in the officer's quarters. The best that they have, and arrange a line of credit for his comfort. The bishop is to have guards with him at all times. They are, however, only to insure his safety and to make certain that he does not betray his identity to anyone. Other than that, they are not to impede his movements. Who is the most close mouthed man in the guard?"

The captain came to attention still sitting down. "Private Williams, Sire. His mother still thinks she's pregnant 'cause he hasn't told her yet that he was birthed and grew up."

Adams turned to Artimus "If that red cloak does not have any special religious importance, I would suggest that you turn it over to the captain. You certainly can't wear it in Austin. If there are any rumors of your visit, we'll send Private Williams out on the street in your robe. He can pretend to be a circus performer or a drunk on his way to a costume party. That will explain the rumors of a monk in Austin."

Standing, he added, "Gentlemen, we are adjourned. Bishop, I hope that your trip will be worth the considerable trouble you must have gone to."

Chapter 11   The Bishop Comes To Dinner

Fortunately, it was Wednesday. Emperor Adams returned to the palace late as usual. It was a night when he and the Empress ate alone in their apartments. Theirs was not an arranged marriage, but something similar. It was also living proof that arranged marriages had a better chance of success than marriages based on sudden and short term passion. When the marriage was arranged for the benefit of the bride and groom, rather than for political or financial gain, the prospective bride and groom were presented with partners who shared the same background and class. They shared the same world view and normally felt comfortable immediately. In spite of American fictions, the arranged couple, if arranged properly, normally came back from the honeymoon very much in love.

The Emperor and Empress of Texas adored each other as much as Queen Victoria and Albert. More important, they trusted each other completely. They were the result of a few hundred years of careful breeding. Texans were not politically correct. They believed that a man could be born bad or good; stupid, smart or crazy; kind or mean. The reasoning was that if dogs came in smart and stupid breeds, and gentle and mean breeds, and horses were born faster or slower, why should humans be any different? Adding a brain didn't mean that people followed different breeding rules than other animals.

The first Emperor of Texas did not want the fate of Peter the Great. The Russian Czar was one of the three or four most effective rulers in history. His son was a dolt who was so lazy that he begged not to be made Czar because it was too much work. He had to be put to death to save Russia.

From the first, prospective additions to the royal family went through rigorous screening. The Texans might not know the term "Genetics", but they were good horse breeders. Candidates were screened for intelligence and competence. Any hint of mental illness or weakness in the family line would disqualify them. Exceptionally bad habits like fiscal irresponsibility, extreme selfishness, cruelty toward servants, or cowardice would keep them from the royal bed.

Texas had not yet bred a separate race like the Tai aristocracy of the Nineteenth Century, but their odds of survival were improved with the good breeding.

All of which meant nothing to Burt and Shirley. They had been in love from the first minute he took her in his arms at the Royal Ball and they began to waltz. The fact that they would never have met if she had not passed the screening was totally unimportant to the young lovers.

The waltz had never ended.

He dropped his crown by the door and hung his ceremonial pearl handled colt 45 on the peg next to his cape. He dropped gratefully into the dining room chair. The Royal apartment was plush but small enough to feel more like a home than a palace.

Dinner was on the table. There were no servants around. Shirley kissed him quickly but warmly. "Anything interesting happen at the office today, Dear?"

As he reached for the plate of roast beef, he answered "Actually, it was a little more interesting than usual. We had a visitor."

"Anyone I know?"

"Not unless you have been to New York. Believe it or not, the son of the showed up in my office this morning. He brought a message from his father."

He began cutting his beef and reached for a baked potato. He was on his second mouthful of salad when his wife threw a biscuit across the table. "You beast!! You can't come in here and say something like that and then just keep on eating! What was the message?"

Actually, it was only partly teasing. He wasn't certain what to say about it yet and he was very hungry. Between mouthfuls he said, "I haven't sorted it all out yet. The Pope sent us a forbidden book and a message that he wants to meet me. Let's finish dinner and then we can sit by the fireplace and think it all over."

They sat in their easy chairs facing the fire. It was the only light in the room. Somehow the world shrank when you were staring at a fireplace. The small and graceful woman at your side, wine in your hand, and the thoughts in your head were all that existed.

He had explained as much as he could of the events of the day. "I don't know where to go next. My gut feeling is that the Pope has a good reason for the meeting. Of course, it could be an assassination attempt or some strange plot to attack our dynasty, but frankly, the Popes have never worked that way. They're our enemies, but they have always been honorable ones.

"For the life of me, I cannot figure out why they sent a forbidden book. I only pray that they do not know about the farm. It could spell the end of the Adams."

His wife looked up at him. "Honey, I have an idea. The decision must be made based upon your judgment of Bishop Artimus. He is his father's son and the only source of information you have. Whatever the Pope is up to, obviously no one but he and his son know about it. Therefore, invite Artimus to stay here. There is no better way to get to know someone than over the dinner table. Give him an apartment in the guest wing. Take him hunting. Watch him dance. Play pool with him. Then make your decision."

"I think you're right. In fact, you are so right that I don't need to think about it. Would you reach over there and ring for the Butler."

The butler was surprised. The Royal couple rarely wanted their evenings alone interrupted by servants. He bowed a little. Texans are not good at bowing. "May I be of service?"

The emperor spoke more firmly than he did with his wife. "Please have a message sent to the officer's quarters. There is an Artimus Jones bivouacked there. Please inform the staff the Mr. Jones is invited to the Palace for breakfast. By the time he finishes breakfast, I want a suite of rooms ready for him in the west wing. He will be with us for an extended period. He is an honored guest. Give him the best we have available. He is about Sir Wilson's size. See if you can scare up some clothes for him. Then call the tailor for a late morning fitting. He's been traveling light and he will need an entire new wardrobe. Tell the tailor to be ready to provide formal, leisure, and sporting outfits. If anyone asks, Mr. Artimus is a member of the secret service and should not be expected to tell anyone where he has been. His missions are not public knowledge."

They were all sitting at breakfast when Artimus arrived. That was stage planning. They wanted to emphasize the informality of the setting and assure

Artimus that this was not a formal occasion. He was shown into the room by the butler, who was, as usual, dressed like a town cowboy in a fringed shirt and string tie. Emperor Adams did not stand. It would have been impolite for an Emperor, but he gestured to Artimus, "Help yourself. There is a good buffet on the sideboard or the cook can rustle up something special if you need it."

When he was seated, the Empress put down her newspaper and smiled warmly.

The Emperor said, "This is the Empress Shirley, my beloved wife. That empty hole down at the end of the table where the food is disappearing is my nephew, Samuel. He is getting ready for a race this afternoon. Everyone, this is Mr. Artimus Jones. He is going to stay with us for a while. He is friend of an old and dear friend of mine."

Looking at Artimus, he continued, "I know that you don't want to be away from your home and family any longer than necessary. However, you can understand that we have to consider this situation carefully so you may be here awhile. We want you to stay here in the palace while we work. It is more comfortable and more private than the officer's quarters."

The Empress chimed in. Her diminutive size and blonde hair did not indicate shyness. "Please eat, Mr. Jones. In Texas, we don't stop eating just because my husband is talking. I want to emphasize that we don't just want you to stay in the palace. We want you to stay with the family. This is a long, lonely trip for you. While you are here, you stay with us. You are invited to share our home, our parties, and our meals. We will try to find some activities to fill your hours as soon as we know what pleases you."

Artimus hid his relief very well. Up until this moment, he wasn't certain that he would live out the day or ever see his wife and family again. However, Texans did not invite you to breakfast with the family, introduce you to the wife and kids, and then kill you.

The Emperor added, around a mouthful of eggs. "I have to get to the office soon. Jeeves will show you to your rooms. You have an appointment with the tailor later this morning. I suggest you take his advice about styles."

The Empress added, "After lunch, Samuel is riding in a school horse race on the East Lawn. I know that it isn't as exciting as your life usually is, but you are invited to join us."

The Emperor's first meeting of the afternoon was with the Archeology Committee. As usual, the meeting was held in the soundproof conference room. The Empress had snuck away from Artimus to attend the meeting.

After the customary repetition of the oath, Sir Wilson opened the meeting. "The first item on the agenda is the progress of Mr. White. Our newest resident at the farm, Mr. White has been with us for several weeks now. I'll let him bring you up to date on his progress."

White Feather, now Solomon White, was missing his feather and was dressed in a typical Texan business suit. His conservative white pipe stem trousers were topped with a bright blue waistcoat and a paisley vest. He wore a traditional leather low slung holster on his right side. The holster was empty as all firearms were left on the table near the door. It was hard for a Texan to check his weapon, but this was a conference about noble treason.

"Most of you know about the shaman healer act that I was using before I was recruited. We have decided that it's too risky to try again. It came uncomfortably close to getting my neck stretched. In any case, even if it had worked, we couldn't invent enough shamans to make a real difference in Texas. We need something more than one by one secret pseudo doctors. We looked at using the medical services that we currently have as a way to start expanding back into real medicine."

There was a startled expression on many of the faces in his audience, so he said, "Don't look so shocked, gentlemen. Texas does have doctors even though the term is a curse word and can get a man killed. The army has surgeons who carefully never identify themselves as doctors. No one complains about someone sewing up a bullet hole or setting a broken bone. If people can understand it, they don't consider it 'medicine'. We also have midwifes in every town. They're not as effective as doctors were, but they do remember that it's important to wash your hands before a delivery, and some of them can even turn a breach birth or sew up a hemorrhage. The leading cause of death among women is still childbirth, but it would be worse if we *didn't* have the midwives. There are also folk cures. People still remember that putting alcohol on a cut can stop the bacteria from attacking it. They think that bacteria are some kind of small invisible evil spirit, but the alcohol still works. There are also many folk remedies on the market. You can get herbal potions for stomach ache, mud pastes for burns, and even magic paste for pimples and warts. As long as it is 'natural', it isn't medicine. Problem is that most of the remedies are less than useless, and the average Texan has less medical care than an ancient Egyptian or Chinaman. If you get sick, you pretty much just die."

Solomon's eyes glazed over a bit and his official voice got a note of sadness. "I am a newcomer here, but I think it's our single greatest problem. Every man and woman in this room has mourned a child or spouse or mother that died too soon."

Realizing he was off topic, his voice hardened. "We have a preliminary plan. It is months or years from working, but at least we have an idea to work on. We have decided to start by introducing herbal medicines with a difference. These will be sold just like the ones we have now, with one difference. They will work. We have been working on identifying medical substances and practices that we can introduce without getting lynched. Most of all, we need what the Ancients called an 'antibiotic'. As some of you may know, neither germs or bacteria are magical little devils. They're like extremely small plants or insects. They're too small to see and, in the right conditions, they multiply almost magically. They can take over and destroy a whole body. They're what makes wounds fester. They are the reason that most men who are gut shot die of the fever days later even if the wound doesn't kill them."

Someone raised a hand for Solomon's attention, "I thought that the alcohol killed the bacteria. What does that anti thing do that's different?"

"The alcohol only kills the bad stuff before it gets into the body. The word is 'topical'. When you pour it on a wound, it kills things trying to get in. If it kills enough, you body can handle what is left over. However, once the bacteria are in your system, the alcohol doesn't do any good. The stuff has already spread into the tissues. Gut wounds kill you because the bacteria are way inside. Even a few of them can cause enough fever to kill you. There are also bacteria that travel through the water and even the air. We think that they cause most of the fevers that kill people. Alcohol won't fight them. If it did, no drunk would ever die. Antibiotics get inside to fight. You drink them or they get absorbed through the skin when you sprinkle them on the wound. They still don't cure everything, but right now deep wounds kill ninety percent of the time. We could get that down to fifteen or twenty percent. We could also save thousands of children a year who die from infections or diseases that antibiotics can cure."

White paused to see if there were any questions. When none were forthcoming, he said, "Of course, the first problem is that we don't have an antibiotic. We have the pharmacology texts that my great grandfather hid for his son. Fortunately, he passed on one that included information on the natural sources of many of the common drugs the Ancients used. The bad news is that many of those sources were plants that are native to China or Europe or other places that we can't reach. There is a note the Nile river mud contains something call Tetracycline that is one of these antibiotics, but we, obviously can't reach the Nile river bank. We are limited to what we can find in the Empire. If it doesn't exist in the countries of Texas, Colorado, Kansas, or NewMex, it's not much use to us. The drug that I used on the boy's hand was called a Sulfa drug. It was one of the first antibiotics made. It was simple enough for me to manufacture, but it is NOT a natural product. We would not want to get caught marketing it. We'll use it if we have to, but it would be dangerous if we got caught manufacturing a drug."

The Empress raised a finger, "Assuming that you do find effective medical substances that can be introduced as 'natural' products, how do you plan to distribute them? We can't very well have 'Emperor Adams Magic Powders' on the market."

"We have the beginnings of a plan. We plan to introduce 'Winnie Wigwams Magic Elixirs' made by Miss Winnie Wigwam herself. You will see her picture on every can and bottle. The silliness of the name is deliberate. If we do get an irate pastor or newspaper editor that takes offense to the "usurpation of GOD'S WILL", he will sound somewhat silly complaining about something called 'Winnie Wigwams Herbal Soothing Powder.' We'll start in a small town. We won't advertise. People will start to realize the powder is "lucky". If we are lucky, the stuff will spread by word of mouth and not be noticed by troublemakers. It is, however, still premature to plan much more because we don't yet know exactly what we are going to sell."

As he sat down, the Emperor took the floor. "Before we adjourn, I want to announce that the Emperor Emeritus Samuel Adams and the Empress Dowager have decided to come a little ways out of retirement. They will be rejoining this committee at our next meeting. I think that you will agree that they will be a great help."

Someone said informally, "Sounds good. The old man was always a creative thinker."

Back at the palace, Artimus had began his morning by being fitted for a Texas wardrobe. The tailor had started the day in an impeccable suit that was now modified with pins in the lapels, yellow measuring tape hanging from the pockets, and sheets of notes sticking out from beneath his vest. He obviously enjoyed making fine clothes more than wearing them. He was saying, "Sir, we have been instructed to provide a variety of appropriate outfits. I hear that you are new to the capitol. Perhaps I could suggest a wardrobe for you."

Artimus was aware of his ignorance of Texan Royal customs, and was the type to take advice rather than take offence. "Sounds good. I have spent my life serving the Empire in Kansas and I really don't know the styles here in the capitol. What would you suggest for a start?'

"This year's colors tend to run to white or pastel trousers, bright blue or yellow coats, and bloused white shirts for both formal and semi-formal wear."

"Tell you what, I suggest that you make up a minimum wardrobe that will get me by for a few weeks. You choose the items. Then when I develop a little more taste, we can do the rest of it."

The fitting, measuring and fussing still took well over an hour. The Tailor then insisted on showing Artimus fabrics and hand drawn pictures for his approval. It took a little longer than he expected because, to his surprise, Artimus realized he was enjoying himself. After two months of tension, it was relaxing to pick out an ascot.

Just as the tailor left the apartment, the butler showed up. Artimus doubted that the timing was accidental. "Their Majesties will be away for most of the day. They have asked that I acquaint you with the amenities of the palace in their absence and offer you a tour." He walked over to table and laid out a printed map. When Artimus leaned over the other side of the table, he turned the map around to be correct to Artimus.

"This is where we are now on the west wing of the second floor. This floor on this wing is devoted to apartments for permanent residents. Anyone you meet here lives in the palace, but the apartments are essentially private homes.

The floor above us contains the Royal Apartments. The extreme west end is the private section that is reserved only for the Royal Family. There are guards at the door and no one enters. The East section of that wing contains the semi-private rooms. There is a private library, pool room, sitting rooms, games rooms, and short term rooms for Royal relatives who are not royal enough for the private section. As you are a special guest, you are, of course, invited to use any of the facilities on that floor."

Artimus' ears had picked up when he heard the word "library". Private libraries were uncommon in this world.

The Butler continued. "The ground floor in this wing contains some offices and rooms that function as sort of a Royal Inn. Short term guests stay there after parties, petitioners, officials visiting for a few days stay there. It is often more empty than filled. The basement levels are utility areas for laundry, repair shops, furnaces and so on."

His finger moved across to the other side of the map. "Of course you saw the grand foyer when you came in. Unless the doors were open, you might not have seen the ballroom behind it. They both occupy all three floors of the center of the building.

The East Wing is a hodgepodge. My offices and some of my staff are there. The officers of the guard and some of the guard themselves are on the third floor.

The main kitchen is on the second floor. Most of the officers and many of my staff eat in the mess right there." He pointed to a large room toward the east end of the wing. "When you are not with their majesties, you can, of course order food to be served either in your apartment or in the semi-private rooms on the third floor. However, you are also welcome to drop into the mess. There are cooks there twenty four hours a day. The food is good, the jokes jovial, and the companionship worthwhile. One of His Majesties complaints about his father retiring was that, as emperor, he could no longer just drop in and have a meal in the mess. There are two areas that you do need to know about in case of emergency. We have not had an attack here in about ninety years. However, there is an armory in the basement of the East Wing. There is a fortified room and a guard contingent on duty at all times. In case of attack, if anything gets past the perimeter wall, get down there and get armed. If you are in the royal chambers, stay put. The walls are also fortified there and you will be safe until the guard gets there."

Artimus was surprised at the amount of information he was being given. Of course, the Papal Secret service probably had some idea of the layout of the palace. It was still surprising to have the household staff lay out a map for him. In fact, Emperor Adams was somewhat of a plunge bettor. He had decided things would go faster if he gave Artimus all the rope he could possibly need to hang himself. Or prove himself. Artimus would find himself fully trusted, and carefully watched.

The butler gestured to the door. "I am on my way to the mess. As you are eating alone this afternoon, perhaps you would like to accompany me. I can point out some more of the amenities on the way."

The palace was a comfortable place. Like many buildings of its time, it was constructed of concrete from three to four feet thick with a thick white tile roof. A layer of brick and stone on the outside and two inches of plaster on the interior walls hid the basic nature of the building.

Inside, there was a conscious effort to look "Western". Most of the service areas were colorfully tiled. Wooden beams, some necessary, some decorative, were in the ceilings of most rooms. Stuffed animal heads hung beside the coats of arms in the grand ballroom.

Wallpaper was an expensive and rare item as there were no power printing presses or roll paper machines, but Texans decorated their palaces and their homes the same way medieval castles and Roman villas were done. All walls were painted. In the more formal rooms, plaster and wood moldings decorated the ceilings and walls. Most of the un-tiled small rooms were stencil painted in patterns that looked much like wallpaper.

The heavy service areas were painted, as service areas have been since the Hittites, with a dark color to shoulder height and then a lighter color for the upper walls and ceilings. Due to the lack of artificial lighting and the expense of good dyes, most large rooms were painted in very light colors and all ceilings were white.

On the way, the butler pointed out the various rooms that they were passing. Artimus wondered if the butler was going to stay with him for lunch. A servant eating with a guest seemed like an unlikely idea.

The mess was, indeed, a warm place. The furniture was heavy and comfortable. A steam table ran along one wall for those in a hurry. Waiters took

orders for custom cooking from those who had time to wait. There were no menus.
A chalk board near the front door listed the special items of the day. If you wanted
something else, you asked for it. If they had it, you got it.

As expected, when they reached the mess, the butler guided Artimus to a table
where several military officers and a civil servant were sitting. "Gentlemen, this is
Mr. Artimus. He is on detached duty from Kansas. You may find each others
company interesting."

Then he left Artimus alone, with Texan military officers and a government
employee across the table. He need not have worried. Texans mostly followed the
Code of The West. Number Three was, "A man never passes up a good chance to
shut up." It didn't stop dinner conversation, but did give Texans the habit of not
asking for and rarely offering personal information.

The remainder of the afternoon was spent touring the palace.

That evening, there were six for dinner. As this was a working dinner, the
servants would lay out most of the food at once and then only return when called.

Wilson made the introductions as the servants began serving. "Mr. Jones you
have, of course, met me earlier. I'm Wilson. The man on my right is Solomon
White. He is a consultant for one of our agencies. Next to him is Sir Robert, who
works for the same agency. Gentlemen, Bishop Artimus Jones." It was the first
time Artimus' title had been used. It was obviously meant to show that everyone at
the table was in on The Secret.

The emperor confirmed that. "Bishop, everyone at this table is fully aware of
your situation and has my full confidence. You need not guard your tongue tonight
any more than you wish."

Artimus had considered this exact situation carefully. He didn't like the
Emperor's belief that his mission could take "a considerable time", and decided that
he would have to plunge in if he was every going to see York again this year. What
he said sounded casual, but had been thought through many times.

He smiled at Sir Robert. 'It's a pleasure to meet you, Sir Robert. It was, after
all, your work which prompted my trip."

The sudden revelation silenced everyone. He continued, "When we heard
about your work at the Archeology institute, we hoped that you were looking for
more than a little more material to feed the holy fires. However, that is conversation
for after dinner. Perhaps we should eat first and talk over brandy."

Conversation was very stilted at first. The Texans did not want to start a
conversation that would leave Artimus out and the two sides, as yet, had little in
common. The Empress solved the problem with her customary courtesy.

"We don't get to meet many visitors from as far away as you, Bishop. I am
certain that we would all love to hear your impressions of Texas."

"Certainly, Your Majesty. It's very different from York. My first impression
was that you Texans are a wild breed. In York, we have more order. Prayers in the
morning. Church from 10 to 12 on Sunday. Workdays begin at dawn and are
required to be over ten hours later. There are laws on how to treat employees,
indentured servants, and customers. Most businesses are licensed and regulated by
the church. Imagine how hard it was for me to get used to a country that only has
ten laws! When I decided to travel as an itinerant tinker, I couldn't believe that all I

had to do was buy a cart full of tools and hit the road. I don't think you know how wild this country is."

The emperor laid down his fork and leaned on his left elbow for a moment while he gathered his thoughts. "Actually, Bishop Jones, we are aware of it. It was planned. The founding Emperor decided that there were two basic ways to look at laws.

"There was the French way. Have a law for everything. One year, the French weavers could not start working for months because the king had not decided what patterns should be made that year. The ancient Americans were the worse. They had thousands and thousands of laws. They had laws to stop you from spitting on the sidewalk. They regulated the citizens bedroom activities. They told you what you could smoke and drink. They even had laws about what jokes and stories you could tell.

"It didn't work. It spawned a plague worse than locusts. Lawyers. With all of the laws trying to predict everything every one could do, there were always loopholes. The richest people in the country were the loophole finders. They had court after court passing judgments on which loopholes were legal and which were not, and then fighting with each other as to which court was right.

"The other way of governing was the Chinese model. You have a reasonable number of laws and then depend upon reasonable interpretation to keep things in check. Chinese administrators were almost independent judges. There were relatively few written laws and the administrator was charged with making individual judgments in each case. As the administrators were screened with tests for intelligence and reasoning power, it worked well until corruption and bribery began on a large scale.

"The danger with that method of government is that it depends upon having intelligent and honest people in administration. The population has to feel that they can trust the judgment they get.

"The founder decided that that was the lesser risk. He wrote down the Code of The West. There were only eleven lines. He could have used any religion as a source, but he decided to use the famous ancient western philosophers like Wayne and Zane Grey to give Texas a feeling that the rules were special for them alone.

"He added some interpretation for each code and then concentrated on forming an educational system and civil service administration to keep things going. It's been a few hundred years, and it still seems to be working."

Artimus smiled and replied, "It seems to work well in Texas, but the uncertainty of having virtually no written laws would make most Yorkers feel completely unprotected."

They continued to talk about the differences in the two countries until the second course was finished. Dinner was a leisurely event at the palace and there was no hurry to finish. It was common and courteous to stop eating often for a little more conversation.

By the third course, venison stew with a thick black bread, they were all relaxed and feeling comfortable with each other.

The empress turned to Artimus again. "Bishop, I am so curious about your trip that I have to chance offending you by asking about your adventures. You don't have to tell us anything secret, but I am dying to know how you suddenly showed up in the center of our capital city. It must be a great spy story!"

"Well," he said, "I am afraid, your majesty, that you may be disappointed. For a great spy story, it had a sorry beginning. I crossed the border near the old Fort Scott. I had decided not to bring anything with me but the absolute minimum, as anything from New York could betray me. I had a sack with Texas gold coin, the book, my robes, a bag of jerky and the letter that I was delivering. I planned to buy clothes, tools, horses and whatever else I needed after I crossed the border.

"I left my unit about a mile from your border station and decided to simply walk around it. We had picked that spot because there was a river that ran parallel to the road and about sixty yards to the north. The water level was down and I figured the banks would hide me.

"Unfortunately, the banks kept getting lower and lower and pretty soon I was beginning my great adventure by crawling on my belly. I was, of course, thinking heroic thoughts at the time. Well, at least until I brushed up against that bush and a bunch of insects shook down onto my back. I did find that itching does interrupt a heroic image.

"Then, when I was closest to the station, a bird landed on my back. Now this is not something that happens in the normal course of human life. However, it wanted the insects, and I couldn't even wave it off because the border guards might hear the noise. I shook it off of me a couple of times, but it must have loved those bugs and been real hungry, 'cause it just landed again and started picking things off of my rump."

"So, I entered Texas for my great adventure crawling belly down in cold water, covered with insects, trying not to scratch, and with a bird on my butt."

No one knew whether to laugh or give sympathy, until the Empress giggled. "Please tell us it got better!"

"It did, but not right away. I couldn't go into any of the villages right up next to the border because they were too small and a stranger would have stood out too much. So I had to hike around them. I hit the ditch every time I heard a horse coming, and that first day I was in that ditch so much I felt like a Jack in the box. After that I cut off the road far enough to be going through the woods. I wasn't so much worried about royal patrols as I was average citizens. The patrol might take me prisoner and lead to a premature end to my mission, but the plague fears could get me hung by any citizen thinking I was from anther country.

"After the first four days, I wished that I was carrying more jerky and less gold. I got back to the road over near New Iola and stopped when I came to an inn that I thought was far enough from the border to be safe. The next morning the inn keeper got me a ride into New Iola with a merchant going that way.

"New Iola is a pretty good sized town. I got a hotel room and mostly hung around the bar for three days just getting used to Texas. I read the local papers, bought some clothes, and tried to act like a normal traveler.

"After a while I got the feeling that everyone was watching me. At first I thought it was paranoia but after a while it was obvious that I was drawing too much attention. I didn't know why, but was certain that I was busted. I was rehearsing, for the fiftieth time, what I was going to tell the Rangers when they arrested me, when I realized that people were staring because I wasn't decently dressed.

"No one told me that a man appearing in public without his firearm was as undressed as a man without pants. I figured it out when I noticed that the town drunk who swept up the boardwalks in front of the stores carried a pistol. It was rusted shut and hadn't fired in about a hundred years, but he was never without it.

"In fact, I don't think I saw a Texan without a firearm until I got to Austin."

Solomon waggled a finger and swallowed. "That fooled me too. I thought they didn't have guns here when I first came here. Actually, they're all armed. It's just that the new fashion is for shoulder holsters. The bulge is, however, just as important as the holster ever was for proper attire. The townspeople must have thought that you were deranged."

"It went away as soon as I completed my wardrobe. However, when I went to the gunsmith, I was amazed at the firearms that I had to choose from. I thought that you would be back to flintlocks. I was surprised that the average citizen could buy flintlock, percussion cap, match lock, and even self contained cartridge firing repeaters if you were rich enough. I still don't know you got that past the anti-techs."

Wilson decided to answer that one. "We didn't 'get it past' the a-techs any more than you did. They wouldn't give up guns either. No one ever gives up guns. In the entire history of mankind, the only people to ever give up guns, even temporarily, were the Japanese during the end of the *Samurai* era – and they changed their minds as soon as they ran into Europeans who had kept theirs. Guns are simple enough for someone to understand them, and they are less afraid of what they can understand. We face the same problem you do. Don't bother to look surprised, we can see that the York cannon facing us range from shell fed moderns to powder and ball muzzle loaders. We are more into personal firearms here than you are in York, but you and us have the same problems with guns. They just get expensive when you run out of machine tools. Any man with a file and a block of old steel out of a pre-dawn city can turn out an AK. It just takes a big part of his lifetime, and then he has to make the bullets by hand.

So, in the war of '37, your Papal troops faced our Rangers with some automatic weapons on both sides, but city policemen have cap locks and private hunters use flintlocks. I am sure that it's the same in York. And, we still believe that your troops retreated because you couldn't afford any more bullets."

Artimus smiled and shook his head good naturedly. "Actually, my grandfather talked a lot about the Persians and the Greeks. He said that Alexander defeated the more civilized and noble Persians not because he was a better general, but because he spent more money on his troops. Every Greek hoplite wore greaves, an iron breastplate and helmet and had an iron and brass shield. All the average Persian soldier had was a sword, helmet and lightweight shield. He fought bare legged and in sandals. It's amazing that they did as well as they did. After 37, grandpa decided on fewer soldiers with more bullets."

The Empress caught his eye and motioned a shush. She reached behind her to signal the servants to bring in fresh courses. They had talked so long that the food on the sideboard was cold.

Two servants refreshed the sideboard and wines. Conversation stopped while the servants worked. Before they left, they served a course of catfish with a side dish of tomatoes and onions. As the servants departed, the Empress said to the table, "I love philosophy and history as much as anyone, but we seem to have lost track of Artimus' adventure. I want to know how you got from New Iola to our palace. Fifteen hundred miles in a strange land sounds so exciting."

"Your majesty, I tried to make it as un-exciting as possible. As you probably know, tinkering has always been a hobby of mine."

They *didn't* know. The pope squad missed that detail.

"I am a fair blacksmith and I've been repairing tin and copper stuff around the castle since I was a small boy. My father encouraged me, and when mother objected, he told her a man couldn't always find someone else to sharpen his knife during a battle. I figured it was the ideal cover so I bought a utility wagon and team. I was able to find everything I needed to be a traveling tinker except a small anvil. All I could get was a blacksmiths anvil and I had to carry the monster with me for two weeks until I got to bigger town. I brought enough money for my trip, but a tinker couldn't just pass towns without looking for work, so I parked in each town and rang my tinkers bell. Then I had to stay while I had visible business.

"Unfortunately, I didn't know what Texas prices were and I priced my services too low during the first few weeks. I had so many customers everywhere I went that I thought I would never get out of town. I particularly remember one very unpleasant woman who brought years worth of broken stuff to me and demanded I fix it. I had to keep in character but I remember thinking to myself, "Here I am on a Mission for The Holy Father and on a great adventure, and I'm arguing with a farmwife about whether this old spoon is worth fixing." I was picturing telling my master that I was not delayed by bandits, storms, deserts, hunger or troops, but I was having a hard time getting past a farmwife with a broken spoon. I am dreadfully feared that this is going to appear in the family history. Of course, I soon learned to charge more and skip the smaller towns. That kept up the character but let me move on faster. I traveled with the wagon for several weeks, until I reached a more civilized area."

By dessert time, Artimus still had not gotten to Austin, but everyone knew each other better.

The Empress decreed the end of the main meal by rising and announcing, "Perhaps you gentlemen would be more comfortable in the sitting room."

The men loaded up with plates of cake, cigars, and wine from the sideboard and accompanied her into the sitting room. The men took seats on the couches around the fireplace while the Empress sat in the chair next to her small desk. She did not excuse herself as most women would have, but wanted to be out of the way of the conversation to come.

They had no more than seated themselves when Sir Robert asked the question that had been bothering him all evening. "What did you mean earlier when you said that my work was the reason for your trip."

Artimus looked toward the emperor, "Your majesty, how free can I be?"

"He knows what you brought. You may speak freely."

Artimus measured his words. "I will not ask you to admit to doing anything heretical or secret. However, we read about your new institution in a copy of the

Austin times."

He glanced around. "It was not great spy work. The paper traveled to New York with a merchant seaman. People can't get through the treaty port, but cargo does. Like you, we pay for copies of whatever the seamen bring back with them. Our Texas squad puzzled over the article for months. On the surface it seemed a noble and proper undertaking. I remember that you personally were quoted as saying you wanted to 'preserve the history of Texas and, incidentally, stoke the fires of Destruction Day with fresh material.' The woodcut showed you standing next to some amorphous mass that was going to the fires. We kept thinking that there was something wrong. Your government has always respected traditional beliefs, but you have never been particularly enthusiastic about the technology prohibitions. In fact, in most things, the Code of The West, Line Nine seems to be your most important rule."

One of the men at the fireplace said, "A man minds his own business."

"Of course," Artimus said. "Then, in the middle of a staff meeting, someone said. 'What a great place to hide! In plain sight. Are the Adams people that smart?' A few weeks later, I was on my way here."

Sir Robert leaned forward with his cigar in his hand. "But why bring us the book?"

"As I specified, it is an enticement for a meeting. I'm afraid that this is the one place that I can say no more. I have instructions to be as honest and open with you as I can be on all other topics except that. Because of the sensitivity of the topic, my master wants to discuss that with your master directly."

There was an awkward silence until Emperor Adams signaled the end of serious conversation by asking "By the way, which of our fine Texas firearms did you end up buying?"

The assembled group happily settled into a few hours of conversation about man's second favorite topic - Guns!

Chapter 12   Breakfast with the family

Artimus had been in the palace for a little over three weeks. He had seen Sam run his race and cheered at the appropriate moments. Actually, the kid was intelligent and game. He obviously learned quickly and never settled for less than his best. He was easy to like and Artimus's cheering was not entirely just courtesy. He learned that Samuel was staying at the palace for a few months while his parents were away on imperial business. The empress doted on him enough to embarrass the adolescent boy.

The tailor had provided Artimus with a few suits appropriate for a northern colonel. His travels through Texas had taught him enough to fake conversation at the frequent parties and balls in the palace. "Colonel" Artimus from the Northern Guard had even become a popular dance partner. The Papacy was more into balls and social events than the Texans and he had learned to dance at an early age.

He spent most of his days in the library. The Texans had collected every book that had not been banned and burned. Their collection included a lot of history, philosophy and fiction. The history books were his favorite. Of course, most books had been edited to remove references to automobiles, airplanes and other obscenities. However, several of the history texts had somehow missed being edited. He played poker with the off duty guardsmen on evenings when his hosts were away and actually began to enjoy his vacation.

The emperor, empress, and Samuel were always together at breakfast. Artimus often took his lunches in the mess hall. Dinner was an adult affair. More often Wilson, Greg or O'Brien would show up. Burt was only at dinner on special occasions.

This particular morning, Burt brought a book to breakfast. He was too polite to bring it to the table, but kept glancing over at it sitting on the sideboard next to the scrambled eggs.

The Empress noticed his not-to-subtle looks. "Burt, darling, are you studying for a test?"

"Yes, Mam. I have a civics exam this afternoon. It's on revolutions."

This was a topic that the Empress had hoped to bring up while Artimus was around. The civics class was central to Texan education. This class and "cons, cheats, and fools" were required for graduation from every school in Texas. "Tell you what, Dear. Why don't you explain the material to us and we'll help you see what you still need to study."

The word "Dear" caused its usual cringe, but Burt when along with it. "Ok. Teacher says this test will be on language and meaning. All revolutionaries say one of a few things. To understand revolutions, you have to understand what they mean. For instance, Teacher says that the most common thing they say is that they are fighting for your 'rights.' That means that they want you to fight so that they get the big house on the hill and all of the pretty girls. The other thing that they like to scream is that you are entitled to have as much as anyone else. Everyone should be the same and you should have a big house too. When they say that, they mean that they will help you steal everything that better men have worked for. If you help them steal it, they will still get the biggest house on the hill and all of the pretty girls, but you get some houses too and the pretty girls' sisters."

The emperor said, "Ok, Burt. What's wrong with that? You get to steal some horses, some money, maybe some land. Even if the revolutionary savior got more than you, you did pretty well."

Burt continued without a pause, "The problem is that you just killed the golden goose. You eat now, but you starve next year. Picture that you have a job in a stable. You make a thousand a year. If you and the other workers revolt, you can steal everything your boss has. However, he isn't around anymore to make payroll so you lose the chance for your thousand next year. Teacher says that is the most successful con job ever done. He says that the communists pulled that one on a third of the world's population and got away with it for over fifty years."

York had a different view of the communist movement. It was taught as a noble but financially misguided movement. Artimus had to jump in. "If the communists did nationalize everything and put it in the peoples name, how was it a 'con job'?"

Burt answered, "Because everyone was supposed to be equal. But the communist party members had private stores, big apartments and better buggies to be equal in, and all anyone else got was poorer. Of course, that was better than the 'noble cause' con. That one is really Teachers favorite."

Brad was obviously enjoying the chance to show off. He said, "All you need is a cause and some suckers. It's always 'freedom for our glorious country' or 'Independence for all people named Jones'. They convince you that you are a Serbian or a Hindu, and that Serbians or Hindus should rule. You revolt, and they get the big house on the hill and all of the pretty girls and then they get to make the laws too. They don't even have to give you a share of what you steal."

Artimus was amused at the simple minded way Texans thought about causes. "Burt, did Teacher tell you that it is always that bad?"

"No, Sir. In fact he made us look for the exceptions."

"How many did you find?"

"I found one, and Nance found one. I found Gandhi. His supporters did well, but he refused to take a dime. He really believed in what he was doing. Nancy found the other one. She found Pancho Villa. He took some stuff during the revolution in Old Mexico, but when it was over, he refused rewards and political power. He went right back to private life. Of course, the politicians had him murdered because they thought he was crazy. Oops, I gotta run."

After Burt ran out, the Emperor turned toward Artimus. "Sorry to put you through the boring stuff. We call them the 'inoculation courses'. From grade school forward, the kids are taught that they can be noble and honorable, but that many people that they meet won't be. During the first few years we teach them about every con from the shell game to the lost wallet stunt. We make them look at how they are done and why people fall for them. When they're teenagers, we have brutal civics courses every year. What Burt is studying now is typical. We also make them think about the dangers of pure democracy, the effects of bribes, and the dangers of a bad emperor.

"At the end of the year, Burt will be taught when you should revolt and how. We believe that no population should put up with the cruelties of Stalin, invasion of personal rights, or gross financial mismanagement on the part of their government. They will also be taught that most bad governments dissolve eventually on their own. When no one will listen to a Ranger or Rangers won't support this government, it will fall the way the Russian and Roman Empires did. It's a lot of hard news. Every year we have to fire a few teachers who don't want to make the world so 'depressing' for the young people. There are always some people who want their children to forever believe in Santa Clause. It seems to work. Our kids don't have many illusions about 'Great Causes', but we haven't had a serious revolt in two hundred years. Every time someone tries to get people to revolt, they are likely to ask 'Yep, what's in it for you?'"

Actually, the emperor did not know it, but Texas had very few revolts for other reasons. A sparse population gave a lot of room for people to avoid authorities they didn't like. The population of the entire area that had been the United States was still only twenty five million people, less than ten percent of what it had been before the plagues. They were also a lot smarter, on the average, than they were before the plagues and flooding. Dumb people had pretty much died before they lived long enough to breed. Pre-dawn students would probably not have understood what the civics classes were about, post-dawn students thought the lessons were obvious.

And, the Adams Family were good rulers who ran a cheap, clean, and honest government.

Chapter 13 Texas Justice

It took only six weeks to make a decision. Artimus' coach arrived early at the Imperial Pavilion. He suspected that the meeting was going to be an important one because it was not being held at the palace.

This time he had an escort when he reached the receptionists' desk. The ranger courier who was escorting him presented his, the courier's, identification at the desk and received pass bracelets for the two of them. If the receptionist recognized Artimus, she was too professional too let it show. The ranger had been Artimus' escort when he was in the officer's quarters and knew vaguely who Artimus was.

The Ranger turned to Artimus and said, "We are a little early. The emperor is still hearing petitions in the Hall of Final Justice. It was suggested to me that you might want to observe the proceedings if we were on time." He smiled and added a personal comment, "It's usually more fun than the waiting room."

As they seated themselves in the balcony, Artimus whispered to the Ranger, "Does His Majesty hear all the cases?"

"No, there are thousands of petitions. Any Texan can appeal any court decision to His Majesty. His staff sorts most of them out. Even the ones that need his attention usually just get a letter. He has these public hearings when he thinks that the lower courts made a serious mistake that needs public precedent set or when he wants to make a point about stupid petitions. Sometimes you get the feeling His Majesty just wants to give a civics lesson. The reporters love this beat because you never know which way the case is going to go."

They looked down on a courtroom that was built a little like a combination of court room and Opera house. In the center of the first floor was the dais that held the throne. It was a traditional tall, gilded, heavily carved, purple upholstered chair. However, it was also possibly the only swivel throne in existence. His Majesty hated to be uncomfortable during testimony.

There was a matching desk to the side of the throne where the Emperor could keep documents and have some workspace. He had often wished that the desk could be properly in front of his Chair, but thrones do not go behind desks.

Below the dais were two railings for testimony and two sets of tables and chairs for the accused and the accusers. Scribes sat at both sides of *the* dais. The first floor seats were utilitarian. The fancy cushioned seats were in the balcony where Artimus and the ranger sat.

The entire wall to the right of Artimus was floor to ceiling windows. Through the small panes of glass, everyone could see Liars Post in the courtyard. A masked bailiff lounged near the post slowly curling and uncurling his whip.

Down below a business man was finishing his testimony, "When we did not get the twelve ton-weight of apples that that the defendant promised, we had to shut down the press rooms and later the distillery. We only had half as much cider as we needed last year and we couldn't make any hard cider. I had to lay off ten men. The defendant offered to return my deposit. However, his failure to deliver cost me a years profit and he owes me what he made me lose."

The emperor turned to the defendant, "Is what he says true? I have your statement, but I want to hear if from you."

The defendant tried to look defiant and respectful at the same time. It made his head bob a lot. "It was not my fault. He tells truth that I agreed to deliver the twelve ton weight. But it weren't my fault that he didn't get them. It was an act of God. There was a late frost last year and then them storms came. My crop was ruined. I didn't get enough apples to feed my family, let alone give twelve tons to Mr. Karris. I didn't deliver but I wasn't my fault and I gave the man his deposit back. I don't owe him nothing else for an Act Of God."

Standing next to the defendant, his lawyer was shaking his head and looking at the ground. In Texas, lawyers advised their clients, but didn't usually talk for them unless they were simple or had a speech defect. The lawyer knew what was coming.

The Emperor was looking at a piece of paper on his side desk. "I have here the contract you signed with Mr. Karris. Does this contract represent your sworn word?"

"Yes, sir. It does."

The emperor made a small show of bringing the paper closer to his face and examining it. "Is there anything you swore to that isn't written here?"

"No, Your Majesty. That's it. Just a standard delivery contract."

The emperor sighed. "Then we have a problem. There is nothing in here that says that you will only deliver if God lets you. Here in Texas, a man's word is good. We depend on it. Your word makes it's own law and you are expected to live by it. We don't make excuses and we don't blame God. You promised delivery and you did not do it. You owe Mr. Karris the money."

He turned to the complainant. "Mr. Karris, I have a statement of damages here in the amount of twenty three thousand crowns. Before judgment is passed, I ask you once only, are these amounts correct?"

There was an uncomfortable silence. Something in the emperors casual tone had warned Karris. Karris could see Liars Post outside the window. A little bead of perspiration appeared on his forehead.

"Well, Your Honor, I mean, Your Majesty, the numbers are pretty close. I mean, you gotta expect a man to leave himself a little room for negotiation and then there was, you know, lawyers fees and such."

The emperor tapped on the case folder lying on his desk. "Very good, Mr. Karris. Your sudden burst of honesty has just saved you an additional trip to Liars Post."

The word "additional" was very scary.

"The report from royal auditors, at the first court, says that you never in your life made a profit of over nineteen thousand crowns. They cannot calculate how you could have made over nine thousand crowns profit from the twelve ton-weight of apples."

He looked at Karris' lawyer. "Mr. Phillips, please explain the fourth line of the Code to your client. We have time for the long version."

Phillips was winging his hands nervously. His eyes looked up at the ceiling and began to recite in school boy fashion. "A man don't lie unless he is fishing. The long version is 'A man don't lie unless he is fishing or his wife asks him if her new dress makes her look fat.'"

He glanced at the Emperor and decided that he was supposed to go on.

"The founder explained that here are social situations where this line does not apply. Men are allowed to tell a few whoppers and the truth is also not a sufficient reason to hurt someone unnecessarily. There is no requirement to tell your best friend that his wife is ugly or to tell a child that you can't see the elephant in his drawing. In all other matters, a man should speak sparingly and no one should ever doubt his truth. A real man don't never lie."

The emperor turned to the defendant. "The judgment, as you know is against you. You will pay the nine thousand crowns suggested by the imperial auditors as a fair price. If you do not pay in a reasonable time, your lands and business are forfeit. Your word has made the law, and we will enforce it. However, you will pay the sum to the town mayor. He will apportion it among the workers who were laid off in accordance to their pay structure."

He looked directly at the complainant. "You, Mr. Karris will receive nothing of the settlement. We cannot let you profit from an attempt at deception. In addition, you have broken your oath three times. You lied to the prefect of your town, and then to regional court. You brought into this court a document that was a deliberate lie. For each dishonesty you are sentenced to two strokes at Liars Post. Because you eventually told the truth voluntarily, half of the sentence is suspended. Remember, for the future, that you took an oath when you approached the court. It does not allow big lies, small lies, half truths, evasions, or exaggeration. Should there be a second offense, the rest of the sentence will be carried out. Bailiff, please have someone escort Mr. Karris to the courtyard."

As the parties were led from the room, Artimus' escort leaned over to him to say, "There's only one more case. His Majesty is almost done."

In the courtroom below, a muscular young man of about twenty five stood at the defendant's rail. A middle aged woman of about forty five was making her way up the aisle toward the other rail.

Through the glass windows, another story was playing itself out. Karris and his lawyer were approaching the grass circle that held Liars Post. Karris stripped his own coat and blouse and handed them to his lawyer. He accepted the leather bit from the bailiff, but waved away the wrist chains. He walked to the post, turned to it and gripped the handholds. He was a crook, but he was still a Texan.

Inside, the woman was making an impassioned plea to the emperor. "He killed my boy. I don't understand why no one will do anything about it. My boy wasn't carrying for more than about a week. He was a polite young man. He never challenged anyone. My boy went to the bar after work to have a few drinks with his friends, and this man murdered him! This man insulted my son, insulted me, and kept threatening him. My boy didn't want a fight, but this man wouldn't let him go. He kept taunting him until he looked like he was going to draw and then he killed him. The bastard even went around town bragging about it and tried to buy everyone drinks to celebrate his 'victory'! I'm a widow. I got no man to avenge my son. You have to help me."

The emperor turned to the defendant. The man had been glaring at the woman during her testimony. His expression was as close to a sneer as the court would allow. "Let's hear your side. Self defense, noble killing, honor killing or murder?"

"Self defense and honor, Your Majesty. The little twerp kept interrupting our conversation. We had words. He could have left anytime, but he stayed. He kept getting madder and then drew his gun. I didn't draw until after he did. I got witnesses to prove it."

"The witnesses won't be necessary. Your word is good in this court."

The sound of the second stoke carried in from the courtyard.

The Emperor continued. "Did the man insult your honor? "

"Yes, Your Majesty, he did."

"Did he call you a liar at any time or imply that you were lying?"

"Yes, he did."

"Would you say that any man who insulted you that way should have to stand up for himself and should be shot if he doesn't apologize? In the same circumstances, would you do it again?"

Bradley stood straight and glared at the mother. "Of course, Your Majesty."

The emperor turned to the now weeping mother. "I am sorry, Mam. There is nothing that I can do for you. This is a civilized society and no man can be required to fight to live. However, when your son put on that gun, he declared himself a man. He demanded the right to stand up to anyone, including me, if he was willing to pay the price.

"I have no doubt that Mr. Bradley goaded your son into that fight. However, your son could have left the bar. He chose to draw rather than walk away. It was his decision and he died by it. I am sorry that I can do nothing."

Bradley smiled smugly. Winning was good. The emperor laid his crown on the side desk and swiveled around on his throne to face the wall behind him. Unexpectedly, the head bailiff rapped his staff twice on the floor and announced, "The Emperor Has Left The Court."

Everyone was confused. Feet shuffled. People whispered. The defendant and the mother looked confused at the rail. After a few seconds, a man stood up from an aisle seat and strode toward the front. He wore a kilt. His appearance was not unusual as many people in Texas paid sincere respect to greatly revered and often fictitious ancestry.

"I'm William O'Brien and I think that you are a liar and bully." He confronted Bradley closely and said in a loud voice, "You may have gotten that boy to draw first, but you are nothing but a coward. I hate it when an ignorant, butt ugly, cowardly jackass like yourself is allowed to walk with polite company."

Ever the bully, Bradley was clenching his fists. He knew he was being set up.

O'Brien was inches away, and said, "Don't breathe on me like that. Your filthy breath smells like farts. Look the other way!!"

Bradley lost it. He reached for his gun before he realized it was checked at the front desk. He settled for a roundhouse swing at O'Brien. O'Brien ducked under the fist and stepped back. Two bailiffs restrained Bradley.

O'Brien said calmly, "I guess we have to settle this like men. I will be in Red Rock on Monday next. I will expect you in the street at high noon."

The head bailiff rapped his staff twice on the floor. "The Emperor Has Entered The Court. All Rise."

On the dais, Emperor Adams had swiveled his throne around and was again wearing his crown. "Be seated. Perhaps I should introduce you two. Sergeant

O'Brien, this is Mr. Bradley, the famous gunfighter from Red Rock. Mr. Bradley, may I introduce Sergeant O'Brien of the Royal Scots Guards. You have something in common. You are the greatest gunman in Red Rock and Sergeant O'Brien is the fastest and best pistoleer in the service. I should remind you that you did state publicly and in front of witnesses that you would draw down on anyone who insulted you and did not apologize. By our customs that means that he is entitled to believe that you intend to kill him. Therefore, if you do not show up for the duel, he has the right – to – hunt – you - down!

"Sergeant, I hear that you plan to be away from your duty post on Monday next. I might suggest staying over on Tuesday to offer your condolences, in case there is a grieving widow or mother to console."

From the back of the room, an angry woman stood up. "I'm the bastards' mother. I've had five sons, and he is the only one that has shamed me so." In spite of her anger, tears flowed down her face. "There won't be no grieving, but you're welcome to drop by for a drink afterward." She dropped into her seat and buried her face in her hanky.

The emperor continued, "I wouldn't worry too much, Mr. Bradley. Not all of Sergeant O'Brien's opponents have died. Sergeant, didn't one live just a few months ago."

"Yes, Your Majesty. The sun was in me eyes. The poor bastard lived for almost two hours."

At a gesture from His Majesty, the head bailiff again rapped his staff twice on the floor and announced, "This court is no longer in session."

And this time, the emperor really did leave.

On the way to the Royal Offices, Artimus asked, "Will Sergeant O'Brien really just execute that man?"

The ranger thought for a second and replied "Well, he can't just execute him. The bully has the same rights as the boy did, but if he fights, he'll die, and he'll probably fight. Bullies don't usually have the courage to walk away in public. Run in private, yes. Back down in public, no. O'Brien will either kill him or hunt him down and make him apologize and crawl publicly. The public humiliation and fear will probably end his life as a successful bully. Either way, humiliation or death, the mother will get the revenge she is entitled to."

By the time Artimus' guide dropped him off at the Imperial office suite, the Emperor was already in his office. He was still dressed in his court regalia but had changed to the working crown and dumped the four pound monstrosity he wore in court.

Sir Wilson and a few other staff were already seated in the office. As soon as Artimus was seated, Wilson said, "We have decided to meet your master. Frankly the decision was much easier than we thought it would be. It is, after all, only an agreement to listen."

It was actually a harder decision than the assembled crew let on. Meeting with a foreign power, with whom you are technically at war, to discuss acts of heresy was dangerous not only to the current emperor, but also to his dynasty.

The dangers were both assassination and betrayal. A premature revealing of the true intent of the Archeological Department could cause enough public outcry to bring down the royal house.

However, Artimus had convinced everyone that he was either as honest as a Texan, or the best actor that they had ever seen.

The emperor took the lead. "Have you worked out how this meeting is going to take place?"

"We have a suggestion. If you could get a map of the north eastern part of the Kansan Territory, up near the Nebraskan border? Thank you. There is a small pre-dawn village north of New Atchison that we could probably get to unnoticed."

The Emperor gestured to one of the men in the room and he went out for a map. "While we are waiting for the map. I assume that you have decided on a way home. Hopefully an easier way than you came?"

Artimus answered, "Yes, I had planned to go home through the trade port at New Galveston. If you could provide me with identification as a quarantined trader to get me into the port, I can handle it from there. I have a code that will tell any Yorker ship to give me passage. If necessary, I can even requisition a ship. That should get me home in about one easy month."

With the raging paranoia about disease, all international trade was done through quarantined trade ports. They were established on close in islands or in harbors with high walled barriers. The personnel lived permanently at the port. Only goods, not people, normally went in from and out to the interior. Texas' international trade port was closer to a city than most. With the rising of the sea level, New Galveston was virtually a suburb of Houston and the best harbor left on the Texas coast.

Most trade was done by island nations that grew immensely wealthy, and sometimes died suddenly when a new mutation of the great plague or a new plague wiped them out. Many large countries did have cargo ships at sea, and Texas had a few hundred. No one had a large navy. The sea was a far less romantic profession when all you saw of foreign lands was the inside of a fortified trade port.

The planning took most of the day. As His Majesty was going to be risking his own royal carcass on the planning, he stayed for the entire meeting.

In the end, they planned to meet in three months. It would take Artimus a month to return to New York. Another two months would be needed for the Yorkers to supply an expedition and travel the sixteen hundred miles to the rendezvous.

They planned for as many contingencies as possible. What happens if the Pope's party encounters a patrol? If the village is leveled or cannot be found? If freak weather delays either party? The planning went on into the evening.

Chapter 14 In A Little Town In Kansas

It was the only structure in sight. Situated in a protected valley and surrounded by grassland on all sides, the large stone farmhouse had been abandoned during one of the border wars. Two imperial guardsmen stood in plain sight on the roof. Inside the emperor and his aid watched the hills to the East. Eleven horses and a few pack mules were corralled in front of the house. A cooking fire sent up more smoke through the chimney than usual, as if someone were using green wood in the hearth.

The aide grunted to the emperor, "Do you think he'll come today?"

The emperor handed the ancient binoculars to his aide. "Could be, Colonel. He's a few days overdue but it's hard to keep a schedule when you're crossing the wilderness and trying not to be seen."

It was only a few minutes later when the colonel pressed the glasses closer to his eyes and said, "Dust cloud in the east. Could be our visitor."

The emperor reached behind him for a telescope and looked where the colonel was pointing. "Looks like them. One man in the front, six riders on each side. They're carrying rifles and crossbows, but no heavy weapons. They've got three pack mules with them. Make that 'empty' pack mules."

The group on the hill slowed to a slow walk, obviously studying the house below. The tall man in the center put up his hand in a stop gesture and turned to the rider next to him. The rider spurred his horse a short way to the rear of the column and spoke to the two rear guards. They wheeled and started back over the rise that they had just crossed.

The colonel was calm. "Sire, I fear treachery. I think that he has sent his riders back for reinforcements now that he knows we are here."

"No colonel, it's not treachery. It's Samurai honor. There is a story, probably fictional, that if two Samurai units met for battle and one had seventy five men and the other had a hundred, that the larger force would send twenty five men to the rear so that no advantage would be taken. When he stopped on the hill, he counted our horses. He saw that I had only brought ten retainers and he had twelve. He sent the others back so that there would be no hint of advantage. That is a classy move."

When Pope Jones and his entourage entered the courtyard, all ten guardsmen were situated around the courtyard. Their personal weapons were present, but holstered. The first man to dismount was Bishop Artimus.

The emperor, realizing that the bishop's mission was to reassure Pope Jones that the real emperor was there, stepped into the courtyard. "It is good to see you again, Bishop. I trust you and your master had a easy trip."

"Thank you for your well wishes. I apologize for our lateness. It turned out to be another interesting trip." Behind him the tallest rider, a man in his fifties with graying hair, was dismounting. Artimus half turned and bowed slightly. "May I present my Master, The Holy Pope John the VI, Protector of the Faith and the Voice of God on Earth. Master, this man I know personally to be Emperor Burton Adams, Emperor of Texas, King of Kansas, Duke of Arkansas and NewMex and Protector of his people."

The emperor shook hands with the Pope. "We've set aside the north wing for you and your men. I'm afraid that it isn't much better than camping out. We couldn't bring many amenities. You may want to settle your men in while my men prepare a meal. We were able to bring some wine and pack in some good food."

"I thank you for the meal. We've had cold camp for a week. Hot food would taste good and wine would be Ambrosia. We'll meet you in the supper hall as soon as the men have taken care of our horses and found places to sleep."

The Pope surprised the Texans by unsaddling his own horse. It seemed that the Adams were not the only men who knew how to keep the guard loyal.

Less than an hour later, the Papal people joined the Texans in the dining hall. There were three tables the room. Two places had been set side by side at the head table, and ten places at each of the two others. There were fresh baskets of bread and flagons of wine on all of the tables.

Before being seated, the Pope led his men in a short prayer. The Texans, unbelievers all, stood silently out of respect for their guests. As he sat down, the colonel thought how handy it was that hunger shortened prayers nicely. There was no fancy service, three rangers brought in platters of beef, baked potatoes and local greens. After a few uncomfortable moments, the leaders set an example by digging into their meals and the others gratefully followed the example. This was camp eating with knife, fingers, and hunger. Then came camp drinking. There had been little conversation during the meal. Both leaders were relieved to see that the wine was loosing up their men. Soon a few toasts were made and then the first ribald joke. If things went well, the first song and old war story should be coming along soon. They should have realized that there would be little friction. These men were experts in the same profession and were not currently at war. Like most men, they loved to talk shop and carouse with men they could respect and relate to.

More and more, they slipped their personal weapons to the floor behind them or stacked them on the rack near the door to allow belts to relax and tunics to loosen.

At the head table the Pope was saying. "For a while I was afraid we wouldn't make it before you got discouraged. The river was swollen and it took us three days to ford it. Then the last cache wasn't there. Either the advance party missed their point or someone got there first. It sure does make this food a feast. Hunger is always the best sauce for any dish."

The emperor gave a polite chuckle. "Can you picture the people back home if they could see us now. They think we feast every night at fancy dress balls with dozens of servants to cut our exotic foods."

The pope smiled "I do have to eat like that. The papacy is very tradition bound. I get about one meal a week with my family, and I hate it when some servant insists on cutting my meat or pouring my wine like I was a child. You know this trip is the best time I've had in years. Sleeping on the ground, eating camp food. When the last food drop wasn't there, we ate food we had killed or gathered ourselves. It's been nice to feel like a man again."

"Where do they think you are?"

"Meditating in the Jersey woods. Some times it is handy to run a theocracy. You?"

"I'm on the way to inspect the troops on the Nebraskan border. I am unfortunately delayed a few weeks due to this unseasonably wet weather. We should have enough time to conduct some business before we're missed."

"That's good, but remember the old saying 'Business Tomorrow, Beer Tonight.'"

It was getting difficult to talk over the drinking songs that were following the mutual bragging and were destined to precede the sad songs of home that would end the night.

They got to work early the next morning. This time there were four at the table. The emperor and the *Pope* were joined by Wilson and Artimus as soon as breakfast was cleared away. The men of both sides had vacated to the courtyard to doze, whittle, spit, polish their weapons, and begin the hard process of waiting.

The pope opened the conversation. "I believe that we should open the discussion by presenting your majesty with the token of good faith that was promised." As he spoke, Artimus was unwrapping a package. "These," the pope said, "are volumes to two through twenty. We are missing chapters eleven and seventeen, but I think you will find these valuable."

Artimus pushed the package across the table. The emperor sat virtually motionless while Wilson leaned forward to accept the package. He handled it with reverence but was fighting a smile with all his will, and losing. A knight accepting the Holy Grail would have been almost as happy as Sir Wilson.

The emperor waited a moment until Wilson's' smile was under control and then looked back to the pope. "I am somewhat puzzled. Your church has been in the forefront of anti-tech for four hundred years. I don't want to offend you, but I have to point out that the church is more likely to burn these books than preserve them. And that doesn't even begin to address why you are giving them to the anti-Christs."

The pope was obviously prepared. "It will take a little while to explain. Let me begin by telling you that the leadership of the church has rarely been anti-tech. That sounds ridiculous when you remember that the church has had heresy trials, burned books, and embraced Destruction Day. However, the church has not often been lead by the dumb. Most popes, including the first American pope knew that there was nothing evil about antibiotics or farm machines. We just had the Urban problem.

"One of my predecessors imprisoned the astronomer Galileo. That pope's name was Urban IV. He told Galileo that he had been convinced that he, Galileo, was right, that the planets revolved around the Sun. But he also told Galileo 'I know your are right, but I have millions of believers out there who are not ready to accept this. If we do not punish you, they will punish us. It will take years to prepare them for it, so I have to stop you.' Knowing he was innocent, Urban nonetheless tried and convicted Galileo, and sentenced him to house arrest for the rest of his life.

"We face the same problem. We can lead people only where they are willing to go. In the days after the plague, there was a world wide hysteria. Everybody was half crazy from losing relatives, loved ones and everyone else that they knew. They had to blame something and they picked science.

"Bishop Charles knew that if he were going to save the church as a moral force for the future, he would first have to save the church itself. And so he did. The pulpits began to sound the back to nature call. When communications completely broke down, he declared himself 'Pope Charles' and tried to keep the church alive.

"We have always had a reverence for history and for books so we tried to save what we could. Books were squirreled away in remote monasteries. As it was too risky to print a lot of copies, several teams of scribes were set up to copy the books. None knew of the other teams. Unfortunately, not all popes were wise and not all teams were trustworthy. Over the four hundred years, most of the books were destroyed. Some new monk would turn out to have the holy spirit of Destruction in him, or one of the bad popes would learn of one of the monasteries and Destruction Day would be hotter than usual that year. Now, too much has been lost. In another generation or two, we will not have enough left to start again."

The pope looked toward the ceiling and said, "In both our lands, one mother in ten dies in childbirth. People are old and toothless by age forty. When we had that long cold spell a few years ago, the two summers that never came, people died of starvation. We no longer produce enough excess food to carry us. People remember bathing, but hot water is rare and flush toilets are not universal. So our people are dying of infections that our ancestors would have considered trivial. Children are crippled and stunted by vitamin deficiencies. We lose loved ones, wives, children, and friends from causes that we no longer understand. Yes, I want the past back. I have never believed that my God, *the God* who loves mankind, could want them to suffer needlessly."

There was a long pause. In each mind was a picture of a lost friend.

The emperor broke the mood. "Alright, let us accept for the moment that the papacy is not really a-tech. That doesn't explain what we are doing here. Although there have been no hostilities to speak of, we have been technically at war since my grandfather expelled all of your priests and closed your churches."

The pope, of course, expected the question. "Time is running out and I still have Urban's problem. None of us expected the hysteria to last this long. We should have remembered that people believed in werewolves for a thousand years, and burned witches even longer. Eventually hysteria becomes 'knowledge' and plants itself in every generation. I have much of the knowledge that I need, but if I use any of it, my own citizens will lynch me with the help of most of my bishops. The renaissance cannot begin in any catholic country, so, to save our people, we have to make a deal with someone. The Adams dynasty has created a government in Texas that has been stable for over two hundred and fifty years and you are not Catholic. That makes you the best candidates for a deal."

It took the emperor a few moments to respond. When someone tells you that the Sun now rises in the West, there is a moment of adjustment required. "We share a noble concern for our people. But there must be some reciprocity in any agreement. What do we have to offer your country?"

He silently congratulated himself on coming up with such a diplomatic way to say, "What's in it for you?"

The pope did not hesitate. He had practiced his answers. "We will benefit when our people know what you are doing. If necessary, I will convince Yorkers that you are a danger to them. They will, hopefully, demand that we keep up with you. Fear of the past is driving them to stay in ignorance. Perhaps fear of Texas can force them out of it."

The pope pretended to think for a moment. "There are two other services that you could offer. During your work, you will obviously learn much of practical nature that is not in the texts. Of course, we expect to be kept informed of your progress and to be allowed to share in your discoveries. In addition, we would want assurances that our priests would eventually be allowed to re-enter your country."

The emperor said, "The sharing of knowledge is obvious. The empire prides itself in fair dealing, and we have never taken advantage of others in a treaty. The other is a problem. Remember that people in the Empire see the War of Thirty-seven as the war that drove the priests out of Texas. However, assuming that we can find a way to meet those requirements, what would we gain?"

"I have brought a few covers of books that you may find interesting." He motioned to Artimus. Artimus opened a leather case and passed the contents over to the Emperor. The emperor glanced at each item and then passed the package to Wilson. The contents were book covers for "The History Of Steam Power", "Great American Railroads", and "The Handbook of Chemistry and Physics".

Artimus cleared his throat. When neither leader seemed to object, he explained, "We chose these because they complete the first step of the renaissance. The electricity course will give you the basics of a new science. You will, however, need a non-animal source of power for any real progress. You will find that steam engines were first made by people with not much more background than we have and they burn unprocessed fuels. Some of the books that survived are less useful because they describe sciences that would take decades to reproduce. I believe that these are the next step."

"You may be right," the emperor answered. "But we still have to know if we can work out an agreement. Your Holiness must know that organized religion is not widespread in Texas. We have enough religion to keep the women happy and comfort those who need it, but it's not organized and it stays out of politics. Part of the reason is the independence we teach Texans. We believe in very little control. Our laws pretty much consist of the Code of the West. We did not see it as appropriate to tell you whether or not to like your parents, to keep a random day holy, to worship any god, or to interfere with your sex life. Of course, while adultery is not specifically against the Code, it is dangerous in a well armed society. That left us the real stuff about killing, cheating, stealing and hurting. Children in Texas are taught that the greatest sin is to get government to make your neighbors do something just because you want to control them. They are taught that the term victimless crime is a nonsense term."

He hesitated for a moment and his expression became slightly painful. "I don't want to sound pompous, but we don't have time for false starts, so let me lay out all of the problems up front. We have freedom of belief in Texas. Now that's not the same as freedom of religion. Freedom of religion has always meant the freedom to accept one of the popular religions. Most often, as with the Puritans, it has meant freedom to be a Puritan. We respect a person's right to believe in Christ, Buddha, Baal, Animism, Atheism, Agnosticism, Satanism or the worship of the Sun God. You can believe that black cats are bad luck, that the dead communicate through mediums, or in the existence of an honest lawyer. Unfortunately for most, your Catholic belief system bestows no special rights. You can believe that a man should have only one wife, but you may not agitate for a law requiring your neighbor to give up his spares. You can refuse to work on your Sabbath, but whether or not you get fired is between you and your employer. We teach our children that the most evil thing you can do is to pass laws just because someone else doesn't like what you are doing. Grandfather tossed out your priests because they were campaigning for laws to make everyone act like a Christian. One damned fool even tried to get laws against sex before marriage. The one that started the Ejection War was trying to get a law passed forbidding suicide, as if a man's life belonged to the state instead of himself. Even if I agreed to let your priests back in, they might not live long enough to be ejected again."

The Pope was obviously ready. "We have been working on it, and I think that I have a solution. I have formed a new order of Monks. By their vows, they can help, but cannot proselytize in any manner except example. They are basically a farming order. We would be satisfied with whatever souls see enlightenment through their example. We would also take satisfaction in the poor who would be helped by the brothers' service. We would guarantee that no member of my church will break or contest your laws, on the penalty of instant banishment in minor cases and painful punishment for major infractions."

It took two days to work out the agreement. They discussed what land the monks could own, how to transfer currency into Texas for their support and the exact rules the priests would have to follow. They also agreed that they would have to go over the agreement with their most trusted advisors and make final decisions after some careful analysis.

During the evening of the fourth day, their majesties were hinting at the possibility of improving trade between the two countries. As with most countries, all trade went only as far as the quarantine posts. Memories of visitors bringing contagion had made a deep impression on humanity. Most countries had ports or border crossings for the exchange of goods, but carefully controlled to see that no people moved inland.

The Pope was saying, "We do have trade and ambassadorial treaties with several Catholic countries. They allow for alien residents, and, after a period in quarantine, direct dealings with inland businesses and ambassadorial presence. If you like, I will send you an example with Artimus. I don't know if making the world smaller would be good or bad. You know, not all countries are at the same level anymore. Because we have believers all over the world, we probably get more and better intelligence than Texas does. We know that Africa is back to the early iron age. They were only two generations into civilization when the plague happened and they went right back to tribal warfare and animism. They haven't been able to keep anything bigger than a brick factory working. Europe is about like us, but Northern China has kept its railroads. Yep, real working steam engines. They have gone back to traditional medicine, but have stopped killing physicians. Fortunately for us, they don't seem to have any interest in progress. They seem to be perfectly happy right where they are. The last time they got in this attitude, they didn't do anything for three thousand years. You know that India is back to subsistence farmers and rich overlords. Our man there says that it looks like the Thirteenth Century. If the world were not so segmented, the differences would not be so pronounced, but I would worry about which country would set the standards."

"Someday it will have to unite," said the emperor as he leaned back from the table. "More than anything else, people want to be rich and to feel safe. International trade makes a lot of money for both sides and international relations can make you feel safe with your neighbors. However, I fear that 'Urban's Problem' will hit us there too."

The next morning they parted in separate directions. The Texans, with the Pope's permission, had sent two men to the nearest settlement for new mules and provisions for the Catholics' home journey. Every trooper had some memento won from the other side. They knew that they probably couldn't speak of this meeting for thirty years, but each wanted a souvenir. The last day, the card games were strangely even as they sought manly ways to exchange a few belongings.

Artimus and Wilson were having a last conference on horseback. Wilson was saying, "Alright, we will meet in the quarter mile between the guard posts in Killer Pass eighty days from today. I will have the official signed treaty with me or I will have a rejection. You bring the books. If either of us is not there, the other will not see that as sign of a rejection, but will assume some hardship has delayed the other. In that case, whomever is there will go to meeting site on every third day until contact is made."

Artimus extended his hand. "Agreed. May God be with you until we meet in Killer Pass."

Chapter 15 A Visit to Yahoo

As the imperial party crested the hill, the first road that they had seen since the meeting was visible less than half a mile away. On the horizon was a large cloud of dust moving generally in their direction.

The forward lookout wheeled back to the main party. He was still holding his binoculars. "It appears to be a ranger troop moving north fast. There's well over a hundred of them and they're stripped down for speed. No supply wagons, no foot soldiers but each man has a spare mount.. They must be in a Hell of a hurry, Sir."

The Emperor gestured towards the road. "In that case, they could probably use the help of a dozen extra rifles. If we cut a little north, I think we can close with them before they hit that bend." No one was surprised at the order to join the fight. The Adams had always led from the front.

The captain of the ranger troop was shocked to see the emperor and his men waiting on the road ahead of him. He signaled his troops to stop and rode alone up to the Emperors party. He was about to jump off his horse for the mandatory kneeling when the emperor stopped him. "Captain, there will be time for formalities later. You seem to be in a big hurry right now. What's up?"

"Your Majesty. We have received an urgent message from Yahoo. They're are under attack by Nebraskan troops. We've been riding twelve hours and Yahoo is still about thirty miles up the road. Our messenger said that the Nebraskans had breeched the wall and that was two days ago. This is every man and mount that we had."

"In that case, you could probably use another squad. Do you mind if we join your expedition?"

"We are yours to command, Your Majesty."

The emperor turned around in his saddle. "Rangers Henry, Martin. Unburden the pack animals and stake them out here. Then try to catch up. The rest of us are leaving now, Captain. Let's move out of here. You lead, we'll follow."

They saw the fires in Yahoo miles before they saw the town. Columns of dark grey smoke marked its location.

The Emperor moved to the front of the column as they approached the cleared land around the town. "Captain, I suggest that you rest your troops before we approach the town. They have had a hard ride. We need to send up a few scouts anyway."

While the column dismounted and prepared for a rest, two scouts went forward on foot. Rangers Henry and Martin arrived while they waited. The scouts returned about forty-five minutes later. "We got up within about thirty yards of the wall. The gates are open, but there's no traffic. We didn't see any guards on the wall or at the gate."

The emperor leaned forward. "How tall is the grass. Can you get twenty men close to the gate without being seen."

The scouts looked at each other for a moment. One said, "I think so. If we move slow. I didn't see any signs of guards at the gate or on the wall. If we kept quiet..."

"Captain, assign twenty of your men to join my Rangers. We'll move around to the back city gate. Then send these men with two groups of fifteen men a-piece to sneak up to the gates. You'll need your best squad leader to lead the squad going for the front gate."

The captain pointed to one of the scouts. "That'll be Sergeant Harrison, here."

"Ok, Harrison. You are going to be the key man on this operation. The Captain will mount up his troops and get as close to the front gate as he can and still stay out of site. My men and the backup squad will do the same thing at the back of the town.

"Your job is to sneak two squads up to the wall on foot. You need one at the back and one at the front. You lead the group at the front.

"You're going to call the play. When you think your men are close enough, run like Hell for the gates. Your job is to keep them open for us. Both mounted groups will move on your first shot.

"I don't need to tell you to be careful where you put that shot. We have no idea what's in there. The Nebraskans could be gone and we could have just a town full of shocked survivors or we could have a hell of a lot of Nebraskans waiting for us to make a stupid play. Be ready to think fast and shoot faster. Alright, lets mount up. One way or another, someone needs us in there."

The dismounted group moved out first. The emperor and the captain sat at the heads of their columns waiting for the right time to go. While they waited, the emperor realized that he need to make an adjustment in firepower. His men had AK47s while the captains' more numerous troops were mostly armed with single shot breech loaders. They could use little more raw fire power. In a moment, two Rangers moved over to the second column and sent two local rangers back.

Then both mounted groups moved out though the woods. They stayed under cover until they reached their positions. For almost a half hour, the only sound was the creaking of leather as men shifted in their saddles trying to keep comfortable and the occasional whinny of a horse.

When the shot came, they burst out of the woods and headed for the rear gate. Then more shots sounded and they knew it was a battle coming. Men urged their horses on faster. Wilson and the locals drew their swords with one hand and held their pistols in the other. The Imperials rode with their knees and held their AK47s in both hands. They got to the gate without taking a single incoming round and swept through looking for targets. The advance squad had dispatched the five or six Nebraskans who were supposed to be watching the gate.

There was no organized force on the other side. However, there a were a few bodies, mostly civilians lying in the streets. A woman was tied to a hitching post. She was alive. Most of her clothes were torn off. The battle became suddenly personal.

They rode two blocks past the squad at the gate before they found their first living Nebraskans. They were ten men looking hung over and disheveled. Two reached for their rifles and died before they could raise them. The emperor signaled for one ranger to take the prisoners. At the first intersection he split his troops into three parts with hand signals and all three groups galloped toward the town square down different streets shooting any armed enemy as they went and peeling off an occasional ranger to take prisoners. They reached the town square about ten minutes later. They had taken only one casualty. The second column got there about the same time and seemed to have taken very few casualties.

Most of the town's population were in a makeshift corral in the town square. They were guarded by soldiers, most of whom had thrown their weapons down when they saw the two mounted columns coming. Several civilians had broken out of the corral and were busily beating the crap out of their guards.

Two blocks away, an apparently sober and professional group had occupied the mission building. They were firing from the second floor windows and were putting up an effective defense. The Captain was watching the building from a protected position. He could see that the building had three foot thick adobe and concrete walls. He signaled his troops to fall back a little. This was going to be a hard fight and there was no point in getting shot by hurrying it.

At the town square, the emperor gathered up ten rangers. "Get to the gates and tell the squads to hold their positions. Their job now is to keep any enemy troops from getting out. I want you men to patrol outside the wall for the same purpose. We don't want any of these bastards getting away."

He turned toward the corral where the civilians were being held. He was momentarily worried about the fact that there were not enough young girls in the mix. "Get these people out of that damned corral, but keep them here. We are going to have to do a house to house and we don't want to accidentally shoot them in their own homes. Lieutenant, organize your men into teams and block out a house to house. Bring any prisoners here. Leave the bodies. We'll deal with them later."

He shouted in a loud voice, "Gentlemen, do not leave this area unless you are with a ranger search team. I know you want to get back to your homes, but we are going to kill a lot of enemy troops and we don't want you mistaken for one. If you feel strong enough, you can pick up a gun off one of the Nebraskans and join one of the search teams."

Then he sat down for a minute and watched other people do their jobs. He considered going to the church to help out, but decided that the Captain could handle it and deserved the chance for a little independent credit.

By this time, explosions were coming from the church. The Captain had decided to keep his men under cover and use grenades to bring the enemy out of the church. It wasn't heroic looking, but in war the only reward for doing things the hard way was written on a tombstone.

Over the next two hours, about two hundred prisoners were brought to the town square. Sporadic gunfire was heard when someone tried to resist. Single shots rang out when one was caught near a woman or a Texan corpse. A dozen Nebraskans were captured outside the walls and about twenty more were killed trying to get away.

The victory was easy. Unbelievably easy. The Nebraskans were in total disarray before the first rangers rode in. Whatever had happened here had destroyed them.

During the afternoon, the picture formed. The Nebraskans had attacked without warning three days before. They had taken a lot of casualties but had finally taken the town. By the end of the first day, the soldiers had started to get drunk and mean. The first rapes happened that night. They looted all the stores and then killed several men they claimed were hiding money from them.

It went on for three days. After the first day, none of the officers seemed to be around and the soldiers got even wilder. The battle was easy because most of the soldiers had been drunk for two days. They had gotten so lax that the surviving townsmen had planned to jump them at about the same time the cavalry showed up.

The officers turned out to be in the group in the church. A major and two captains were delivered to the square just before nightfall.

The meeting was in the town hall. The emperor sat at the center of the dais. Captain Franks on was on his right. They were listening to the report by the mayor of Yahoo. "So far we have identified one hundred and fifty civilian casualties in addition to the six rangers that were posted here. About fifteen buildings were burned or destroyed. We can't count the assaults against the women, and we don't want to. It will be hard enough for them to live with without us questioning and writing down who was and who was not attacked. Another ten or fifteen people are missing. I cannot describe the three days of humiliation, beatings and torture. It's already dark and the sun would be up before I was done. Your Majesty, these men were animals. I hope that they will be tried as war criminals."

His Majesty sighed, "No, there won't be any trials."

Before the shocked looks turned into verbal protests, he continued. "Trials are what we use to determine guilt or innocence. We are sitting in here smelling the smoke of burning buildings, listening to women sobbing, watching the carpenters prepare caskets in the square. Guilt has been determined beyond a reasonable doubt. A trial would be pointless and I have always encouraged Texans to avoid pointless ritual. Tomorrow I will pronounce and execute the sentences."

Later, in private, he would say to Wilson, "The worst part is none of this makes sense. We aren't at war with Nebraska, or at peace, and for a hundred years we have just ignored each other. I don't think that they want a war. Even little wars like '37 are rare. Not many people want to invade a foreign country when your troops are likely to bring back a foreign disease that can wipe you out. We have over a hundred and fifty dead today, more will die tomorrow, and we don't even know why." That night the crown was heavy. Tomorrow would be a very bad day.

There were rangers all around the rim of the small valley. The emperor was sitting on his horse and facing about two hundred Nebraskan prisoners. The day had just begun, but he already felt the fatigue of a sleepless night spent contemplating a bad day to come.

Addressing the prisoners in a loud voice that hid his fatigue, His Majesty asked, "Who is the ranking officer here?"

One man stood. He stepped forward briskly and stood at attention. "I am Major Talbert. I commanded this party."

Emperor Adams dismounted and crossed the short distance between them. As he walked, he slipped the hammer strap from his forty-five. He stopped a few feet from the major. "Major, you have led your men to murder." Gesturing over his shoulder he said, "The evidence is abundant and irrefutable. I therefore find you guilty of murder, rape, battery, theft, and arson and sentence you to death."

He gestured to a ranger behind him who came forward with a small folding writing table and chair. "Do you wish to write a letter to your family before sentence is carried out?" Talbert's eyes were sad but calm. "Yes, I would. I do not protest the sentence, but I want my family to know what happened."

"Take as much time as you need." The emperor backed away several paces and sat in another folding chair. Talbert wrote slowly. Occasionally he would look up at the horizon at think for a moment. He was finished in less than twenty minutes. He arose, folded the letter, and held it over to the ranger who had brought the table.

The emperor walked forward. "Do you want a blindfold?"

"No, I'll leave as I lived, with my eyes open."

Knowing what was coming, Talbert turned his back and looked up. He clasped his hands behind his back. His lips moved in a silent goodbye. Texans didn't use firing squads. The squads were mainly ways to avoid admitting that you were the one that took a life. Texans were taught that if something had to be done, you did it and you took responsibility. The emperor hoped that the wobble he felt didn't show in his walk. Taking a human life this way was the hardest thing a man had to do. Execution was different than battle and he knew he was in for nightmares again. And it was going to get worse before the day was over.

He raised his forty five and carried out the sentence.

Back on his horse, he addressed the prisoners. "You think that you are prisoners of war, and you could have been. But, you came here and raped, wounded and killed over a hundred and fifty villagers, most after the battle was over. I prefer to avoid generalities. Sergeant, hand me the list of victims. The first name on this list is Winifred Armbruster. You raped and killed her. If you had attacked me and my men we would have treated you as prisoners of war and eventually traded you back to your country. If you had even let her live, we might have been able to spare all your lives. But you didn't do that. You killed Winifred and over a hundred other innocents. The blood spilled requires a blood payment."

He turned his horse to face a ditch thirty feet behind him. "Emperors Guard at the ditch!" Twenty rangers dismounted and took standing positions on the other side of the ditch from the emperor. Turning back to the prisoners, he said loudly but calmly "You now have two minutes to choose twenty men to stand by that ditch." Almost if it were an after thought he added, "If you fail to comply in that time, you will all be shot."

It took the prisoners a moment to realize what he had said. Then a hundred voices babbled. Some determined, some calm and some just scared. In just over a minute the victims began to walk, or be shoved, forward. The first ten marched, the next six walked with unsteady gait, and the last four had to be supported by their companions.

Adams was visibly disgusted. He hoped it would be misinterpreted. If the world was only reasonable, these men could live. It was time for him to play Texan. "Get those last four cowards back in the mob. Who is in command after Talbert?"

A trim middle aged man stood up from near the front of the prisoners. "I am Captain Carter. Now in command."

"Do you not, Captain, have four more men with the courage to walk forward without help?"

"Yes, Sir. Myself and my two aides will take their places. Others will follow."

Gesturing to the men next to him, Carter walked calmly to the ditch. He and his aides took positions at the center of the line, stood at parade rest and looked calmly at the firing squad. As he glanced right and left, the other men stood a little straighter and dressed their line. Two more prisoners stood without a word and joined each end of the line. Adams looked at the line of prisoners. "Nebraskans, face your own men, and kneel. You are not soldiers on trial here." The prisoners turned their backs on the firing squad but looked for a moment as if they were going to refuse the order to kneel. Then Captain Carter slowly kneeled to the ground and bent his head forward. The rest followed suit.

The emperor scanned the lines of rangers surrounding the prisoners and then his hand arose above his head. When his hand dropped, it was all black powder and noise. When the smoke cleared, only the twenty-one kneeling men survived.

"You have been spared because you were the bravest and the most noble, and probably the stupidest of your group. Now you bury your dead and go home. You will find shovels in that quartermasters wagon. Bury them, but leave no markers. When you are done, you will find four mules packed with enough provisions to get you to the border, if you hurry. So long as you do not pick up a weapon or molest one of my citizens, you have free passage for the straight line between here and nearest border. You are spared to tell your people that we do not consider the murder of innocent civilians to be an act of war. We do not do this to others and do not allow it to be done to us. I don't care if you call it war, police action, freedom fighting or jihad and I don't care if you are in uniform, out of uniform, or stark naked. If you attack the bystanders, there will be no quarter."

With that he turned his back on them and rode to join his officers at the crest of the hill. "Pick one ranger that can track well and leave him behind to follow them. Tell him to stay out of sight. I want them to think that we're so confident that we aren't even going to watch them go."

The aide made a rotating motion above his shoulder. The rangers around the valley began to turn their horses and disappear. Below them, the quartermaster had finished handing out the shovels. As the men began to dig, he staked out four heavily laden mules and then slowly took his wagon out of the valley.

It was like striking a stage set.

As they rode away, the emperor noticed the messenger and his lathered horse. "What's so important that you ran that horse half to death?"

"Sir Eric sends word that you are needed in Austin as soon as possible. They have received news that requires your personal attention. There is no written message, but I am instructed to relay the message code twenty-three".

Chapter 16 Code 23

Code twenty-three roughly translated meant Come straight home. Have news of danger to the nation. The danger is not immediate, but we need to get moving on it now.

As a result, the Imperial party left at first light and moved in the shortest direction toward Austin. It was assumed that Sir Eric would be moving north with a party. Texas was about as big as could be administered as one county. Strong local officials and a benign government allowed the empire to govern in the fashion of the old Chin Empire, but communications were measured in days or weeks rather than minutes or hours.

They had their horses re-shod with highway shoes and moved down along the ancient highway 35 toward Austin. The Ancients had built well. Most of the highways were still useable and all were recognizable. The surfaces were rough where the blacktop had crumbled, but most of the concrete base was still intact. It was hard enough on the horse's feet that most travelers who did not have wagons chose to ride along the grassy shoulder.

They moved faster near Wichita. The Kansas administration had managed to resurface one lane of blacktop for over thirty miles in each direction from the capitol.

Sir Eric had been moving north since shortly after the messenger left Austin. The two parties met in Wellington, Kansas.

The Imperial party was bivouacked at the local ranger station. The station normally held thirty permanently stationed rangers, but there were quarters for twice that many in case of emergency. There were better quarters in town, but using them would have required more ceremony than they had time for.

Dinner had just been delivered from a local restaurant when they heard a group of horses approach the station. Sir Eric came in followed by two rangers and a fourth man in an ill fitting uniform. The fourth man was about fifty. He had a grey beard and a deep tan. The wrinkles on his face testified to a long life in the sun.

Eric and Wilson smiled, shook hands, pounded arms and did the other rituals of men meeting. Wilson started. "Good to see you Eric. Let the locals take care of the horse. His Majesty is in the mess hall. He will be happy to see you."

Eric and his party started for the mess hall. Wilson hung back for a second and got the attention of one of the local rangers. "Better send someone down for more food, and a considerable quantity of wine." Then he headed for the mess hall himself.

When he got there, Eric and the older man were standing at the emperor's table trying to decide how formal they should be. Wilson stepped into the breach. "There is no better forum for important news than over a hungry meal. I suggest that we four move into the commander's office for a quieter venue."

The emperor picked up his plate and said, "Sounds good. Lead the way, Wilson. You gentlemen get some food and refreshment and come on in."

When they had pulled up chairs and seated themselves around the commandant's desk, Eric spoke up. "I apologize before we start. This information is still important, but it would have been better if we could have found you while you were still in your meeting." Obviously the older man was not in on the details of the meeting with the Pope. "We didn't know how long the meeting would take and hoped that we would be there in time. However, what Captain Teague has to report is still both important and timely." He gestured at the older man. "This is Captain George Teague. He commands the Pecos."

Like most countries, Texas had a small merchant fleet of it's own.

"He has left quarantine to be with us. Captain, please tell these gentlemen what happened on your last trip."

Teague laid his fork aside reluctantly. It had been a long days ride and lunch had been in the saddle.

Wilson intervened. "Captain, I know you had a long ride today. Please enjoy your meal before you report. The world will not end in the next twenty minutes." Despite Wilson's reassurances, the meal was hurried by hunger and decorated with thirst. They soon got as far as cigars and wine. It was time to talk.

Fortunately, they had found four large chairs to pull up to the desk. With the meal over, all four men leaned back with a sigh, as men have since cave man days, and digested their meals. Each had a cigar in one hand and wine in the other. The world would be right for a few minutes.

The captain sensed it was time to start. "We ran into something unusual on our last voyage." And then he thought to himself, What a stupid thing to say. Of course we saw something unusual! Otherwise why would I be here? He paused for a second and started over. "We were running south down the coast of Florida about a hundred miles offshore. We were on a broad reach and traveling fast. In fact, I remember that my first mate had just commented on how easy the trip was going. The crows nest saw the ship a long way off. She was a big three-masted barque. Biggest I ever saw. She had to be over two hundred feet long and over a thousand tons. They were running on a starboard tack and it looked like they were going to pass several hundred yards off of our bow. Then we got closer and saw what it was ahead of us. She was a steel ship! She wasn't showing a flag, but we could make out her name with a glass. She was the *Star Of India*.

"At first, we thought she was just another armed merchantman. When she passed in front of us, we could see that she had four cannon mounted on deck and a swivel gun next to the wheelhouse. Then we made out the twelve closed gun ports on her port side. She was a twenty four gun powerhouse. Just about when we noticed that, she heaved over and went to a port tack. She was trying to cut us off. We figured we had about ten minutes before she cut right across the bow. We laid on all the sail we had and got even more speed up. We managed to pass by before she cut in front of us. We didn't think that she could turn around for hours, but the second mate put a warning shot over her stern with the swivel gun just to warn her we weren't an easy target."

Sir Eric stepped in. "The problem is, that this ship can't exist. Not in this world. We've checked with shipyards, steel wrights, and all of our engineers. No one could have built that ship. We have all the refined steel we want in the old cites, and we can't do it. The problem is that you can't make that much formed steel plate without powered equipment. You need rolling mills and presses and power hammers to do the job. All of that stuff has been outlawed for four hundred years.

But, someone seems to have a steel mill going. That means that they have some sort of power plant and some kind of industrialization. That ship flew no flag, so they don't want to be found yet. We know, however, that she was no pirate ship and not a private venture. The resources to build her would require at least a medium sized country behind you. She was also armed to the teeth. This ship was not built for trade, it was a war ship. Somebody out there is moving ahead. They already have one ship near our waters and they could be coming for us."

The emperor thought for a few moments. "I can see why you wanted to get this to us. It adds a certain air of urgency to our negotiations. I'm not particularly worried that they, whoever 'they' are, will be coming for us soon. They still have the problem of getting troops to go into foreign lands and the problem of letting them come home. For now, I would expect them to use the ship for protected commerce or coastal defense. However, the fact that someone can build it is disturbing. History records that countries that come in second tend to disappear. Countries that have power tend to use it, and these people have power. Someday they will come!"

Chapter 17 The Truth About The Star

The *Go For Broke* was almost broke. She was an old wooden barque out of Scotland. High seas and old age were killing her. The captain decided to make a run for an abandoned shipyard on an old map. Perhaps there they could find a dock and material to help them make it home.

They didn't have much hope of finding the shipyard. Since the sea levels had risen, a lot of islands had disappeared and the ones that were left didn't look like they used too.

This time they got lucky. The Curacao ship yard was, surprisingly, a little higher than the surrounding land. It extended well below the old sea level, but was built big to service the mammoth cruise ships of the Ancients. Most of her yards were still above water.

The first mate led a crew ashore to see if there was anything useable in the yard. They weren't gone over thirty minutes when one of the crewman came running back, yelling as he came, "Captain, Captain, you gotta come see this! Captain."

Captain Moore left the bridge of *the Go For Broke* at a fast walk, about all the hurrying he did at age fifty five. "What the Hell is so important?"

The crewman was breathless. "We found a ship! An iron ship!"

"So, we've all seen iron ships, but those rusted hulks never have anything we need."

"No captain! This one is in the dry-dock and she looks like new!! AND SHE SAILS!!"

Now the Captain did hurry. In a few minutes they were able to look over the lip of the dry-dock at a two hundred foot long steel sailing ship with the name Star Of India painted on her bow. Even though she was the biggest boat in the world, she did look a little like a sailing skiff in a dock built to handle the worlds biggest cruise ships.

She almost gleamed. There had been a little leakage through the dry-doors, but not enough so that the puddle under the ship never got over four or five feet deep.

The first mate had tears in his eyes. "Ain't she beautiful? She looks almost like we could sail her away."

The captain looked back and forth from stern to bow and finally said, "If she's as good inside as she is out, maybe we can. She looks barque rigged. If her own sails aren't there, we might be able to use the *Go For Broke's* to get some headway. You two go back to the ship for the rest of the crew. Tell them to bring rope ladders. The rest of you look for some tall ladders that will get us up on deck once we are down in the dock. Let's get going."

The entire crew ended up in the bottom of the dry-dock looking up at the Star. The captain yelled for attention. "We don't want any accidental damage or anything spoiled. The first and second mates, and the carpenter, Mr. Samuels, and myself will go aboard first and inspect the ship. Then you can all come take a look. While we are gone, inspect the hull, but be careful not to damage anything. This is an old ship."

It was a ninety minutes before the first mate stuck his head over the rail and called for everyone to come up to the deck. By then they'd had time to notice that the hull was perfect. No rust. No barnacles. No problems. They were into wondering how the Ancients had made it so durable.

When they were assembled on deck, he addressed them in a voice loud enough to carry to the two hundred and fifty men and women on the deck. "I've spent an hour going over a metal plaque and some papers left on the bridge. The mates have walked the ship from end to end and the carpenter has been up on the rigging.   She is in great shape. Better than great shape, and it was intentional. According to the information on the bridge, this ship was made in 1863 AD. She sailed the seas for a hundred years and then was in a museum for fifty years. The museum people brought her here during the sailing interregnum in about 50 New Era. They knew that they couldn't keep her up any more and wanted her preserved to sail again. They made is us a present of her. They preserved her. They filled the hold with spare rigging and sails and they gave her to us. She is the biggest and best ship in the world today and she's ours. We are all filthy rich!!"

He paused for a second and looked over his shoulder. He pointed to the cruise ship sized doors at the end of the dock. "At least we will be if we can figure out how to open those damned sea doors."

The Ancients were helpful. There were instructions on how to find the valves that let the sea back into the lock, and how to bypass them or blow them if needed. Knowing that welding, at least in the ancient sense, might be lost art, they had welded pockets in several places on the inside of the sea doors where explosives might free up them up.

It took three weeks of backbreaking labor to get the valves open and free the Star Of India.

They then spent a month re-rigging her and transferring their cargo, plus all the tools, clothes, cloth and kids from the *Go For Broke* to the *Star*.

The carpenter was the first one to voice the obvious worry. "Captain. This ship will be ours only as long as we can defend it. The Go For Broke only had four cannon and one swivel gun. That's plenty to defend a ship no one wants but the Star of India is a big prize."

"Do you have any ideas?"

"Yep. Of course we'll transfer the four cannon and the swivel, but the smart thing to do is to avoid a fight. Me and a couple of the boys are pretty fair artists. What say we paint on a few extra gun ports, say ten on each side. We'll make 'em look like closed ports. Then anyone coming for us will think we are the biggest ship in the world AND the best armed. Better to bluff than fight."

A month later they were trying to get back to their home for a cargo and some real cannons. They were tacking South looking for the westerlys that would take them across the Atlantic. With the change of climate, the jet steam only ran reliably in the southern hemisphere.

They were having a hard time. The ship was too big for the crew to handle and their lack of experience was showing. They were good sailors and had sailed a barque rig for years, but this was bigger and clumsier than they were used to. They weren't able to set more than half the sails and a barque is a hard ship to get on tack even with a crew who knows her well.

There was a man in the crows nest, but he was busy watching the struggle below. He never saw the Texas ship that was approaching downwind. They were zigzagging more then they needed to because they wanted to practice running the ship. They changed from a starboard to a port tack slowly and everyone's attention was on the rigging. They didn't realize that they were on a collision course with the sloop and didn't even see her until she had laid on more sail and passed to their stern.

In fact, they might not noticed her at all if there hadn't been the boom of a deck gun from the sloop and the whistle of a ball going overhead.

"Jesus, they sure take it hard when you cut them off!!". The captain called out to the carpenter, "There goes your theory about scaring our way out of a fight. We better learn to sail better or get more guns in a hurry."

Chapter 18   To Be or Not To Be

One of the generals opened the discussion with pessimism. "I think that we have to be very careful. This man is a religious leader and that makes him completely untrustworthy."

Someone asked, "How do you justify that reasoning?"

The general snorted. "Because he is not responsible. If an atheist or a Texan screws you over, he has to take responsibility for what he did. Look, if I kill a man, the blood is on my hands and mine alone, I have to answer for it. It isn't like that for a person with a cause. He can cheat you, double cross you, or even kill you without the least problem with his conscience because he did it for 'the greater glory of God', or 'the noble people of Serbia' or some such nonsense. Christians and Moslems both have even killed women and children and said it was okay because they did it for God or Allah. I'd rather deal with an atheist any time. I mean, how can we trust this man is telling the truth, let alone that he'll keep his word?"

The emperor emeritus, who had traveled from Houston to attend the meeting, decided to address that topic. "I believe that Jones is telling the truth. It's the very nature of religion that puts him in that spot." The emeritus seemed to fated to eventually look like Benjamin Franklin. In retirement, his hair was thinning, his face rounding, and his paunch growing. However, the Empire had prospered during the reign of Emperor Samuel Adams, and he commanded respect not related to the title of Emperor Emeritus.

When the expressions around the table told him that he was not being understood, he continued, "Some of you may have read The Founders beliefs on human nature. For those of you who have not, let me say that his belief was that humans were much more closely related to cows than to coyotes. He noted that you sometimes see a lone coyote when you ride down the road it night. You never see a lone cow, or a lone buffalo or a lone gazelle. They are herd animals that live and move as part of a group, and humans are the same. We live in families and groups and clans and nations. It's so unusual to see a human live alone that when we do see it, we make fun of them and call them names like 'hermit'. Children who are raised without human touch and adults that live without human contact suffer terribly. In fact, one of our most severe punishments is simply to put a person in solitary confinement and deny them the company on other people. The punishment is so cruel that it's outlawed in Texas.

"Most people realize that, but they don't look at what it means. It defines us. We not only want to live with others, our most powerful drive to be like others and to make them be like us. That's why we have fashions. That is why every woman wants to wear the same color bonnet and every man wears a ten gallon hat and a gun, and why sports fans will be rabidly loyal to sports teams that they have absolutely no logical connection to. It's also why humans kill so easily. All you have to do is to convince people that we are 'Armenian' and the other guys are 'Turks' and, therefore, not a part of our herd, and we can kill each other almost without compunction.

"It's also why most laws in other countries have nothing to do with protecting people from evil or preventing harm. Outside of Texas, a vast majority of laws enforce 'morals', that is, tell you how to behave as part of the herd. They tell you what clothing you can wear, who you can have sex with, who you can marry, what words you can say, what drugs you can use to get drunk on, when you can gamble, when you can drink, what body parts you can show in public, and a million other things that logically should be no one's business but your own. But, people are not logical. Our biological urge is to part of the herd, not to be free. As a race, there is nothing we claim more of and want less of than freedom.

"That is why we have religion and why Pope Jones is in a bind. Most people think that the function of religion is to promise eternal life, to protect us from the darkness. The problem is that some of the oldest and most tenacious religions, like Judaism, never promise a single day of afterlife. The real purpose of religion is to make everyone else behave the same, dress the same, and talk the same and blame it all on God. Every majority opinion is attributed to God. Christ never said a word condemning slavery, the showing of woman's breasts, or the use of cocaine. However, generations of preachers have invoked his name to control everything from the content of books to the length of hemlines, all in the name of GOD. God only gave the world ten commandments, but the priests have enforced a thousand morals, all in the name of Christianity.

"That gives credence to Pope Jones statements. As the role of religion is to enforce public opinion as Divine Will, he has the problem he claims. The people of York were, and are, afraid. They were afraid of doctors and machines and of the world ending again. It therefore became the job of the church to make that fear holy and correct. If the church refuses to sanctify public beliefs, they just find another church. That is the purpose of religion.

"If Moslem men want women to hide their face in public and want to kill Jews, the job of the Moslem cleric is to claim that Mohammed wants your wife to be a slave and that he wants you to kill Jews. The fact that Mohammed specifically forbids most killing and never mentioned a chadri is conveniently forgotten. If the people of York are afraid, it's the job of Pope Jones to say that anyone who acts differently is blaspheming. He has the same problem that we have, that he has to change public opinion before he can change what he supports. It's even worse for him, because he is the official guardian of public morals."

Down the table, General Armbruster harrumphed. "The substance of what you say may be right, but I doubt if either religion or the Pope's problem is all that simple. I seem to remember that you also said once 'when a man gives you a very simple solution to a complex problem he is either very perceptive, or too dumb to see the real problem, or running for office.' The Popes obviously have some moral authority. I remember that one of the crazier ones actually declared that priests had to be celibate."

The old emperor smiled, "Of course, the Pope does have influence about like we do, the same as any respected leader of the community. But they can't and we can't just declare public opinion. By the way, the celibacy that the crazy pope declared wasn't actually enforced for a few hundred years, until the public swayed that way. And before anyone else objects, yes, I understand that religion has other functions after it is established. It makes people feel special, gives them a place to meditate, and in the case of Christianity does relieve the fear of death in some people, but that does not change its basic nature or the basic problem that Pope Jones has."

Armbruster shuffled some papers in front of him. "Maybe we can accept that his problems are real, but, more important, can we trust him?"

The emperor looked around the table, inviting comment. The chief of intelligence cleared his throat. "I have had copies of some relevant entries in our Pope file made for each of you. Our direct contact with him has been limited as we are officially at war with them, even though it has been thirty years since we shot at each other. If I can address you to the summary page, we can find no significant promise that the Papacy has broken during his reign. He is a bit of a hard ass and has less humor than his sons or his father. He, for instance, graduated from Annapolis with only nine demerits in four years and, he has publicly been a stickler for Papal tradition and moral values. He advocates a strong and intrusive priesthood that publicly judges everything from the citizens drinking habits to their spending habits."

Armbruster pointed at the folder placed in front of him and asked, "What does it say in here about his family life?"

The chief cleared his throat again. "There is not much in here about his family life. We didn't know if it would be relevant. However, he has been married for thirty-two years, and has three sons and one daughter who lived. You have met his eldest son. We have discussed Artimus Jones at length in this council and agreed that he is trustworthy. They are a close family who gather for holidays and birthdays. What else would you want to know?"

Armbruster asked, "Is he faithful to his wife?"

"Yes, Sir. As far as we know. We only have information from newspapers and court informants, but we have never heard of any improprieties. I must say that I don't see how that is relevant to our current discussion."

Armbruster responded, "In my mind, everything. He is the most powerful man in his country and can therefore have any woman or as many women as he wants. If he takes his oath to his wife seriously enough to stay faithful in those circumstances, I will believe that he respects his word like a Texan."

The discussion continued for two hours, but, in the end, the fidelity of the Pope and the character of his offspring were the deciding factors. The consensus of the council was that the Pope could be trusted.

The emperor then moved the meeting to the discussion of the treaty. "The information sharing is obviously no problem. Texas always deals fair. We do need to discuss the requirement that we allow papal abbeys to be re-established in Texas."

The elder emperor took the lead again. "Dangerous, damned dangerous. That's what the war was all about. Those bastards attacked the very basis of Texan society. Those of you who have studied history know that the Founder and the first privy counsel worked hard to preserve a belief in real independence. They deliberately reached back into history to a partly mythological time when freedom and independence were valued more than at any other time in our history and modeled their world after it. We live in a West based on both fact and myth, but we have the freest society in history.

"Freedom isn't natural, so we have to fight every year to keep people believing in it. Our school systems repeatedly warn our children of the dangers of letting government make laws, we limit our laws to the Code, and we warn people that the greatest evil is to let government butt into anyone's business.

"It's an uphill battle that we will lose someday. The real danger of the priests that caused the war of '37 wasn't just that they offended Texan beliefs, but that people might get to like the simple solution of passing laws for everything. That's why we had to kick them out so fast. Letting them back in is like letting a poisonous snake sleep in your bed."

The current emperor finally got a word in. "Maybe we need to be snake charmers this time. If we can figure out a way to keep from being bitten, the payoff is very good. It could save us lifetimes of work. I also believe that the pope will not press his rights for at least several years."

The emperor emeritus looked skeptical. "What makes you think that we won't have priests meddling in our affairs next year?"

The younger emperor gestured at the treaty he held. "Because this is a dumb treaty negotiated by a very competent man. I think that this section is window dressing for his counsel back home. Look at the section on when the abbeys will be established. It says 'as soon as normal relations can be established.' We haven't even started working on a peace treaty yet and they haven't asked to. Now look at the section on where the abbeys can be placed. It has some specifics about the rights to purchase farmable land and access to roads, but it includes the phrase 'locations mutually agreed to.' Texas is a huge empire and Pope Jones has to realize that we can choose to 'mutually agree' only to locations in NewMex or Kansas that are so far away from civilization that the buzzards won't be able to find their bodies if they die. I also have to report that as bad as those provisions are for the Yorkers, Baron Wilson will testify to the fact that they were very easy to negotiate. It makes me think that they are window dressing to make the deal look better with his counsel or to convince us that we are getting something very valuable."

The older emperor sounded like Armbruster when he harrumphed. "Window dressing or not, they will still be here someday."

His son answered, "Yes, Sire. And we will stick them in NewMex and kick their butts out the first time they preach a sermon. Remember that they are also forbidden to proselytize."

With the older and younger emperor leading opposing sides, it took the rest of the day to reach a consensus.

Chapter 19 Back In Nebraska

Captain Carter stood at attention before the Court Marshal board. He was wearing his dress buckskins and leather Jones hat. His leather epaulets were freshly oiled and his boots freshly polished. Spectators looking for a sign of fear or even nervousness were disappointed. His face was impassive as the lead court officer spoke to him.

"Your written report seems to be relatively complete and honest. I am impressed that you did not claim any heroic feats to explain the survival of only twenty men out of a company. However, I do have a few questions for you. I have before me a copy of the orders given to your major. I assume that, as second in command, you were aware of those orders. Is that correct?"

"Yes, Sir."

"Captain, would you tell me what you remember of those orders."

"Yes, Sir. We were to make an incursion into Texan territory. We were to avoid direct combat but to make enough trouble to provoke a response from Austin. We were then to retreat to the border while gathering intelligence regarding the strength of the Texan response."

"Very good captain. You were supposed to tickle the Texans to see how hard they would respond. Now where, may I ask, is that part of the orders that told you to massacre civilians, burn towns and rape women?"

At first, Carter's eyes were passive as he explained. "The major led us about eighty klicks into Texas. As I stated in my report, he wanted to make certain that the Texans saw the raid as more than a simple border incursion.

"He decided that we would hit the ranger station in Yahoo. It was a small ten-man station in a backwater town. The plan was to lay siege to the station but allow them to get a message out to the imperials.

"We planned to be gone into the hills before the imperials came. We were going to leave a scout or two on the roadway to count the imperials and report their response.

"Things went wrong even before we got to the city wall. Someone spotted us while we still outside the wall. We weren't worried. The major had figured that the civilians would scatter and the rangers would hold up in the station. We would settle in for a few days of easy siege, a little target practice, and out of town before anyone showed up.

"Things sure went wrong. By the time we got to the city gates, bullets were thicker than hailstones. Emperor Adams made a big deal about us "attacking innocent civilians" but the only unarmed Texan I saw was a seven year old girl child, and I suspect that she just forgot to bring her gun. Instead of ten Rangers, we were in the middle of the nastiest firefight you ever saw with three or four hundred of the meanest bastards on Earth."

Wilson's calm was breaking a little and his voice was higher. "We'd have retreated, but your back makes an even better target than your front. We had to go on. By the time we burned the ranger station and subdued most of the 'civilians', we had suffered almost fifty percent casualties. Worst victory I ever saw.

"The men were enraged. They all lost friends. They felt cheated that what was supposed to be an easy assignment had turned so rotten and scared them so bad. They acted like all scared men. They got mad. They blamed the Texans. They started talking about 'getting even'.

"Within a few hours incidents began to happen. A few houses started burning. A prisoner or two 'tried to escape' and by nightfall the women started to scream. At first the major tried to stop them but he soon realized that they were almost crazed enough kill him too.

"He told me and Captain Smith to do what we could to quell the violence, without getting ourselves killed. It wasn't very much. He stayed out of the way. He was no coward, but he knew when to stop fighting the tide."

Wilson face was still calm, but his eyes were in Texas. He shuddered slightly. "It is amazing how long it takes to destroy a town that size. The burning and shooting and screaming went on all night, and the next day, and the next night. I felt sick, and helpless, and weak. Then you just go numb.

"The Imperials showed up the third day. It wasn't much of a fight. I guess it's hard to set up an effective resistance when two of you are holding down a woman and the third is on top of her.

"You know the rest from the report. Major knew they were going to execute him. He didn't mind much. He knew that it had been his job to shoot his own dog. It was a blood debt that he was willing to pay."

There was an awkward silence as the court waited to see if Wilson were through. After a few seconds, his head drooped for the first time and he stared at the floor. An uncharitable observer might have implied that one of Wilson's eyes glistened just slightly.

The court officer spoke in quiet tones. "Captain, you are a problem for us." He shifted on his chair. "You stood by while your men massacred a town. If the Texans hadn't punished your command, we probably would have.

On the other hand, you redeemed yourself when you offered to die for crimes that you had witnessed but not participated in. It ended up saving your life, but you didn't know that when you volunteered. You also became a public hero when you lead those last twenty men out of Texas. The newspapers love you."

The court officer looked down at the document in front of him. His expression was that of a child who had just been told that he was having liver and broccoli for dinner. The disgust in his voice was masked, but not well.

"So, we're going to call it a draw. No medal, no punishment. Your current tour of duty is up in less than six months. At that time you will quietly leave the army. Between now and then, you are posted to the War College. You will work with the leadership specialists there to understand just what went wrong and how it could have been avoided.

"An army that cannot be controlled is more dangerous than any foreign power."

Wilson saluted as the officers arose without further comment and filed out of a door behind the bench. The spectators drifted out in silence. Then he was alone. Still at attention and still staring at the bench.

Chapter 20   Moving The Farm.

It was the first meeting of the archeology committee since the meeting with the Pope. The committee had grown to sixteen with the addition of the Emperor Emeritus and the Empress Dowager. In her middle forties, the Dowager was considered "middle aged", but her rich chestnut hair and hard won slender figure made her look younger than her years. There were also now others in the Empire who had hints of the work. The scientists of the committee had now had three weeks to pour over the books that had been provided by the Yorkers.

The emperor opened the meeting by beginning the usual round of oaths "*Know ye that we intend to conduct business both secret and desperate . . . .*" The oath had become more important as the committee worked. When you are surrounded by curious and enthusiastic scientists, it's easy to forget the penalty for forbidden knowledge.

When the oaths were done, the emperor turned the meeting over to Sir Greg with the question, "How are things on the farm?"

"As you all know, we have decided to prepare for a higher level of activity. With the news that we have competition and the possibility of help from the Yorkers, we anticipate working on a larger scale than we have done in the past. The old farm is too close to Austin for comfort. Therefore, we have decided to establish a new facility on a royal ranch at Sweetwater. We will have six thousand acres of privacy and access to the Sweetwater River.

"Workers have already started work on the charcoal plant that we plan to use for cover. Everyone knows that the plant puts out a lot of smoke and noise so we'll have good cover for our other activities, and some fuel.

"Solomon's office will stay at the old farm, but we plan to manufacture Winnie Wigwams products at the new facility. Eric is working on plans to make it look like the stuff is being shipped from somewhere else up the Sweetwater river. With luck, even the barge captains won't know exactly where they are loading it. I would like to turn the meeting over to Mr. White. He will fill you in on the progress of his project."

Solomon arose from his chair and moved back a few steps to stand by an easel. "We have decided on two simple products for our first try. We are going to package Epson Salts first. Epson salts are actually soluble magnesium sulfate. If you soak a wound in them shortly after it happens, the salts draw infectious material from the wound and can prevent an infection taking hold.

"We are also going to market a bottle of purified alcohol. Winnie will sell it as the "miracle infection stopper". We hope that someone will challenge the "miracle" part and force her to admit that it's really just alcohol and red dye.

"We will start with these items because they are already known and used by some people. We'll purify them, package them and popularize them. We will also firmly establish that Winnie is a harmless native woman selling traditional herbal cures and not medicine.

"We are already working on the process to make large quantities of sulphanilamide. The ancients called it 'Sulpha' for short. It was the first 'anti-biotic' that was discovered. One text that survives says that it was eventually made in five thousand varieties. It can be used as a pill, mixed with water, or spread on a wound as a powder or gel. A man can often actually survive a gut wound if it's used right.

"I have managed to make small quantities myself. The powder form looks like a common chalk powder. That is it's greatest advantage. It looks like chalk powder. I have a little here that I made in the lab."

He reached behind the easel and brought out two black match boxes. He slid them open and handed them out left and right. "Pass this around and give it a look."

He paused for a moment while the people at the table looked in the boxes. The Empress stuck her pinkie in her box and tested the texture. Wilson took a little on his finger and looked for a minute like he was going to taste it. If so, he changed his mind and passed the box on.

Solomon looked at Wilson as he passed the box and asked "Sir Wilson, if I hadn't told you want that was, what would you think that you just looked at."

Wilson thought for a few seconds and said, "Some sort of talcum powder, or maybe the stuff my wife puts in the soups to thicken them up."

"Would you believe that we get it by grinding up bark from a desert tree?"

"Sure, it looks like a ground up powder. Maybe from some dried out plant material."

Solomon smile broadly. "That is why it's so good. Actually, it took me several days to make what you see in those boxes. It took beakers and tubing and chemicals and heat and thermometers, but you can't tell it. We'll sell it as a magic powder that you can sprinkle on or drink and we will show people pictures of the Sulpha Tree right on the label. Nobody who is sick is going to object to dried tree bark, especially when it's sold by an Indian woman named 'Winnie Wigwam'."

He had started to sit down when the Emperor Emeritus raised an index finger. "Have you worked on how Winnie looks and how it will be packaged?"

Solomon was half way in his seat and had to do a ballet step to start going up instead of down. He reached for the Easel." I almost forgot. We had an artist draw up a sample Winnie." He flipped the cover paper over. There was a picture of Winnie. She was an Indian woman about twenty-five years old, dressed in a long buckskin dress and boots. On her head was a beaded band with a single blue feather in it. She had a nice smile and enough curves showing through the buckskin to catch a mans eye without offending his wife.

The ancients would have recognized a Disney image of an Indian, but now there were real Indians who dressed that way. With the blurring of memory, many fictions had become realities.

The Emperor Emeritus went on. "Have you planned the packaging and distribution, the business end of this?"

"No sir. No one here has any experience with business – except you." The emperor showed a wry smile. Solomon went on. "It is well known that the Imperial businesses prospered under your able hand. We were frankly hoping that you might advise us on that end of the business."

It was a very familiar way to talk to your emperor, even if he was retired, but a mutual oath of heresy and treason gave privileges not granted to people outside this room. The conversation about Winnie lasted until they took a break to get lunch from a sideboard. Everyone filled a plate and returned to the table.

Then it was Eric's turn. He was so anxious to start that his plate sat untouched. As soon as he stood up he got a school boys grin. "Gentlemen, as you know, we have only had a few weeks with the books from York. In such a short time, it's hard to expect much. I must therefore report that WE UNDERSTAND IT ALL!!. IT IS SO SIMPLE!! We have been all the way through the books several times.

"The good news is that there are only about four basic parts and three or four basic rules to the whole thing. It is so simple that I cannot understand how the knowledge was lost in the first place. It was like being blind and having sight restored. We can already look at pieces that were just garbage last month and have an idea of what they do and how they work.

"Now the bad news. It's like chess. Anyone in this room can learn the moves in less than an hour. To become a chess champion takes years. The basics are simple, but knowing how to apply them is complex.

"We have also learned something else important. We now know what is on those destruction items people call 'circuit boards'. Believe it or not, those little black plastic pieces have millions of tiny parts in them. I'm serious. Millions. What's important is that we know not to waste time on them. It will be a hundred years before we have the tools to build anything like that.

"It gets even better. I can prove we understand it. Ladies, I do have to apologize for the language that I have to use. Please try to remember that we are talking about real concrete things and not just swearing. After years of wondering what a gen.., uh, generator would look like, I have built one."

He expected applause. Instead, there was a stunned silence around the table. He continued on into the silence.

"It was easy. It is a few feet of wire, a couple of pieces of brass, and a handle to turn it. We used one of the gauges from the silo to see that it worked." His voice had begun to fail. No one seemed excited. No one moved.

The emperor leaned forward at the head of the table. "Gentlemen, relax. You all knew that this day would come. This is where we were going. That's why we take the oath every time we meet."

A colonel across the table spoke quietly. "It's different to plan to raise the Devil than it is to see a horned man with hooves and a pitchfork standing at your door. I think we are all in shock. I thought we were going to plan things before we did them, get agreement from the committee members. We've just opened a forbidden science and we didn't even know that we were doing it."

The Emperor Emeritus spoke from the foot of the table.

"Gentlemen, we are sixteen adventurers in the same boat. You were chosen for intelligence, courage, and competence. There is not one weak or foolish man or woman at this table. You are in a room of people, every one of which you can trust to guard your back. If Sir Eric made this decision, it was a good one. Trust each other. This may be the only time in your life that you will be able to trust every member of your team. As for myself, I have been using that swear word all my life and I am damned curious to see what it was I was talking about. Sir Eric. Now that the team has its breath, please tell us what a 'generator' is."

Eric continued in a much more subdued manner. "It's a simple idea. We all know that things are made of up of atoms. On the outer layer of atoms are small particles called electrons. In some materials like metals, the electrons can leave the atom that they are on and move to the next one over. When they do that, they try to push the electrons already on that atom over to the next one. When they move, they carry energy with them.

"Picture pouring a bucket of water in a trough. It would run off the other end. If you had a water wheel there, the water would turn the wheel. It would keep turning the water wheel as long as you kept pouring water in.

"A generator is kind of like that bucket. It makes electrons move. Then there are devices that work like the water wheel and get turned by the electrons.

"If anyone, or everyone, is interested, we can stay over for an hour or two after this meeting and I can explain almost all of the basics of electricity to you. The generator I built is about 4 inches square and weighs only a few ounces. I would have brought it to show you, but I don't think ANYTHING that we don't want seen should ever leave the farm.

"I assure you, that the only thing this generator does is to move a needle on a gauge when we turn the handle. Nothing more will be done until this committee approves it."

All of the members of the committee except the two Empresses stayed after the meeting for over two hours to listen to Eric and Greg's explanation. It might be scary, but everyone loves to be in on a secret.

Chapter 21   Meeting In Killer Pass

Artimus was enjoying a pipe under the tarp that he had staked out against the cold mountain drizzle. Looking For all the world like a man with no cares in the world bigger than waiting for the rain to stop.

Wilson was in his tan weather coat with the hood cinched around his neck. His horse walked slowly up to the spot that Artimus had staked out on the side of the road. He waved to Artimus as he approached, but did not say anything until he was seated under the low tarp. "Well, believe this. We both got here on the appointed day."

Artimus took the pipe out of his mouth. "From your presence, I assume that the emperor decided to accept the treaty."

"He did. I have the signed document with me."

"Good. We'd better burn it before we get on the road."

Wilson was aghast "Burn it? Doesn't the Pope want the treaty?"

"Certainly, he does. But if the word of a king isn't good enough, the paper it's on will be no better. The emperor is, after all, a Texan. Code of the west, A man don't lie unless he is fishing.

"There is a greater danger that it should fall into the wrong hands. I'll send up a signal flare to let the border guards know that I am leaving with you. No other verification is needed."

As they fed the red banded document to the fire, Wilson looked at Artimus. "I brought new identification papers for you. You are now Artimus Jones, Knight of the Imperial Service. I also have your knight's ring and a copy of the newspaper clipping that was published when your ringer went through the ceremony. I think you will like what they wrote about you. You will be in service to Baron Wilson. By the way, do you have the books with you?"

"I thought that I saw a Baron's Medallion when you opened your coat. Congratulations on your promotion. The books are in my saddlebags. Do you want to transfer them now?"

"No thanks. You've brought them this far. I doubt that you'll lose them now. We had better strike the tarp and send up your flare. By the way, what color is your flare?"

"Red, is that important"

"Not if it's red. I just wanted to be sure that it wasn't a color that would mislead the imperial post."

When the two of them reached the border station, twenty rangers were mounted in double file ready to escort them on the two day trip to the canal. They carried twenty of the four hundred remaining AK47's in Texas. They had been ready to rescue Baron Wilson if he had sent up the trouble flare that he had in his backpack. But there was no reason to mention that.

The trip down the mountain side was cold and wet. Even the rangers huddled inside their rain gear as the horses picked their way down. About an hour before sunset, they set up camp in a protected hollow at the base of a cliff. The cliff behind them and boulders on three sides gave some protection from the miserable weather.

It was hard even then to keep a campfire burning. Supper was undercooked and the coffee was watery. Something about such weather makes a tent or a canopy as wonderful as a palace. You can sit there warmer than you were before and almost dry and feel the warm sensation of beating nature. It takes a spell of misery to make a man that happy.

The next day the weather was worse, but, they were now down past the timber line. They were following the wide path though the forest that was once a highway. They stayed on the shoulder to protect their horse's hooves from loose concrete. There were steep hills on both sides of the road and some bare cliffs too steep to have vegetation. They were traveling in a pass between such hills. Out front two rangers took the point, staying just within sight of the following men. Two were forward outriggers and two trailing behind as rear guard. That left fourteen men and Wilson escorting Artimus down the road.

When Wilson first heard the sound, he thought it was thunder. Like everyone else, he hesitated a second before he looked up. Then the outrigger yelled, "Avalanche! Avalanche! Get the Hell out of there. Move fast or die! Wilson hesitated a split second longer to see the Artimus was in motion and then spurred his horse. They were in an area of sand and loose rock. The horses stumbled as they tried to get into a gallop. Looking down, he saw a round shadow covering his on the ground and getting larger. His last fully conscious thought was We're not going to make it. And he didn't.

Lying there semi-awake under the body of his horse he heard the sounds of gunfire. Just before he drifted deeper, he thought "Gunfire? When do avalanches shoot at people?" ....

He came too looking up at the ranger sergeant. He rolled over a little and saw he was lying on a blanket laid out just beyond the pass where the avalanche happened. "What happened? Is everyone alright?"

"I'm sorry , sir. You don't seem to have any broken bones and Sir Artimus came to about an half hour ago. It was a bandit ambush. They started the avalanche and about ten men hit both the front and rear guards. We fell back to the canyon mouth and regrouped, and then it took us about an hour to send them back up the hill.

We lost seven men and most of the horses in the avalanche and one rear guard was wounded."

Wilson suddenly realized what happened. "Where is Artimus' horse?" He was almost yelling.

The sergeant pointed to a spot about half way up the cliff. "There he is. One of the bandits tried to steal him, but the horse was limping. They got about that far when the bandit decided to take the livery and leave the horse. By the time we were ranged in, the horse was dead and the bandit gone. We also lost three AK's."

"Is Artimus able to talk? I need to confer with him."

The walk to Artimus' side was the most painful he could remember. He tried to console himself with the fact that he was able to move and nothing seemed broken. It was a poor consolation. Artimus was in the middle of being bandaged by a ranger. He had cuts on his head and left leg and gave the impression of a bruised doll, but seemed to be breathing alright. "Did you hear that a bandit got your saddlebags?"

"The ranger told me when I asked about my horse. You know we have to get them back. There's five years of work and a few men's lives in those bags. If we have to arrange all of this all over again, it will delay us for at least two years."

Wilson put his hand on Artimus' leg. "Are you up to travel? It'll be by shanks mare and across rough trail."

"The cut doesn't seem too bad. I'll have the private pour some spirits on it and bind it tight. If you'll have someone cut me a crutch, I'll keep up."

Wilson called all of the men together. He did not insist that they stand. "Rangers, the bandits have taken a pouch with an important treaty in it. If we lose it, lives could be lost as well. The treaty we are seeking is in a pair of saddlebags that have a large golden 'A' emblazoned on the flat. The case was locked and the contents must be kept secret for the good of the realm. We are going after them."

The sergeant came to attention, or as much at attention as a man with a dislocated shoulder can do. "Baron Wilson. They also have three of our weapons. No ranger has lost his weapon in two hundred and thirty years. We'll find them. Now."

In the end, they sent one ranger on horseback down the mountain for reinforcements. The other two horses were loaded with the wounded ranger, Artimus, and what supplies they could salvage. Before they left they built a small pylon of stones to show the relief column where they entered the forest. Private Gomez led the way as he was the best tracker in the squad. They started up the hill.

The country was heavy wooded. Tracking was relatively easy because of the pine needles and small shrubbery that was abundant in the forest. They blazed a trail for the reinforcements to follow behind them. The trip started out as a journey of misery for bruised and hurt men, and rapidly got worse. Texans were taught that there is a connection between the body and the mind and that a proper attitude can control much of the pain that the body feels. By mid afternoon, every man had tested that to the limit. Rangers do not complain, but they do hobble and occasionally stumble when reaching the limits of human endurance.

They were gaining on the bandits. Even though most of the bandits were mounted, they were slowed down by the ones who had not gotten horses in the battle and were probably overconfident. Maybe they were not in a hurry because it was obvious that the rangers were too hurt to pursue them.

The men were taking turns hanging on the saddles of the two horses. One man on each side would grip the saddle horn and stumble along. When it was Wilson's turn, Artimus asked him "What do we do when we catch them?" Wilson answered, "We'll try not to catch them. They must have a camp somewhere around here. We'll follow them to the camp and watch them until the reinforcements arrive. There are no extra points in this game for doing it the hard way, so we won't take them on with thirteen men if we can wait for fifty more to show up." Fatigue made him speak slowly between deep breaths.

They stopped near sunset when they could see the bandit's bonfire a few miles ahead. They were too fatigued to close the gap that night and settled for a cold camp and sleep. A few hours after sundown, there was the sound of an AK clip being fired in the bandit camp. A minute later there was the sound of a large caliber cap

and ball pistol being discharged. The sergeant glanced sleepily toward Artimus.
"They seem to be having an ownership discussion regarding our guns. I hope no
one gives in easily."

Leaving at dawn, they passed the bandits camp from the night before. There
was a body casually tossed aside. It had powder burns on its arms, a lot of holes
from AK ammo, and part of the skull gone from single black powder ball. Private
Adams gave it a cursory look. "Looks like the moron tried to grab an AK from the
wrong end. Looks like some friend administered a mercy shot for him, and the rest
of the human race."

Day two of the pursuit was like day one, only harder. No one had been
unscathed by the avalanche, and now bruises and abrasions were responding to the
constant pounding. There was a rumor that a ranger could march a hundred miles on
a broken leg. It was, of course, a lie but today it felt real.

Shortly before the next nightfall, the tracker motioned them to stop. In a quiet
voice he said, "I think they stopped over that next hill."

The rangers slumped gratefully to the ground while the tracker went ahead. He
was back in about twenty minutes. "They've got a camp in a clearing. It looks
pretty permanent. Besides lean-to's, they've got a couple of log cabins. They've got
two guards out, but they're such amateurs that a blind man could see them from a
hundred paces. Sir, I heard what you said about watching them. I might suggest that
there is good cover and slightly elevated position on both the north and south sides
of the meadow. You might want to set up squads in those two spots."

"Good idea." Wilson looked at the sergeant. "Take six men with you to the
north side, and Artimus and I and the other five will cover the south. Don't kill the
guards unless they see you. We don't want the camp wondering what happened to
them."

Artimus and the wounded ranger got off the horses, with a little help, and
walked unsteadily towards the meadow.

One of the men walked the horses back into the woods and staked them out far
enough away to be unheard. As an afterthought, he took the lasso from one saddle
and, on the way back, strung it between two trees across a path he had crossed. He
put it at about knee level.

The rangers knew they would need sleep if they were to function the next
morning. Each group set up one rotating guard while the others slept. The guard
was as much as prevent them from snoring as it was to watch the enemy. The night
seemed endless until it did end, and then sore muscles made it seem as if the night
had been tragically short.

Shortly after daybreak, a large man came out of the larger of the two log
cabins. He was shirtless and in stocking feet, but wore his pants and a gun belt. He
stretched his arms and yawned while he urinated into a hillock behind the cabin.
Suddenly he became very loud, yelling for someone named "Jack" and cursing. The
rangers thought that they had been spotted, but the big man was not drawing his
weapon. "Jack" had apparently gotten up, along with others who couldn't sleep
during the bellowing. A good sized argument was underway.

Private Adams was watching over the top of the hillock. "They seem to be
arguing about that horse. The big guy keeps pointing to it and screaming at the little

guy. Wait, he's pointing at the brand. That's one of our horses! He must have just realized that the little guy took on a ranger column. He's got his gun out. We might just be loosing one bandit. Nope, the big guy just pistol whipped the little guy and started barking orders to everyone else. Everyone seems to be in motion. You might want to see this, sir."

Wilson rolled over and levered himself on his elbows. "Shit. They're moving out! Two of them are jogging to the corral for the horses and the rest are screaming at the people still sleeping. Rangers, pick your targets right to left, no duplicates, one volley and move!."

Seven guns roared, seven bandits fell, and the rangers were over the hill in dead run. Within seconds, the firing was echoed on the other side clearing. In ninety seconds, crossing the meadow would be suicide, but by the time the bandits picked up their weapons, the rangers were firing into the lean-tos and the cabin windows. A few bandits got off shots before the end, but none who took time to aim survived to fire.

At the meadow's edge, Artimus realized that he could not keep up with the ranger assault, so he hobbled fast toward the corral and the two bandits who were saddling horses. At twenty paces, one of the men noticed Artimus charging at him. Aiming from a galloping hobble with a forty five pistol was hard so it took Artimus two shots to put him down.

The other bandit was moving around the corral using the horses for cover. He was safe only so long as he kept his head down and was either too smart or too scared to expose his head to take a shot. Artimus had just reached the corral when the bandit made his break. He leaped on a horse and spurred it though the gate at full gallop. Artimus' shot went wide. The bandit's horse was carrying a saddlebag with a big "A" on the side.

As he jumped on a saddled horse, Artimus yelled, "He's got the case!", and spurred after the fleeing bandit. The bandit was across the meadow and leaving on a wooded trail when Artimus got close. His pistol now only held one ball. He steadied the pistol barrel across his left arm, timed the bounce from the horse and fired his last ball.

The horse went down with the rider. He thought, "After I missed the first one, I was worried about losing my touch, but I'll be bragging about this shot to my grandchildren."

Then he reined his horse up next to the fallen bandit and saw the lariat that had tripped the horse and broken the bandit's neck. "Well, it'd be a good story anyway." The firing had stopped behind him. He reached the fallen bandit and decided that he was unable to kneel down to check a pulse, so he kicked the bandit in the crotch with his good foot. "Either you're dead, or you're more of a man than I am." Balancing on his good leg, he leaned over to pick up the saddlebags from the ground.

Of the forty-three bandits, eleven had survived by doing the only thing that would get you though a ranger assault. They threw their weapons as far away as they could and laid flat on ground with their arms outstretched. Holding a weapon, having a weapon in your holster or looking capable of reaching for a weapon all had the same results. Jack was one of the survivors.

Artimus looked down at Jack from horseback. "This pouch is still sealed. Just curious. Why did you steal it and then never open it?"

"We was saving it for Big Phil. We knew he'd be pissed about us hitting a ranger column. We wanted to make sure he knew we was splitting the loot fair. Didn't make no never mind no way. He was still pissed."

About that time, the sergeant took over. "We have some cleanup and sanitation work to do. You men will get your comrade's bodies and put them in that cabin. Rangers Walton and Jones will accompany you." When the bodies were in the cabin, Jones dowsed them with coal oil and sent fire to the cabin.

Artimus said the prayers. He ended with "We hope, Oh Lord, that you may know something of these men that we do not know. And therefore do not need to send them directly to Hell. Good men or bad, they now rest in peace and in your care."

They formed up as a two mounted columns. The prisoners rode bareback, two to a horse between the columns. As the column left the clearing, the fire was still blazing behind them.

Chapter 22   Back Home At The Palace

It was a tired and dusty group that rode up the path to the palace. Baron Wilson had left the group as they approached the city. His wife and daughters had not seen him in much too long. He was anxious for a hot bath, clean clothes and a night in his own bed. They had ridden hard since the battle with the bandits. The near loss of the books had given them all a sense of urgency.

The emperor, Sir Artimus, and the troopers continued on to the palace. The Empress, and nearly everyone else in the palace, had known for hours that the party was returning. However, the trooper who had ridden ahead with the news also carried a message to the Empress that they were too tired for ceremony and just wanted to clean up and get a simple meal.

They were seated in the private Imperial dining room an hour later. Artimus was a little disappointed that Samuel seemed to be no longer in the palace. In fact, Samuel had finished his testing and been returned to his family. He did not know he was being tested, but had done well. Texans had come up with their own solution to the emperor problem. Empires and Kingdoms had often fallen because of the problem of succession. Kings and emperors generally ruled from an age when most men were retiring, up until their death. This usually left an inexperienced but late middle aged ruler on the throne, often fighting for his life from the first day.

Texan emperors retired as soon as they new generation was in its prime. Their willingness to do so was the hallmark of an Adams. They assumed the Emeritus role that allowed them to assist the new ruler that they, the old ruler, had selected with the advice and consent of the Adams family. It was normally the eldest son, but could be any family member. The new ruler had backing both politically and practically.

If he turned out to be a loser, the old emperor was around to rally the cause for the younger man's removal. This had only happened once. The third Adams had turned out to be a coward. Like all cowards with power, he became a bully and had to be replaced. He opted to fight it out rather than retire, but his grave was placed with the usual honors in the family plot.

Until Emperor Burton Adams produced an heir, his two brothers and one nephew would be periodically weighed as possible successors.

The empress smiled at Artimus, "It's good to have you back, Sir Artimus. From the looks of the two of you, your second trip into Texas must have been as good as your first one."

Sir Artimus and the emperor filled in Her Majesty on the battle with the bandits. She was fascinated. Like most well bred Texas women, she was a contradiction of dependent femininity and frontier woman. By the time they got to the wine and fireplace end of the meal, the story was told and they were catching up on family gossip. The Empress was saying, "I do feel sorry for your family. It looks like you are going to be gone at least another year."

Sir Artimus smiled a little, "I'll miss them, but they have their uncles and my father to help them along. Of course, they're too young to bring here. They couldn't handle the deceptions. My father has agreed to send one of my brothers to take my place next year so that I can rotate out home. These trips across country have been fascinating, but I can use the packet boats and get home in less than three weeks. I might even get holidays in New Manhattan."

As the only other person of royal blood in the castle, Artimus was entitled to an apartment in the royal rooms. However, they decided that he should keep a lower profile so he returned to his old apartment on the floor below. After the strenuous trip from the border, it felt as good as home.

At breakfast the next morning, the Empress announced that they had a busy morning. Artimus was invited to a meeting of the Royal Archeological Society.

The meeting was held in the usual sound proof room. The table was filling up. There were now twenty senior members of the group and more personnel working at the farm.

Artimus had already met Bishop Wilson, Greg, and a few others. The rest were new to him. At first, there was the usual chatter of gossip and small talk. When the last servant left the room, all fell suddenly and completely silent. The Emperor and Empress were sitting at the head of the table. The Emperor and Empress emeritus were at their right. Artimus was on the left. He would soon know the reason for the seating arrangements.

The emperor stood and began in a serious voice. "Know ye that we intend to conduct business both secret and desperate. I swear by my right to rule that I shall not betray this body or its secrets. May I lose my throne if I fail to honor my oath."

He sat and the Empress arose, "Know ye that we intend to conduct business both secret and desperate. I swear by my honor and my life that I shall not betray this body or its secrets. I will lose my life before I will betray this body."

One by one, each member arose and repeated the oath, substituting whatever was most sacred to them in the oath.

"I swear by my God...". "I swear on my family honor as Scotsmen and my right to wear the kilt." The oath was personal and individual. The long version of the oath was, obviously, for Artimus' benefit.

Eventually the oath giving got to Artimus. All eyes were on him. He looked around the table at all of the faces. He said, "I cannot, of course, swear allegiance to a group who's purposes I do not know. I can, however, swear that I will reveal nothing learned here today to anyone. Will that suffice for today?"

The elder Adams responded, "It is all we can expect today."

Artimus rose and placed his hand across his heart. "I swear by my God that I shall keep all learned here today secret. May I be damned if I break this oath."

The younger Adams hit his fist on the table. It was not impolite or angry, just the Texas version of a gavel. He turned to Artimus. "You already know the basic purpose of the Archeology Committee. It is as you guessed in our first meeting. We are also trying to solve Urban's problem. This you know, but, up to now it has not been appropriate to fill you in on the details of our actions."

He turned to the group as a whole. "As you know, gentlemen, we are going to use Artimus's first visit as a chance to review our progress and plans. You make speak as freely as if he were always a member of the group. In fact, you may need to add a little more detail than usual. As most of you know, one of the agreements that got us the new books was a promise to share all progress with the Papacy. I intend that we should honor this in full. 'A mans word is his worth'.

"Artimus has a means of sending detailed coded messages back to the Papacy. He will be given free access to all of the progress notes, formulas and plans that we have. Greg, why don't you start by bringing us up to date on the farm?"

Greg remained seated, but leaned forward to be better heard. "We now have thirty workers at the farm. That is about as many as we can count on to keep a secret no matter how well we screen them. Unfortunately, the old farm is too close to Austin to keep secrets easily, too far away from Lone Star to transport new product to, and too small to hide the new projects coming up. We have, therefore, acquired a large tract of land near Sweetwater. We have six thousand acres on a river front.

"The current plan is to put in a charcoal plant. Charcoal Coke plants create large amounts of smoke and require heavy volumes of river traffic to operate. It's almost a perfect cover. We'll establish three zones. There will be an outer perimeter of Rangers dressed a private guards. Near the river there will be a section devoted to the coke plant and support facilities. No one there will need to know about the third zone. In the center of the farm, we will set up our secure manufacturing and research facilities. Everyone there will be a part of the Archeology Committee or a cleared spouse. There will be housing for all personnel and they will be discouraged from leaving unnecessarily. We should have preliminary plans for the new farm and new labs available at our next meeting."

The emperor leaned forward. "Thank you, Greg. Mr. White, how is Winnie Wigwams health these days?"

"She is healthy and doing well. Thanks to our chief, the Elder Adams, we have a distribution network up and running. We started in a small town in the panhandle, and there were no problems. At the Chief's suggestion," he nodded at the Emperor Emeritus, "we started whisper campaigns in the bars and churches about how lucky Winnie Wigwam was. We were sold out in a few days and started getting orders from nearby towns within a few weeks. We really haven't had any red flags or resistance so far, but we're going to wait until Winnie is firmly established in Austin before we put out the next product.

"Most of Winnie Wigwams current powders are made in Lone Star. They really are natural products, so we don't have to hide anything about them except the ownership of the company. The lab at the new farm is being setup to produce the new product. As you know, there is no Sulpha tree, so we will have to produce the Powder of the Bark of the Sulpha Tree at the farm. We'll ship the powder to Lone Star for packaging. We have decided that the less we try to hide, the fewer problems we will have. So everything will be public knowledge and record except the actual production of the powder."

The emperor leaned forward on his elbows and gestured at Mr. White. "Mr. White, please be certain that Sir Artimus has all of the information that his people will need to produce the Sulpha powder. It is as badly needed there as here. You used this once, you said, as a powder to cover a wound. Can it also be ingested?"

White responded. "I am not certain of the efficacy, but I think that it can be. It might lose some effectiveness going though the stomach, but I think it would still work. I do remember a reference to the Ancients using it as a liquid so it must be ingestible."

The emperor looked at Artimus. "When you pass this on, you might suggest to your principals that some communion wafers might be made to be luckier than usual. That way the priests can give the dosage as part of a religious ritual without even knowing that they are dispensing anything except God's love."

Artimus smiled. "That's as tricky as a Texan. I will pass on the suggestion."

The meeting turned to Greg. He explained that his group, thanks to the books from the Papacy, had managed to get something called a telegraph working. He described it in some detail. It was, he said, a marvel that could send messages from one end of Texas to the other instantly. Unfortunately, no one could figure out how you hide several hundred miles of wire from public view. For the time being, the device would remain a laboratory curiosity.

The meeting went on for two more hours before they broke for a meal. As Adams slapped the Texas gavel to end the current session, Sir Artimus stood and cleared his throat. "Gentlemen, I have now witnessed the full scope and intent of this group. I thank you for your candor. I know now what my father would expect."

He raised one finger to indicate that he was not done, and reached inside his cloak. He brought forth a small bible and laid it on the table. Placing his right hand on the bible, he began, "I swear by my God that I will not only keep the secrets of this group, but that I will also support the goals of this group as far as my God will allow, even to my very death. May my soul be damned forever if I fail in this oath."

There was a moment of silence. Texans respected a promise and knew a big one when the heard it. Then a few people said, "Welcome, Sir Artimus," and the servants were allowed in to serve a meal.

Chapter 23   The Trip To Sweetwater

Artimus was in the fifth month of his stay in Texas and in the fifth day of his first trip to Sweetwater. The way to Sweetwater was a northward trip on the Colorado River through both manmade and natural lakes.

The Nacogdoches was equipped with several modes of power. When on the lakes, square sails were hoisted on the two masts. Poles and rudder moved her downriver. The trip to Sweetwater was, unfortunately for the crew, upriver. They had offloaded the mules and were dragging her along. Fortunately, the Ancients had built roads along the river banks throughout Texas, so their mules had a cleared path to walk almost all the way. Unfortunately, the ancients had also been prolific bridge builders, so the crew spent a lot of time passing the tow cables under bridges.

Artimus and Wilson were settled back in deck chairs on a deck built over the aft steering house. Each held a beaker of Bourbon in his right hand and had an expression of relaxation on his face. Their escorts were scattered around the deck a few feet below, tanning, gambling, polishing weapons and napping. For a fleeting moment, Wilson felt a pang of conscience for the way he had described the upcoming trip to his wife, "Honey, it's a lot of hard work and very uncomfortable but I'll be thinking of you all of time." However, it was an old tradition. Neolithic man had probably told his wife, "Honey, You know that I would rather stay home with you and the kids, but the boys and I are out of flint and we have to make this trip..." Somehow, the temporary absence of even the most loved and kind wife allowed a man to relax even in the face of danger.

Artimus roused himself. "Do you think that we will make the farm today?"

Wilson looked at the sun and replied, "Unless we run into something unexpected. We'll actually dock about five miles past Colorado City. Cargos going to Sweetwater are offloaded at Colorado City and go by wagon into the city. The farm is about five miles further up the river and it has its own docks. We'll leave the boat there."

Artimus swiveled his head to look up and down the river. "Seems like a lot of traffic on this waterway. I can see three other barges on this side and several going the other way. Are you certain that it was wise to establish the farm in such a heavily traveled area?"

Wilson half opened eyes did not look up, "It was a deliberate choice to put it a traveled area. We felt that trying to hide it would make anyone who ran across it too curious. It's still actually more hidden than is apparent. The ranch is several thousand acres. Most of it's in a valley surrounded by low hills, and we added ditches and fences to the valley walls. From the river, you will see a large area near the river where we have the docks, warehouses, offices, and worker's barracks without getting too close the lab. The coke plant is the cover for any noise and smoke that we generate. It's inland a ways and is just barely visible from the docks. A rather small road leaves the coke plant to go to the interior. The coke plant itself hides the road from anyone of the river. The workers think that the road goes to a VIP barracks and office building that is supposed to be just around the bend. Some of Winnie Wigwam's natural herbs and medications manufacturing facilities are also located there. You will want to see their operations."

They both decided to doze off not due to lack of desire to be productive, of course, just to husband their energies for the tasks ahead.

They arrived at the farm on schedule. The smoke from the coke plant was visible almost as soon as they left Colorado City, a thoroughly misnamed little bump on the river. The warehouses and docks covered almost a quarter mile on the riverfront. There were several boats docked loading coke, unloading fuel and unloading supplies for the workers. It had a very busy and public look to it.

There were several covered passenger wagons waiting at the dock. They looked somewhat like horse drawn versions of the street cars of San Francisco, when there was a San Francisco. Artimus, Wilson and their escorts boarded one marked "Executive Office Building". They were of course, the only passengers. There was room on the rear cargo deck for all of their luggage.

It took almost over half an hour to get to the lab. They passed several guard towers, crossed a bridge and passed through several fences of increasing size. From the outside, it looked like an easy trip from the river. From the inside it looked like Fort Knox.

The main compound had to be large, larger than Artimus expected. There were only fifty or so workers there, but most of them lived on the grounds. A few family men lived near the river with their families, but the others wanted to be close to their work. There were barracks that were more apartment houses than military barracks, a small store, a two story office building, stables, a barn, outbuildings, and a building that an Ancient would have mistaken for an aircraft hanger. There were smoke stacks poking through the roof of that one and the sound of blacksmith tools inside.

There was a big stream, almost a river, running through the compound. Toward the back of it there was an older rough wood building housing an undershot water wheel. From the sounds, it was operating a blacksmith hammer inside.

Sirs Eric and Greg greeted them at the wagon stop. They were now full time residents of the Farm except for their monthly trips to the Archeology meetings. Sometimes, they might not both make the meeting, preferring to keep working.

Sir Greg greeted them especially warmly. Although he was one of the most intelligent men on the committee, emotionally he was always a little like a boy wanting to show off what he could do. "We have meetings with all of the department heads set up for tomorrow and several demonstrations. I figure that today you will want to freshen up and rest from the trip. Your quarters are in the executive building. The porters will show your men to their barracks. Dinner is in an hour and I hope you brought our wives a lot of gossip from Austin."

He had not stopped for a breath while he took Wilson's arm and started walking. The non-stop chattiness occurred so often that his acquaintances sometimes speculated that his lungs were larger than normal.

There were about fifty people at dinner. It was supposed to be a casual affair, but the women rarely had a chance to show off their party clothes to a stranger or get gossip from the court, so it turned out to be fancier than expected. Artimus hoped that it would not be like this every night.

Instead of the usual cafeteria style food and simple table settings, the dinner was served by the cooks and placed on white lace tablecloths. Artimus and Wilson were seated at the head table with Sirs Greg and Eric and their ladies. The women pumped the visitors for news of Austin, and the lives of the Royals, and what color bonnets were in fashion. Fortunately, as gentlemen of the court, they knew enough to pay attention to such details and they were, therefore, popular at dinner.

Wilson felt sympathy for the women. In an era without television, gossip was the breath of life. Contact with your fellow man took the place of contact with Walter Cronkite. As the women had no work here and few other women to converse with, the fact that they stayed part of each year was a testament to their devotion to their husbands. Greg and Eric were rich men by any important measure.

There was no business that night until the women left and then it was bourbon business. No one wanted to spoil the presentations due over the next couple of days so they settled for the time honored tradition of solving all of the world's problems before the last drink was drunk. With full bellies and great cigars, agreement was possible on anything.

The next morning the work began in earnest. The first working meeting took place in the Disk Lab, so called because it was where they worked on the mysterious disk found in the silo.

Sir Eric introduced James Kawamoto, the current project manager and then stepped back. James had met Artimus at one of the committee meetings in Austin and knew that he was supposed to hold back nothing. He was a tall thin man dressed in a traditional yellow lab coat. He began with a briefing about how the disk had been found. He covered everything from finding the newspaper article in a destruction day pile and included the burying of Bones. He filled in Artimus on the information theory that he needed and then showed him the ruined mechanism. "We have decided that there is little to be gained from the mechanism itself. Thanks to the books that you brought, we now know that it would take hundreds of years to decode the internal workings of the chips. You saved us a few years of work."

He moved the discussion to a lab table on the other side of the room. The disk was held in a jig that looked like a four foot long lathe. It was held between two padded brackets on wooden arms. Both arms had handles on the outer sides of the spindles to allow the disk to be turned without being touched. A large binocular microscope was sitting near it on the bench. It was mounted on a jig that would allow it be held steady at height of the disk.

"We are actually a long way ahead of where we thought we would be. It didn't take long to figure out that the disk is written with dots. We couldn't see them until we got the most powerful microscope in the country and then augmented it with extra lenses. If you look carefully, you can see that the disk changes color near the outer edge. That is where the dots end. It is like looking at a record and seeing where the sound stops."

Wilson interrupted. "How long will it take you to read the dots?"

Kawamoto shrugged, "Years, lifetimes perhaps. At first, I thought that it was going to be easy after we figured out how it was written. After all, we can assume that the language is Ancient English and that the dots represent letters in a language we know. If you look at the mechanism, you can see that the writing is done in a circle around the edge like a sound record. Duck soup. The writers weren't trying to hide anything. They would make it as simple as they could. Then we started to realize the problems. Someone noted that if we were writing a book like this, we would add a lot of pictures. We don't know how they coded pictures. I figured that we would see groups of dots that were black and white codes like eight hundred lines of eight hundred dots that formed a picture with eight hundred tiny lines of eight hundred tiny dots each. Hard to figure out, but doable with enough time.

"Of course, we didn't realize at the time that they might have encoded music, voice, color pictures, and things that we don't even know exist. However, with enough time, we could still learn to real all of it by doing one type at a time. So we set up our best microscope and began to take a look. We couldn't see anything. Oh, after we augmented the microscope with better lenses, you could sort of see a blur of dots which kept shifting as your eyes tried to focus. We also couldn't keep track of where we were when we spun the wheel. The biggest problem, though, was that we just don't have a scope with the power to see the dots clearly."

Sir Wilson tried to sound encouraging. "Well, you know basic optics. All you need to do is to upgrade your microscope until you can read the dots. Then pick a small area and work on it.

Greg snorted. "There is one more problem that Mr. Kawamoto has not gotten to yet. One of our techs did an estimate of the number of dots on the disk. It's hard to be very accurate, but there seem to be between twenty and fifty billion dots. That's 'billion' with a 'B'. Our grandchildren will be working on it."

That brought the mood down a little. However, Kawamoto chimed in with a semi-cheerful, "Well, the title was How EVERYTHING Works. You have to print very small to get everything on one small disk."

They spent some time looking through the microscope at the little blue blurs on the disk. Finally Artimus said, "It's a big job, but, if what you say proves out, there could be more information on that one disk than we have in all of our secret libraries. It's definitely worth working on."

Their next stop was the electronics lab. This was one of Eric's favorite places. "I still can't believe how easy it is. Over here we have our first generator. As you can see, it's only about four inches long. You crank it with that little handle on the end. About the only thing you can do with it is to make a needle move on one of the Ancient gauges. We've come a long way in the four months since we built that.

"We have been using that device in the corner to get power to play with. It's called a battery. In that box there is a pile of metal sandwiches with wet sponge fillings. There about two thousand plates in that box. It gives us steady power as long as we keep the sponges wet. With that, we have been able to make or find resistors, capacitors and other parts.

"We have been waiting for wire to make a real generator. We have been able to salvage a little useable wire from inside the walls of Ancient buildings. It's very old, but some of it has a plastic coating that has survived all of these years. Let me show you our most interesting project. This one is pure magic."

Kawamoto lead his guests to a table near the window. "Stand here and watch this device." He returned to the battery and connected two wires to terminals on the wooden side of the battery and then sat at a table near the other end of the room from the observers. "Sir Wilson, could you give me a number from one to ten?"

"Seven."

"Watch the device." The device they were watching looked like a small balance beam with a nail in the end. Two wires were connected to a thimble sized coil of wire under the nail. After a moment it clicked. Once. Twice. Seven times. They were amazed.

Wilson called over his shoulder, "Can you do that again? Make it click two groups of three." Three clicks, then three more clicks.

Sir Greg nudged Wilson. "It gets better. Were you an Indian Scout as a boy?. Good. Did you learn the secret knock language? Well, listen to this."

They all stared at the device. It began to click short and long clicks. Short, short, pause. Long, short, pause. Long, short, short, pause. Wilson's smile almost broke his face. If I remember my code, that think is spelling out 'Indian Scouts' in our 'secret' knock language."

Sir Eric was bustling across the room. "And I was all the way across the room. Once we get more power and wire, I could do the same thing from one side of Texas to the other. We could run a wire from here to Austin and do the same thing, as soon as we have the wire and work out a few other details."

Wilson was impressed. "I can't believe that you are moving this fast. We will have to change your name to Merlin."

Eric managed to look sheepish. "I once heard someone use the phrase 'Standing on the shoulders of great men.' That describes us now. Not only were we given a thousand years of discovery for free, but we got the wire from the Ancients. It would have taken us weeks just to pull that much copper and I have no idea how they made that plastic cover. We look good because we have help."

Eric closed down the telegraph key and joined them on their walk to the machine building. As they crossed the yard to the building, they passed the sorting pile for Destruction Day. Greg gestured to the pile of junk, "Everything interesting from the digs and donations comes here for sorting. In the last four months, we have learned enough to change our ideas of what is useful to keep. All of the circuit boards are useless but we are keeping all wiring that looks like it's good condition and all gauges and coils. What we can't use goes back to the towns for the annual fires."

They entered the larger building and the visitors were surprised to find it virtually empty. There was a blacksmith fire going in the rear corner and two men working on something that looked like it was going to end up as a large gear wheel. On a work bench, four men were polishing brass pistons and fitting them into cylinders. The cylinders had levers and bars attached at odd angles.

Between the work benches was a large table with an apparently assembled machine on it. Several men in lab coats were fussing over it. It was so odd that is was hard to take in all at once. It looked somewhat like a big tea kettle sitting on the floor with a wood fire under it and tubes attached between it and some cylinders on the work bench.

Sir Greg gave his guests some time to look around the machine. The smiths stood back to allow Wilson and Artimus to touch, poke, and examine the machine. They stared at the parts and burned their fingers on the steam lines.

When they had had sufficient time to look at all of it, Greg asked them, "Gentlemen, if you will stand back a little we'll show you how this works. Don't worry, it's not dangerous. We're only standing back to get a better look."

Two of the smiths used thick gloved hands to turn valves between the tea kettle and the cylinders. Steam surrounded the cylinders and bubbled in the lines and the flywheel started turning. In seconds, it was turning too fast to see. The escaping steam and the noise of the rods moving back and forth made it hard to hear Greg say, "Thing worked almost from the first time we fired it up. You attach a propeller or a wheel to that flywheel and you can go anywhere without a horse or an oar. Attach it to a trip hammer or a lathe and you don't care if the stream is running or not." He waved for the smiths to turn the valves off. Everyone was happy to hear silence again.

When the machine had slowed to a stop, Artimus said, "That's pretty impressive."

Sir Greg replied, "It looks good, but we're new at it. There are some serious problems that we haven't solved yet. It takes about fifteen or twenty minutes to get the kettle hot enough to use. Then when you are running it, it's very inefficient. It takes a Hell of a lot of wood to keep it working. It's because of all that steam that you see escaping. The pistons aren't tight enough in the cylinders and they waste a lot of steam. Come on over here. I'll show you what were gonna try next."

He walked over to the bench where the Smiths had been working on pistons and cylinders. He pointed to a piston in a foot operated lathe. "You see that grove that we cast into this one. Fredrick's truing it up so we can try to put a gasket in it. We'll try rubber first, but I don't think it will last long enough. If we can get this thing tight enough and it still works, we'll have a practical engine."

They spent the rest of the afternoon examining and testing the engine. They tried to start it with them holding the flywheel. They put belts on the flywheel and tried to turn a lathe and a corn sheller. They tried to get the water to boil faster by filling the tank only half full and then adding cold water once the engine started working. They tested how fast they could make it run. As with all men, the line between "examining and testing" and "playing" was a blurry one.

The next day was harder for Artimus. One of Solomon's alchemists walked him through the steps to make Sulpha. It took most of the day. At each step he wrote down the procedure and compared his notes to the ones provided by the alchemist. The second day, he went through the procedures with the alchemist watching but not helping. At each step he carefully followed his notes from the previous day. He made two mistakes and the batch was ruined. The alchemist pointed out the errors and he corrected his notes.

The third day, he succeeded in producing a small but useable quantity of the drug.

The fourth and fifth days were taken up in encoding the instructions for transmission back to York. He used an old but almost unbreakable code. As a religious man, he carried a small copy of the Bible in his pocket at all times. Unknown to most was the fact the this was a rare edition. Not very many of that exact edition existed in the world and the other copies were all in the hands of York intelligence.

It was an old but almost unbreakable code. The words were three number sets xx, yyy, zzz. zzz was the page number, yyy, the line number and xx the word number on the line. 05007298 was page 298, line 7, word 5. You needed another copy of that exact bible to read it. There were also codes for spelling out unknown words and writing scrambled numbers. Simple, used for centuries, and still damned near unbreakable.

It was also slow. It took an entire day for Artimus to encode his notes to check all of the encoding. The next day, he encoded them again and compared the two copies to find any errors. Then he filed the originals in a cabinet that would never leave the farm.

Artimus would, however, leave the farm and sleep half the way back to Austin.

Chapter 24   The Trouble Starts

The trouble didn't start until after they found the poppies. Solomon had assistants out canvassing gardens, roadsides, and weed patches for useful plants. The cover story was that they were looking for some poisonous plants to be destroyed. They carried hand reproductions of pictures from Solomon's books.

A nice little grandmother in Houston was growing an herb that she liked because of it's pretty purple flower. She also liked the taste of the dried poppy seeds in her cakes and tea. Five hundred years before, she would have gotten life in jail for growing opium. Now she got a thank you and a request for a few samples.

Solomon announced the find at a meeting of the Archeology Committee. "We have found a source for one of the most powerful drugs in history. The good news is that it's an herb, actually a poppy, and we should be able to produce a natural appearing product that Winnie can put on the market. The bad news is that the drug was so frightening to the Ancients that they jailed a huge percentage of their population for using it without government permission.

"Now, I admit that I do not know how it could be that a drug would be dangerous if you took it by your self and would be harmless if a bureaucrat gave you permission to use it. We do know that the poppy was used to ease pain, cure coughing, stop vomiting and, strangely, also to produce vomiting when needed to get poison out of your system. The only thing that I can think of that they might have objected to is that it is also a sort of super loco weed if you use a lot of it. Maybe the Ancients just hated fun."

The Elder Adams was a history buff. Fortunately, while technical texts had been burned, many books on other topics had survived.

He addressed Solomon. "I don't think that you have to worry, Solomon. I have read about this stuff. I never thought I would actually know what it was. Knowing we have it is like hearing someone announcing that they brought a unicorn home. I can tell you what happened, but I can't promise it will make any sense. The old books don't talk much about the medicinal value of this stuff. They had a lot of names for it, but the most common was 'dope'. All the books talk about is the 'evil of addiction'. Apparently this stuff works on human beings like alcohol. You know, most of us like a little drink once in a while and we pour whisky on our wounds, but it isn't really important to us. However, every town seems to have it's town drunk. Some people start to drink and they can't stop. This dope stuff was the same. I don't really know why that upset the Ancients so much. They never mention more than ten percent of the population using it and even less than that being drunks, or whatever they called it. I think they called them 'addicts'.

"However, the Ancients loved laws. They must have loved a law more than a woman. If we could get a complete set of their laws in one book, we could probably heat the palace all winter by burning it.   The damned fools outlawed 'dope'. They said it was for the public's good, as if the government had a right to tell you if you could get drunk. When we have a drunk here in Texas, they get jobs shoveling manure at the stables. They make enough for booze and a little food and everyone gets a good laugh. When the Ancients outlawed 'dope', it got expensive to buy and the drunks, or addicts couldn't make enough money to get it by shoveling manure.

Pretty soon they were forced to steal or kill to get what they needed. Pretty soon, they had most of their police and rangers chasing criminals that they created by outlawing 'dope'. They didn't have time for real criminals any more.

"I did see one reference that grudgingly reported that the people who grew the dope, used it regularly, and never had a problem. Of course, they didn't outlaw it in that country, and neither will we. If you decide that this stuff is good for us, we can handle it."

The elder Adams was a history buff, but the records of the first anesthetic use had been lost to history. Even when the books existed, most people thought that anesthesia began with ether in 1846 when Dr. Henry J. Bigelow used it in his dental practice. They ignore that fact that anesthesia had been used for hundreds of years in other cultures. In fact, a country doctor in America had performed an operation under anesthesia as early as 1786. He was castigated by the church for "denying the patient the pain that God intended." The public outcry was so great, that anesthesia was not used again in western medicine for another 80 years.

Chapter 25   The Poppies Return

The nice lady had been very flattered that the empress wanted to grow her pretty purple poppies in the royal gardens. She had given almost her entire crop to Solomon's agent. By growing them in a greenhouse at the old farm, Solomon's team had several bushels within four months of their discovery. When the seeds were harvested, some of the plants could be used for laudanum production. Laudanum was marketed widely during the Victorian age. It was the first pain killer widely available in the west.

The production of laudanum was marvelously simple. The poppies were dried out for several days. Then you put them in a crock and heated it gently. In a few hours, the laudanum would sweat out of the poppies. The fluid contained a high percentage of morphine. It was a marvelous pain killer, mildly addictive, lethal in larger doses, and tasted awful. To make it palatable, it was usually mixed with sugar for children or alcohol for adults.

It was widely used until aspirin and heroin were commercially produced. A similar and also simple product called paregoric was produced by adding camphor and aromatic oils that seemed to enhance the effect of the morphine.

Solomon was telling Sir Artimus that he would be happy if he could just get commercial quantities of the simpler compound.

"This is an ideal product for Winnie Wigwam. It really is a natural product so simple to produce that anyone could have the feeling that they understood it.   In fact, part of the plan is to actually grow and display the poppies in the empress' garden and let out the secret of laudanum to the population. Winnie would then be marketing the professional version of a drug that everyone knew about."

Artimus was intrigued. "Just how good is this stuff?"

Solomon asked, "Ever see a man get a limb amputated? I've seen men die from the shock and pain when you cut his leg off. With this stuff, he would feel the pain, but it would be bearable. If you use both this and Sulpha, you can reduce the death rate from surgery from thirty five percent down to almost none. It also cures headaches, soothes women's problems', and helps tuberculosis."

Artimus responded, "I assume that we are going to send some seed and some instructions to York."

"Yes, Sir. I want you to send both some seeds and some dried poppies so they know what they should look like. We'll also send instructions for the laudanum production. I have been thinking that we should also reproduce the pictures that my agents used to look for useful plants. You may find things in York that we don't have here. This stuff is so simple that you can probably send it without even having to code it."

Artimus wasn't certain that he would send anything without coding. He was, as always, anxious to see what new toys they had at the farm. "What cute stuff have you done in the five months that I have been gone, aside from the gardening?"

Solomon took Artimus by the arm and headed for the door. "It's been very busy. We have three teams going. We have one group still working on the steam engine, another group working on electric power, and a third group working on something new, a way to send signals through the air. Oh, we still have a group working on that disk we found, but they aren't getting very far as yet."

As they walked across the yard to the hanger building, Solomon continued, "I think that you will have some significant coding to do this time. We are making some real progress over here."

Entering the building, Artimus could see that things had been rearranged. The center of the floor now held a steam engine on wheels. The wheels were on a pair of steel ribbons about fifty feet long. The entire back wall seemed to be a smithy working on engine parts. The wall in front of him held benches with wires and gears. There was a strong acid smell coming over the half height partitions. To his right, three smiths were working at desk height work benches. They also had batteries and wires on their desks. There was an occasional smell of burnt rubber from that area.

Solomon headed for the steam engine first. This was much more impressive than it had been on Artimus' last visit. The boiler was now mounted on the front of the carriage. There was a water storage tank and a wood bin on the rear of the machine. There was now a cylinder on each side and they were attached to the front wheels. Artimus was impressed and said so.

Solomon pointed to the boiler. "This is how we solved the problem of getting it to start before noon. This is not actually a water tank. Inside there is a fire on the floor and it heats water that runs though in tubes. That way there isn't too much water in it at one time and the fire gets to all parts of the tube at the same time. It will start up in less than five minutes now. We didn't invent it. It was in a picture in one of your books. However, one of our guys figured out a way to save fuel. In the books, they let the steam escape after it has turned the wheel. One of our boys got the idea of running the spent steam under the water tank. It preheats the water and saves fuel. Come on over to the bench and I'll show you something else that wasn't in the books."

The smith had a piston and cylinder laid out for Artimus' inspection.

He told Artimus, "You remember that the last time you were here, we tried to put grooves in the piston and seal it with leather. It worked but only for about ten minutes. We had hoped that the steam would keep the leather moist and pliable. It was a fool's hope. Then we got lucky. One of the archeology teams brought in a small ancient motor. It was, as usual, pretty much of a rusted lump, but just a little less rusted than most of them. We soaked it in oil for several days and then chiseled it apart. The outsides were not recognizable, but we did get a recognizable piston. It had grooves in it like our steam engine, but from the residue in the groove, it looked like it had used a metal ring for sealing. That didn't seem possible at first, but we experimented and found that springy steel would work. You have to use at least two of them and make certain that the gaps don't line up, but you get a damned good seal with the right metal. All of a sudden, you don't need to cut down an entire forest to travel to town. It probably wasn't mentioned in the books, because they would have figured that everyone knew how to seal a piston. I figure your people would have the same problems we did getting the engine to work so we have a description of what metal we used and how we sealed it."

Artimus asked, "How soon do you think that you will have that engine working?"

The smith answered, "I think that it will work right now. We plan to test it outside as soon as we get some more rail up here. We have also built a couple of model sized engines and he have the parts almost finished for two stationary engines. Those two buildings behind here house water driven trip hammers in one and water powered lathes in the other. We plan to try out the stationary engines there within a few weeks. We're moving fast, but we have the Ancients to help us."

Over at the electrical department things were also moving along. The smith there was also eager to show off his toys. "The problem we had with the books you sent was that they were about electronics and we how know that electricity is a little different than electronics. They are related, however, and the theory chapters gave us enough to work on. I think that I am allowed to tell you that we also have a few pictures and some Destruction Day material that has helped a little.   First things first. We can't depend upon Ancient wire for everything we need. We have found a way to make our own. We draw the copper first and any good smith can do that. It does turn out that the size of the die is important. You need different size wires for different things. Now the wire has to be kept separate from other wires, even when they are working very close together. It's called 'insulation.' We have found two ways to insulate. You will need to tell your people that after the wire is made, you can dip it in molten rubber for a good insulation. Rubber is sometimes hard to get, so we also tried dipping the wire in tar and then coating it with cotton cloth. You have to use a tar that won't harden up, but it when you do it right, that also works. We now have all of the wire we need with or without the Ancients.

"We also have some good batteries and ways to charge them. Your people probably already know how to make generators once they have the wire, but you should give them the plans for these batteries. They are rubber boxes with zinc lining and lead plates. They need to be fed electricity from the generators. They store it and give it back where you need it. You can turn the generator with anything, including your own arm, but it gets tiresome after a while. If you look above you, you can see that we have wires running through the ceiling. One of the boys salvaged a water pumping windmill and put it on the roof. One of our generators is up there on the windmill right now charging those batteries next to you. It saves your arm real well. We don't have much working yet except the generators and batteries. We are hoping to have some motors working before the end of the year. Of course, we still have no idea of how to show this stuff to people without being burned as witches."

At the third stop, Artimus was handed a pair a headphones. "These go over your ears, but don't do it yet." He gestured to the apparatus on the bench. "This is what those first books you sent us were all about. This is our Radio work bench."

Artimus knew well what was in the books, having had plenty of time to read them on his trip to Texas and having as much curiosity as anyone, but he felt that it was polite to keep quiet while the smith showed off his work.

"It seems that small amounts of electricity will go through the air as well as metal. The book is very clear on the theory. However, they use tubes with a vacuum inside and lots of stuff that we don't have the tools to produce. However, there was short history section that mentioned an earlier type of radio. It was called a spark gap and it doesn't need as much to build. This is an experimental rig that we set up to test the theory. It's interesting to see it work even though it doesn't do much yet."

Artimus asked, "What does it do?"

The smith answered, "It makes clicks, magical clicks. Let me show you. See this coil of wire. It's attached to the battery over there. When you close the switch, it makes a spark jump between these two points. Part of the spark goes into the air like the electricity in the telegraph. You can hear it in the earphones. Fred, you click the key when we get over to the antenna. Sir Artimus, if you will accompany me and bring your earphones."

He lead Artimus about twenty feet away from the bench to another table. "We need to attach the earphones to the long wire. It just goes up into the air to pick up the clicks." Actually, only one wire from the earphones went to the ceiling, the other was attached to a pipe in the floor. "Pick a number between one and ten".

Artimus answered "Six."

The smith held up his hands with six fingers extended. Fred, still at the bench, closed the switch slowly six times.

Artimus looked surprised. "It's just noise, but I can definitely hear six clicks. How far will it work?" The smith answered, "When we get it right, clear around the world. This time next year, you'll be sending your messages home without leaving the farm."

Artimus seemed distracted the rest of the day. He always enjoyed his trips to the farm, but this time he seemed distracted. That night at the dinner table, he announced to Greg and Wilson, "I would like to have a meeting with your electrical and radio teams tomorrow. Perhaps we could use one of the offices on the second floor."

Artimus spent the evening alone in his room. The next morning, the meeting was held in workroom in the office building. Tables and chairs had been brought in and, at Artimus' request, a blackboard hung in behind a podium at the front of the room.

Artimus began without preamble. "Is one of you a stenographer? I would like to have a record made of this meeting for His Majesty." A hand rose in the back. "Good. The only person here who was at the original meeting between our masters is Baron Wilson. At this time I need to review some of the points of our agreement, if Baron Wilson agrees that such things can be discussed with this group. Baron Wilson, do I have your permission to discuss the terms of and reasons for our agreement?"

The Baron nodded his head, "You may proceed on your own judgment."

"Basically our agreement was that York would provide such books and knowledge as we could to help Texas begin rebuilding a modern society. In return, Texas, you, would keep us informed of your progress and render whatever assistance you could in convincing our population to accept changes. Our problem in York is that our people have reacted more violently even than Texans when we have tried to introduce new things. Our proposed solution is to hope that Texas can eventually make public progress. Then the fear of Texas would convince our people that they would have to accept changes to keep up. In the mean time, we would parallel

Texas in secret technology and be able to introduce the changes quickly when the time came. There was, however, no agreement to share information about York itself, only what was necessary to help Texas make progress. Before I left home, I was given additional instructions. My instructions were to evaluate the honesty of Texas and, if I felt it wise, to offer whatever additional information about York and whatever help that I could, above and beyond the original agreement.

"We are now in that situation. You have, as a group, shown that you intend to honor your agreements in the broadest possible sense and have displayed nothing but eagerness to help all of us. You have, in a sense, made this a common cause. With that in mind, Sir Eric, I believe that I can guarantee that I will send my reports back by spark gap. I will have a radio transmitter delivered here before I return from my next trip. We have four of then in York and I will send one to you.

"Let me explain a little more of our situation. No one has asked what we have done with these books in York. Perhaps because of our public image, you assumed that we had not actually built anything with these books. In truth, we have done very little except preserve them. However, they have been copied again and again over the years. It was inevitable that some of the monks who copied them also read them. As a result, we do have some abbeys where the monks have a rather excellent grasp of scientific principles. In most cases, we can do nothing with the knowledge.

"The last time we tried to introduce modern medicine, we had riots in the pews. About a hundred years ago, a charwoman saw a monk working on a model steam engine such as the one you have there, and the parishioners tried to burn down the Abbey. They were convinced that the Devil had taken over the Monk's body.

"We have not, as a result, been able to accomplish even as much as you have in practical terms. What equipment we have is cobbled together from Destruction Day offerings.

"One exception is in electronics. The parts are small and easy to conceal and it's mostly theory. Monks have a lot of time for theory, and they seem to have capacity for it. Before I came here, I visited an abbey where they had working radios. They had about the same experience that you did. They had the same theory books but did not have the expertise to create vacuum bottles with fine wire grids in them. They ended up with the same solution that you did. They described it to me as a spark gap transmitter. However, it was something called a 'rotary spark gap'. I am not a electrical theorist, but I think that I can draw what I saw. It might save you some time."

He turned to the blackboard and took chalk in hand. "One of the things they told me was that alternating current was better for building a transmitter. The most successful transmitter that they built looked like this." He drew an oval on the board and then drew a circle attached to the front of the oval. He was definitely not a great artist. However, the drawing did end up looking like an electric fan with a metal circle mounted on the front of it. "This is a motor that spins at a set speed. The speed is not important except that it's best to keep it steady. There were several protrusions, like quarter inch bolts arranged around this disk on the front." He drew a circle on the board with ten smaller circles arranged around it. "These are arranged in pairs. You'll see why in a minute. In front of the plate there were two contacts mounted on the base plate. They were attached to the generator with very heavy wires and a telegraph key. When the plate turned, sparks would jump across the gaps between the contacts on the base plate and the contacts on the rotating plate.

"When I listened to it in the earphones, it sounded different than yours. I could hear a note, almost a musical note, at the frequency of the sparks. It would go on and off with the key, but it was still more of a tone than a spark. The monks told me that it made it easier for the receiver to pick it up. They were able to tune in on the signal with a variable capacitor.

"They were hoping to eventually build a carrier wave set like we saw in the CIE manual, but in the meantime, this was buildable and workable. The abbey was in South Carolina. The monks told me that they could contact an abbey in Florida with the wireless. I have to tell you, however, that this thing was big. If you are going to build one, don't think small. The generator was about this big." He spread his arms out as far as they would go. "I think it was salvaged from an old ship. I don't know how it survived. The radio used an antenna that consisted of ten wires each about one hundred feet long. The abbey tested it at night and took it down during daylight hours until they decided to disguise the antenna as a clothes drying line."

Someone in the audience raised his hand, "Sir Artimus. How did they power the generator?"

Artimus shrugged, "SAP. It's a power source unique to religious orders. Semi-intelligent Animal Power. Basically monks walking a capstan. I offered to build them a water wheel or at least a horse powered wheel. They said that 'walking the generator' was good for meditation. Only monks would do that. I suggest that you use a waterwheel."

Someone asked, "Have the monks tried to send and receive actual messages?"

"Yes, they have. They used what you call the Indian scout secret language. As you guessed, it was designed for such messages by an Ancient named 'Morse'. By the way, if you plan to use the transmitter, you should know that it makes a hell of a racket and a strong ozone smell. Between the generator noise and the sparks jumping several hundred times a minute, it is noticeable."

There were several other questions which Artimus answered as best he could. They discussed the radio and then the monk's attempts for electric light. Artimus told them that the monks had finally gotten an arc light working, but that they decided that gas mantles were more practical. They had produced a few working light bulbs, but they also were less useful than the mantles.

Artimus left the meeting saying a silent prayer of thanks. One of the problems with working with extremely honest people is that they expect the same from their partners. He knew the second that he saw the earphones that the entire project was in danger. It might be awhile before the Texans could make a transmitter, but the receiver was easy. Sooner than later, they would be listening when the Carolina or Florida radios were transmitting. The appearance of deception, even though technically legal within the agreement, would damage the relationship, perhaps fatally. Thank God, he had been able to act first.

At lunch, he said to Wilson, "I will be going home in a few months. I will suggest to His Majesty that I bring back one or more of the more talented monks to join the crews here. I hope that you will support the proposal."

Wilson answered, "We will have to give it careful thought, but my first impression is that I would support it. A monk should be able to handle the isolation of the farm and shouldn't be much of a security risk. While you spoke, I also had thought that if we get these radios working, we might want to set up communication between the Farm and the abbeys."

Artimus took a second to swallow before he answered, "I had the same idea, but we would have to encode anything sensitive. Radio waves go everywhere and if we have a receiver, someone else could too."

Chapter 26   Some Things Never Change

Things seemed to be going well. The new opium powders were easing pain throughout the empire and the empress and dowager began to campaign subtly for better training for midwives. The Empress's Ladies of Charity began to gossip about the possibility of improving care for mothers and children. Wicked and dangerous gossip was, after all, the most delicious kind.

However, some things never change. A midwife in Watsonville used the new opium powder to ease the pain of a young mother in childbirth, and the local preacher heard about it. Your grandmother would have recognized the church. It was only big enough for two hundred parishioners to crowd in. Even at that, it was rarely full, as Watsonville was a small town and few of the men would attend the services. The audience of bonneted women and old men sat with looks of grim determination on their faces as they listened to the sermon.

"Brothers and Sisters, God is angry! Mankind is again usurping God's holy place. You have heard how Winnie Wigwam's powders took from your sister Helen, her God appointed pain of childbirth. You all know that the pain of childbirth is God's judgment on womankind due to the evil actions of Eve. It has always been so. It must always be so! This is not the first evil done in the name of this witch. It is God's place to say who lives and who dies. Now, people believe that this witch's powder will stop the infection of wounds with the Devil's evil red demons. We all know that only God has the right to say who lives and who dies. Only prayer can drive away the demons! These evil people are challenging God!"

His angry arm was raised, his accusing finger pointing toward the downtown area. His face was red with anger and bright with sweat. "You must stop this evil now! If the general store won't stop selling this evil, you must stop them! God demands his respect!!"

In the pews, the angry women gritted their teeth and jutted their jaws in righteous anger. God's will would be done in Watsonville. Of course, pain would go on and wounds would continue to kill, but who would dare question Gods will?

Three hundred miles away in New Austin, the Reverend Diaz heard about the sermon in Watsonville. He was a well groomed thirtyish man with regular features and more strength in his face than most expected for a minister. He dressed neatly and wore matching pistols with plain black handles. He had read the newspaper accounts of the demonstration and near riot that had caused the local store to publicly burn it's Winnie Wigwam products. Reverend Diaz was a much more sophisticated man than the preacher in Watsonville. He had been educated in a real seminary and ministered to a large congregation in New Austin. He was the type of evil hardest to deal with, an honest and principled man who was terribly misguided, hurting people with the only the best of intentions.

Throughout history, small men have used religion to do small minded evils and blame them on one or the other God. The reverend was not such a man. He was more humanity loving than God fearing. He did not believe that demons infested cuts and knew that prayer did more to change people than it did to change God's actions. He also knew in the depth of his soul that medicine and doctors had caused the great plagues and nearly wiped out humanity. He loved humanity and would fight to the death to protect it. He was a very dangerous man.

A less than generous soul might have made note of the fact that his church lived on contributions. A popular cause brought in more people, lead to more contributions and allowed the reverend to do God's work a little more comfortably. It also got him noticed in the newspapers and gave him more influence to protect his flock from evil ways.

He began his holy crusade much the same way that the preacher in Watsonville had done his. He began from the pulpit. His pulpit was in a larger church. It had a balcony for the choir and another for the overflow crowds. He could preach to seven hundred souls on a Sunday. His people were not the bonneted women of Watsonville. His women wore lace trimmed bonnets in the latest styles, carefully coordinated with their wide, checked skirts and their silk blouses. Every parasol matched every bonnet and every high button shoe was shined to perfection.

"Ladies and Gentlemen. It has come to my attention that we, as a society, are in danger of repeating our most serious mistakes. It has been over four hundred years since the great plagues smited the unrighteous and brought humanity to the brink of extinction. We seem to be forgetting the wisdom learned from those times.

"It's hard to watch pain and know that the ancients could have stopped it. It's wrenching in your soul to see a child die and know that the ancients might have saved it. However, we know what eventually happens when you open the gates and allow meddling with nature. Even before the great plagues, we know that the ancients were complaining that their potions were losing power. The forces of evil and disease had learned to overcome the potions and were ever more powerful. More and more children were being born defective in mind and body. Eventually, the evil in nature became so powerful as to almost wipe humanity from the face of the earth.

"We must be ever vigilant to assure that our children and our children's children will always be born strong…."

The empress threw her morning paper down hard. "Damn that Diaz! Why can't we stop him?"

The emperor looked up from his breakfast and answered, "Because we're Texans. We fight wars to make sure that no one can muzzle Diaz or anyone else."

She snorted angrily. "I know that we have to be an example of high morality, but there must be a reasonable limit to anything. You can't let these people do this. They are responsible for thousands of deaths."

Artimus was the third person at the breakfast table. "I have to say that I am tempted to agree with her. There must be some limits on free speech. That man is a menace."

The emperor sighed through a mouthful of pancakes. "That's just it. There cannot be limits on free speech or you end up with Stalin's freedom. In the old soviet union, they had one of the world's worst leaders. Man called "Stalin", killed ten or twelve million of his own people. The constitution of his country guaranteed free speech, and they had it. As long as what you wanted to say was how wonderful Stalin was, you could speak all you want. It was 'Stalin's Freedom.'

"A lot of countries have had it. The old United States had it worse than Russia.

They complained about the Moslem countries forbidding free speech, but they had laws about what jokes you could tell, what you could say about your neighbor and even what you could print. They called it being 'politically correct.' Anyone else would have called it being censored. It's the worst enemy freedom ever had.

"Since no one likes to hear the opposition, it is the most common kind of horror that governments commit. We spent too long fighting it to commit it."

He belatedly realized that he had just offended his wife by preaching at her and must have offended Artimus, who came from a theocracy that certainly must have heresy laws. Like every embarrassed husband and friend in history, he was hit with the urge to extricate himself by shoving his foot deeper into his oral orifice. "I'm sorry, Honey. I know that you know all that and if it weren't for your condition," the empress was visibly pregnant, "You would be lecturing me on it."

Artimus carefully kept silence. As a trained military man, he knew a minefield when he saw it. He had always been slightly embarrassed by his country's heresy laws. As a young man, he had asked his tutors, "If it's true, why do we have to force people not to say anything else. Isn't the truth powerful enough to win?" He never did like the answers, but learned early that you could not foster religious tolerance and still be the leader of a theocracy.

However, he did want to relieve the emperors all too obvious embarrassment. "Maybe there is a way around him. You know that you won't change his mind or bribe him and you couldn't threaten Diaz with a platoon of Rangers. I've been to his services a few times. He is intelligent, honest, and a Texan. He is the most noble and difficult of enemies, but he does have some weaknesses."

The empress looked interested. "Weakness? Like gambling or drinking? Maybe he is a skirt chaser?"

Artimus almost chuckled. "No, My Lady. He is a good family man and a good Christian, as far as I know. But my family has been in the same business as he is for a long time and I can tell you, he has weaknesses. You weren't there when my father explained to His Majesty why wer'e giving our treasure to our enemy. However, we head the church in York and we couldn't do the things there that we are doing here.

"Except for those times in history when the church is backed by military power, we are forced to follow more than we lead. The honest truth is that churches are forced to follow the lead of society on most moral matters. We are able to influence, but not normally to dictate. Look at the history. Five hundred years to a thousand years after Christ, the church supported slavery. We just campaigned for better treatment of slaves. When the improving economies swung public opinion against slavery, we became abolitionists. Had we made the switch a few hundred years earlier, we would have been ignored or replaced. The early church prized celibacy for the holy and gave it public support, but also supported prostitution and libertine sexual activity for the masses until the Victorian age, when we suddenly remembered that it was against God's will.

"The important thing to remember is that Diaz can only reflect what the people around him want to believe. Picture him as sort of an echo chamber repeating and amplifying opinions. So you sidestep him. You cannot change him, but if you change his parishioners, he loses power. He follows more than he leads.

"So, you continue as you have done. You and the ladies of your social circle have more real power and influence than he does. Sooner or later you will find some way to show your opinions and people will try to follow you."

The empress did not look happy. "It's nice to feel that we have a winning path, but it would be so much more satisfying to see him standing at Liars Post."

Both men attributed her meaner than usual attitude to "her condition" and decided, wisely, to change the topic.

Chapter 27   The Delivery

The labor was a hard one. He sat with his face in his hands and worried. He had been worrying for over three hours. Hearing his wife scream in pain had driven him to the edge of despair. Over and over he wondered what good it was to be emperor when he couldn't even help his wife.

The noise had stopped a few minutes before. Now he waited to find out if he was a husband and father or widower. The midwives appeared in white aprons and caps. He worried that the downcast stares were not merely from Imperial respect.

"How is she?"

"She rests. It was a hard labor, but she rests now. There was some bleeding, but we used Winnie Wigwam's powders and there should be no infection."

"And the child?"

"The baby is early. It was not due for at least another month". She paused.

"It does not breathe well. I'm very sorry, Sire."

The empress was sweaty in her thin white gown. Her damp hair caressed the baby in her arms. She looked up with a tired smile. "Meet your son. Hamilton, this is your father, Adam. You are going to like him."

"Sally, you know it's not good luck to name him for the first few months."

"I don't care. He is Hamilton. He is a strong boy." Her hand brushed the baby's cheek. "Someday he will grow up to be emperor. Honey, I'm so tired. I can't stay awake."

It was three am. He was still sleeping in the chair and holding his wife's hand when the baby stopped breathing. He was awakened hours later by the noise below the window. The bed was empty, the covers askew and still showing the damp outline of the recent mothers sweat. There was a commotion below the window. He had just gotten to the window when the chamberlain and a guardsman broke into the room.

"She's gone!!" He didn't have to ask who. In the courtyard below, his wife was shoving aside her lady in waiting and mounting a horse. She was dressed in a flowing skirt and silk blouse. She had a bright red cape around her shoulders but she had not fixed her hair. The lady in waiting was still crying and holding her mistress's foot when the empress looked down coldly, kicked the lady's shoulder and spurred the horse out of the courtyard.

"Your Majesty, you have to stop her! She just delivered a baby. If she rides far, she'll start bleeding. She could die."

They were bolting down the stairs. Emperor, midwives, guards, and ladies jostling together, privilege forgotten in their haste. "What the hell happened?"

The breathless midwife gasped out. "She got up about an hour ago looking for the baby. She was terrible hurt when she found out that it had died. She wailed and cried and then just suddenly she grabbed her cloak and ran out the kitchen door."

Within a minute the breathless party was at the ranger station behind the house. Several horses were kept saddled for emergencies. The emperor got the first one, the midwife and the next five runners got the others. As they rode out of the gate, the rest of the party was heading for the stables.

The Monday morning congregation didn't recognize the wild eyed woman who ran in the front door of the church. It wasn't until she walked slowly across the back of the church and up the side aisle that some of them recognized her. She stopped at the end of the aisle and looked over at Reverend Diaz. There was a long silence. Diaz was concerned but confused. He waited politely for her to speak.

"My baby is dead."

"What?"

"My baby is dead. You killed him. My baby would have lived if there had been a doctor. You killed him. Now you've killed your last baby."

The empress threw her cloak back across her shoulder. Strapped low on her hip was a service revolver. Her eyes were as cold as her voice was loud. "Fill your hand, you son of a bitch, or die with it empty!"

Diaz was startled. He threw his hands in front of him palms forward. His voice was incredulous. "I can't draw on a woman!" He gestured to the crowd. "Someone stop her." No one moved.

The empress drew and fired faster than most men could. The shot buzzed by Diaz's right ear. He slowly lowered his hands to his side. His voice was calm again but his eyes were moist. "I will not kill my empress." His eyes glanced past the blood trickling down the empress's leg and pooling on her shoe.

Her gun hand was drooping. It took two hands to make the second shot go by Diaz's other ear. "I won't miss again, you son of a bitch!"

"And I won't draw a gun on you. My Lady, you are injured."

The room was quiet. Outside, horses were coming, fast. The room was spinning a little. It was hard to keep her balance. "And my baby...", she was slowly falling, "is dead." She couldn't seem to aim.

The guardsmen got to the room too late to stop her fall, but in time to surround her. The emperor and the midwife followed at a run. The midwife knelt by her side and lifted her soggy dress. Without a word the guards turned to face the crowd and shield the empress's modesty as much as possible. The emperor kneeled beside to hold her limp hand in his.

The midwife cared nothing for modesty. She tore her apron loose and stuffed it where it would stop the bleeding, modesty be damned.

"Will she live?' he asked.

"I think so. This bleeding is not a hemorrhage. She has lost blood but it's slowing down. She may be alright."

His eyes never left her face. "Reverend Diaz?"

"Yes, Sire." the voice behind him answered.

"If she dies, I will remove my crown and kill you personally."

"Yes, Your Majesty."

The empress continued to improve. Her color returned in a week, but her smile did not. She continued to take her meals in her sick bed. Even when she was well enough to sit on the couch and talk with her friends, she did not return to the imperial bedroom. She explained to her husband the she felt too weak to share a bed and needed a little more time to heal. She was loving but distant.

She was visited several times a day by the ladies in her circle. At first, they came with expressions of concern and false cheer showing on their faces. Their visits became longer and more numerous as the empress's health improved.

Finally, after three weeks, the emperor awoke to his wife's voice saying, "Shove over, won't you? You're on my side of the bed." They slept in each others arms until their limbs hurt. When he awoke, she was gone.

She was also missing at breakfast. "Jeeves, is the empress still taking her breakfast in her sick room?"

"No, Sire. She and the other ladies left before breakfast this morning. I assume that they are going to have breakfast together somewhere."

The emperor asked, "What ladies? Where did they leave to?"

Jeeves looked apologetic, "The ladies that have been visiting her in the sick room. You know, Her Ladies of Charity. About ten of them showed up before dawn with their servants and some other women. They left over an hour ago. They took wagons and seemed to be headed for Austin."

"Jeeves, find the empress's secretary and see if she knows where my wife has gone."

Jeeves returned in a state of agitation. "Your Majesty, Her Majesty's secretary is missing, as is my wife, Sir Greg's wife and the empress dowager. They all left before dawn!"

The emperor was out of his chair and heading for the door, "Oh shit, this can't be good. Notify Sir Greg and Artimus to meet me at the stables."

The three men and a ranger escort galloped into town about an hour after sunrise. It was the time most people were going to work and the shops were beginning to open. Here and there a coffee shop or bakery was serving men headed to work. A few hacks were carrying bankers and executives to their offices and an occasional horse drawn bus carried office workers to work. Even though it was a city, downtown Austin managed to look like a western town. The lack of elevators kept the buildings down to one or two stories and the hitching posts, wooden walks, and covered porches completed the western look. The emperor was headed for Diaz' church. It was a block off the main street and nearly in the center of town. He had a feeling that whatever the women were up too, it probably would involve the unfortunate Diaz.

He was wrong, but close enough to find the women. Even at this time of the morning, they had gathered a crowd. They were in front of a store building. It was a typical Texan business building. The front of the store was paned in two foot square window glass, giving the look of a picture window without needing huge glass panes. The second floor was offices or storage depending upon what kind of business you ran.

A few things made this building look different. In front of it were ten armed women. Now, Texas women were often politely armed with purse pistols or derringers, but these women carried shotguns and had bandoliers of shells crossing their neat silk covered bosoms. Each and every one had forsaken her bonnet for a full Stetson and she wore it with a matching angry look. Above the women, a new sign was in place. It read in neat, clear, bright red letters large enough to cover most of the second floor, "Midwife School." On the door hung a plaque that read "Enough have died." The women stood in front of windows clearly stocked with obstetrical tools and Winnie Wigwam's Natural Potions.

The sight was curious enough to bring onlookers who, seeing the expression on the women's faces and the guns in their hands, then stayed on the far side of the street.

The emperor dismounted and approached the building leading his horse. He motioned his escort to stay back. His wife and his mother were standing on the wooden walk in front of the store. He motioned for his wife to step forward for a private conversation. She glanced quickly at the other women and then came near him. When they were reasonably alone, he said in a loud whisper, "Honey, what are you doing?"

She did not look directly at him, but answered though clenched teeth, speaking only loud enough for him to hear, "I'm testing Artimus' theory. If we're right, the guiding lights of Texas are on this porch. Diaz is a dead man or a winner as of today. I couldn't tell you because you and dad have to be able disavow us if we are wrong. Now you have to get very angry and stalk off. I'll be home in a few days."

Sir Greg looked as confused as the emperor felt, "Sire, what's happening to our wives?" The emperor began to lead his horse away as he motioned for Greg and Jeeves to follow. "Let's go over to that restaurant and I'll explain." In fact, by the time they reached the restaurant, the emperor had decided that his wife was right, they had to separate the empire from the women for the time being. He, Jeeves, and Greg ended up at the imperial offices several blocks away. As they left, the reporters from the Austin Times and Houston Chronicle were already approaching the new Midwife School.

The last thing he heard as he left was the empress saying to the reporters, "Damned right! Enough women have died! You put in your article that anyone who wants to protest better come armed and armored, because we are going to put holes in them."

By nightfall, a platform had been built in front of the school. Speeches were being made. Flags waved and bands played by torchlight. It had the look and feel of a small town election and, in a way, it was.

The empress was speaking again, "Enough! Enough! If we keep going the way we are one out of three of us will die in childbirth. You there, do you want your daughter to die having a child? How about you, Ma'am? Do you want to die and leave your children alone? Half of our children will die before they reach a birthday. I am tired of watching my friends die and my babies die! This school will make sure that every woman and every child gets the best care that we know how to give."

The women cheered.

"And by the way, Reverend Damned Diaz, the next damned man who tells me that my pain is what I owe for the sins of the past had better be ready to pass a pumpkin through his penis because until he does, I'M NOT LISTENING!!"

The fact that Diaz would never have said such a thing didn't matter a bit. The women hated him for it and cheered again.

It started on Wednesday and was not over until Sunday morning. The editorials the first day were incredulous or critical. By the second day, some columnists were asking why they couldn't make better use of the natural medications, and why not train midwives better? After all, midwives were already trained, just not very well. It helped that the empress and empress dowager and every stylish woman in Austin was on the side of the school. By Friday, any reporter who criticized the school or Winnie Wigwam was sleeping alone. Saturday, midwives began to show up for training.

Diaz surrendered on Sunday. He looked out over a small crowd of defiant women and surrendered. "This has been an exciting week in Austin. We have a new school and talk of new ways to ease the pain and suffering of our women. Contrary to what people often believe, Our Father never says anywhere in His Word that suffering and death are good things. He is a loving parent and a loving parent does not want to see his children harmed. We must, however, curb our arrogance. In the past, we stepped too far and hurt ourselves despite God's love for us. As we step onto this path again, let us go with caution and avoid the mistakes of the past."

Of course, he was only talking about midwifing and childbirth. A doctor was still fair game for a lynching. It was, however, a good bet that once the wife had care, the husband and children would not be far behind.

Sunday evening, the empress returned to a passionate reunion with her husband.

Chapter 28 The Plot's Afoot

The empress and her husband had been virtually inseparable in the three days since her return from the school. They entered the Archeology meeting hand in hand to find all of the other committee members standing at attention behind their chairs.

"Hip, Hip, Hooray!" rang out to rafters. The empress blushed as her husband stepped back to join the cheer. "Hip, Hip, Hooray! Hip, Hip, Hooray!" The applause continued until the blushing empress sat and begged for it to stop.

"Gentlemen, I came here to apologize for acting without consulting with you all. I know now that it was very risky and very wrong and I can only plead my extreme emotional state as an excuse."

After they all sat, the elder Adams leaned forward. "Nonsense. You and the Dowager had a good sense of timing. You had the sympathy of the entire population. If you had waited for a consultation, the moment would have passed. We are all grateful for what you did."

Solomon joined in. "The orders for Winnie Wigwam's Natural Potions are ten times what we can ship. Item number two on the agenda today is deciding what new products to introduce and item three is trying to figure out how to ramp up production. I think we are past the hump."

The emperor was still smiling broadly as he pounded the table for order. "Gentlemen, our first order of business is on the table. As you know, Sir Greg has returned from the farm with an idea for out next project. Sir Greg, you have the floor."

As Sir Greg strode to the blackboard at the end of the table, he motioned to the envelopes on the table. "Gentlemen, if you will open the envelopes at your seats, we can go over the proposal for our next step. Of course, it might seem a little tame after that last one. You will remember that we began with established three general goals. First, reestablish the healing arts in Texas. Second, reestablish manufacturing with powered machinery and tooling. Third, reestablish communications and travel throughout the realm.

"The subcommittee on technology has come up with a plan that may advance our second and third goals. We have now had almost a year to read the books from York and we have learned much from them. Some of you have been to the farm and seen the progress. Let me bring the others of you up to date.

"One of the books provided by Pope Jones was 'The History of Steam Power.' It was well chosen by the Pope's advisors. We have now built several steam engines. If you will look at the photographic plate in your envelopes, it will show you what a steam engine looks like." There was one photo plate in each envelope. The print was made by combining four negatives to print a collage. "The picture in the upper left corner is a steam engine that we built at the farm. As with the electricity, it turns out to be simple technology that the average school boy could master in a day. As with electricity, it could take years to master the subtleties, but we can, and will, show each and every one of you, today, how it works. In fact, we have made a working model small enough to carry in a suitcase and we will be demonstrating it after the meeting."

This time, Greg had cleared the demonstration in advance with key committee members. They were also now a much more sophisticated audience than they had been a year ago.

"The machine in the photograph is about two meters long and one meter in height. That big tank you see is the steam supply. Most of the bulk of the machine is just a boiler and fire pit. The working parts are those tubes that are attached to the flywheel. We were able to build the first model in less than three weeks. It's powered by the same firewood or coke that you burn in your fireplaces. Of course, there are some problems. Artimus, you saw this machine work on your last trip to the farm. How would you describe it?"

Artimus thought for a second. "It was a screaming, fire breathing, smoking demon, the sight of which could cause miscarriages in women and nightmares in children."

Greg smiled and waved his hand toward Artimus. "That, Gentlemen, is our problem. I am certain that by the standards of the Ancients, this machine is quiet enough and not disturbing at all. However, everyone who sees it for the first time, including such brave men as Sir Artimus and Master Sergeant O'Brien, see it as a frightening machine. We dare not put one in front of the population until we learn how to control it better and how to get them to like it.

"If you look at the picture at the upper right corner of the page, you will see one of the ways that the Ancients changed their lives with steam power. What you see there is an early, for them, steam carriage. They called it a 'locomotive'. You can judge the size by looking at the human figure in its control room. It was a conveyance that ran on rails. You can see the rails extending out in front of it. They are iron or steel bars about two meters apart. With one of these, you could travel from Houston to Austin in two hours and be in the Kingdom of Kansas tonight.

The implications for the Rangers and for business are obvious. Of course, we can't build them yet, but Mr. Wayne has a proposal for you that may get us closer. Mr. Wayne, would you take the floor."

Jonathon Wayne was a muscular man of about thirty. His usual profession was sales. He worked for the elder Adams in developing the marketing campaign for Winnie Wigwam and had displayed enough intelligence and creativity to get invited into the secret group.

"I was hoping that Sir Greg would cover those last two photographs, as he was the moving force behind them. However, I will do my best. On my last visit to the farm, Sirs Greg and Eric showed me the steam engine that they were working on. It was the same one that you see in the first photograph, but they were trying to mount it on a wagon to create a locomotive. They have made a wagon and about a hundred meters of track and they are building the engine right on the wagon.

"I happened to notice that the smiths working on the engine were able to move it around rather easily. It took two of them to get it started, but then one of them could push the wagon with the engine up and down the track. It was like it was on ice. You can see from the photographs that this is a heavy piece of machinery.

"I mentioned this to Greg and he decided to find out how much easier it really was. The result was the picture that you see in the lower left corner. The pony you see hitched to the wagon is Susie. We picked her because she has one of those big hearts where she will almost kill herself to please you. She will pull until she can't pull anymore.

"We tested her on a standard wagon first. She can pull about seven hundred kilograms on level ground. However, when we hitched her up to the wagon on the rails, we had a hard time getting enough weight on it to stop her. She pulled four times that weight. And once she got it moving, she pulled it fast.

"It turns out that even without the locomotive, the rail road thing is a great idea. Once you got her on rails, the horse can pull almost as fast as she can gallop. You might not make Houston in a few hours, but you could be there tonight with a big load of cargo or troopers. Even best of all, we know that there won't be much protest from the population, because we already have some of these in Texas."

Someone from the other end of the table spoke for the group. "If we have any of these, I haven't seen them, and I think that I would have noticed a railroad."

Wayne was smiling like a school kid. He loved it when a pitch was going well. "That's because you don't spend much time in mines. In fact there aren't many mines anymore. The usual way of getting metals is to scavenge from one of the old cities and melt down what you want. However, there are a few mines left in NewMex where they get borax and silver and a few underground coal mines in Texas. When they are tunneling underground, they bring the ore up to the surface in donkey powered carts that run on wooden rails. It's just that no one ever noticed before.

"My idea was that if we could build a rail system for horse powered cars, we would get a boost immediately and we would have the structure in place for steam engines when we figure out how to introduce them.

"The last photograph on the sheet is a copy of a page in a history of Kansas. It's a street scene in about 1880 A.D. If you look into the center left background, you'll see a horse drawn carriage that is running on rails. The Ancients had steam engines by then, but must have found the horse drawn cars valuable enough to keep them.

"Thanks to the old roads, we have ready made road beds. We can build such a system faster and cheaper than the Ancients by far. The best thing is that we won't even have to hide it. Of course, we can't hide it, but what I mean is that as soon as people find out how much faster and cheaper it is to travel by rail, we can form stock companies that will build these things all over the empire."

O'Brien signaled for attention. "Laddie, I like your thinking, but, like you said, even if something like this exists now, no one here has seen one before. I'd like a little plan about what to do if the public reaction is like it was for Winnie Wigwams pain killer."

Wayne was beaming, "Got you covered. We do have a plan. As you know, I grew up in the Kingdom of Kansas. I was lucky enough to get home for Union Day this year. The Elder Adams and the Empress Dowager were also making their annual appearance at the celebration. I noticed that the women had only two topics of conversation when they got together, their children, and the royals. They gossiped about the royal family as if they lived in town."

He looked down the table at the royal family and nodded to the Empress Dowager. "I don't know if you are aware of the concern that the people of Kansas, particularly the women, have for their queen and the queen mum. Their love runs deep."

Now it was the Dowager's turn to blush. In truth, she had earned that love. As a young queen she had tackled the job as seriously as anyone in the long line before her. In addition to the usual charities and church work, she had bandaged more than one soldier with her own hands and had personally cared for plague victims during the last outbreak. Unlike other wealthy women, she had cared for her children herself and took them with her whenever possible. Every woman in Texas wanted to be her. She was also modest enough to deny it all and blush beautifully when she was younger.

"Your Majesty, my plan depends upon that. If you will bear with me, the explanation is more complex than the plan. I got the idea when you came to the meeting in August on the handle of a cane. You had hurt your ankle playing tennis and had to hobble for a month.

"I checked with your secretary. When that happened, you received over nine hundred get well cards, most of them from people who have never met you. I also noticed that, in spite of your pain, you made it to the All Saints Church every Sunday and to the All Saints Women's Charitable Society on the first of the month. Not only did I notice, but all of Texas, or at least the female half of Texas, noticed. They would therefore be very concerned if something happened to you that would keep you from your church work."

"Mr. Wayne, I hope you are not planning to break my legs. The torn ligaments were bad enough."

"No, Your Majesty, but Solomon could probably fake up a pretty good looking cast. Then he could tell the reporters that your leg couldn't stand the jostling of a trip to the church. The public might demand that we find a way to help you. The path from the Bowie Palace to All Saints Church is right down the main street for about three miles. In order to help the Empress Dowager, we lay rails from one to the other. That allows her to get to church in a nice smooth rail car without being jostled, and people would love it.

"We start with a single carriage on rails being pulled by a pony. The second week, you invite some of the ladies of the church to join you and we have to use a bigger wagon like the one in the photo. If no one complains, you mention after you heal up, that it's a shame that the more elderly people cannot get to church easily. We run more rails to help them out. In appreciation for the public support, you declare that anyone can use the rail system now that it serves the entire downtown.

"Soon we have street cars serving the entire city. Within a year, the rails would join cities. Some day we'll figure out how to add steam power but in the meantime, we revolutionize our transportation system."

He looked at the emperor, "Your majesty, if we had had this system last year, we could have gotten to Yahoo in hours instead of four days."

The empress dowager leaned forward slightly for attention. "You have thought it out well. I admit to having some reservations. In all my time as empress, I was never dishonest with my people and I hate to take advantage of their concern for me. If we do this, we will be committing a fraud that will cause upset for many people. They will be genuinely worried about me, while I am lying to them. It tastes like sour bile in my mouth. However, you are right. It will eventually be good for them. We will do it for the people of Yahoo. However, I want Solomon to make it clear from the start that I am in no real danger. We will worry our people as little as possible."

It was a long meeting that day. They broke twice for meals. In addition to the items on the agenda, most of the men stayed for the lessons on steam power. They then ended up playing with the toy steam engine for hours while they smoked cigars and drank good bourbon.

Chapter 29   The First Ride

The plan had worked well. The newspapers received a tip that the Empress Dowager had fallen from her horse during an afternoon ride. Solomon had wanted to make the accident be something dramatic and noble, but the empress had insisted there be no lies bigger than needed. When the reporters politely inquired at Bowie house as the condition of the empress, they were introduced to her personal surgeon, Solomon White. The reporters were, of course, polite. Public figures in Texas were not available for public amusement. Crawling over fences, getting secret pictures and printing lies were all actions that could potentially have permanent and deadly consequences. Libel suits were far less common that duels. Freedom of speech also included the freedom to back up or eat your words.

Solomon explained that the empress had fallen when her horse was spooked during an afternoon ride with her husband. Her leg had been, unfortunately, broken and she was suffering from severe strains to her back and side muscles. Solomon and the empress social secretary answered endless questions about the empress's comfort, details of the accident, details of the cast, and so on. The questions were all polite but there were a lot of them. As predicted, Royal Fever ran high among Texas women.

Solomon and the secretary managed to work in twice that the Empress's main concern was that she would miss attending her church. It was well known the empress was a sincerely pious person who took her faith seriously. They also mentioned how much she would miss her friends and the work of the Ladies Charitable Committee. Solomon explained that the empress was quite willing to endure the pain of a carriage trip to the church, but that he had been required to forbid it because the jostling of the carriage could keep her bones from healing properly. The reporters realized without having to have it said that this was probably due to the empress's age. At forty-seven, she was considered rather elderly in Texas.

With a little help from tips given to the Austin Times, the public began to demand that help be found for the empress. The leg could take two or three months to heal and they did not want the empress to suffer that long. Various plans were printed to carry the empress on a paladin or in the arms of admirers. All were rejected to the lack of dignity involved. Then someone suggested that if only the road could be made smoother and a special carriage built, the empress might be able to go to church. Perhaps, one prompted reporter said, something like the carts used in mines.

Within a few days, the rails that had been in storage were being laid into the pavement of the main street. They were sunken into the pavement flush with the surface and were exactly as far apart as the old railroad lines. The workers were strangely competent for people who had never done this before. Within a week, a special carriage was presented to the reporters. It was a fancy white carriage with extensive scroll work and two plush purple seats facing each other, one with a footrest for the empress's leg cast. It was pulled by a dappled grey pony. It seemed that the entire city turned out to see the empress carried to the carriage for her first ride. They cheered as she was carried to the church and she smiled outside and cringed inside, still bothered by the lie.

The empress did not like riding alone and asked for various ladies to accompany her on her twice weekly and then daily trips. Wayne's plan worked perfectly. Before the leg "healed", the empress had requested and received extensions of the street car lines to the homes of several elderly ladies who just happened to live in areas that needed a street car line.

The next meeting of the Archeology Committee was devoted to the plans for expanding the rail system.

The emperor emeritus was presenting his business plan. "We all feel that it is time for us to move on with the rail system. Right now we have engineers laying rail on the docks in Galveston and at the new farm. Since we plan to eventually tie all of these tracks together, the engineers have developed a set of standards for them. It seems that the Ancients had one exact width that they used for all of their track. All rails were four feet nine inches apart. We don't know why they picked that exact measurement, but since they had hundreds of years of experience, we have decided to use the same measurements."

In doing so, the emperor had no idea that he was continuing the tradition of using a Roman army cart as a standard. All over Europe there were rutted stone roads with the ruts four feet eight and a half inches apart, worn there by the wheels of Roman army and postal carts. That had formed the basis for the first rail systems and now a nameless Roman official was picking the gauge for a railroad built two thousand eight hundred years after his death.

"The next step is to get the business of railroading going. We have, at least temporarily, good public support. The fact that these things are easy to understand has lead the public to accept them quickly. The royal city councils in New Galveston, Austin, Houston, and Fort Worth have all passed resolutions to put street railways in their cities. We are going to leave those as Royal services. The crown will finance them and charge a small ticket price to recover the investment. I suspect that sooner or later even Yahoo and Watsonville will want them.

"The real changes will come when we start putting in the interurban runs. I have formed a stock company to finance the national railroads. The Adams family has provided the initial capital, but we will be selling as much stock as possible. Frankly, we don't need the investment, but we want to have as many people as possible investing in it. Every investor is also a proselytizer. More people. More support.

"That leads us to a small matter that I want to handle before we go on. I beg your patience for an irrelevancy. Part of the Adams family stock will be distributed to each and every member of this committee. We have also incorporated Winnie Wigwams Enterprises now that it is safe to go public with it. In this weeks envelope, you have each received a stock certificate for shares in Winnie Wigwam Enterprises. We have failed to consult you on this matter because we, speaking for the Adams, knew that most of you would refuse to accept personal gain for what you are doing. We have not taken these risks for money, but for the good of our people.

"It is, however, my personal opinion that if others get rich from your work and you do not share in the wealth, there could eventually be feelings of regret. These feelings could eventually slow down or hurt our work. Therefore, there will be a distribution of ownership in any enterprise that we start. The distributions are all equal for all members of the committee. Whether you are a committee head or a smith, you take the same risks and the rewards are the same. The distributions will, of course, not be public knowledge and will not occur until we are certain that the company has gained public acceptance.

"Now, back to the business at hand. We expect that the railroads will expand rapidly. We have found some historical books with articles about the building of the railroad net in the old American States. The major part of their work was the building of the roadbed for the track. Thanks to the remnants of the old highway system, we have all of the roadbed we need. We have relatively level roads going everywhere and even have intact bridges in most places. I read that when they built the railroad between the oceans, that they had two companies compete. The companies were given land on both sides of what they built. One chapter claims that one of the companies built as much as twenty miles of road in one day in an area where they did not need to build roadbed. I don't know if we can do that well, but I expect freight and passenger traffic to be moving between New Galveston, Houston, and Austin by this time next year.

"Later this year, the privy council will bring to the emperor a recommendation that the Rangers finance the construction of routes out to our borders and along the coast for use in case of invasion. While invasion is, of course, only a remote possibility, it does give us a reason for public financing for the longest routes.

"The project managers will be Sir Bradley and Mr. Barnes. Sir Bradley will manage the overall project flow while Mr. Barnes will supervise the actual design and construction of the railway and the rolling equipment. They will be the only Archeology Committee members involved as this project is, as of now, almost totally in the public domain. I will now turn the meeting over to Sir Bradley who will cover some of the engineering plans."

Sir Bradley was an engineer in an era when slide rules where high tech and paper and pencil more common. As with most engineers, he had mostly designed buildings, water works, and water powered factories.

"We have one great problem left. Thanks to Mr. Wayne and the empress, we have wide public support and, thanks to the business acumen of the emperor emeritus, we have the funds and resources for building. Now we need ten thousand miles of rail. The standard rail is twenty four feet long and you need two of them. That is about four million, four hundred thousand rails by the time the system is ten thousand miles long. That is a lot of rail.

"We ordered the initial rail for the empress's street car from a foundry in Austin. They did it a special order item. Obviously we will need something more extensive for our thousands of miles of rail. We, therefore, propose to establish two new iron mills. The first will be on a tributary of the Colorado river. It will mine a previously unused landfill near Georgetown. There is enough water flow to power six wheels for pounders and shredders and one wheel for the bellows. It will ship rail down the river to Austin. From there we can build out toward Dallas and San Antonio. We are looking for second site somewhere near Woodland. From there we can reach the old highway 10 to start building a line from San Antonio to Huston. In the long term, we will probably need a third mine on the Red Rock River to serve the northern part of the empire.

"There are two items that specifically concern this committee. The first is a minor subterfuge. We know that if we are successful, that we will someday be running steam engines with heavy cars on these rails. That requires a much heavier rail line than does a simple horse car service. Captain O'Brien has therefore designed a rather unnecessary but very heavy freight car for the Rangers. It's designed to hold several cannons with ammunition. If we actually build it, it will take a six horse Clydesdale team to pull it. The ability to service this car will be part of all specifications for rail contracts. That way the rail will be built heavy enough for use when we mechanize the lines.

"The other subterfuge is much more dangerous. If we decide to do it, it will require a vote of the entire committee. It is potentially magic and potentially deadly. We have set up a demonstration over by the wall. If you will accompany me, we will show you what we have in mind."

Eric stood near a twelve foot long table up against the wall. A blue cloth covered whatever was on the table. As they jostled to stand around the table he said, "I know that some of you have seen this before, but we want to make certain that everyone gets a look."

He pulled the cloth back. On the table were two twelve foot sections of railroad track held in the air by a pair of stands. On one end of the table there was a battery and a switch. The battery was wired though the switch to the outer rail and grounded to the inner rail. On the other end was the clicker, looking like a miniature oil pump wired between the rails.

Eric continued, "This is a working model of what we propose to do. It is called a 'telegraph'. Let me show you how it works. This battery will energize that coil down there to make the arm jump and make a clicking noise when the current flows through these wires."

He demonstrated with a series of slow and long clicks. One click when the switch was closed, another when it was opened and the arm fell back. "We have found that with a little practice, you can send messages using the Indian Scouts Secret Code. In fact, we are beginning to suspect that the code was invented for this device."

He clicked a few more times for effect. "This device is only twelve feet long, but we have reason to believe that if that rail was twenty miles or a hundred miles long, it would still work. The Ancients used this device to send messages for hundreds or thousands of miles. We have known how to use this device for months, but we have two problems. The Ancients hung wires on poles to carry the clicks. We obviously cannot do that because there is no way we could explain what we are doing. We have to hide it because of the second problem. It sure looks like the old magic. This one is not as easy to understand as a street car.

"We do need it. If the *Star Of India* people enter New Galveston harbor, this would tell the troops in Dallas within minutes. If we get attacked on our northern border again, Austin could know in hours and troops could be on their way the same day.

"While working on this, we realized that with a very slight change, the rails could take the place of wires. It does require a little subterfuge as there are normally gaps in rail roads at the switches. However, we can come up with some excuse about lighting and get the builders to bridge the gaps with wire.

"Unfortunately, we will have to create secret rooms in the major cities and staff them with reliable staff to send and receive the messages. If anyone got wind of it, it could get nasty. For that reason, it would require the thoughts of this entire committee."

They all returned to the table. The discussion was a long one. The risks of discovery were as great as the need for the communication. By nightfall, they had a decision. The emperor banged the table. "Alright, then this is our decision. If anyone present does not concur, let him speak now. We will have the rails constructed as suggested by Sir Eric. Sir Eric and his team will create a key and bar set for each potential location. They will create them in such a way as they can be disassembled and, when stored, will look like some common objects such as art or kitchen utensils. They will test the installation at each location and then disassemble and store the equipment. We will have it available for national emergency, but will not yet implement it. Do we have agreement?"

He passed his hand in half moon arc in front of him, looking at each member in turn, giving the impression of an auctioneer closing the bidding. Then slapped his hand on the table, "It is so decided."

Chapter 30 Changing of the Guard

It had been a busy year, but it was time for Artimus to leave. It was a tailgate party. Artimus, Baron Wilson and the Baroness, Sir Eric and his lady, Sir Greg and his lady sat at folding tables set up next to the traveling wagons. Servants relaxed at the ready nearby. Picnic food and beer covered the tables. The wagons were set up near the quarantine gate of New Galveston. The white city walls were close enough to dwarf the wagons. They were waiting for Artimus' replacement.

Sir Wilson and Artimus were watching the gate through hooded eyes. Each held a glass of wine in his hand. In these days, getting the right day, give or take two or three days, was considered an on time arrival. One of the troopers who was, like others in the escort, dressed as a servant, was reporting. "They just posted the list of new arrivals. There are two Yorker ships on the list. We might get lucky today."

Another hour passed before Artimus said, "There he is."

A tall and rather handsome man was presenting his credentials to the guard. He had, unlike other gentlemen, only two large wheeled cases of personal goods. The guard was somewhat surprised. Normally only cargo and the drivers went through these gates, and the drivers lived in the city. They always came back within a few hours. Anyone wanting to leave the city permanently went though quarantine in a separate section of the city and left by the passenger gate. This man was carrying an imperial pass allowing him special rights to leave the gate immediately. The guard decided that he was seeing his first real spy and stepped aside.

Artimus was hurrying to his brother as fast as dignity would allow. "Jeremiah! Over here!" The troopers with Artimus fell behind. By the time they reached for Jeremiah's cases, the brothers had completed the handshaking, arm pounding and hugging part of meeting and were back to showing all the dignity as you would expect from a grinning drunk. Artimus took his bother's arm and pointed to the wagons. "The nearest town is ten miles away, so we brought some camper wagons. We're going to stay in them tonight. Come on over and meet your new friends." Except for the troopers rolling the cases, the rest of the party had held back to give the brothers a private moment.

Artimus did the introductions. "Jeremiah, this is Baron and Baroness Wilson, Sir Greg and his lady Jane, Sir…" When he had completed the introductions, he waved Jeremiah toward a wagon seat. The troopers already had most of the tables and chairs struck and packed away. "Take a seat, we are going to travel about a half mile down the road and then camp out. We'll have one whole day to catch up."

An hour and a half later, the troopers had almost finished setting up a campsite. The fire pit was full of wood and the cook was unpacking food for dinner. Tents were going up and folding furniture unfolding. The brothers were sitting in one of the first tents to go up and sharing news of home and Texas. As soon as he reassured Artimus about his family and friends, Jeremiah asked, "I've been reading your dispatches. Are you certain that these people are as honorable as you have said? They look too good to be true."

Artimus replied, "It's a lot like York. In York, everyone claims to be a Christian. You and I both know that in reality, we have some very good and devout citizens who believe and follow the commandments and then we have those who ignore the commandments and those who use them for their own purposes. Texas is different only in that the percentage of people who believe in their ten commandments is higher than normal. The Adams have made the Law of The West a religion and they themselves set an example of following it strictly. Most of the people you will work with are going to be the best you could ask for. One warning, they keep their word one hundred percent and they will expect you to do the same. They make no excuses for dishonesty, white lies, partial truths, or evasion. To them is it all the same. Your word is good or you aren't. Keep our word good."

That night over the campfire and until late the next day, the men brought Jeremiah up to speed. He had gotten the dispatches, but face to face conversation was better at getting him acquainted with their situation. They described the situation with Winnie Wigwam and the midwife school, the tricks they had pulled to get the railroad going, and the general progress at the Farm. As much as possible, they filled him in on the social customs and people he would meet at court and instructed him in his new identity. With Artimus' help, they were able to fill in information that was not written, such as the fact that the deception done by the empress dowager should never be mentioned in her presence.

By evening of the second day, it was time for Artimus to leave. He approached the gate with trunks that contained "plants for the papal garden", samples of Laudanum and sulphanilamide, and instructions for their manufacture. He also carried one of the books of drawings use to find the poppies in Texas. They would use it to carry out the same search in York. He also carried an intense longing to see his wife and children again.

Chapter 31   The New Member

Jeremiah was not surprised when the meeting of the Archeological Committee began with the long version of the oath. Artimus had told him of the expectations. When it came his turn, he stood and took out his bible. "On my oath to my God, on my immortal soul, and on my chances for salvation, I swear before my God that I will never betray this body or anyone in it and that I shall takes its secrets to my grave. So help me God."

With that, Emperor Adams began the meeting. "As most of you know, Bishop Jeremiah is, as was Artimus before him, now Sir Jeremiah and he serves as a captain in the Kansas Rangers. Most of you know this, because, according to the newspaper accounts that I read, most of you were at his elevation ceremony. Sir Jeremiah, if you have any messages for us, we would happily give you the floor before we begin the regular agenda."

He knew that sounded a little stiff. They were determined to like and trust Jeremiah, but he had simply not yet sat under a rainy tarp or been shot at with anyone in the room. Such things bind men together and had made his brother a firm friend of all of them. The emperor hoped that Jeremiah would have an equal chance to prove himself.

Jeremiah stood. "I would like to fill you in on what I have brought with me while the entire committee is present. First of all, I have brought some additional books. The first item is a copy of 'The Handbook of Chemistry and Physics.' This is a rare book because it takes over a year to copy. Essentially, it's a set of tables on things such a tensile strength, chemical formulas, specific gravities and other information for scientists. It was a reference book that an Ancient engineer would have kept on his desk. As establishing radio contact between our countries is desirable, I have brought two books on amateur radio. The books for amateurs are good because among the Ancients, the hobbyists often constructed their own equipment. They also did not have the tools that professional companies had, so they give instructions on how to improvise or work with simple tools.

"My master asked a monk who knows more about chemistry than we can admit to, to find a text on basic principles. We have been only partly successful in that. We had some high school and college text books, but they all assume that you can order graphite or whatever else you need from a chemical supply house. I brought one text from one hundred years before the new era and one from just before the new era started. The older one is the more valuable. It is the best that we can do.

"In appreciation of the idea for Winnie Wigwam, I have also brought seed for a plant that treats diabetes in adults, a plant with diuretic seeds, and one that treats congestion. These are all natural products that our monks have been using as folk medicine.

"I also bring the personal thanks of the Pope for the Winnie Wigwam idea. We have begun a similar enterprise and it is working well. One of our orders has begun marketing Monk Marvin's Holy Potions. They are normally distributed by priests who are making house calls, but they are also available in stores. We have had some difficulty in getting the priests to use them, but the public has accepted them very well. We have already begun to see the death rate from infections and fevers fall.

"One other idea has made its way to York. We tested your idea for a horse drawn railroad and then spent a few days wondering why we didn't think of it a hundred years ago. We now have three mills turning out and storing steel rail. We are going to introduce it on Destruction Day. We are prepping the news by planting stories ahead of time about how railroads are used in mines and factories already.

"You know that Philadelphia is our biggest city. It also has the biggest Destruction Day fire. To celebrate this year, we will build rails for the cars that are delivering Destruction Day material from the warehouse. Frankly, most of the stuff is reproductions now as we have cleaned our country down to bedrock. Anyway, the material will be delivered by three large carts coming on three separate sets of track. Before the ceremony, we will use a papal coach mounted on rails to bring in the Pope. After the ceremony, we'll replace the work carts with passenger cars and give people rides on the new holiday amusement.

"By this time next year, we hope to have rail lines running from Philadelphia to Albany. I do not want to distract from our agenda, so I will answer any questions that you have after the meeting. I will be here for awhile."

In fact, the plan was for Jeremiah to spend a year as the Papal liaison to Texas. Then Artimus would return for another term.

The meeting was, again, a long one. Now that the new farm was the center of activity, it took two days to make the two hundred twenty five mile trip from the farm to Austin and longer to go back upriver. Meetings of the whole were therefore less frequent and longer. The first two hours were taken up with progress reports. The rail ventures were going well. The Dallas, Houston, and San Antonio triangle would be operational within the month. As expected, it was going fast due to the fact that the roadbed already existed. The Rangers had suggested that a coastal line should be the next one. The committee agreed, but decided that the next line after that would run along the old highway 20. That would connect Sweetwater, and therefore the farm, into the rail network.

The reception to the street car lines had been universally good. Businessmen were now beginning to use the lines for freight. In Houston and Dallas, the agricultural associations had asked for lines to be laid out to the farm lands. It was almost too easy.

The emperor emeritus reported on the more difficult business side of the railroads. "The biggest problem that we face now is to keep the support of freight carriers. If we let the people who now carry freight get hurt, we will create of core of protest. We have started a number of policies to deal with that. The Imperial Texas Railway has a policy to purchase the equipment of any independent hauler at a premium to fair market price and then to offer the hauler a permanent job with the ITR. Freight companies are being offered cheaper rates on the rail than they used to pay on road traffic." The mornings meeting dragged on with enough business reports to sound like more like a corporate board meeting that a heretical secret society. Lunch was a relief.

After lunch came the technical session. It was always more interesting than the business plans. Emperor Adams opened the discussion by recognizing Sir Greg.

He began with, "We now have several steam engines working at the farm. The mills there are running with steam power and we have three locomotives ready. The locomotives are being tested on a quarter of a mile track that we have built around the compound. They improve as we learn more about steam and are able to implement more features. The current engines are what the Ancients called 'triple expansion' engines. That means that the steam is used three times before it is exhausted. The engines are much more complicated to build now, but they use less than half the fuel of the first models. Our emphasis now is on developing manufacturing techniques for the engines that we have. We plan to develop final plans for a small and a large stationary engine. That would be one small enough to run an individual grist mill and one big enough to, say, power a small ore processing plant. We will also finalize a design for a locomotive capable of pulling twenty fully loaded carriages at twenty five miles an hour. At that point, we will manufacture as many as we can afford to hide away and continue to look for a way to introduce them to the public.

Our problem is still to produce a plan to get the public to accept them. If any of the committees have any suggestions, this would be the time to present them." He looked around the table hopefully but not expectantly. After a moment, Jeremiah tentatively raised his hand and said too softly, "I do have something to suggest to the committee."

Sir Greg gestured and said cheerfully, "Sir Jeremiah, the stage is yours."

Jeremiah was uncertain as to how one normally presented a plan to the group, so he settled for leaning forward over the table so that the other members could see him. "I believe that if you look at what motivates a luddie, there is a next step that logically presents itself." Only Emperor Adams understood the reference to "Luddite", but most members figured it out from context.

For his part, Jeremiah realized that the people at the table could not hear him well, so he stood up and leaned on his chair. "This problem has been around for a lot longer that this Empire. For thousands of years, people have resisted change. It might be stronger now, but it has always been here."

As he felt more confidence, Jeremiah began to move toward the foot of the conference table. "I suggest that what motivates these people is simple fear. In fact, the simplest fear of all. The fear of the unknown. Look inside yourselves and remember how you first felt when you began to dabble with the dark arts and compare it with how you feel now when you see a radio or a generator. Now you are amused, but if you are really honest with yourselves, you will remember that even you felt different before you understood what you were looking at.

Therefore, maybe the first step is to arrange for people to understand these things."

He saw the shocked looks around the table. "Please, I am not suggesting that we go public with what we are doing. I'm suggesting that if we demystified steam engines, people would not be scared of them. Look at our experience in York. If the parishioners had understood that the steam coming out of the engine was just heated water, they might still have disapproved of the engine, but they wouldn't have thought that the monk was possessed by the Devil. The disapproval would have been much easier to deal with than the fear.

"This group is proof that it doesn't take years of training to conquer the fear. I just watched you as Sir Greg described a triple expansion steam engine and no one here looked confused. From my understanding, the only training shared by this entire group was a one hour description of the workings of a simple engine and a couple of hours experimenting with one. That is enough to understand the simple basics. A person who understands that much may not be our ally, but he will have lost a lot of his incentive to be our enemy."

The expressions around the table were starting to look positive, tentative, but positive. Someone asked, "Have you any ideas on how you educate a population that will hang anyone who brings up the topic?"

Jeremiah replied, "We do have a plan that we have been working on in York. You would have to change it to fit Texas, but it might actually be much easier here. In York, I represent a church that is the official censor forbidding such knowledge to be acquired. We are our own worst enemies.

"The basic plan is to take advantage of a human emotion that is often stronger than fear. People love to be in on a secret. There are few things more satisfying than the feeling that you know more than your neighbor. We plan to publish a 'secret' book and let people get access to it 'in spite of our best censorship efforts.' The book will be called something like 'Secrets of The Ancients. How they controlled the world.' It will be mostly a description of what their world looked like, but it will contain simplified chapters on steam power, electricity, radio, telephone, telegraph. The chapters will have a lot of pictures and we hope to include examples of how to do hobbyist experiments. Of course, those sections will contain warnings about the dangers of black magic and how the reader should only use his knowledge for good. It will contain warnings about how dangerous all of this stuff is. It should be a best seller. Even people who hate it, will want to read it."

John Wayne was smiling, "My God. You're thinking like a Texan, this is beginning to make sense. How do you plan to distribute the book when you are the ones censoring it?"

"We plan to use the pornographers. I'm sorry. I hope that I did not offend the ladies." He hadn't. Pornography was the definition of legally forbidden images and text. No one told a Texan what the could read, at least not twice. Jeremiah was confused by the committee's confusion.

The Elder Adams jumped in to help him. "In York, pictures and stories of an erotic nature are forbidden. You can be jailed for printing or reading forbidden material." The Texans were amazed, but willing to accept that the Yorkers were that crazy.

Jeremiah continued, "Even though such things are illegal, they have existed since the beginning of time and the church always loses this particular battle. A man can walk into most book stores or cigar stands in York and purchase such material from a box underneath the counter. Since it is illegal, the publishers are, of course, anonymous and hard to trace. We plan to use such a publisher to print and distribute the book.

"We feel that we can get sufficient publicity to sell a lot of them if we arrest a few cigar store owners and have public trials for selling the book of 'secrets.' Of course, we will allow the sellers to publicly repent and get by with small fines. If the book is profitable, we are certain that more will be sold than the holy fires can consume."

The debate was spirited for the rest of the afternoon. Within an hour, the committee decided that the Yorker plan made sense. Of course, the fact that they had no other idea of what to do next made the plan sound even better. It took them several tries to figure out how to publish the book anonymously. They decided to follow the York plan there also. Even though erotic material was legal in Texas, many women still objected to it. Therefore, the distribution channels were less public than for other types of literature. It was decided to open a legal and apparently public company owned by totally fictitious people. It would print and ship one large run of the book and be closed before the reporters came calling.

They then selected committees to compose each section of the book, set up a review process, chewed over the details of how to print the book and disappear and generally spent the afternoon in happy scheming. After all, everyone loves to be in on a secret.

Chapter 32   Jones Phones Home

It turned out that Jeremiah was less comfortable at court than Artimus had been. Where Artimus had been closest to Baron Wilson and Emperor Adams, Jeremiah developed his closest relationships with Sir Greg and Sir Eric. He tended to spend more of this time at the farm rather than at the court. Jeremiah was like his brother in that he was not afraid to get his hands dirty and do practical work. This made him popular with the smiths.

However, impatience had led him and Eric to the bench they were at. The decision had been made to begin the production of vacuum tubes and powered amplifiers. Glass making was a common skill and the smiths were becoming proficient at the accurate machining that would be needed to make vacuum pumps. It was taking longer than they liked and that lead to the device on the table in front of them. Like early scientists, they worked in polished woods as much as with copper connections. The device they had built was once called an electrolytic detector. It used two contacts submerged in dilute sulfuric acid to detect and rectify the signal.

Sir Eric was listening intently to the static in the earphones as Jeremiah moved the adjusting knobs. Both of their eyes were on the clock on the desk. "Got it. Right there." Eric's eyes were lighting up. Jeremiah looked mildly confused. "That's odd. They aren't due on the air for another ten minutes. Monks are usually very timely." Eric handed the headphones to Jeremiah. "Here, listen. It's faint. It comes and goes, but it is definitely code."

Jeremiahs eyes squinted as he listened intently to the earphone. After several seconds he said, "You're right. It think it's code. It comes and goes. However, it isn't the abbey! Here listen again." He handed the phones to Eric. "It's clicks. Just clicks. The abbey sounds like a tone that starts and stops. It's a seven hundred and fifty cycle tone. These are just clicks."

No scientific researcher was ever more excited than these two men. They sat through the evening and into the night trying to hear more. Occasionally the clicks would return for a few seconds. Once, Eric even thought he heard a word spoken.

They speculated again and again about what they were hearing. Eric asked, "You were at the abbey. Did they ever mention hearing other signals."

"Never. Not once. Either they weren't paying attention or their rig couldn't pick it up."

Eric stirred in his chair. "Well, we are two thousand miles west of them. Maybe the source is west of here or down in Central America. It could be that the ship people are south of here."

Jeremiah looked puzzled. "The ship people?"

Eric answered, "Yep, the ship people. You must have read the reports about the *Star of India*. It has been three years now and we haven't heard any more news of it, but we are still prepared to see it again. They have to be years ahead of us and, if history is any guide, those who have power tend to use it. Since no one else has seen a ship like it, we are hoping that they can't build many of them yet. We could have years before they come, but it feels like they are out there."

Jeremiah was not convinced. "I don't doubt that the ship exists, but I think that these transmissions are probably from someone passing himself off as a wizard, or a couple of hermits trying to hold on to the old days. Maybe it's from a coastal watch from some small country that has held on to a military secret for hundreds of years. Whoever they are, either they are a long way away, or their rigs are very weak. I don't think we have to worry about them. Let's close up and head for the dorm."

Two months later, they had the rotary spark gap transmitter and a super heterodyne receiver working. They were both surprised at the huge size of a generator that was required. The project had been delayed while a new steam engine was built to power it.

This time they heard the weekly transmission from the abbey clearly. They also had a great time imagining the monks faces when they suddenly started receiving a transmission that started, "Bishop Jeremiah Jones with a coded message for the pope, as follows…" A message direct from the holy ghost wouldn't have surprised them more. Until that moment the monks had no idea that there were more radios in the world than the two in Yorker abbeys.

During the first week, they communicated daily with the abbey in South Carolina. They were able to receive the Yorker broadcasts every day, but the weaker crystal radios of the Yorkers often lost the Texas signal. During one of the clearer transmissions, they made arrangements to send a diplomatic box to the abbey with the parts for a super heterodyne receiver. They would seal the parts in a box filled with cotton. In the box would be diplomatic letter about the rare Destruction Day offering being made to the people of York by the Emperor of Texas.

While they were waiting for the receiver, the monks moved the primary transmitter from South Carolina to Albany. Before Jeremiah left Texas, he was able to have daily conversations with headquarters. He took back with him the parts for several more receivers.

Chapter 33 A Little Light Reading

The workers just accepted that executives always had screwy ideas. The rail that they were laying was obviously a waste of money. It was obviously much too heavy for what they needed. Then there was that screwy little guy who kept testing the plates between the rails for tightness. It was the same screwy little guy who told them that the gaps had to be bridged with wires to "keep lightning away from the passengers." What bull. Just something to make the bigwigs feel important by making you do extra work.

They had some fun that day. Just before lunch some skinny guy in a black suit had stood on the roadbed and screamed that they were doing Satan's work. Fred wanted to point out to the man that Satan didn't care how the horse pulled a wagon, but the other workers didn't have even that much patience. It was the black suit's bad luck that he had picked a bridge to make a stand on. It was his good luck that there was water in the river below, and it was a small bridge. The workers held their laughter until they could see him swimming below.

Lunch was brought out on a rail wagon with more ties. The cooks set up the tables and dished out stew and bread, lots of it. They had to serve fast or get bitched at by the men. Lunch was as short as gulped food could make it and work was dawn till dusk. They were laying two tracks with two teams. There was a bonus for the most track laid every day and another bonus for being furthest ahead. If you won, the pay was great. If you lost, it was still good.

They had to build a crossover switch or a turnout about every other mile. It allowed empty supply wagons to be returned past the incoming full ones. They still often built five miles a day. One day when things went perfectly, they built ten miles of track.

Passenger traffic started running as soon as the tracks reached each town. People were anxious to travel. It was only twice as fast as the old coaches, but it was smooth and comfortable. If it hadn't been a swear word, people might have said it was 'modern'. The standard coach car was twenty-four feet long, ten feet wide and had glass windows in the front. In bad weather, curtains would protect the passengers from the elements. It was drawn by either two or four large horses. Compared to a stage coach, it was heaven.

Larger teams of horses pulled two or three freight wagons hitched together. Some of the freight wagons were enclosed, but most were flatbeds. The normal procedure for shippers was to rent space for a standard four, six, or twelve foot crate. The box would be packed at the shipper's location, sent by wagon to the railhead and then loaded by crane or ramp onto the freight wagon. Shippers were charged by the size and weight of the crates. As one driver and one team could handle several shipments, it was cheaper to use the rail freight over long distances even when you counted the cost of loading and unloading the boxes.

Fred was surprised when one of his mates said, "You know, the ancients had railroads like this and they traveled a hundred miles an hour."

Fred knew a campfire story when he heard one. "Bull. Anyway, how would you know what an Ancient did?"

His mate looked conspiratorial, "I bought a book on it. Back at Temple city."

Fred snorted, "There ain't no such book. No one really knows what the Ancients did, except that they got themselves killed off."

His friend smiled like a man with a secret. "There is too. I'll let you read it when I'm done. It's called 'Secrets of the Ancients.' and it's got all kinda stuff in it. Of course, they warn you that you gotta keep it to yourself. The shop keeper told me that they don't just let anyone buy one of these books. I got it 'cause one of the chapters is on railroads and I'm a railroad worker. They had big engines that run off steam and they'd pull a hundred cars at a time. Top speed about a hundred miles an hour."

Fred was still not a believer. "You couldn't go a hundred miles an hour. The human body couldn't take the strain. You'd fall apart like a broken egg."

While Fred and his mate argued and jawed, a lot of people were reading that 'secret' book. Most figured it was a fantasy. As predicted, some read it because they were interested, some because they were outraged.

The emperor emeritus carried the ball for the imperial family. He had nowhere near his wife's problem with lying in a good cause. He told the reporters, "A book on the Ancients? No, I haven't read it. Even though I am retired, I don't have much time for reading. What would I say to the people who think the book should be banned? I'd say that it isn't fitting to try and tell any Texan what he can read or what he can think. A man minds his own business!

"I would also remind those who don't like the book that I will support their right to say so. They can complain to the publisher, challenge the writer to a duel, burn as many copies as they can buy or throw them on the fires next Destruction Day. I will support their right to complain the same as I support the rights of the readers to read. Texas is a free country. Someday I might even read the book myself just to see what all the excitement is about.

"As far as forbidding people to know things, I never saw an advantage to keeping a man stupid unless he was your enemy. Free people can't be kept dumb. I might also point out that knowing and doing are two different things. Knowing is a man's right. Doing is what can be dangerous. You there, Harold isn't it?" The emperor pointed at one of the reporters. "I bet you have had more than one impure thought today when you saw the beautiful women out on this lovely spring day. Don't deny it or I'll pull out a bible and make you swear! You think your wife should leave you? Of course not. Thinking is one thing and doing is another. Knowing is a mans right. If anyone does anything dangerous, we will be watching."

The battle wasn't won that easily. There were protests in the streets and lectures from the pulpit. Some books were burned and some store owners were threatened. In the end it just made the book more sought after. It did both sides good. The Texans, mostly younger men, defended their right to do what they damned well wanted to do. The fearful, mostly women and ministers, held on tight to their new cause and trotted it out whenever they needed something to complain about. In four or five months, both sides were worn out. Like the battles that ended because the participants ran out of ammo, this battle stopped because they ran out of energy.

Funny thing is that they never were able to interview the publisher. It seems that they fell on hard times and had to close up shop even before all of the books were shipped.

Chapter 34   Baron Artimus

This time Artimus brought his wife when he returned to Texas. The first dinner at the palace was a small one. Only Baron and Baroness Wilson and the imperial couple dined with Sir Artimus and Lady Linda Jones.

When the empress learned that Lady Artimus was with her husband, she insisted that they stay in the royal section of the palace. Artimus' preference for the officer's quarters was unimportant compared to the ladies wishes. The women were dressed in semiformal court attire. The men were in uncomfortable pipe stem pants, stiff shirts and paisley vests.

The empress was leaning over toward Lady Artimus. "You must tell us about your trip. I've never been on a ship. Were you scared?"

Lady Wilson put her napkin in her lap, "Not really. It was hard to get used to at first, because it never stops moving. Artimus was very sick the second day out." Artimus was blushing inside. Only a wife could tell such a story and the wife was still talking. "After the first few days, you stop noticing it. You just sway with the boat and keep on walking. In fact, I loved it. It was the first time that Artimus and I have been alone since we got married."

The empress interrupted, "Alone, I hear that there are a hundred men just to move the sails. You must have been very crowded."

"Not really. We had our own cabin and, thank God, we had to leave our servants behind. The cabin was only ten feet square, but there was a lock on the door and no one outside of it. You cannot know how little privacy there is in the Papacy. Why, a servant walked into our room during our honeymoon to deliver a hot water bottle. Even when you lock them out, they sit in front of your door waiting, guarding, and listening." She put her hand on her husbands arm. "I know that my husband has a lot of work to do, but this trip has been the honeymoon that we never had."

Inside, Artimus suffered. Listening to your wife or your mother talk about you is just about the worse thing that can happen to a man's pride.

The empress gestured at the walls around them. "Here in Texas, we maintain some privacy. This suite, for instance, is for invited guests and family only. His majesty and I also have our private apartments that even servants don't normally enter. It is almost like having our own home.

You know, we do like having you and Artimus here. He is an old friend and I am certain that you will also be one. However, we do have a very nice home in the city. My husband used it during his bachelor days and it has been empty since." Actually, her husband had used it for quiet meetings with pliable females, but that was never discussed. He had not been there since he and the empress visited it during their courtship. "Perhaps you would like to use it during your stay here. You could still spend your time here when Artimus is on the road, but you could also have your own home."

Lady Artimus was obviously excited. "Could we do that, Honey? Could we have our own home for awhile?" At home, she would never have publicly addressed her husband as "Honey."

Artimus thought fleetingly about how much we liked the simplicity of the officer's quarters and enjoyed the easy company of the cafeteria, and said with a smile, "Of course, Dear." What else could any man say?

The empress was irrepressible tonight. She and Lady Artimus seemed to be old friends ten minutes after they met. Perhaps it was because only a handful of women in the world could share the experience of marrying the future ruler of their country. "You know, we will have to adjust your status. Sir Artimus was perfectly happy to be a knight of the empire, but he really should have a little more status now that you are here. Being a Baroness would explain why you are staying in the imperial apartments."

Her husband interrupted. "Actually, we have been debating that. We are considering a status of 'Ambassador From York'. It may be time to drop the charade. It has been over three years since his first trip. Perhaps the time for the deception has passed."

Artimus leaned forward. "You may be right, but I do value my work with the committee and it's easier if I do not have to assume consular duties. We may have to drop the pretense during my trip here, but I would prefer to stay a Texan a little bit longer."

The empress patted Lady Artimus hand. "We will announce to the papers tomorrow that Artimus has been given the title of 'Baron of Las Cruces' in appreciation of his service to the Crown. We'll announce that the ceremony has already taken place in NewMex, but we can still have a reception party here at the palace."

The men were grateful when dinner was over and they could retire to the smoking room. This time the empress and the ladies went to the parlor for sherry and women's conversation.

Once they relaxed in overstuffed chairs and had their cigars lit, they asked Artimus how things were going in York. "Not as well as here in Texas, but I may have some important news for you. One of our sea captains has sighted another steel ship. She damned near ran down one our ships. They were on the outbound run to England when they spotted her running abeam of them. She was a lot faster than they were, but they kept her in sight for almost a day. She must have been out of the same yards as the *Star of India*, but she was armed different. You said the Star was a barque about two hundred twenty feet long. The captain said it had twelve gun ports on each side, and had about four deck guns. This ship was the 'Go For Broke II'. She was also a barque about two hundred feet long, but she was built without gun ports. She carried ten cannon on deck and four swivel guns. She also looked like she had a 50 caliber machine gun on a mount. The owner had to be a government or be pretty damned rich to afford that kind of armament. Some one out there is far in advance of us. Whether or not they are currently hostile, we need to be on our guard."

They talked into the night about railroads and radios and wives and guns. Artimus recounted his ocean voyages and Adams recounted his battles with Nebraskans. They talked until the women insisted that they go home.

Chapter 35   The Dogleg

It was no longer practical for the entire Archeology Committee to meet in Austin. The original members were often heading up work groups in other parts of the county. Many of the new workers were not even sworn conspirators and were only troopers or state workers sworn to secrecy. Artimus' return, however, was a special occasion and all of the original members did attend the meeting. All were anxious to hear about York and all wanted to help plan the next step. It felt good to look around the group and see every face in place just as it had been three years before.

Artimus began by summarizing the progress in York.

"It will be somewhat harder there. I'm afraid that our people are not as fiercely independent as Texans. We published the book we planned but I am afraid more went into the holy fires than went into homes. We even had to have a few heresy trials of people who sold it. Of course, they repented and were forgiven. We have started a railroad from Albany to Florida. The abbeys have been encouraged to build sections to link themselves together. We do not yet have as centralized a plan as Texas, but there is good progress.

"The radio tubes that you sent have been very helpful. We now have working radios in three abbeys. One of the three is powered with a steam engine.

"We have been working on a new concept. We have been working on the assumption that all technology would start alarm bells among our more conservative subjects. However, some of our Bishops theorized that many technological products were lost not because of fear of technology, but simply because the skills were lost.

"As you know, all glass in both York and Texas is blown by tradesman. That means that it's expensive and the largest pane you can get is about five feet by four feet. Even that is very rare. We found plans for a glass making machine where the glass is made by pouring it onto a pool of molten tin. Even without a power source, you can make virtually any sized pane of glass quick and cheap and with semi skilled labor. People love it. One of the abbeys has licensed out the plans to several private companies and no one has objected.

"That will be the new direction in York. Instead of trying to introduce electric lights in one step we will try getting people used to changes one step at a time. First we improve gas mantles, then we talk about electric bulbs. We learned from the emperor emeritus that letting people make money creates allies, so the improvements will be farmed out to private businesses as much as possible."

He also told them about the new steel ship and they discussed the ramifications of another industrial powerhouse in the world.

Sir Wayne presented his new plan for technological acclimation. "Toys. What could be less threatening than a cute little toy? and what parent wants to tell his child he can't have the toy he wants for Christmas? This Christmas, children will be able to have an aeolipile. The aeolipile was a sort of steam engine invented by Heron of Alexandria, a Greek philosopher, over two thousand years ago."

Turning to the easel, he said, "It looks like this. Just a ball with two bent arms sticking out. It's attached to a kettle of water. When you heat the kettle over a fire, the water boils and the steam makes the ball rotate. It is perfectly and visibly harmless and a good lesson in steam power. The team at the farm is also looking into other toys."

Sir Greg summarized for the Texans. The new farm was building steam engines as fast as possible and then storing them away for later use. They had completed ten locomotives and twenty stationary engines of various sizes. Currently they were stored at the farm until a plan to introduce them was developed. There was a permanent facility where two skilled smiths made electronic components. Vacuum tubes, capacitors, and resistors were now available to the smiths working on radio.

They still had not been successful in producing a good light bulb, but generators had been made from parts that they produced themselves. Things were moving very fast. Toward the end of the formal meeting, Baron Artimus took the floor again. "I have heard that you have tested the telegraph links as the railways have gone in. As you know, our radio links are also getting much better. We now have clear telegraphy connections, and hope to have voice transmission by the end of the year. Unfortunately, a radio rig with its huge antenna and noisy steam engine would be rather impractical to place here in Austin. I would, therefore, suggest that we activate the telegraph links between here and the farm and between New Galveston and the farm. That would give us dogleg connection into Albany and Florida. We could send or receive messages by telegraph between here and the farm and then transcribe to or from the radio rigs into York. In addition to allowing a closer cooperation between our countries, it would allow an early alarm to be sounded if the ship people approach either of our countries."

Either it was a very good idea that did not need discussion, or the members were anxious to get to dinner, as the suggestion was adopted immediately.

Chapter 36   The War Wagons

This would be the empress's first visit to the farm. In the past, the prospect of an upriver boat ride was enough to make her decide to stay in Austin. Now both she and Baroness Artimus were joining their husbands for the trip. The reason was the new rail car. Nothing like the imperial rail car had been seen for over five hundred years. The private car was only thirty feet long, but it had room for comfortable couches, a small dining table, a tiny kitchen, and a water closet. You could even walk around while it was moving. The windows were glass on all four sides. It was pulled by four horses harnessed in a single line to give them more hoof room between the tracks.

While the empress and the baronesses were having tea inside, the men decided to take a little rum and some cigars outside where the air was fresh and the voices quiet. They sat on the jump seats that folded down on the tiny rear platform and puffed away.

Artimus spoke first, "You, know, we are going to have to make the big step soon. We can go on like this for another year or two, but sooner or later, we have to go for the big ones like opening medical schools or using steam engines."

Wilson was staring at the tracks receding behind them. "I know, and we are about out of ideas. This railroad is the only real visible difference we've made. The funny thing is that the backlash hasn't been nearly as bad as we expected. Maybe the old emperor is right. Men who are making money don't have time to make a fuss."

Artimus looked wistful. "That is more of a problem in York. Your father was able to sell stock in the railroad before it was even done and now Winnie Wigwam is making a lot of people money. Unfortunately, in York, over a third of our industrial production, and our money, is tied up in the abbeys. They act like the old time plantations, growing corn, raising kids, and manufacturing buggies. They are almost self contained towns and that makes them almost self absorbed."

The emperor looked mildly surprised. "I'm amazed that you can get so many men to live the monk's life. Most of our men like their women too much to join a monastic order, no matter how rich the order is."

It was Artimus turn to chuckle. "You don't know the monastic life in York. Monks gave up celibacy at the same time priests did. These are all married men and if you don't have a wife, the abbey will find one for you. The second American pope declared celibacy to be an affront to God. He said God needed a lot more children and it was our duty to produce them. It's now a pretty good life with fresh air, family, and neighbors."

They were both silent for awhile. Finally Wilson leaned back from the rail. "Well, maybe the ship people will come. No one will complain about a steam engine or a telegraph if it's saving his life."

Artimus and the women were impressed by the changes in the farm. The private coach rolled right through to gates and up to the main compound. Tracks now went through a station at the road side before continuing on to a small rail yard barely visible behind the compound, and there were sidings at each of the factory buildings. The farm itself was more impressive than ever. In addition to the new passenger station, the hidden buildings now included a new barracks and two new factory buildings.

All three wives were strong, competent, and capable partners for their husbands, but they were still wives. While the men toured the factories, their wives did their job of filling in all of the other wives on the news of Austin. It was time for tea, cakes, and all of the gossip that wasn't fit to print in the newspapers.

Out in the yard, the men were all sitting in the cab of the latest steam engine. Artimus was asking Greg, "How many of these do we have now?"

"Fourteen done completely and two more in progress. It's getting easier to build them as we get more outside part suppliers up to speed."

The emperor glanced at Artimus. "Actually, Artimus has another idea that we discussed on the way up here. His suggestion was we that build some kind of steam engine that could be retrofitted into existing boats. We could then store the engines near the shipyards and convert to power as soon as the time is right."

Artimus took over. "My reasoning is that any threat that either country faces will probably come from the sea. It's not that the sea people with the steel ships are imminent, it's just that our borders with each other are safe and we are in no danger from our other neighbors. That means that any threat would come in from the sea and attack our coasts."

Greg looked thoughtful. "What makes you think that, after five hundred years, we are in danger of invasion? No one does that these days."

Artimus answered, "The radio signals. You and Jeremiah heard some faint signals when you set up the new radio. Now that we have the super heterodyne receivers in York, we are also getting occasional hits. They don't happen often and we don't know where they are from, but there are other things going on. You know we have contacts with some other Catholic countries. Last year, Northern China built at least two steam powered riverboats. In the middle east, there have been some serious border wars, people actually invading and occupying other countries. Things are happening out there. I get the feeling that after five hundred years of darkness, we aren't the only ones trying to light a few candles."

Greg was chewing on his lip. "I know, I've had the same feeling ever since we got those signals. Tell you what, Eric, Mitch and several other members of the committee are here now. Maybe we need to set up a working meeting tonight. Do a little brainstorming."

The meeting was rather large for being done on the spur of the moment. Even the new 'Lieutenant' O'Brien was there as he had been working with the security teams at the farm. The three wives did not attend the meeting as the Baronesses were not formal members of the committee and the empress did not want to insult them with her abandonment. The emperor opened the meeting with his concerns about possible progress in other countries, including his concerns about the steel ships and the radio transmissions that had been received. "In conclusion, it is the opinion of several members that we should turn our attentions, in part, to projects that could strengthen the nation's defenses. Of course, the rangers will develop programs with conventional weapons and tactics. Our work here will be to provide the edge, to develop whatever new tools we feel can help. Of course, it will probably take several months to finalize our plans, but it's handy that we are all together to begin the process. This meeting is now open for discussion."

Sir Eric spoke first. "I agree with you wholeheartedly, but perhaps not for the same reasons. I don't believe that the radio transmissions necessarily mean that we have competition. It's possible that we are hearing scavengers using, but not necessarily understanding, Ancient equipment."

The emperor, as did others, looked doubtful. "How can they be using five hundred year old equipment? Did the Ancients actually build that well?"

"It is theoretically possible, Sire. During the last fifty years of the old era, most electronics were made of solid pieces of material. Given the right conditions, they would never wear out." He paused for a moment. "It would, however, still mean that they were not A-techs and that they certainly have no fear of electronics. Perhaps it's irrelevant where they got the radios."

The emperor continued, "Perhaps that is also the point. It doesn't matter exactly what is going on in the world, there is enough going on where we need to look to our borders. Do we have any specific suggestions at this meeting or do we need to form a work group for the next meeting?"

Mitchell leaned forward. "The mention of steamboats in China suggests an idea for us. We are not ready to build steamboats quite yet, but we could build conversion engines. Most of the coast guard boats are schooners built to two standard plans. We could design a steam engine that was ready to bolt in, something where the boiler and firebox went to the hold and the engine bolted to the deck or the sides. It might run a pair of water wheels at the back of the boat or maybe we could design a propeller shaft that went over the side or back of the boat. Since there are only two types of boats that it would have to fit, we could make one or two designs and have as many powered boats as we need. We could test the designs here and then warehouse them in ports ready to install. If we have to show these to the public, it would be to a public that is getting shot at and likely to be grateful for the help."

The emperor brightened. "Excellent suggestion. Unless the committee objects, you can put together a work team and start on the project. Next?"

One of the smiths had the next idea. "Cannons. Less than half or our ports have defensive cannons. Right now, most of our artillery pieces are cap fired muzzle loaders. They are good enough as field pieces, but slow to load and not very accurate. We have a few rifled breech loaders, but they are just too expensive to produce without power lathes. If we set up a large steam powered lathe here, we could turn out some large rifled cannon barrels for port defense. We wouldn't have to make the whole cannons here. We could tell people that we have the world's biggest set of water wheels driving a metal lathe, and contract with private companies to finish the cannons elsewhere. If we can get cannons large enough to throw shells four or five miles, we would have an effective coastal defense without needing many of them."

As it was an evening meeting, there was only time to flesh out the first two ideas and reject a few others. The emperor closed the meeting with, "We will be continuing this discussion at the next meeting. If you cannot attend the meeting, please feel free to submit your comments through a coworker. Now, it's time to rejoin the ladies."

Two days later, they were back on the railroad heading for Austin. There was a low bench built into the roof at each end of the car where the trainman could sit with his feet dangling over the edge. The emperor and Wilson were sitting on the rear bench with beakers of gin, clutching their coats around them, and watching the track disappear behind them. It was not a talking time, but after a while Wilson said, "Remember that ride to York? Remember how sore we were when we got there?"

"Yep. I remember it was like an all day stampede followed by a marathon. Mostly, I remember how saddle sore I was when we rode into town."

"Do you think it would have been as exciting if we had ridden into town on a streetcar?"

Chapter 37   Time To Go

Three more months passed before they found out how right they were. They were at dinner in the imperial suite. Even though the Baroness Artimus loved her little house in the city, the four royals, the emperor and empress, 'Baron' Artimus and 'Baroness' Artimus, ate together as often as not. Artimus no longer had the luxury of cafeteria dinner and poker with the boys. It was now a servant supplied dinner and polite conversation or quiet plotting.

The empress had noticed a fleeting sadness cross the Baroness' face and guessed the reason. "You shouldn't worry. I am certain that your children are fine."

"Oh, I know it, but I miss them so much. I probably miss them more than they miss me. My oldest loves his uncle Jeremiah and his cousins. He's probably in heaven now. His sister loves Jeremiah's wife and her grandfather and now she sees them every day. I just hope that they won't change too much before we get back."

Artimus was reassuring. "It's only another six months before we rotate back and you will be surprised how fast it goes."

It was at that moment that the servant showed up in an agitated state. "Your majesty. There is a trooper in the hallway. He insists that he has a message that you will want to see now."

"Show him in. I'll meet him in my office."

Less than five minutes after the emperor left to meet the messenger, the servant returned to the dining room. "If it pleases you, Baron Artimus, the emperor requests your presence in his office."

The emperor was at his desk, holding out a message. "Believe it or not, this is our first dogleg message. This is a transcript of a radio message that was sent from Albany to the farm and then by telegraph to the ranger station. It's for you and it's not good news."

Artimus took the message. It was addressed to "Bishop Artimus Jones, Commander of God's Southern Army." It was short and pointed. "Naples attacked by enemy fleet. Tampa threatened. You are recalled immediately."

"It's the news that we feared. I will need to return home immediately. I will be leaving tomorrow if transportation can be arranged."

The emperor was trying to think fast. "Our coast guard has some fast sloops in Galveston and Port Arthur. The rail line goes as far as Port Arthur. We'll send the private car there and then assign a flotilla to get you home. You probably don't want to go directly into the war zone, but we can get you to Tallahassee or Clearwater. If the Tampa radio station is still up, we can get some situation information from them."

They hurried back to the dining room. Artimus blurted out, "Honey, I have to go back to York tomorrow. We have been attacked in Florida and I have to rejoin my command."

"I'll start packing now, or can we leave the luggage?"

"You can't go. There is an enemy fleet between here and home. I'll be sailing into a war zone."

"I am not afraid."

"I am. We cannot chance making orphans of Joseph and Cindy. They don't like their uncle that much. You will have to stay here until it is safe to travel."

The empress put her arm around the other woman's shoulder. "You do not understand. She will worry herself to death about the children if she doesn't get home. Sire, can't we arrange something that won't go through the war zone?"

The emperor tried to be reassuring without making a commitment. "When we have more information from Florida, we will try to arrange something. We need to know where the war zone is before we can plan to avoid it. Now Artimus and I need to get down to the telegraph. We may be late coming home."

The telegraph office was a small windowless storage building in the rail yards. The only thing at all odd about it was that the "ground wire" from the rails was apparently grounded under the building. There were two men manning the key. The emperor asked, "Is there anyone up at the farm?"

"Yes, Sire. The station is manned twenty four hours a day. We got the message for you about an hour ago."

"Get on the key. Tell the farm to fire up the rig and try to contact Tampa. They will keep trying until they get through. Baron, what message should we send first?"

Artimus reached for a sheet of paper and pen. "Send this: Bishop Artimus returning by sea. Request Situation report. They should keep sending it until they get answer. If Tampa requests identify verification, tell them to send the code: prodigal son."

As the telegrapher reached for his key, Artimus and Adams found chairs and coffee. It could be a long night. The answer came back in a little over an hour. "Tampa wants to know what code to use."

Artimus said, "Reply: No code. Send in clear. Have no time to decode and enemy knows where they are. Repeat the identification."

This time less than five minutes passed before the key began to clack. "Situation Grave. Enemy fleet estimated as many as two hundred vessels. Coastal attacks occurring at Coral Gables and Naples. Goal seems to be major raiding. Extensive burning of outlying towns, missing civilians. Suggest landing no further south than Crystal River. Suggest you send landing location in code."

Artimus said, "Tell them to ask if the enemy has steel ships and if they are getting any radio transmissions from the fleet."

This time the answer took longer. "No steel ships sighted. Estimate fleet consists of about fifty heavy ships of the line, fifty armed cargo carriers, fifty or more support craft and coastal sloops. No radio traffic."

The emperor sighed. "It could be worse. At least they are not likely to have any super surprises. They are a conventional fleet. Of course, they could be hiding the fact that they can pick up our radios. Better switch to code before you ask where your troops are."

"Good idea." Artimus reached for more paper and wrote for the telegrapher, "Code B1. Send disposition our forces."

The communication slowed down then as they had to decode each incoming message before they could reply. It turned out to be very difficult to keep the strings of numbers accurate enough for translation. Random numbers are hard to check. Within an hour, they had established a protocol wherein Tampa sent to the Farm, and the Farm sent the entire message back to Tampa for confirmation before sending it on. Long messages sometimes were sent three or four times. They then had to repeat the checking process on the telegraph leg. Sometime during the evening, the emperor sent a rider to Port Arthur with a message to prepare three coastal sloops for sailing the next day.

By morning, they had gone through a second shift of telegraphers and Artimus had a picture of where his troops were, and in what condition, and had a plan to join them. They were too tired to ride their horses back to the palace and settled for sleeping though a buggy ride.

Chapter 38   Where The Heart Is

He returned home early in the morning. Night work was rare in a society without electric lights, but not unknown. Gillis worked under the big gas lamps as a switch man in the rail yard. The rail cars had to be prepared all night for the early morning departures and sometimes cars came in at night, guided by oil lamps mounted on the tops of the coaches. His wife had arisen with the sun to prepare his supper. Their home was a comfortable one with a pump in the kitchen and an inside water closet with a drain to the Ancient sewers. Both children were still asleep upstairs in their bedroom. In his bedroom, his wife had placed hot bricks under the covers of their bed.

As he sat down at the big oak table in the kitchen, his wife was serving his supper stew of potatoes and beef. "How did it go at work tonight, Dear?"

He shook his head slightly. "I don't know, there's something strange going on in that yard"

"What do you mean strange, Dear."

"The emperor was there last night. He and some man I never saw spent the whole evening in a storage shed."

"Oh, you must be wrong. Are you sure that it was Emperor Adams? It must have been someone else."

"No, it was the emperor, alright. I've seen him before, and that isn't all. Something funny is going on in that building. I kind of accidentally walked by it. There were evil smells coming from that place. It smelled like sulfur and brimstone in there and I heard a woodpecker pecking all night. I tell you, wife, there is something evil going on."

His wife had sat down opposite him while he talked. "Now, Gilley, Emperor Adams is a good man, just like his father. I'm sure that he has a good reason for anything that he is doing."   She looked around the comfortable kitchen with the copper pans on the walls and the iron stove. "Besides, this is the first steady wages you've gotten in a long time. I don't want you to let silly thoughts get you fired. Now you finish your supper and get to bed while I get the children off to school. Then I'll be in with a little something that will get your mind off all this silly stuff, if you're not too tired."

While Gilley struggled with his conscience and his fear, Artimus and Adams struggled with timetables. Artimus was listing to his wife sniffle while she packed his bag and trying not to be impatient. Adams was pacing around the room. "It's two hundred miles to Port Arthur. If we take a light rail car and change horses at Galveston, that's about fifteen hours, maybe ten if we can get fresh sets of horses on the way. We might make it in time for you to sail on the tide tonight. The *City Of Waco* is getting ready to sail. With good winds, she'll have you in Clearwater in about three days, five days if the winds are bad." He knew he was talking to himself, but even emperors get cases of nerves occasionally. "We'll get Linda to Albany as soon as we know the way is clear."

Artimus was ardently repeating, "No, Dear. You can't come with us. This will be Mongol riding. It's just me, His Majesty and the driver and if the driver's weight slows us down, we'll dump him off on the trackside. We have to make that tide."

The empress took her arm. "It's alright, Dear. We'll be able to hear from Tampa when he gets there. Remember, we have the radio now. In the meantime, we'll sit here and do what soldiers wives always do. We'll try not to worry them too much."

The gentle reminder of her duties almost stopped the sniffling, but the tears still ran down the baroness face. "All right. You're right. Artimus, Dear, don't worry about me, I'll be safe here with Her Majesty until we meet in Albany. I feel a little foolish for crying like a schoolgirl." Her resolve returned and her tears dried as she remembered that she, too, had married a future king and current warrior. Weakness was not allowed.

Two mounted troopers waited at the front door with two saddled mounts. The servant handed Artimus' duffle up to one of the troopers. The wives clung for a few long moments to their departing husbands. The empress said, no, Shirley said quietly to Burton, "Take care of him. Linda is very scared, and so am I." Then they were mounted, and, suddenly, away.

At the nearest station, an inspection wagon had been prepared for them. It was about the size of a surrey with two bench seats, a windshield, and a small cargo platform at the back. It had been hastily re-rigged with an in-line four horse harness, and two picnic baskets had been tossed on the rear cargo deck. The station master was waiting by the wagon. "Your advance riders went though here about three hours ago, Your Majesty. They will have the track cleared and spare horses waiting when you need them. Good Luck and a safe journey, Sire." The driver and one trooper took the front bench, Artimus and the emperor the rear seat. There was barely time for a "Thank you, well done," before they were pulling away from the station.

It was a fast trip and uncomfortable, but compared to horseback, almost enjoyable. They changed horses about every thirty miles. About two hours into the trip, they cracked open the first picnic basket and had a dinner of sandwiches, beer and fruit. As the horses did not need constant attention, the driver was able to turn in his seat to join them. Darkness fell about the time they hit Galveston but they rigged the oil lamps and kept on going. Two years before, such a trip would have been a symphony of aching butts, chapped thighs, and painful guts. On this trip, they had time to catch a guilty nap.

They arrived in Port Arthur in just over fourteen hours, having passed their advance riders about thirty miles out. They took local horses and went immediately to the harbor. The first messengers had reached the port about an hour earlier and the *City of Waco* was the center of activity as she prepared to sail. A crew was always on board the coast guard ship, but she was not always provisioned for a voyage of unknown duration. They had two gangplanks out to the dock and men were carrying boxes and crates in the gaslight of the docks. A squirrel cage crane was loading powder and ball down to the gun deck through the cargo hatches. The first mate and the captain were supervising from different ends of the ship.

Captain Granger recognized the emperor before he got the ramp. "Your Majesty. Over here. We will be ready to sail in an hour." The emperor and Artimus hurried up the gang plank and over to the captain. The emperor returned the captains salute as he approached, said, "Bring the first mate and the purser. We need to meet in your cabin", and he kept moving aft. A few minutes later the captain, first mate, and a younger officer entered the cabin to find the emperor and Artimus already seated in front of the Captain's desk. There was a awkward moment before the captain decided that the fact that Artimus was seated meant that they should also be seated. The emperor began without delay. "Purser, please be ready to write out your orders. I will dictate them now and sign them at the end of this meeting." The younger crew member turned around and took paper and pen from the writing table and laid it on the desk. "Ready, Sire."

"Start writing when I signal. First, Captain, do you recognize the man with me?"

"Yes, Sire. He is the Baron Artimus Jones of Kansas. We met at the Christmas Ball in Austin."

"I now inform you that this is also Bishop Artimus Jones, Heir Apparent To The Papacy of York, Ambassador of York to the Empire of Texas, and a valued ally of the Empire. He is also a personal friend."

Captain Granger was too Texan to look surprised. He bowed slightly from where he sat. "Welcome aboard Your Eminence."

The emperor continued, "I will not be sailing with you. Your first objective is to get Bishop Artimus home. There is a fleet of unknown origin attacking the west coast of Florida. His eminence needs to rejoin his troops. Your orders are: You are to return Bishop Artimus safely to Florida. Your fleet will operate in accordance with his wishes until you have completed the first objective. Your second objective is to gather information about the attacking fleet. Your third objective is to harass that fleet whenever it's safe to do so. If you meet a Yorker warship, you will raise the parlay flag and offer joint operations. You will, however, avoid combat unless you have overwhelming strength. Purser, write that out for my signature. If my instructions got here in time, two smaller ships will sail with you. On a personal note, when dealing with Bishop Jones, you may want to keep in mind that he has been in combat for the Empire and has earned its respect."

The captain felt mildly insulted by the warning but realized that the emperor was under the stress of haste. "I have always respected Baron Artimus and I do welcome the chance to serve with Bishop Jones. We will get you home, Your Eminence. With your permission, we sail in less than an hour. Once we are at sea, we can discuss where you want to be placed. Your Majesty, may we be excused to complete our preparations?"

The purser stayed behind to complete the transcription of the orders. The emperor and Artimus stood by the ship's railing silently marking the passage of an era. Baron Artimus would never return and the committee had suddenly become an operational institution. Artimus voiced it first, "They aren't afraid of the plagues. They're big and nasty and not afraid to invade. The world is changing."

Adams answered, "It's a good thing we got a head start. I better get on shore. They will be leaving soon. I'll try to keep Linda here as long as possible. If that fleet leaves, it will be easier to get her home, but, if we have to, I'll send her overland on a caravan."

Artimus' chuckle was forced. "I'm not worried about her. She and Her Majesty can spend two weeks trying to figure out how many more dinner invitations 'Her Imminence' gets compared to 'Baroness'. Just keep her busy."

They shook hands knowing it might be the last time they did so and the emperor strode out to his horse. Unwritten rule thirteen of The Code was *Real men don't look back.*

Chapter 39   Hi, Ho, Away We Go

The trip was as fast as they had hoped. The wind was good enough to make over ten knots most of the way. The captain laid on most of the sails in the locker. Artimus was in the bow admiring the spinnaker when the captain came up behind him. "Beautiful isn't it? You know, when you told me that you were in the secret service, I assumed it was the Texas secret service. When this is over, I would love to hear the story. I have good news. If this wind holds, we can be near Crystal River in about three days. Problem is, we'll have to leave our escort behind because they can't keep up with us if we crowd on that much sail. Do you want to chance it?"

"Sounds like a good idea. We'll run from anything we see anyway. You can rendezvous with the other ships after you drop me off."

Despite a close attention to the horizon, they never made contact with a Yorker ship. That was not surprising as most national fleets were astonishingly small in an era where invasion was virtually unknown and travel unpopular. Their small flotilla was a significant percentage of the Texas fleet. The raiders would have to be stopped on the beaches and they could pick any beach they wanted.

The good news was that they didn't meet any raiders either. As predicted, they arrived off the coast at Crystal River just three days after leaving Port Arthur. They were greeted with a cannon ball that fell well short of the ship. The captain was calm as he shouted out, "Raise the parlay flag! They must think we're part of the pirate fleet! Bishop Jones, how do we announce our presence?"

Artimus answered, raise the flags 'B', 'S', and 'P' and hope they believe you."

"I might suggest that if we do this again, that you mention the cannon a little earlier in the trip."

"I would have, but we didn't have any cannon here when I left. Hell, if they had had them longer, they might not have missed."

The firing seemed to have stopped. Even for amateurs, it was a long time since the one round had been fired.

The captain looked through his spyglass. "It seems to have stopped. We'll try putting a boat over the side. I want to send a marine squad with you just in case those aren't your friends. If they are your friends, try to get a message up and down the coast that the Texans are the good guys."

Artimus had donned his bishop's medallion and ring before he threw his duffel down to the boat and climbed over the side. His thought as we went over the side was, *It looks like it will be another interesting trip.*

It turned out that there were a hundred fifty papal troops manning two cannons in the town. The civilians had been evacuated inland and the troops were under orders to retreat if the cannons did not discourage a landing. There was nothing left in the town worth killing and dying for. The commander of the town had been told that the main army was moving toward Tampa on the old highway 75. He provided Artimus with a fast horse and a ten man escort for his move inland. He cut inland and made the highway the next day. The road was jammed with wagons and carts headed north and hundreds of people without wheels were walking along the side of the old highway. The main body of troops seemed to be about two hours closer to

Tampa so he headed south with his escort.

By the end of the second day, he was approaching the rear guard of a large column of troops. He and the escort stopped for a half an hour to rest their horses and themselves before the final ride and then caught up with the rear of the column. As he passed the rear guard, he shouted over to the sergeant leading them, "Soldier! Where is your commanding officer?"

The soldier looked as if we was not going to answer and then changed his mind when he saw the bishop's medallion on Artimus. "Everyone is in a command wagon about a mile ahead. Bishop Jeremiah is in charge." A command wagon was like a house trailer. Similar contraptions had been used by the Romans, Mongols, Chinese, Americans, and Germans. It's advantage today was that is was easy to find. Even though the army was moving at a walking pace, it took almost another half hour before they reached it.

Artimus brought his horse up to wagon and then swung aboard the rear platform without dismounting. One of his escorts took his horse as he left it and moved into position behind the wagon.

Inside, his brother was at a map table with several other officers. He tried not to look surprised when Artimus opened the door. Future kings, even backup future kings, do not look surprised. The "Glad to see you, how are the kids?" would have to wait until later. "Artimus! I didn't expect you so soon, but I'm glad you made it. Steward, His Eminence could probably use some refreshments after his long ride." He sat down and motioned to the officers around him to follow suit. "We've got a lot of briefing to do. Why don't you eat while we go over the situation?"

"Thank you, it's been a hungry ride. Could someone tell the troopers with me where they can find some food and rest?" They waited politely until Artimus was seated with his beer and sausages before they went on. "As you probably know, they hit us about two weeks ago. The first place they hit was Naples. They came ashore in force and ransacked the town. They spent three days stealing everything in town and raping all the women. Once they had the town secured, they fanned out into the countryside and did the same to the biggest abbeys in the areas. After a week, they gathered up every healthy person that had not fled and took them aboard their ships. We assume they took them as slaves. Before they left there, Coral Gables was already under attack. They seem to be leapfrogging their way up the coast. Their ships have already scouted Tampa harbor so we figure that Tampa could be next.

We don't have a lot to stop them with because virtually all of our forces are scattered on borders hundreds of miles away. I was in South Carolina when we got the news from Tampa. The garrison there was only three thousand men. We've been picking up men as we moved, but we still have less than seven thousand troops and half of them are virtually untrained. I've managed to drag forty artillery pieces with us, but they are going to be outranged by the shipboard cannon. Between Tampa and Naples we may have another five thousand men waiting for us. They've got ten to twenty thousand heavily armed and well trained men backed up by a several hundred ship's cannons. We have to cover the entire coast and they pick where they fight."

Artimus was still chewing despite the bad news. "Do we have any advantages?"

"A few. About a thousand, maybe more, of our troops are cavalry and once the enemy hits the beaches, he's on foot. We also know the landscape so we have an advantage when the enemy leaves the coast. We have most of the coast evacuated except for the soldiers. I decided that it's a lot easier to replace buildings and town treasuries than it is to replace wives and children so we're not fighting for ground unless we have an advantage."

Artimus put aside his plate. "Where do you want me to stand?"

Jeremiah motioned to the other officers. "Gentlemen, could you leave us alone for a minute." The men in the wagon shuffled toward the front to them a largely fictional feeling of privacy. "Brother, you are the senior Archbishop on the scene. You stand anywhere you want. This expedition is yours to lead."

Artimus disagreed. "I may be a year older, but you know the situation here and you've handled it so far. As I remember it, Annapolis gave you the same diploma that they gave me."

In fact, Jeremiah was aware that he had much less experience in leading troops than Artimus, but he realized the discussion was over. "We have a lot of coast to cover and we can't keep our troops all in once place, so I will command this force and you assume command of the Tampa garrison. The enemy seems to be operating by leapfrogging two units up the coast, so that gives us a matching structure." It also put Artimus in command of the bulk of trained troops.

They returned to the map table and asked the other officers to join them. A captain who had been stationed at Saint Pete's resumed the briefing. "We have seen two ships scouting Tampa bay, but there is still a chance that they could attack Port Charlotte or Sarasota before they reach Tampa. We have confirmation that both of those cities are virtually empty now. We figure to hold them at Tampa. Fortunately, they are bound to their ships. They have not been willing to penetrate more than ten miles inland. Unfortunately, there are a lot of sandy beaches on the coast that allow small boat landings near a lot of farms and abbeys."

Artimus looked at the map and measured with this thumb and forefinger. "We can do it. If we assume that they want the big cities for booty, then we can expect them to hit Tampa. There are only about a hundred and twenty miles of coast between where they are now and Tampa bay. You said that we had about a thousand horse so far. There must be five hundred or more mounted troopers in Tampa and we can pick more as we travel. I suggest that we take those and as many more as we can find mounts for and divide them into five groups. I would guess that between existing mounted men and the number that we can mount on local horses, we should end up with about two thousand cavalry. We send one group to Cape Coral to harass the enemy if he is still there. The others we place at roughly twenty mile intervals up the coast. That gives us at least five hundred cavalry an hour's ride from anywhere they land. We can't stop a landing in force, but we can make any small landings short and bloody affairs. We then fortify the Tampa-St. Pete's area and make the real stand there."

The group thought about it for moment and then Jeremiah said, "I think that's a good basic plan. We might have a way to speed up the response time. We don't have any warships in these waters that can stand up to the pirates, but St. Pete's has one of the best catamaran racing clubs in York. They have three or four times the speed of the warships. We can load them up with signal flares and send them out to shadow the fleet. They'll be hard to hit if they keep moving and they can send up a flare if they see the enemy moving toward the beach. Hell, they can swoop in near shore and send up a flare every hour to show where the enemy is even if they are not landing."

One of the captains pointed at Cape Coral. "We brought some signal flares that can be seen at least twenty miles over the horizon. How about we make the Cape Coral troop a little bigger and then have it shadow the main fleet by following the flares from the catamarans? Then we get an even faster response."

The discussion went on for over an hour. They discussed where to place the cavalry, what supplies the cavalry would take with them, where they would defend Tampa, and as many other details as they could think of quickly. They decided that Artimus would leave one hundred mounted men behind, to act as messengers and scouts, and take the rest with his column. At one point Artimus told them, "If you succeed in getting the catamarans to sea, tell them that there are a few Texan ships in the area that might also be shadowing the pirate fleet. They are on our side and may help in a crisis." As the meeting drew to a close, Artimus told them, "Remember that you don't have to defeat them. This is a raiding party. They are not fighting for home and family or God and Country. All they want is booty. If you make it expensive, they won't want it. If history is right, we only need to kill or disable about ten percent to get them to leave. One thousand kills is all it takes to end this."

Artimus gathered the mounted troops and moved off ahead of the column. By nightfall, they were at the turn off to Tampa. He had the men make camp and then gathered all of the officers in front of his tent. "Gentlemen. We are in for some hard riding tomorrow. Before we face the enemy, we all need to know who is at our side. Many of you have joined this column from small posts or home guard levies. I will therefore ask you to raise your hand one at a time and tell us your name, rank, specialty, and a one sentence description of what forces you command."

The answers were quick. "Colonel Jamison, Cavalry officer. Three hundred mounted troops armed with Smithson repeaters."

"Captain Gregson. Eighty mounted with lance and buntline. Two gatlings with fifteen hundred rounds."

"Home Colonel Jessup, eighty volunteers from Gainesville. Armed with a variety of personal weapons."

Artimus made quick notes as they counted off. The total was higher than he expected, one thousand seven hundred men, most professionals. He handed a stack of paper to the nearest man. "Pass these out to all of the officers. Gentlemen this is a signed authorization for each of you to requisition all horses that you find and to enlist any and all papal and home guard troops. As we are a mobile force, only those who are mounted or who can be provided with mounts will join this force. All others should be directed to begin moving toward Tampa to join the forces there."

He then divided the column into three units, each with a mix of professional and home guard troops. The strongest unit was sent to Coral Gables. "At first light, pack two days rations and ride hard. Remember that you may be riding into the demons of Hell when you get there. If the enemy is still in town, you are to make at least a noisy, hell bent charge into town. Your first job is to make the enemy know that we are going to fight him. You are to harass the enemy any way you can, short of pitched battle, until he leaves Coral Gables. You will then proceed twenty miles north along the coast and wait for further orders."

The other two columns were assigned positions on the coast. "Set up camp and then patrol the beaches. Move the civilians inland. We have reason to believe that this is a slave raiding party that will not stray far from the beach. If people move inland fifteen or twenty miles, they may be safe. You are to ride down hard on any enemy landing. We want them convinced that stepping onto the beach is a bad idea. You don't need to defeat all of them, but you must establish a heavy cost for landing.

"I can't promise when or if you will get reinforcements. Our northern troops are at least days or weeks away. I will be riding to Tampa and I will be sending the mounted troops there down the coast. They will, however, have their own sections of beach to defend so you can't count on them for help."

"Keep watch on the ocean horizon. We are going to send out ships to shadow the enemy fleet and they will try to send up flares to mark the enemy fleet. Remember that your job is to introduce them to the Devil and not for you to meet the Lord too soon. Tomorrow will be hard. Sleep soon, sleep hard, but don't sleep too long!"

Chapter 40   Unwelcome Tourists

Colonel Jamison's command had swollen to twelve hundred men as he rode south along the old highway 75. Most of the men he picked up from abbeys and villages along the way were inexperienced and lightly armed but determined and willing to fight. His main concern was that only his professional troops had armor. Willingness and courage were a lot less effective then good steel plate when you were riding down on an enemy.

It was a sad anticlimax. Cape Coral was a mausoleum almost empty of living souls. They came riding hard down the main road and then slowed to a walk when the smell from the city told them of the horrors ahead. The soccer field on the outskirts was littered with the bodies of men and boys that appeared to have been executed. Bodies of defenders lay behind failed barricades. Bodies of women, often without clothes, lay on the streets. Bodies of the men were everywhere, some still clutching the improvised weapons that they had died with, some had just been shot as they ran. A few crying children wandered the streets and the very few who had hidden successfully cried over the bodies of their friends and family members.

They learned that the enemy had left the previous night, taking with them a thousand or so Yorkers, mostly women, as slaves. They had made the men and boys carry everything of value to the boats and then killed them. Despite the horror, they could not stay to help. Their job was to help the living in the next town.

They rode north twenty miles, leaving two man teams of observers every mile on the road. They camped on the coast and sent twenty men further north to set up more observation posts. Flares in the pre-dawn light sent them north a second twenty miles the next day.

That afternoon, a rider from the forward post rode in on a lathered horse. "The pirates are landing in Port Charlotte." Jamison learned that pirates had come ashore in Port Charlotte at first light. They anchored five large warships and five armed merchantmen in the harbor and offloaded twenty five longboats full of attackers. Fortunately, the second column of cavalry had gotten to their positions in the Port and were well hidden among the docks and behind barricades. There were a few cannon already there and this was the column with the gatling guns. The pirates were totally taken by surprise. The troopers had waited until they beached their boats and then wiped them out in a one sided twenty minute battle. Then the warships opened up with cannon fire. Once the pirates realized that they were not in danger of hitting their own men, or realized that they didn't care if they hit their own men, they started to bombard the shoreline with the ship's cannon. The Yorkers had been forced to pull back and were setting up a new defensive line in the city.

They were only an hour away from Port Charlotte. When they were more than a mile from the city, they could hear that the bombardment was still going. The area south of Port Charlotte was dense tropical forest. Colonel Jamison stopped his men at the edge of the jungle barely within sight of the city. He studied the city with his spy glass for several minutes and then called over on of his messengers. "Private, I want you to ride into the city and contact the commanding officer of the garrison. Tell him that I suggest that he set up his defensive lines on the east side of the old highway. If he can hold or delay the pirates on the highway, we can ride in and flank them."

A few hours later, the second wave of pirates landed. This time there was no opposition as they left the beaches. The garrison put up token resistance until the pirates approached the old highway, and then stiffened the line to hold them. The Yorker commander waited until the pirates were bunched at the roadside and then made a show of abandoning his positions and retreating. The pirates swarmed across the highway and then stopped when the troops that had not retreated opened up with the gatling guns. They were pinned. On the edge of the forest, Colonel Jamison watched from horseback. When he saw the phony retreat start, he took his lance in one hand and his buntline in the other and, guiding his horse with his knees, led a thousand men, twenty abreast, sweeping up the highway toward the pirates. It took long enough so that some of the pirates had time to retreat to cover, but most of them were ridden down in the first wave. There weren't any left for the third and fourth units to kill. From there, it was street by street, chasing the remaining pirates back to the beaches. Less than a hundred pirates made it back to their boats. Only fifty Yorkers fell in the battle.

Then the bombardment started again, this time on the city center and the highway. Jamison met with Captain Watson, commander of the second column, in a basement near the edge of town. Watson was grimly cheerful. "It's been a good fight so far, but I think it's time to go. We stopped the first two waves, but there are only five warships out there. They can bring in fifty more. We won't surprise them a second time. The civilians are gone and we should follow them."

Jamison agreed. "I suggest that you keep the machine guns and cannon here. You can set up a perimeter to harass them if they start to move inland. I'll take my group north toward Tampa in case they come ashore again." The pirates were still bombarding the empty town when the Yorkers pulled out.

Jeremiah and Artimus met in the Tampa abbey. The abbey was a citrus plantation about ten miles northeast of Tampa. One hundred and five monks and their families occupied the farm houses flanking the main drive. The main building was an oversized red brick and tile structure that held the administration offices, chapel and library. There were two secret subbasements that held the secret libraries, electronics labs, and radio room. The brothers met in the radio room.

The problem was not the ground war, it was the ships. The ten thousand Yorker troops were lightly armed and often inexperienced, but they had the defender's advantage. Even though they might face twice their number of heavily armed professionals, the home court advantage in war was often ten to one. The Alamo held out for a week against forty to one odds.

The problem was that the ships could stand off and pound any defensive line in the city until it crumbled. There were no bunkers in the city and no time to build any. Despite defensive walls, gallant soldiers, and the willingness to die heroic deaths, the city could not be held.

The two brothers sat at a large conference table. Around them, the bright light from the gas mantles illuminated work benches and book shelves. Two radio operators sat at the console and the smell of ozone filled the room. Jeremiah was writing on a message pad. "In Tampa. Eleven thousand troops Tampa. Two thousand guarding coastline. Artimus here. Enemy sighted in harbor. Expect attack tomorrow. Cannot hold city long. Signed: Prodigal two."

He handed the message to one of the radio operators for encoding. "Send this to Albany. Address it to the Pope."

They waited for less than five minutes before the operator announced "We have message confirmation from Albany, Your Eminence." Less than a minute later, he announced, "Message confirmation from Austin, Your Eminence."

Jeremiah looked startled. "Austin?" He looked at Artimus. "Can they read our code?"

Artimus shrugged. "I provided Emperor Adams with my copy of the code book when we parted. I knew that we might have to communicate with them during this crisis and it was the only code available."

Jeremiah was visibly upset. "But they are infidels! We have lived among them and we know that they eat without thanking God for their abundance, marry without blessing, and even let their children die without the sacrament of baptism. It is all right to treat with them or even visit with them, but we cannot be allies with infidels."

artimus was mildly disgusted and hoped that it did not show. "We have lived among them. Have you even seen a Texan break his promise?"

Jeremiah knew the question was a serious one and gave it some thought. "Only once. At the farm, one of the boys made a promise to a friend and then broke it. The others boys wouldn't speak to him for a week. I'll admit that they seem to be honest. I even admit to a certain fondness for some of the Texans that I worked with. However, you are talking about letting a heathen country read our most secret messages."

Artimus shrugged again. "We have other codes if we need them. However, the world is changing and strong friends are a good idea, no matter what they name their God. If you don't believe me, kick the question upstairs."

The next message was in a second code. It read "Texans can read code one. J counsels caution."

This time the answer took longer and was also in the second code. "Bad Times require strong friends. Remember the Alamo. Go back to code one. H.F.E."

Artimus showed the message to his brother. "Holy Father on Earth has spoken. That makes it official. Until he decides otherwise, we're partners with the Texans."

He handed the paper he had been writing on to the radio operator. "Send this to Austin. You don't need to code it." The message read: "To Her Eminence. Am in Tampa. All limbs present. Do not worry. A."

They spread a map on the conference table and began to look for a solution to their problem. They had help, but it was on the end of a frustratingly slow line. The emperor and the military members of the committee were in the rail yards in Austin, the Pope and his trusted bishops in Albany. The exchange of ideas was slow and patience was wearing thin. At one point the Texas end asked, "What estimate range pirate cannon?" The answer went back, "two miles". Answer again, "How do we get enemy troops to attack two and half miles inland."

Eventually, the plan was painfully woven. They would begin by defending the city as hard as they could. The pirate would have to be convinced that was the main battle. They knew that the pirates had come for booty and slaves, mainly gold and women. Their job was to convince the enemy that there was plenty of gold and a lot of slaves just over the hill. They picked a spot on the Hassle River about three miles from the bay. It was an isolated abbey nestled in a valley on three sides and fronting the Hassle River on the fourth. The river would make it easy for the pirates to approach in strength and make it more enticing while the hills surrounding it would make it easier for the Yorkers to set up an ambush.

They then concocted a story that the treasuries of the city and of several abbeys had been moved to the Hassle River site for safe keeping. The story would be given to all of the troops to use a bargaining chip if they were captured. In a final step that Artimus considered the silliest idea that he had heard, the Pope suggested that in the hours remaining before the invasion, that the newspapers distribute an edition with the front page reassuring the citizens that all of the valuables of Tampa were safe at Hassle River. They could even show a map on the second page, showing the Hassle River Abbey as being near a large convent full of potential female slaves. The longer Artimus thought about it, the more juvenile it sounded, but it was better than any idea he had.

When they reached Tampa they saw that the people had been building beach defenses night and day. Sandbags, wagons, lumber, rocks, dismantled fences, all went into the beach defenses. Elsewhere, they reinforced the lighter defensive walls on the north and south to defend from flanking attacks. Every able bodied citizen worked until he dropped. The half dozen cannon already in place were sandbagged and ringed with concrete walls.

Artimus and Jeremiah set up headquarters in the city hall. Two days later, Artimus was inspecting barriers near the beach on the south end of the city when he heard horses approaching. In the distance, a tired column of mounted troopers was riding into town, lead by Colonel Jamison. When he saw Artimus's party, Jamison and two troopers spurred their horses and rode ahead.

He saluted as he reached Artimus. "Colonel Jamison reporting, Sir. We followed the flares all the way up the coast and ended up here. If the flares are right, this is where the fleet is. We have some prisoners that will interest you." He turned to the man next to him. "Sergeant, bring the prisoners forward." He turned back to Artimus and continued, "They were captured by our forward guard yesterday afternoon. Twenty of our boys ran across a party of raiders that were in the process of leaving a village that they had just ransacked. Most of the raiders were in boats headed back to their ships, but about fifteen of them were still on shore. They were leading a line of prisoners down to their boats. Our boys spurred into them and got within about thirty yards before the raiders opened up. It was bloody but when it was over we had three prisoners and they didn't have any. We lost most of the patrol, but the boys did their job."

The sergeant had returned with two men tied on the back of a horse. They were short, dark skinned men with dark curly hair. They weren't negro, but their skin color would have told anyone that they weren't Yorkers either. They were wearing torn yellow uniforms. Artimus looked them over. "I thought that you said there were three prisoners."

Jamison shrugged. "There were. One of them didn't want to talk to us. He ended up talking to Saint Peter, but I'll have you know that we said a proper prayer over him. They claim that they are members of the Royal Brazilian Expeditionary Force. They speak something pretty much like Spanish, and they do talk a lot when properly asked."

Artimus gestured at the city. "The place is pretty much empty. Bivouac your men anywhere you see space. Then take these prisoners to our headquarters at city hall. Let them know where you are so they can send supplies and I'll meet you there to continue the interrogation. From the bandages that I see, you must have had more than one encounter with the enemy. Well done, Sir."

Chapter 41   The City Of Waco

The City of Waco was under full sail. On the eastern horizon, the sails of the pirate fleet were barely visible. For three days she and the two smaller Texas ships had tracked them, out of range and ready to run. Captain Granger was standing at the rail watching the horizon when the call came down from the crows nest, "Sail Ho. Small Ship at two o'clock." It took some searching with the spyglass before he found it. It was a small boat moving faster than he had ever seen anything move. It looked like two canoes with platform lashed between them. A large triangular sail had it heeled so far over that a crewman was hanging onto a rope to try to keep it from capsizing. After a few minutes, he could make out the flag of York on the mast and the name *Weekend Pain* painted on her side. The first mate came up next to him. "I think that she is trying to rendezvous with us."

The captain looked out to the horizon for other ships. "I agree, Mr. Costner. I think we should see what he wants. Signal the other two ships to heave to."

Twenty minutes later, all three ships were hove to under just enough sail to keep steerage and the little boat was close enough to hail. The little boat looked as it was made of bamboo, netting, and teak. It was obviously made for speed. There were military signal rockets strapped to the roof of the cabin that rode between the canoes and a launch tube secured to the forward mast. The sailor on the *Weekend Pain* threw a weighted rope over the side of the *Waco*. Before they could lower a rope ladder, he scrambled up the rope and vaulted onto the deck. Seeing the captain, he saluted. "Captain Samuels of the papal scout *Weekend Pain*, may I come aboard?"

Gardiner was looking over the side while he returned the salute. "Welcome aboard. What in the hell do you call that thing?"

"It's a catamaran, Sir. There are about a dozen of us out here watching the pirate fleet. Whenever they move more than a few miles, we dart in near shore and put up a flare for the ground troops."

Gardner harrumphed. "I am amazed that you aren't all dead. There are no guns on that thing."

Samuels shrugged. "We can hit twenty five knots in a good breeze and they don't shoot so good at moving targets. They haven't come close to us yet. We also tack better. The warships are built to run downwind and Weekend Pain runs best cross the wind. However, we could use some help. We had to leave in a hurry and we are short of food and water. Can you provide us with some supplies?"

"Certainly, how much can you store?"

"It's a small cabin. We've got a twenty gallon water tank for the two of us and we have about enough space for one good sea chest."

Gardiner turned to the first mate. "Get a twenty gallon cask of water up here and have the cooks put together a large sea chest of provisions. Tell them dried meat, canned crackers, canned fruit and whatever else they can fit in."

After the mate left, Gardiner turned to Captain Samuels. "What are you finding out there?"

Samuel replied, "There are about a hundred ships in that group over the horizon. Half of them are war ships, the other half armed merchantmen. The merchantmen are filled with marines. They also have a couple of one kind of ship that I have never seen before. It's a big gunboat. It's made wide like a carrack, but its got so many big guns that it waddles like a fat duck in the water. I can't imagine that it would do well in a fight."

The water cask had appeared on deck. Two crewmen rigged a net to the crab and swung the cask over the side. Below, the crewman on the Weekend Pain struggled to catch the swinging net. By the time he had the cask stowed in the cabin, it was time to do it all over again with the sea chest. While the others struggled with the cargo, Samuels got Captain Gardner's attention one last time, and gestured to the north. "If you are looking for an easy prize or some information, you should know that they sent out scouts about twenty or thirty miles ahead of the fleet. The scouts are light schooners and not very well armed. If you get between them and the main fleet, you should be able to run one down easy." Then he was over the side, climbing back down the ladder.

The next day, they re-supplied another catamaran and pulled a Yorker crewman off debris that proved that the pirates didn't always miss.

Then Gardner decided it was time to go hunting. Judging from the flares, the main fleet had stopped near Tampa. When they didn't move for a day, he decided it was time to take out the scouts. He put on more sail and set a north-northeast course that should take him near the shore north of the main fleet. It took less than three hours to find the scouts. They were sailing north at a leisurely pace about two hundred yards apart. He sent one of his smaller ships wide on each side to prevent escape and then steered for the space between the two ships. They saw him coming and crowded on sail, but it was much too late for them. The pirate on the left broke crosswind into a tack and tried to break free. He left her to the smaller Texan sloop and pursued one still running abeam. His cannon were loaded with chain, two balls of steel connected with a steel chain. It was designed to dismast the enemy and leave them afloat.

Before they closed, the *City of Waco* began to take fire. The pirate ship carried a three pound swivel as a stern gun. It wasn't likely to sink the Waco, but it made the Texans keep their heads down. Marines in the rigging of both ships began to exchange fire at about two hundred yards. The Texan ship closed relentlessly. When they were even with the pirate, they took a broadside from the pirate before they let go a single volley of chain from the ten port side cannon. The pirate stopped dead in the water as her rigging fell into the ocean. The second Texan ship, the *Hopalong Cassidy*, had fallen slightly behind. As she neared the pirate, grappling hooks flew and planks fell. *The Hopalong* sent a final broadside into the pirate before the sound of small arms announced the boarding. The pirate was only able to fire three of her cannon into *the Hopalong* before they were silenced by the boarding parties. Unable to stop immediately, the *City of Waco* veered off to help the *Tex Ritter* with it's target.

The same scenario played out again, except that this time the Starboard guns dismasted the second pirate. There was no attempt to board her. Girard decided he had all the prisoners he needed so he and the *Tex Ritter* continued to pound the pirate until it was obviously afire and sinking. It took a lot of pounding as it has always been hard to actually sink a wooden ship. It might be debatable as to whether the pirate crew was unwilling to surrender or simply unable to find anything to fly a white flag from. Debatable but irrelevant.

By the time the two ships managed to rendezvous with the *Hopalong Cassidy* and her prize, the cleanup was progressing on the pirate. The rigging had been cut away to clear the decks and the surviving pirates were gathered on the foredeck. As Captain Gardner boarded the ship, the captain of the *Hopalong* was seated at a folding table with a man in a garish costume. The short, dark haired, dark skinned man was wearing a bright yellow tri corner hat and coat, both decorated with enough orange braid to make a whore house owner proud. The bright green pants with the yellow stripe completed the ensemble. The Texan captains saluted each other.

The *Hopalong's* captain pointed to the garish prisoner. "This tastefully dressed little man claims that he is not a pirate. He has explained to me that he is Jesus Ricardo, Captain of the *Virgin Lupe*, ship of the Royal Navy of Brazil and that he should be treated with the respect of a captured officer, prisoner of war. Brazilian is a lot like Spanish. He can understand and answer if you talk Spanish slowly."

Gardner did not want more than two or three prisoners, but he was trapped. "We don't know that these men have participated in any landings, so we will give them the minimum treatment due to prisoners of war. Maybe they haven't raped an pillaged yet. Search this ship for maps, orders, any paperwork that will tell us anything, then fire her up. Move the prisoners into your forward hold and burn this thing to the waterline. Send the bright boy captain and his first mate to my ship. I'll question him as we sail. If he doesn't talk, I'll drag him behind us on a rope until he does."

Chapter 42   The Battle For Tampa

In Tampa, their prisoners were very informative. "How many ships? How would I know? I saw the belly of the one I was in and maybe fifty or more around us when we landed. No one tells us anything. Why were we here? Well, the kingdom is running out of serfs. They die early, you know. Lots of the young nobles they can't get an estate 'cause they got no money and they got no serfs. So the king, he puts up this fleet. He tells the young bucks that they can use it if they give him twenty percent of the booty and some money for each serf they find. Then they tell us soldiers that we get a hundred reals for every slave, excuse me, serf we bring back and we get ourselves twenty percent of the booty we find. It beats being home with the wife, don't it? Guess I ain't gonna get home in three months like they promised, am I?"

The fleet did not come until five days after the Yorker army arrived in Tampa. Some of the men from the surrounding farms came into town to help dig shelters for the troops. There was even time to pour concrete barriers and shelters in a couple of areas. They dug in. They waited. The farmers evacuated.

When the fleet came, it did so with deliberate speed. Warships entered that harbor and anchored offshore. Then five strange lumbering monsters anchored themselves outside the harbor, out of range of the Yorker artillery. They anchored themselves in the shallows where St. Petersburg had been before the waters rose. They used four anchors each and then winched the anchor chains as tight as the swells allowed. Watching from a hillside, Artimus thought how easy it would be to sink them if he had any artillery that could reach them, but they were safely out of range. Later in the day, the troop ships had appeared and anchored near the waddlers. They waited like wolves waiting for the prey to weaken.

The second day, the gun ships opened fire. They were so securely anchored, that they were almost glued into place and still they rocked heavily with every blast. The first volley from the first ship took out two hundred yards of beach fortifications with grape shot. The Yorkers had never seen anything like it. By the time all five ships had fired their first volleys, the Yorkers were in retreat. Mushroom clouds rose behind them where high explosive and shrapnel shells were wiping out sections of the shoreline. Standing on the hill near Artimus, Jeremiah had the calm to notice that the Brazilians seemed to be sparing the warehouse district. Pointing at the beach, he shouted at Artimus, "The pirates are leaving the docks alone. They want the stuff in the warehouses. If we can get some men there, they can bloody the first wave when it lands." Before Artimus could protest, Jeremiah was on his horse and moving toward the town. He gathered up several platoons of the retreating troops and six gatling guns and headed back to the beach under the artillery barrage. He abandoned his horse immediately to lead the men on foot. They ran through the street crouched over as the noise of the barrage deafened them. When they reached the warehouse district, they found about a hundred troops in the bunkers who had not retreated. They had realized that the barrage was not hitting them and decided that it was safer where they were. Jeremiah was amazed that he felt no fear. This sort of action was much more typical of Artimus than him. All he felt was a sense of determination and a feeling of urgency.

He and his troops hunkered under the concrete barriers as close to the ground as they could get. The barrage went on for another hour. They passed canteens without raising their heads and if a man had to piss, well, he tried to piss in the other direction, but he didn't stand up. Then the silence came. When they were certain that the barrage was over, they found places to make their stands. The gatlings went into sandbagged revetments where the operators could hide from the incoming boats. Two troopers managed to sneak down the shore and bring back a small artillery piece. Jeremiah had them keep it out of sight behind a warehouse. The Brazilians had to think that everyone had left.

Then they held quiet while they waited for the boats. Jeremiah and his lieutenants could see the shoreline through a warehouse window. They watched the boats land and saw several hundred yellow uniformed pirates get out of their boats casually and saunter toward the warehouses. The Brazilians were grinning like school kids and pounding each other on the back. They were like kids at a picnic. They felt that way until they were less than fifty feet from the first warehouse. That was when the first gatling gun opened up. The Yorkers were firing from everywhere. Rooftops, beach walls, sandy dunes, warehouse windows were all deadly. Within a minute, the three pounder put its first shell in the middle of the landing boats. The Brazilians were well armed and plenty tough, but a third of them were dead before they reached for their weapons. They raced back to their boats but less than a third of them made it that far. A yellow stripe just makes such a good target.

As soon as the first boat pulled away, Jeremiah was shouting for his men to follow him. It was time to get the hell out. Sure enough, the Yorkers were less than two blocks from the shoreline when the gunboats opened up. A half dozen Yorkers too entranced with battle excitement had followed the Brazilians onto the beach. They were vaporized in the first volley. The rest kept moving, fast. Some of the Brazilians on both sides of the warehouse district had not retreated and they were also in the middle of the barrage.

When they reached the edge of town, Artimus was waiting with a cavalry company. Each man held a spare horse, ready to mount a rescue mission or just provide a ride to get the Yorkers out of the city. When Jeremiah's men had mounted up, they rode into the hills. Behind them, the artillery barrage continued. All the Brazilians would get out of those warehouses was powder, ashes, and broken junk. They left pickets and retreated to the Tampa Abbey.

At the abbey, they reported events to Austin and Albany. They also learned that the Yorker fleet was coming, much too late help them. Every Yorker ship that could be contacted was gathering in the Florida keys for a combined attack. It would be at least two more weeks before enough of them gathered to have a chance at stopping the Brazilians.

They had planted the newspapers suggested by Pope Jones in the magazine stands around Tampa, but did not really believe the Brazilians would fall for such an obvious trick and move inland.

It finally came down to the fact that they had ten thousand troops that had nothing else to do. They needed badly to bloody the Brazilians, but the bulk of the Brazilian fleet was in Tampa Harbor and virtually untouchable. The Brazilian troops were in Tampa scraping up goodies under the protection of the gun ships and were not assailable. In the unlikely event that they fell for the ruse, they could be hurt, otherwise the Yorkers could only wait for them to leave.

When Artimus and Jeremiah reached the Hassle River plantation, two colonels were already surveying the area with their field glasses. The abbey here was similar to the Tampa abbey except that there were fewer monk's houses and they were spread out down a dirt road between the river front and the main building. There were low hills on all three sides and the jungle came up to the top of the hills on both the east and west sides. The south side of the river, away from the abbey was also heavily wooded. If the Brazilians were dumber than tree stumps, it was a good ambush place. The abbey was totally abandoned as the residents had left as soon as the plan was announced.

They decided to divide into four companies. Two, containing most of their forces and the few artillery pieces they had salvaged, would dig into the jungle just beyond the east and west hills. The third, smaller, company would dig into the forest south of the river. The fourth group was the cavalry. The obvious place to put them would be on the road going north. It was the main road in and out of the abbey and was hidden behind another set of hills. The problem was that a charge down that road would make them traverse cleared fields where the enemy would see them coming and there was no cover.

It was decided to place the cavalry farther up the river. They would charge down the riverbanks if needed and try to catch the Brazilians at the river's edge. The plan, such as it was, was to let the invaders get out of their boats and approach the main building. When they were close, the east and west companies would start firing from the tree line, charging if the invader line did not break. The company across the river and the cavalry would attack as the invaders tried to get back to their boats. At the last minute, they formed another small group to hide in two of the worker's houses hoping to surprise the invaders with close in fire.

Bishop Jeremiah asked to command the group on the south bank. They all dug in, and waited.

In Tampa, Admiral Gomez was sitting in Jeremiah's seat in city hall, meeting with the most influential captains and nobles in the fleet. He and several others were looking at copies of the Tampa Times. He snorted. "This is a trick. It's an obvious trick. They are trying to get us to abandon our artillery cover and attack inland."

One of the younger nobles looked excited. "Maybe not. They couldn't have known that we would conquer the town the next day. Look. They printed it in English. How would they know that we could read it? I think that they were trying to reassure their citizens and we just kicked the crap out of them faster than they expected."

One of the other young nobles leaped up, "This has not been a good expedition. We have made crap so far, and this is a chance to recover our investments. My men are out there digging through busted buildings and ransacking private homes trying to get enough loot to make it worth coming."

Someone else spoke up. "We captured less than three thousand serfs so far. It's going to be hard to start estates with that many. Even if this is a trap, I suggest that we go kick the crap out of them. If the army is there, we'll kick their butts and take them for serfs. It's one way to get some bodies to take home."

The admiral made one last plea for sense. "It is true that we haven't been as successful as we hoped in some areas. We never realized how many of the serfs would evacuate instead of fighting and being captured. The next time, we will bring horses and do some real shore operations. Now that we know what to do, next time we'll cut off the population from running and capture more of them. For now, I suggest that we take what we have, maybe do one more landing before the Yorker fleet has time to arrive, and then head for home."

He was shouted down. The passions of youth do not conform well to sensibility. Finally, he asked for a map of the area. "This abbey is about four miles up river. You know that you could be ambushed in the boats and that it will be hard for the gunboats to help. However, if you are going to do this, prepare a of list of the groups that want to participate and we will provide boats and what cover we can."

Of course, he did not offer to provide supplies as each noble hired and supplied his own company of men.

Chapter 43   The Battle of Hassle River

In the end, a hundred longboats were required to carry the five thousand volunteers upriver. Each noble had been torn between the desire for more help from the other nobles and the desire to keep a larger share of the treasure. Eventually, about half of them, mostly the younger ones, decided to make the attack. They carried one mortar for each group of a hundred men, each soldier had a lever action rifle, and most nobles carried sten guns. Everyone had steel armor. They felt more than equal to any army they would meet.

They were allowed to travel up the river unmolested. The Yorkers wanted to give them the feeling that they were moving through an empty landscape. Arriving at the abbey, the Brazilian commander saw the scattered homes along the road and the main building in the distance. Around the administration building he could see breastworks, gun emplacements and what appeared to be soldiers hiding behind barricades. In fact, the building was as empty as the suits that had been propped up to look like defenders. There was no one there.

To the surprise of the Yorkers, the Brazilian commander offloaded his weapons and men but did not move forward. His men milled abound the river front while he watched the admin building through his field glasses. After a while, he consulted with two men who erected a launch tube for a six foot long rocket. He sent it skyward where it burst with a bright green light, clearly visible in the daytime. Artimus was on the western hill five minutes later when he heard an ear pounding screeching and then saw a section of the valley below explode. The shells hit between the river and the administration building. He yelled at the messenger by his side, "The bastards can hit us. We're over four miles from the coast and those bastards have help. Private, get over to Captain Jamison and tell him: Change of plans. Go on my second red flare, one charge, and then everyone up the river. No sniping from the tree line because the artillery will open up. Tell the cavalry to go on the first red. This battle just got shorter."

While they were talking, the Brazilian had set up a second flare. It went up arcing to the north and few minutes later a second volley came in placed further north. It was impressive as Hell, but Artimus guessed, correctly, that there wouldn't be any more. The Brazilian wanted to scare the Yorkers away but didn't want to destroy the treasure building. Still surprised at the fearlessness of the fake York troopers, the Brazilians formed up and began to march on the town. They started firing two hundred yards short of the main building.

That was Artimus's cue. He yelled for his men to take cover and sent up the first red flare. That brought immediate heavy fire from the Brazilians, but also drew their attention in the wrong direction as the cavalry column began its charge down the river bank and into their rear. When they heard the horses, the men hidden in the houses along the dirt road opened fire. The artillery from both hills was sending shells into the Brazilian soldiers. The Brazilians had mortars set up near the water front, but weren't certain where to fire them.

The cavalry took out several of the mortar crews as they made their turn north into the Brazilian rear. As soon as the cavalry passed, Jeremiah's group opened fire on the mortar and boat crews from the opposite river bank.

For a last minute plan, things were going well. Then the Brazilians got organized and began putting out fire toward the cavalry column. At that point Artimus sent up his second flare and led the charge into the valley. They had to get among the Brazilians before the invader's superior fire power wiped them out. The few precious minutes that the invaders were paying attention to the cavalry gave them their only chance.

Half of the cavalry died or went to ground on dead horses before they closed with the invaders, yet the charge disorganized the Brazilians enough to let the other two columns of Yorkers close on the enemy.

Then it was hand to hand, pistol to pistol and lance to saber. The Yorkers fought well, but the Brazilians were better armed and had better armor. At first, more Yorkers fell than Brazilians, a lot more.

Then the real Yorker advantage started to work. The Brazilians were looters who cared nothing about each other and who had no desire to die, while the Yorkers were fighting for their families and wanted blood, lots of Brazilian blood at any price.

The Brazilians began to fall back toward the boats in spite of the greater number of Yorkers falling. Artimus led his men to cover and shot at the Brazilian backs from behind hillocks, fences, and rocks. The Brazilians couldn't take cover and run at the same time, and no one was going to volunteer to stay behind "for the good of the corps".

It turned into a rout when Jeremiah's men opened up again as the Brazilians approached their boats. Of the five thousand Brazilians who had come for the easy victory, less than half made it back to the boats.

Walking the battlefield, Artimus could see that it was a costly victory. They had killed half of the invaders, but had lost at least as many men of their own.

He was sad to see Jamison lying on the battlefield, bloody sword in one hand and empty pistol in the other, along with thousands of his men.

Artimus himself had taken a grazing hit to his left arm, but hadn't noticed until the battle was over. Jeremiah sought him out on the battlefield.

"We won, brother. It doesn't look like it, but we won. These yellow bastards won't want to fight us again."

Chapter 44   Down On The Range

This meeting was a large one due to the urgency caused by the war in York. Everyone's chair was filled and a podium had been set up at one end of the room so that the speakers could be better heard. The emperor began the meeting with, "We have a lot to do today. Let's start with the progress reports. Please keep to the point. I would ask that this time only members keep their suggestions until later in the meeting. Perhaps you would start Sir White, with the news from the medical area."

Sir White walked to the podium. "We have nothing but good news. In addition to the midwife school, we have opened two surgeon's schools. As you know, the population has always accepted simple surgery such as stitching wounds and setting broken arms. Now that we have opiates and the Sulpha drugs, we can teach surgeons to handle a much wider variety of illnesses. We are also teaching them basic pharmacology. Winnie Wigwam now sells sixteen potions. Most are effective herbal or natural medications, but we also sell three kinds of Sulpha. I am happy to announce that we have competition. Two diuretics which are natural plants have been put on the market for 'women's ills' and there is now a second marketer of Epson salts. Things could not be better. Our hope is that surgeons will eventually take over all of the functions of doctors without having to use the nasty word 'doctor'.

"In part, the lack of problems is associated with the good results. With better training and medication, infant mortality at the one year mark, has dropped from fifty percent to twenty percent in the central areas. We have enough happy mothers to shut up any Diaz that rears his head. It seems that many deaths that we thought were due to the remnants of the plague were actually from simpler and more treatable causes.

"It is my belief that within a year, the only function this committee will have in regards to healing will be to decide at what pace we release the old knowledge. The progress will shortly be self sustaining. Thank you."

The next up was Sir Greg. "At the farm, we have been concentrating on three projects. The first is well underway. We have set up powered machinery to make gun barrels. These are rifled breech loading coastal defense guns that are larger and more accurate than anything we have made before. It is our hope that their high rate of fire and their accuracy will make each one do the work of five older muzzle loaders. The work has not gone as fast as we had hoped. As you know, the cannon are actually cast and assembled elsewhere. They go to the farm only for boring and rifling the barrel, and tapping the breech mechanism. The construction of the lathes and other machinery as well as the engines to power them came in on schedule. However, it turned out to be more difficult than we had anticipated to produce the high quality bits and grinding heads that we need. We have only managed to turn out three finished barrels a week. We hope to increase that to five a week in time.

"On the steam engine side, we have now completed twenty locomotives and have them stored at the farm. We are not building any more until we find a way to start using them. We are now building engines for our Thirty five coastal boats. We have designed a rig that bolts on in about one hour. You remove the mast and rigging, lower the boiler and firebox into the hold, and bolt the engine and side-wheels to the deck. We have tested the conversion on the reservoir at the farm and find that we can make as much as fifteen knots with it and it does not matter if you are going upwind or down. We propose to mount swivel cannon on the bow when they go into use. Because of the news that we are here to hear today, we are building them as fast as we can.

"The third project is radios. We are building receivers for some of our larger ships. They will come with batteries and hand cranked generators. We hope to have transmitters available within a year, but at this time, they are simply too large and take too much power to be put on the ships. The radios will be mounted on the ships, but no one except the radio operator will be made aware of their presence until they are needed."

Sir Greg sat down to allow Baron Wilson to take the floor. "I also have mostly good news. The toys that we designed for Christmas were a hit. More than half of the population has now seen a working steam device. There were protests from some preachers and some newspaper columnists, but the kids loved them and the Diaz's couldn't find much to complain about. There have been an increase in sermons with the theme of 'humility for mankind', but not much else in protest.

"The books sales have dropped off. That is, however, because everyone seems to have read it. As you know, this one did cause book burnings, spankings, and sermons when it first came out. Now it is simply gossip.

"Following the lead of the Yorkers, we have begun to sell glass making machines that use a float system to make clear, smooth, large sheets of glass cheaply. The same dummy company sells a paper making machine now. The new machine is hand or animal cranked and uses a screen in a bath of pulp to make a continuous sheet of paper as long as you want it. It has reduced the cost of paper production by over ninety percent. To make certain that the new machines would not spark protests from the businesses that could not afford them, they are sold below cost and on terms that anyone can afford.

"The combination of events, the railways, the new machines, the new book, the toys, the new medicines, all introduced carefully seems to have had the effect that we wanted. Most of the population is now accepting of changes and while queasy, is no longer automatically frightened."

As Baron Wilson sat down, the emperor stood. He did not leave his spot at the head of the table, but he leaned over with his palms on the edge of the desk. "I suggest that everyone take a deep breath and look around the table. Remember this time and the people around you. Do you realize that in less than five years, you have brought this country from the dark ages to the renaissance? I had barely hoped that we would get this far in my lifetime and we have done it in less than five years. We only have two steps to go. When we introduce steam engines and the telegraph or the radio, we will have brought this county into the industrial age. Both the means and the necessity will be next on the agenda. Congratulations.

"From this point on, we will be returning to the usual rules. Get your coffee and drinks now, put a sandwich at your place, scarf down a roll, light up a pipe. We have work to do. General Armbruster will fill you in on what we know so far."

General Armbruster arose and went to the podium. "You all have at your seats, copies of the messages that I hold here. You can go over them in detail at your convenience, but let me summarize the high points.

"The Brazilians hit York with between ten and twenty thousand troops and between one hundred fifty and two hundred ships. Their objective was slaves and booty. They did not have the steel ships that we feared, but they did have a few gun boats that could fire rounds at least five miles inland. They savaged much of the coast. Their normal tactic was to go in under the cover of the gunboats and that limited them to a narrow strip of land near the coast.

"The Yorkers beat them back. They had at least one minor and one major battle and the Brazilians seemed to have lost their interest. Beyond that, the news is not good.

"The raiders got to more small villages along the coast than was thought at first. The last estimate is over eight thousand prisoners were taken back to Brazil, and more than twice that are dead or wounded. They also looted four large cities and many coastal abbeys and villages. The Yorkers were only able to get twenty ships into action. They tried to intercept the raiders as they passed the Florida Keys on the way home but the Yorker ships took a lot of losses and didn't do much damage to the invaders.

"The foot soldiers all carried lever action rifles similar to our Winchesters and the nobles all carried something similar to a sten gun. They were all well armored. The soldiers were, apparently, paid mercenaries working on commission and the officers were mostly young nobles attempting to amass slaves and money for estates.

"I should point out that although the invaders left, they are not beaten. All but about three thousand of them made it back to the ships. All but six of their ships survived to go home. They have been discouraged, but not severely wounded. On a more personal note, both Jeremiah and Artimus were in combat in Tampa. Artimus was slightly injured but both are now fine."

The emperor interjected, "General, would you briefly fill in the committee on the steps that the rangers are taking."

"Yes, Sire. Texans civilians would not be the easy pickings that Yorkers were. Most Yorkers were unarmed and every Texan carries a personal weapon and usually knows how to use it. However, no matter how tough they are, no local ranger and his posse are going to be able to stand up to heavily armed and armored soldiers. Even though our population has grown to over two million people, we still have only twenty thousand full time rangers, so we have begun a recruitment campaign to double the number of full time rangers and we are organizing home guards that will add another seventy thousand men during emergencies.

"The railways have been completed along the coast and we are establishing forts every one hundred fifty miles. This is where the majority of the rangers will be stationed. That puts a ranger battalion not more than three hours away from any point on the coast.

"We are also upgrading the armor and armament of the troops. The approach to fighting in Texas has always been sorta personal. We have less than five hundred rangers with automatic weapons and not one of them wears body armor. It just wouldn't be fitting to face down an enemy in the street wearing the stuff. Now we will have to change and the Emperor Emeritus has been working with the armorers to come up with a quick and effective solution. They have designed a coat of plates that is a good balance between protection and practicality. It's essentially a leather vest with steel plates riveted inside and cotton padding near the skin. Of course, we had to make changes from the medieval version. Ours have two levels of overlapping plates to stop shrapnel and most bullets, but they are still quick and easy to make and they don't have to be made to fit each individual. Head protection is a problem. It takes at least a day and usually two for a blacksmith to turn out a steel helm. The production rate is very slow.

"The Yorkers are sending us a sample of the Sten gun the invaders used and we have plans of a similar Ancient German gun called the MP41. The gun was a cheap stamped metal firearm for the Ancients. The problem is that they had stamping mills and we don't. We can reproduce it, but slowly, and it burns a lot of ammunition. We will have to find a way to produce larger quantities than we can now put out. Those problems still need to be solved.

"We have ordered more ships built, but there is no chance that we can match their fleet in less than two years, and we must assume that the Brazilians will keep on building on their lead.

"For those of you who want more detail, it is available from me or my office. Frankly, we are here to see what ideas this committee can offer to help the preparedness effort. In that light, the discussion is open to the floor."

Sir Greg spoke up first. "It's obvious that we are going to have to chance more powered machinery. As I see it, the only question is how we are going to do it. I have been thinking about the helmet problem. We could solve it if we had even a little powered machinery. There is an industrial scrap yard out in NewMex that has never been mined. It's a damned long way from anywhere. Seems the Ancients liked to hide scrap where no one could see it. Now that we have a couple of lathes working, we should be able to use them to build some presses and powered hammers. Even a good powered hammer would make it possible to pound out twenty helmets a day."

After two hours of discussion, everyone agreed that Greg was right. It was time to move on. They agreed to establish a second place with steam engines and powered equipment in the deserts of NewMex and to depend on the sheer vastness of the desert for cover. They also formed a committee to look at production of the sub machine gun. 'Stamped' sounded like a simple process that would get very complicated when they actually did it.

At Baron Wilson's suggestion, it was agreed to activate all of the hidden telegraph stations near the coast. From now on, twenty four hour instant communications would be maintained.

Sir Eric had been looking thoughtful during the discussion. Finally he said, "General, I am not a naval or military expert, but I think that logic tells us that we should not spend any money building ships yet." The General looked very skeptical as Greg continued, "Think about it. We have the home court advantage. They have to build ships that can carry twenty thousand men ten thousand miles from home to find a fight, but we know that they are coming to us. Aside from scouts that we already have, we only need boats that can fight within twenty miles of home. I suggest that we concentrate on some small gun ships designed to sink bigger ships close up. We could build a lot more of the small coastal boats than we have steam engines for. Rather then build ocean going gun platforms, we add a little armor and a bigger gun to the small ships. It's cheap and easy, and we could build a lot of them. I don't mean that we never build a navy, just that for now all we need to do is defend."

That idea took a lot more discussion, but eventually even the General saw the logic of it. They did agree, however, to test a prototype as soon as possible."

The emperor emeritus finally tossed in the damp towel. "This is all good. We have an action plan and I am beginning to feel that Texas will not be an easy target. However, we have forgotten the problem of not getting lynched for black magic. These things we are talking about are a lot noisier than a toy steam engine. People are getting more sophisticated in Texas but remember how Artimus described that locomotive. 'Like the fires of Hell coming!' or something like that."

Baron Wilson leaned forward. "Sire, we have a possible solution. It is, I admit, one that I am not happy about. Somehow it feels bad. However, I have been communicating with Jeremiah. He had a photographer make photographs of several of the atrocities committed in Naples and at one of the coastal abbeys that was attacked. Along with the Brazilian armor and guns, he is sending negatives of several of the pictures. In York, they are making copies to be posted in every church in the country. They say that are asking for prayers for the dead, but in reality, they are gathering sympathy for any measures that they have to take to counter the invaders. In Texas, I suggest that we release the pictures to the newspapers. They can publish woodcuts and descriptions. It should garner public support for anything we have to do."

The emperor emeritus made a face. "You're right. It has the taste of bad bile to use the dead like that. Maybe we have no choice."

It was a bad tasting end to a meeting.

Three days later, they were saying goodbye to Linda. When it was certain that the invaders had left for Brazil, the emperor had arranged for two ships to take her back home. After considerable debate, they had decided to let it be a public event. The empress felt that her Eminence would have less time for worry if she was leaving as the popular representative of York rather than as Linda returning to Artimus. The two imperial coaches sat on a siding at the naval yard along with several other private and first class railcars that had brought over a hundred guests to see her off. It had been a grand and gala sendoff party, but now Her Eminence was alone with Her Majesty and it was just Shirley saying goodbye to Linda. "I know that Artimus is going to meet you with a Yorker ship, but these captains have orders to escort you all the way to Albany if you will let them. We all know that York is short on ships now and we'd feel better if Artimus lets us escort you all the way home. We'll miss you. Oh, his majesty loaded several chests of stuff for Artimus. Some of it is committee work, but four chests are Texas spices, cigars, Texas whiskey and such stuff. Don't be surprised when they offload more than you brought on board." In fact, her eminence had brought twenty crates of furniture, bedding, dishes, clothes, and other souvenirs from Texas herself. Royalty travels well.

The latest royal railcar had a tiny but separate smoking lounge at the rear. While the women enjoyed tea and gossip in the front section, Wilson and the two emperors were enjoying after lunch cigars and whiskey and the absence of the women. The elder emperor raised his glass. "To our wives, the source of our two greatest pleasures, when we see them and when we avoid them. Wilson, you have been looking worried lately. Aren't your plans going well?"

Wilson sipped his whiskey. "Oh, things are going very well. While we were distributing the atrocity pictures to the churches and newspapers, Wayne had a brilliant idea. He suggested to a reporter that they start printing letters from the readers with suggestions about what to do to defend Texas. Now the papers are printing letters from worried people suggesting everything from a two thousand mile long coastal wall to an atom bomb. They are also printing the letters from Diaz warning about the dangers of such thinking, but overall we have enough public support to do almost anything in the face of an invasion. We're winning. That's what worries me lately.

"I like Texas. For all of our problems, I feel like I was born in Shangri-La. I have had a life of more freedom than most places in history and more responsibility than most. I like my horse, and my gun, and my hat, and I like living in a world where home town sheriffs can handle justice and ten laws are all you need. Look out there and squint your eyes and look twenty years into the future. What do you see?"

Both emperors involuntarily glanced out the window. "In less than twenty years, we'll have smokestacks all along the horizon. We'll have armored rangers instead of home town sheriffs, steam locomotives instead of horses, and commercial law instead of honorable men. I'm not certain that I'll like it."

The younger emperor leaned forward. "I think you're worrying too much, Wilson. It isn't the hats and guns that make Texas, it's the attitude. One thing that we learned from our Yorker friends was that it is possible to screw up a society with hundreds of damned laws and restrictions without a single working steam engine. I personally like the Joneses, but can you imagine living in a country where the government tells you that you have to stay in a marriage that you want out of, and tells you what hours and days you can operate your own business. No, someday Texas will be a lost paradise like Camelot, but it won't be for a long time and I am just going to concentrate on enjoying living in Camelot while it lasts."

The elder Adams stirred. "Romance is great, but here we are having cigars and whiskey on the way home. I'm happy. Of course, I'll be a lot happier when we get the coastal defenses done."

The younger emperor sipped his whiskey. "You know, Dad, I've been meaning to ask you to take over more of the day to day stuff in Austin. I need to work on those coastal defenses and Wilson needs to be at the farm. There just aren't enough heads to handle things these days."

"You, my son, are the emperor now. I serve at your pleasure. However, as soon as the crisis is over, I would appreciate being released to return home. Frankly, at my age I would rather hand out opinions than hand out judgments in the papal court." He was quiet for a moment. "You know, this war won't be like the Yorkers. You can't let them get away with their men and ships intact. We have to sucker them up onto the land and kill them all so they never come back."

Chapter 45   Uninvited Guests – Day One

Four months later, Ranger Barnes was having a hard time keeping awake. The first light glow of dawn was filtering through his sore and sandy eyelids. He had spent another long and chilly night manning the a cannon on the walls of Corpus Christi. It was not the glamorous service that he had hoped for when he joined the Rangers. He was suddenly awake when a loud screaming sound came from the sea and passed over his head, followed by a load explosion from the city.

"Jesus Christ, Sarge, what the hell was that?" He looked out to sea and saw dim spots appearing on the horizon.

The sergeant had his glasses out and was leaned over the parapets. "Looks like it's what we have been waiting for. Looks like a dozen or more ships about five miles out. Start loading."

"Shouldn't we tell someone?"

"Do you actually think there's anyone within ten miles who doesn't know?"

On the parapets, all ten gun crews were preparing to fire. Barnes looked harried, "How we gonna hit 'em five miles away?"

The sergeant was still looking out to sea, "Never said war was fair. All they got to do is hit a city four miles wide and we gotta hit a ship eighty feet long. Set your range five point one miles." More shells were incoming now. Only six of the ships at sea were firing, but the shells were incoming every few seconds now. The Texas guns were firing more slowly as they looked for the range. Behind them were the sounds of a city under attack, bells, alarms, screaming children, the sound of fires crackling and buildings crumbling, all punctuated with explosions.

After twenty minutes, the shelling stopped. Barnes asked, 'You think it's over Sarge?"

"Na. They just overheated their barrels firing too fast. They'll start again pretty soon."

That was about the time that the empress heard the banging on her bedroom door. Her first reaction was irritation. It was one of those half asleep, romantic, warm in the bed, spooned with her husband mornings. Suddenly she realized that no one ever banged on the door of their private bedroom!

The same realization hit her husband as he bolted from the bed and grabbed his robe. He was at the door before his robe was fully closed. As he grabbed the door open, the chamberlain almost yelled, "They're here! Corpus Christie is under attack."

Behind him, the empress already had a shower turned on and was reaching in his closet for clothes. The ninety second shower finished waking him up and his military uniform was laid out by the time he stepped out of the shower. As his wife helped towel him off he said, "I'll be in the telegraph room. Don't know when I'll be back." His horse and escort were waiting at the front door.

The imperial office building now had a telegraph room hidden in the basement. The signal ran through the street car tracks and a special siding built for the building.

The room was partitioned into a conference room and a smaller room for the actual telegraph. There were now twenty staff in addition to Wilson and Armbruster who knew about the telegraph and most of them were there on duty. As he entered, General Armbruster was ready with an update. "About a dozen ships appeared off the coast of Corpus Christi at first light. They have been shelling the city off and on for about two hours. The shore batteries are firing back, but they report that they have done no damage yet to the fleet. There have been no reports of additional ships and no reports of a landing."

The emperor sighed. "They're out there. Telegraph the other coastal cities to prepare for attack. Activate phase one and tell the farm to ready phase two. Tell the southern fort to reinforce Corpus Christi. They can be there in two hours on the railway."

Armbruster called over the signalman. "Send a message to the commanders at Corpus Christi, Brownsville, New Galveston, Victoria, and Port Arthur: Prepare all boats. Do not launch until invader fleet closes in. Send to the farm: Invaders Here. Wraps off. Prepare phase two. Await destination orders."

At the farm, train crews rolled out of bed and headed for the locomotives. By noon, all were filled with water and fuel and had small fires heating their tanks.

At the Corpus Christi docks, the crews of a dozen coastal boats stood on the dock and resisted the urge to duck for cover as they were told to make a trip upriver. "Move fast. Sail if you can, row if you have to, drag if you have to, but move fast. Your destination is the new warehouse ten miles up the Nueces. You can't miss it on the north bank and they will have men out to signal you. Now move out before we lose any more boats."

It was a grueling fifteen mile trip. They were all able to sail the five miles to the river mouth, but then it was rowing and towing the rest of the way. The explosions behind them kept them working full speed and they arrived at the warehouse too exhausted to climb out of their boats. A captain they had never seen before was waiting on the dock. "I imagine that you are a little tired after your trip. As soon as you get your breath, you will find beer and sandwiches inside."

Amazing the rejuvenating power of the magic word "beer". Within a few minutes they were all filing into the warehouse where a long table held platters of sandwiches, bowls of fruit, and steins of beer. The amazing thing, though, was the boat on a display stand between the table and the warehouse wall. It was a full sized coastal boat on stands, tilted toward the table.

The captain was smiling. "Gentlemen, get your sandwiches and come around the boat. I'm going to show you how to kill a big ship with small boat – and never have to row or tow again."

One sailor gestured with this beer stein, "What the Hell is that thing? Its got wheels on it and a chimney. Ain't no boat."

The captain was still smiling. "Gentlemen, this is what all of your boats will look like tomorrow. Those wheels are paddle wheels. The chimney is for an engine like one of those your kids got for Christmas, only this one burns coke and turns the paddle wheels. She carries two main weapons. That tube thing up front is a rocket launcher. The rockets don't carry a lot of weight, but they have a heavy charge of powder or incendiary. That cute looking gun mounted on the center platform is a rapid fire seventy five millimeter cannon. It's belt fed with explosive rounds and capable of putting nice holes in wooden ships. In those crates over there, we have conversion kits for all of your boats."

One crewman stepped forward with a grim look on his face. He was fingering the cross on the chain around his neck. "Captain, with all due respect, this isn't right. This is black magic and we got no business messing with it."

The Captain never stopped smiling, "Sailor, what's your name?"

"Harrison, sir."

"Harrison, this thing is no more magic than that pistol on your hip and you don't seem to mind using that. Now if it scares you too much, you can wait in the guard shack while the real men complete their work. On the way to battle, we can drop you off in town so you can explain to your kid that you were too scared to defend him. Corporal, escort Seaman Harrison to the guard room. He has a weak stomach. Anyone else?"

The crews for these boats had been deliberately picked from atheists, nonconformists, troublemakers and other men of good quality. There were no more objections among the other fifty nine men. Apparently Harrison was either a mistake or a last minute replacement.

The Captain continued, "When you finish your meals, beach your boats and start moving the crates out. Each of you will have a new crew member that will help with the installation and then man the engines during your run. Each crew will do its own conversion but you may have to team with the crew next to you to move some of the heavier pieces into place. Work carefully, but remember that every hour we are here, more people are dying. When you get the rest of the rig installed, you'll need to pull your boat up to the dock where the cranes will lower the boiler into the hold. If you finish your rig, try to help the others."

On four other river banks in Texas, other crews were working on their boats. In the other warehouses, six other seamen refused to participate. Two of them tried to attack the sample boats with axes and had to be restrained. One man ran up and down the beach screaming "Blasphemy! Blasphemy!" until someone patiently cold cocked him and handcuffed him to a pipe far enough from the beach to muffle his panicky screams. There were no other problems.

The farm had prepared the kits well. Nothing had to cut or fitted and everything was clearly marked. It was a bolt in job and by nightfall, all of the boats were converted and the boilers fired up for the first time. The crews practiced until it was too dark to see and then moved inside to be trained on operation and maintenance of the new engines and cannon.

Back at Corpus Christi, nightfall brought a halt in the shelling. All day long, the shells from the boats had fallen at the western edge of town, furthest from the shore. When the shelling let up, the garrison commander walked the ruined city walls inspecting the damage. As deeper night fell, a glow was apparent on the western horizon.

His aid pointed to it, "What do you think that is?"

The commander stared a the glow for a moment, "It's an army. A big army that wants us to know that it's there. Get some scouts out to see just how big it is."

The commander was still up at midnight when the first scouts returned and reported, "It's big, alright. About five thousand men and horses. Nice man we talked to said that they landed two days ago in an empty area near Kingsville. They've been moving fast since then, just taking time for gathering slaves and killing people. He complained that they haven't even been given time to loot properly. After the bastard told us about the slaves, he broke his neck getting off his horse. He did say that they were told that tomorrow would be a big payday."

In Austin, the word went out on the telegraph to move all of the troops south of Corpus Christi up to defend it. Even with the rail cars, the additional two thousand men would not be in place until the next evening. The invaders did not wait that long.

Back at Austin, more people had gathered into the command center. The old emperor was pacing. "The worst part about that damned telegraph is that you know where the war is and you're still too far away to help. The rest of that fleet has to be out there somewhere. I don't believe that they came all this way with five thousand men and a dozen ships. They leapfrogged the coast in Florida, and they're going to do the same here. Corpus Christi is a diversion."

The younger emperor looked up from the message he was reading. "We all agree with you. The message went out this afternoon to evacuate all of the women and children near the coast. Unfortunately there are only nine telegraph stations on the coast so it will take about twenty four hours for everyone to get the message."

At the same time that Corpus Christi was being shelled, a dusty rider fell off an exhausted horse in front of the sheriff's office in Brownsville. When the deputies picked him up and he got his breath, he gasped out "Bayview. Foreigners attacking. Lots of them. They need help."

Sheriff Garrett didn't wait for more. "Scott, get the posse bell ringing. Harry, get out to the ranger station. Tell them we need everyone. We'll ride in an hour." Within twenty minutes, two hundred mounted rangers showed up in full gear. They were wearing the new armored coats and fifteen were carrying one of the new sub machine guns. Within the hour all five hundred twenty seven able bodied men in Brownsville were saddled up and in front of the sheriff's office. The sheriff had one of those voices that you could hear over a waterfall. "Anyone short of ammo fill your bags from the boxes over there. Take plenty of ammo, this isn't a bank robber. These are soldiers we're going after. Everyone needs to be armed long and short. See the deputy if you need a better pistol, the rangers brought spare rifles in the wagon over there. Don't be shy." As they moved out, Garrett assumed his other title of Colonel of the Home Guard.

It was only twenty miles to Bayview, less than a two hour ride for men in a hurry. It was a small town with not more than two thousand inhabitants. Today it was a funeral pyre. The smoke could be seen more than a mile from the town. The Brazilians must have surprised the inhabitants. There were bodies on both sides of the main street, but no one alive. In one place, it looked as if some of the town's men had surrendered and then been executed. The slaughter was worse in the town square, littered with the bodies of the very old and very young. Garret kneeled at the bodies of two small children, shot and left to die. On a sidewalk bench an older couple had died arm in arm. "I understand killing the men, but why did they kill these people?"

His sergeant said "They were too old or too young to make good slaves. They didn't want to bother carrying them back to Brazil."

Garrett shook his head, "Damned animals!"

Scattered among the bodies were a several yellow uniformed corpses. Nearby one of them showed signs of life. Garrett shouted out, "Get the Padre up here. Padre, he speaks something like Spanish, ask him where they took the prisoners."

The Padre kneeled by the wounded invader. The invader's arm had been shattered by a bullet, but his soon to be fatal wound was a gut shot. The padre took his bible from the pocket of his buckskin coat and kissed it. He spoke to the invader, "Son, you are going to die soon. You cannot meet God with this on your conscience. Tell us where they took the people so we can rescue them."

The invader groaned and glared at the priest. The padre leaned forward again, apparently oblivious the fact that his one knee was pressing hard on the invaders wounded arm. "Son, you must confess for the good of your soul." The invader screamed twice and then blurted out, "Vista, Laguna Vista. Get off my damned arm!"

"Son, do they have prisoners with them?"

The invader looked wolfish, "Yes, father. Good looking women. You need one old man?"

The priest looked sympathetically at the wounded man and accidentally leaned on his wounded arm one last time. "My son, you have earned absolution. Do you wish to be cured of your pain? Good. Here is my derringer. It has one bullet. Do what you must."

Garrett swung up on his horse. While they were examining the town, forty more men from outlying ranches caught up with the column. "They are headed back to Laguna Vista. Their boats must be there. Let's go get our people back."

He lead the column west out of town, trying to be professional, trying not to let the anger he felt show in his eyes.

The invaders, well over five hundred of them, were there with their captives. There were horses tethered between the beach and the tree line, still yoked to wagons. The wagons had padded benches about the size to hold ten men on each side. Apparently the yellowbellies had learned something from their raid on Florida. Most were lounging on the beach and some of them were holding down screaming women. They seemed to have about two hundred captives roped and chained together, mostly women. They also seemed to be waiting for something, probably the return of their ships. There was no cover in the tenth of a mile between the tree line and the beach, just scrub brush. Garrett called over the ranger captain for a conference. There was nothing fancy to be done. They decided on a simple plan. The Posse would form a long line in the woods and then charge from a position behind the Brazilian wagons. The Rangers would form a second column and come out of the tree line near the beach where they could move faster. They would depend on the slight cover of the Brazilian wagons and the sloth of the invaders to let them close.

They mounted up abreast, scattered inside the tree line. Garret took his pistol in his left hand and his saber in his right. Raising the saber over his head, he gave the order never before given in Texas, "No Quarter! Charge the bastards." They burst out of the forest in a long line and galloped for the beach. The invaders jumped up as they heard the charge coming. The rangers came out of the tree line near the shore and charged up the beach, hitting them on their flank. The fire from the invaders was sporadic but deadly. The sten guns immediately took out the first ten men in the Ranger column and several horses and men from the posse.

When the prisoners heard the horses, they began to kick at their captors and bite the ones close enough. They pulled on their ropes and upset some of the invaders. Most of The invaders couldn't decide whether to hold on to their captives or look at the Rangers. The confusion was fatal. Some prisoners managed to land hard kicks to the privates of the invaders and several ended up with invader guns in their hands. One woman threw her ropes around the throat of her captor and climbed on his back to strangle him. Then the horses were among them. The invaders soon realized that the Texans were not interested in prisoners, and only one side would leave the battlefield alive. Even mercenaries fight hard for their own lives. During the battle Garret thought several times about how much more satisfying the saber was when dispatching animals.

When the battle ended, two hundred fifty two Texans, including Garrett, the ranger captain, and the Padre were dead but there were no breathing Brazilians in sight and not one Texan had been taken into slavery.

The ranger lieutenant took command. "There is still work to be done. I know that you have all suffered greatly, but their friends are still alive. We need to get them too. Everyone help clean this beach up. Take our wounded and dead to the tree line. Prop up the yellowbellies."

There were loud protests and cries of "You can't be serious."

He stood his ground. "Do you want to do this again next year? Or do you want to avenge your dead today?"

Grudgingly, most agreed. They moved the wounded and as many of the dead as they could into the woods. Then ten rangers stripped Brazilian officers and donned their uniforms. The remaining one hundred fifty surviving rangers sat on the beach with ropes dangling from them as if they were captives. Most rangers had a submachine gun or sten gun near them. Around them, the unmoving yellowbellies looked to be lounging or sleeping. Two hundred members of the posse remained ready in the tree line. Five women convinced the lieutenant that the scene would not look convincing without female captives and insisted on joined the rangers on the beach. One removed her top to complete the illusion of slavery.

They had less than an hour to wait. A virtual fleet of longboats appeared at the headlands and rowed for the beach. They were accompanied by several clumsy flat bottom boats that were apparently intended to transport the wagons and horses. The yellow clad rangers jumped up and down and fired pistols into the air in mock celebration. Two of them went about kicking the dead as if they were trying to wake the men up for departure. It was perfect.

The longboat commanders were so confident that twenty of them beached almost at once and the laughing crews jumped out onto the beach to congratulate their fellow invaders. Seconds later the rangers opened up with the confiscated sten guns and raked the beach clean. They threw off their fake chains and ropes and charged the boats to make certain that no one escaped. Several of the boats had not yet beached and they rowed back hard to get away. It did most of them no good. The posse had kept all of the long guns. They rode out from the tree line when the shooting started and went to prone firing positions on the beach. As the sailors tried desperately to row away, the Texans calmly held a turkey shoot. They later found out that only one man on each boat was armed with a rifle, the rest carried only sailors knives. Didn't seem to matter much. A slaver is a slaver even when he was dumb enough to bring a knife to a gunfight.

Chapter 46   Uninvited Guests – Day two

The next morning a rider in a garish yellow uniform and a plumed orange hat showed up below the Corpus Christi city walls. The mayor and the garrison commander rode out to meet him. His offer was simple, "You have seen what we can do to your city. We have been merciful so far and only destroyed your walls and a little of the center. If you do not surrender, we will flatten your city block by block and kill all you, and your families, and even your horses and dogs. You have until noon."

As the Brazilian turned to go, the commander rode around in front of him. "We are honorable men in Texas and I cannot kill you under a flag of truce. However, I believe that I can express our feelings clearly." He reached over the horse's head, grabbed the officer's tunic and threw him to the ground. "Now, as you walk home, remember you are in Texas. You want to live, you leave now." With that, he took the Brazilian's horse and rode back into the city.

Back in Austin, they were trying to figure out where the main invasion fleet was. There had been no news from the fleet and even with overnight reinforcements, only two dozen ships had been sighted at Corpus Christi. They had all slept on cots the night before and the atmosphere was getting stale. The two emperors, Wilson, and Armbruster took the lead, but there were ten other staff members there. Wilson had his tired head in his hand. "Look, the cat is out of the bag. We activated the steam launches yesterday so we might as well let the locomotives into the war. We can send them to Houston. They have to pass through there anyway, wherever the damned fleet is."

The emperor knew that he was making a major decision. One that could live in history as the salvation of Texas or the end of the Adams. He wished his voice did not sound so weary as he voiced it. "The Baron is correct. Signal the Farm: Fully activate phase two. Proceed all assets to Houston. Further orders there. General, would you fill us in on our status."

The general shuffled his papers. "We have now received reports of a dozen small landings by the Brazilians. They have been using wagons to move inland and have been attacking remote towns. So far the local forces have been able to handle the problems. No one has asked for additional help.

"Corpus Christi seems to be the first big battle. The Brazilians landed five thousand men there. Apparently they plan to use the gunboats to force a surrender of the city. We have just twelve steam launches to handle the invaders.

"Baron, you are most familiar with the boats. Do they have a chance against ships of the line?"

Wilson answered, "I think so. They plan to sneak up behind them and blast them in the butts. That is not as trivial as it sounds. The warships are hard to maneuver under sail. Our boats can go upwind or crosswind, keep out of the line of fire of the warships and shoot them in their most vulnerable spots. Remember, even these monster gun boats usually only have a couple of swivel cannon that can fire sternwards. If the launches work as well as we planned, it's at least an even bet."

The elder emperor looked at this pocket watch. "If they left on time, we should have news in a few hours."

The General continued, "We have a thousand rangers in Corpus Christi and about two thousand posse members. By this afternoon, they will have two thousand more reservists arriving by rail. Unfortunately, we didn't have enough horses ready to transport, so the troops coming will have to fight on foot. If we can handle the ships, they have a good chance to win."

Back at Corpus Christi, they were getting ready to "handle the ships." The boat crews were up at first light, stoking the fires and loading ammunition. Breakfast was hot, well prepared, and strangely tasteless. All minds were on the boats. An hour after dawn they headed down the Nueces for the ocean. The boats were harder to handle than they hoped. The paddlewheels tended to overwhelm the rudder and make the boats hard to turn. They soon learned that the best way to turn was to use the clutches on the paddlewheels. Most boats ended up with two men in the stern. One handled the rudder and the other sat behind the two clutch levers. They could only make five miles an hour on the river and keep the boats under control.

Things were better when they got to the ocean. They didn't have to handle currents and narrow places. They sped up to twelve knots and found the boats easy to handle. The only problem was waves. The paddlewheels were rather small and they found that they would sometimes lift out of the water on a heavy swell. That would slow the boat down or make it fishtail. They headed straight out to sea for a mile and then turned south toward the warships. If all went as planned, the warships would be sitting parallel to the shore readying for a bombardment. They would come in downwind and get a least one shot in. Even if they were seen, it would be hard for the sailing ships to move into or across the wind to attack them.

By the time the warships were in sight, they had learned that the faster they went, the less problem they had with the swell. Most boats were up to fifteen knots. They scattered left and right and made no attempt to keep order. In the lead boat, Seaman First Class Erickson was manning the launcher on the *Suzy III*. The lack of a sail over his head made him feel strangely exposed and his nerves were showing. The noise and speed were nerve-wracking. "Damn this thing moves fast. I keep waiting for us to swamp."

His loader shouted back, "Just keep your eyes on the warships, the captain will keep us afloat."

The rockets were four foot long versions of the signal flares they were familiar with. These had vanes on the back and were fired by pulling a string that set off a percussion cap. Unfortunately, they had no where near the effective range of a cannon. This would be close in work.

They would have to attack the warships from the stern and hope that their speed would keep them safe from the stern chasers. The plan was to get in close, fire up or sink a ship and then retreat upwind before they got sunk. They were belching smoke like a badly lit campfire and had no hope of escaping detection. If they got abeam of the warships, their smokestacks would make highly visible artillery markers.

The *Suzy III* was the lead boat. There had been no chance to practice with the rockets, but Erickson reasoned that the trajectory of the rocket would be lower than an artillery shell and lowered the launch tube to an almost horizontal position. When they were about four hundred yards out, the Brazilians seemed to realize that the approaching boats were not burning wrecks and opened fire. Fortunately, most of the ships on the north end of the formation were anchored with their sterns facing the approaching boats. With only one gun, the stern chaser, on each ship able to fire at the newcomers, they weren't going to get off many shots before the boats closed. The first rounds from the ships overshot and went wide in every direction. At three hundred yards, a few ships got off rounds that were close enough to make the Texans duck. Looking back, Erickson could see that one boat was dead in the water. It looked as if one round was close enough to swamp the boat and put out the boiler fire. Everyone else was still coming. At two hundred yards, Erickson's gunner opened up with the rapid fire cannon. The first rounds hit high on the stern. The second burst seemed to take out the stern chaser. At about a hundred and fifty yards, Erickson tried to put a rocket into the water line. He misjudged the delay in the launch and the rocket went high over the stern when the boat rose on a swell. He was still staring at it when his loader shouldered him aside to put another incendiary in the launch tube. The second rocket was timed better and went into the center of the stern with a satisfying "whump". At first there didn't seem to be much damage aside from some broken windows, but then the fire started in a line from the rocket to the waterline. As they closed, the gunner put more rounds into the area hit by the rocket. They were loading the third rocket when the boat made a sharp sliding turn. Erickson would have landed in the water if the loader hadn't gotten one hand on the launcher and another on his crewmate. Lesson two. Fast, nose heavy boats turn very slow and plow into the water, and they don't have brakes. As Erickson looked behind him, he saw that several of the warships were burning. At least two on the other end of the formation were setting sails, apparently preparing to give chase.

Twenty minutes later the eleven surviving boats were rendezvoused about two miles from the warships. The commander of the flotilla was speaking through a megaphone. "The turn was a bad idea. When we slow down to make the turn, we are good targets. They can't hit us when we are close to them, so this time we go all the way through, no stops. The big waddlers are the most important ones to hit. Be ready to swivel the launchers when you go by, that's one of our advantages, they can't aim their big guns. Gunners, your job is to keep the small arms fire off of us. Now stoke up all the speed you can and we go again."

The boats turned clumsily and lined up like stock cars waiting for the signal. Then the commander blew his steam whistle and they were off. This time they took more fire earlier and one boat, the *Sweet Matilda*, dissolved into firewood from a direct hit from a stern chaser. The rest kept going. All Erickson could see were the ships growing larger. At two hundred yards, he started firing the rockets. The first ship they approached was already ablaze but he put one more onto its deck. Then he swayed back as the steersman put them within ten feet of the side of the monster. The gunner raised his gun to rake the gun ports as they passed. They were along side the next one before he could get his wits together for another shot. He waved frantically for the crew to duck as he swiveled the launcher around and fired a rocket almost over their rear deck. At twenty feet, it was hard to miss. The rocket turned out to be an explosive charge placed right at the waterline on the bow of the ship. On both sides, he could hear small arms firing and rockets whooshing as the other boats did their work. One time he heard his rocket hit a ship at the same time as another one took it from the far side. It wasn't all one sided. The big ships had swivel guns and small arms they could use. Ahead of him, he could see one of the Texas boats aflame and drifting. He kept thinking that they had to be through soon. The line of ships just kept going on. Then they reached the ships that had set their sails and cut their anchors. Two of them had managed slow turns and were almost broadside to the Texans. Erickson's gunner poured fire into the wheelhouse of the closest one. Then the warship let loose a broadside that made the water explode twenty yards behind them. The ships couldn't depress their guns far enough to hit the Texans. At least not yet. If they were still operating as the Texans moved away, there would be a lot of dead Texans. Erickson fired rockets at the gun deck as fast at the loader could get them ready. It didn't matter what they were, explosive or incendiary, they just had to destroy that deck. A glance showed that the other warship that had turned was taking a lot of fire from the other boats. Then they were past the Brazilian formation. Eight boats out of ammo, out of rockets, with crew bleeding from small arms fire, moved away as fast as they could. They took two more salvos from one of the ships that had turned and one more boat exploded into splinters. Behind them, the Brazilian fleet was in flames. The one ship that Erickson had made the lucky bow hit on was sinking at the bow, the rest just burned. Erickson looked back at his own boat to see that the steersman manning the clutches had taken a hit and been replaced by the engineer. Everyone else seemed unscathed.

It seemed doubtful that the Brazilians would be shelling Corpus Christi that day. The boats returned to the city docks to the cheers of the garrison. The crews all smiled and waved thanks, but inside, the commander was anxious to tell Austin what they had learned about tactics.

In Austin, the news caused every man in the command center to stand up and cheer. The Corpus Christi fleet had been reinforced overnight and the Texan boats had disabled at least fifteen ships. They immediately sent messages to the other boat crews describing the tactics used by the first boats. "Go in fast and close. Remember you can fire to the side. Keep moving through. Incendiaries most effective. Remember the Alamo and don't do it again."

General Armbruster suggested a second message, "Now that the cat, as you put it, is out of the bag, there is no longer a reason the keep the locomotives in Houston. I suggest that we scatter them between Corpus Christi and Port Arthur. Put one or two in each town or fort where they are likely to be used. That will cut down on the time it takes to get troops into the action."

The emperor said, "I tend to agree with you. What are your feelings about the equipment train?"

"Leave it in Houston. The most probable place to need it in New Galveston and that's only twenty miles from Houston."

The emperor looked around the table. "Anyone have another plan? Is this the consensus? I do so order. We are in it."

At the end of the table, Sir O'Brien cleared his throat. "Sire, I think my place is with the troops now. I request permission to join the troops in Port Arthur."

"O'Brien, I envy you. This modern warfare doesn't seem very manly. You have my permission to join your troops. Remember the Alamo."

"And never let it happen again. Thank you, Sire. I'll be leaving now."

After O'Brien left, the emperor turned to his father. "God, I really do envy him. I'd love to get my hands into this fight."

Wilson rapped on the table. "You forget that Houston is only six hours away now. We could leave tonight and move this entire operation to Houston well before morning. Then we would only be twenty miles from the probable center of battle."

The emperor emeritus perked up. "That's right. What are we waiting for? Let's start getting ready to move."

His son put a hand on his arm, "Dad, We aren't waiting for anything, but you are. Texas can't afford to have both of us near the same battle. Someone has to stay behind."

The emeritus momentarily looked sour. "Tell you what, son. I'll stay in Houston, well behind the lines and you can go on the battle when we find out where it is. At least I'll get to see your mother tomorrow."

The emperor was not fooled. His parents loved each other dearly, but the elder emperor was no more in a hurry to get home than a child was happy to leave the playground. "Alright, Sire. We go to Houston together."

In Corpus Christi, the reinforcements had arrived by two o'clock in the afternoon. Two thousand men on eighty rail cars. A fast thinking colonel sent over five hundred horses along in a cattle drive. The horses weren't trained to work in teams and couldn't pull rail cars, but they could be driven along like cattle. Relieved of the burden of riders, they moved easily behind the rail cars and arrived fresh. They now had enough mounts to go after the Brazilians. The problem was to find the Brazilians. When the expected artillery barrage failed to materialize, the invaders had disappeared. The scouts reported that the invader camp was empty.

Fortunately, the Brazilians had depended on firepower more than brainpower. Their wagons left deep ruts that they had not bothered to conceal.

The garrison had about one thousand rangers when the bombardment started. Over nine hundred were still battle worthy. There were one thousand mounted reinforcements and horses for about five hundred more. The call went out for a posse. By four o'clock another twelve hundred men were saddled and armed. The commander decided to leave behind five hundred men to guard the walls and rode out to the invader camp with the rest of the men and a dozen mortars strapped to pack animals. The scouts rode ahead to follow the easy trail. The captain rode at the head of the column with his lieutenants at his sides.

At nightfall, the scouts estimated that they were less than a half hour behind the invaders. The commander decided to stop for the night and attack in the morning. It would give them time to scout out the opposition and pick the best place for an ambush. The Texans fixed small sheltered fires and extinguished them immediately after dinner. The fires in the invader camp were easily visible a few miles away.

The officers sat around a very small fire planning for the next day. One of the lieutenants pulled his coat tight around him and looked at the fires in the distance. "I figure there are five, maybe six thousand yellowbellies and about thirty five hundred of us. Don't seem like a real fair fight."

The captain shrugged. "What do you suggest we do, fight with one hand behind our backs?"

Chapter 47   Uninvited Guests – Day Three

The next day, they found out where the enemy fleet was. It was off the coast of Galveston. The ships stretched from horizon to horizon, troop carriers, cargo ships, war ships. This time they came for booty and bodies and they came big.

The bombardment began without warning, posturing, or bargaining. The gun ships seen off Florida anchored themselves two miles out and began to shell the port. The city batteries answered immediately. There were twenty of the new naval guns in place. Unlike Corpus Christi, they occasionally hit ships in the fleet only because there we so many of them. The Brazilians were again using their superior fire power to shell from extreme range.

In Galveston itself, the population moved into the new tunnels and shelters. The buildings, the docks, and the ships might go up, but the people were basically safe.

In a change of plans, the commander of Galveston, Cornell Peterson sent a message to the coastal defense guns to lay low. He ordered them to stop firing one by one as if they had been hit. They would be more useful as surprises when the yellowbellies tried to land.

The steam launches were ordered to move away from the docks until a coordinated attack could be launched.

Then they sat down and listened to the ground shake.

The orders went out from Houston. All steam launches except Corpus Christi were ordered to make their way to High Island, thirty miles north of Galveston. By counting the hulls, they estimated that the Brazilians brought between fifteen and twenty thousand troops. The locomotives were ordered to bring all but skeleton crews from every fort and city between Galveston and Port Arthur.

In Corpus Christi, the commander was too far away to get his orders. His day had begun an hour before dawn when he and his soldiers moved toward the invader camp. They left their horses a quarter mile from the camp and moved quietly down the trail. Just out of sight of the camp, they moved into the woods surrounding the meadow the Brazilians were sleeping in. Most of the camp was still asleep and the sentries seemed deaf and dumb. He could see that in addition to the campfires, they had erected tents for the officers and still dragged mess wagons along. There was no sign that they had dug a ditch or protected themselves with a barricade or palisade. As General Schwarzkopf said, "It helps to be fighting the Iraqis."

They had decided on a simple strategy. Surround the Brazilians and shoot a lot of them. The mortars were useless because there were Texan captives in the camp, it would have to be done personally. Full dawn was still a few minutes away when Garrett walked into the clearing carrying his AK47 at waist height. Seeing him on the move was the signal for the rest of the men to move. There was no shouting, no running, almost no sound. It took several seconds for the sentries to notice the silent line of men. Then it took longer to recognize that it was an attack. A few Brazilians called out, but there was no general panic for almost a minute. By that time, the Rangers were almost to the edge of the sleeping camp. The commander shouldered his weapon and fired a three round burst into the nearest standing Brazilian. Three thousand Texans did the same. They kept walking toward the camp firing calmly as they walked. By the time the first real resistance came, less than half of the Brazilians survived. Most of them were asleep and too amateurish to have gun or armor on them.

The invaders around the officer's tents were not so easy. They seemed to be an elite corps and they were on their feet and firing their sten guns before the Texans reached them. The Texan commander made an overhand gesture and dropped to the ground behind a handy body. A dozen of his men had dropped from the Brazilian fire, now the rest sought cover. The sten gun fire was heavy, but inaccurate. The Texans responded with Ak47s and Winchesters. For the next thirty minutes, the toll rose on both sides. Then the Brazilian officers began to call out for cease fire and surrender. White flags appeared and some small groups of Brazilians stood up with their hands raised. That was a problem. Most Texans just won't kill a man with his hands in the air, even if he does need it pretty bad. Firing from the Texans tapered off and the battle ceased. Almost fifteen hundred invaders had managed to successfully surrender by throwing their weapons away and either prostrating themselves or putting their hands in the air. Eight hundred forty Texans were dead or badly wounded. In addition to the fifteen hundred who surrendered, the Brazilians were allowed to tend to almost four hundred living but wounded troops on their side.

It took the rest of the day to bury the invader dead and begin the trip home. Almost three hundred Texans, mostly women, were found chained in the wagons and ten women were found in the tents of the officers. All but one had survived by hitting the ground and staying low, but one Texan woman had died from a stray Texan bullet. One of the ten came out of her tent smiling and waving at her rescuers. Then she walked over to a Brazilian officer and continued to smile while she drove a knife deep into his abdomen. She was still smiling as she walked away, brushing her hair back.

Fortunately, the invaders had brought enough slave manacles to outfit them all for the trip home. Well before nightfall, the column moved out. Dead and wounded Texans rode in the wagons, along with the captives too bruised to ride horses. The Brazilians marched manacled together in the center of the column. The pace was slow and tired.

By the evening of the third day Sir O'Brien had ridden down to Port Arthur on one of the steam locomotives. The workers at the rail yard had put together two trains of twenty excursion cars in spite of their frequent complaints that there was no team in existence that could pull twenty cars. The cars had ten parallel bench seats for up to sixty passengers. There were half height doors and sliding curtains at each bench. Two groups of eight hundred men apiece were camped out next to the sidings waiting to board. O'Brien had decided that a flashy entrance was needed so he rode on the front of the first engine as it approached the sidings. He made certain that he was very visible, standing tall and calm, holding onto the front headlight. He was dressed in his customary green kilt and was wearing a coat of plates that had been tailored to compliment his kilt. His green helmet carried both Captains bars and a knightly coat of arms. He jumped down lightly and approached the troops. You don't sneak up in a steam engine, particularly in a pre-industrial world, and every man was on his feet staring and pointing at the "Smokey III".

His voice boomed out cheerfully, "Gentlemen, if you will strike camp and get aboard, we will all be in Houston in plenty of time for the fight."

A voice from the crowd said, "It's a god damned dragon. I ain't riding that damned thing!"

O'Brien's cheerful voice boomed out, "Why it's just a little steam engine, like your kid got for Christmas." He walked around with an exaggerated swagger. "I've been riding this dragon all the way from Houston. Do I look dead? Because, if I'm dead, I want to someone to write my mother in Lone star so's she can come to my funeral. She wouldn't want to miss it. Now let's get aboard."

Several voices sounded, "No way. We're not riding in that thing."

O'Brien called out, "Who said that? Someone have the balls to come forward."

A middle aged ranger stepped out from the crowd. "I said that. I'm Sergeant Porter and I'm not getting on that evil thing."

O'Brien looked at the Sergeant. "Well, then turn in your guns and leave. You won't be needing them any more."

The sergeant looked defiant. "No one takes my guns!"

O'Brien looked patient. "Sergeant, a lot of good Texans are going to die in the morning if we aren't there. This is the only way we can get everyone there in time. If you're a coward, the rangers don't need you and you don't need a gun."

For a moment it looked as if Porter was going to draw. "Are you calling me a coward?"

O'Brien said calmly and almost respectfully, "No, Sergeant. I said 'if' not 'when'. There's still a seat up there for you and a fight tomorrow for all of us."

It was a close thing, but the sergeant walked to the rail car and defiantly swung aboard. In the next fifteen minutes, the rangers decamped and over seven hundred boarded. The ones who quietly slipped away were carefully not mentioned.

Before they left, O'Brien walked the train. "I know you men won't be worried, but just for the record let me tell you that this thing really doesn't go much faster than the horse cars you've all been on. It just doesn't have to stop and be changed like the horses. It makes a lot of smoke and noise, but it is just smoke and noise and don't hurt nothing. We'll be in Houston in less than four hours. There's food and drinks under your benches. Relax and enjoy the ride."

As they pulled out of the siding, O'Brien could see that the train on the other siding was almost finished loading. Apparently his counterpart had also been successful.

All eighteen locomotives made at least two trips that night, bringing over fifteen thousand troops to Houston by morning. Some of them came from as far away as San Antonio and Dallas. It sometimes took creativity to avoid confrontation. The commander in San Antonio put female nurses on the cars to pass out food and drink. Not one man was willing to appear cowardly in front of the women. A passing preacher who saw the women on the train yelled out "Harlots, Witches!" and went home missing his front teeth. No one insults a Texan woman in front of Texan men. Nationwide, less than a thousand men refused to board and there were no mass protests.

On the way, the sights and sounds of the trains caused a lot of people to pray, curse, and believe the end of the world was coming. The train crews in a hundred depots learned why the railroad had overstocked on coke for the heaters, water for the passengers, and excursion coaches. It was a night that few would forget.

Chapter 48   Uninvited Guests Day Four

The emperor and General Armbruster sat on horseback and looked down at the Port Of Galveston. Shells were exploding in the center of town about twice a minute. The general looked and shook his head. "Can you believe that over half of the traders refused to leave quarantine? They think that the Brazilians will honor their neutrality."

The emperor looked mildly disgusted. "There seem to be no limits on human stupidity. We need to get in there."

The general flinched at the noise of another barrage. "This may not be the best time, Sire."

"No, I meant the we have to get troops in there before the landing. The garrison is only about a thousand strong. They can't hold out for long. How much space do we have in the shelters?"

The general thought for a second. "If they are as bomb proof as we think, we might get another five hundred or so into them. Depends on how many civilians went to the shelters instead of leaving."

He turned in his saddle and looked past the mortar installation. "I suggest that we have the troops dig in over there and then they can charge in the back gate when the yellowbellies are on the shoreline. The boys inside should be able to hold the city long enough for the reinforcements to come in."

The emperor got down from his horse and walked around the hilltop. "We can use this to signal the third column. You, over there." A young ranger looked up from where he was sitting on the grass. "I have an important task for you. Are you up to the most important job of they day? Good. You get some flares, big ones. If you don't have any here, there are plenty at the station about a mile down the hill. But you have to move fast. Sometime today those bastards are coming. When they do, you send up four or five flares. You be ready to duck, it may draw fire. You see that small hill north, northeast of here. That's between us and Todville. There is a naval force at Todville that has to know when those boats are on the way. Your job is to make certain that they do. The entire battle may depend upon it. Good luck, Son."

He turned to his escorts. "Sergeant, pick two men to ride to Todville. There are boats tied up at the dock there waiting to hear from us. Make certain that they know to watch this hill for flares. If there is time before the attack, they may want to send their own observer back here. The rest of us are headed back to camp."

In the early morning light, another group of Rangers was getting the surprise of their lives. They were standing on a dock in Todville looking down at eleven fifty foot long steel tanks floating in the water. A twelfth was hanging in a sling just above the water. Ranger Captain Watson stood near it. "Gentlemen, when we asked for volunteers, we asked for men who could swim well and who were not afraid to work in small spaces. This is why. It's called a Hunley. You row it by sitting inside and turning a crank that's attached to that propeller thing at the rear. That's your job. You will have an experienced captain to steer and you row for him. Now the thing that keeps you safe, is that this thing goes under water. Don't worry, you can still breath. Those two long tubes sticking up are called snorkels. When we are rowing underwater, one of you will be turning a fan to bring air down for the rest of us. The tubes on the front hold something called torpedoes. There're like rockets, but they use compressed air to put twenty pounds of explosive into another ship. You have to get close because they don't have much range. I am not going to lie to you. I have been in these things a lot of times and it's scary. It feels as safe as a gunfight with O'Brien, but there are ships out there with guns almost big enough to hit Houston and this is the only way we have to stop them. If you go, you'll have a story for the grandkids, but if you win a medal, we'll probably send it to your widow. Now, you all volunteered blind so if any man wants to change his mind, there is no shame attached. Anyone?"

When it was obvious that no one was going to move, someone asked, "How are we going to see where we're going?"

The captain asked, "You ever put two mirrors together and make a periscope when you were a kid? We got something like that attached to the front tube."

Someone else asked, "Do you use those wing things to go up and down?" For the next half hour, they looked over the hanging boat and asked questions. Then it was time to drop it in the water. In fact, the boat was only related to a Hunley. Someone had found the description of the submarine in a history book on an early American war. The engineers had followed the old plans, but used lighter materials than the Hunley brothers, increased the size by twenty percent, added the snorkels and periscope and made other improvements. The result was a new but proven design.

One of the rangers asked, "When do we leave?"

The captain pointed in the general direction of Galveston. "Watch for flares from the Port. They will tell us when to go."

Ranger Corporal Ted Garrett did not yet know that his father had fallen in Corpus Christi. Even if he had known, he had more immediate problems. He was standing with about five hundred other rangers watching the city walls of Galveston. Explosions were still coming from the town. In front of him, the captain was pointing to a small creek where the railroad had been cut by a lucky hit. "That's your first objective. You'll go in batches of fifty. When you hear the barrage hit, you run like Hell for that ditch. Hold up and wait for the next barrage, then run like Hell for the walls. Hit the ground at the base of the walls and then run for the tunnels after the next one. The yellowbellies are getting off a barrage about once a minute. Don't dally. First squad up!"

When the next barrage hit, the captain yelled at the group of rangers kneeling on the ground next to him, "Run like Hell. Now!" Fifty more rangers moved up to wait for the next barrage.

Garrett was in the third group. His legs felt like rubber as he ran and he stumbled part way to the ditch. He ended up scrambling the last fifteen feet on his hands and knees. Then he had to run again. This time he dove down right at the base of the city walls. Then he followed his sergeant through the gate and hoped that the man knew where the tunnels were. The tunnels were crowded and dark as they followed an officer to what he said was a stairway next to the docks. They rested by sitting on the concrete floor and leaning up against the wall.

When the attack came, the emperor was back up on the hill with a signal man. He had hoped to be in the front of the fight, but finally realized that his job was to coordinate it. The barrage had been stopped for about fifteen minutes when the fleet started discharging boats. One wave pulled away and another started loading. He turned to the young man he had sent for the rockets. "Send up the signals for Todville."

Turning to the signal man, he said, "Signal the garrison to hold fire." By the time the first wave got within a two hundred yards of shore, the sea was filled with over six hundred white landing boats in two waves.

"Signal the garrison, open fire on the second wave." Below, the six surviving cannons of the garrison opened fire with carronade shells, thirty pounds of explosive shell backed up with a thirty pound cask of grapeshot. Halfway between the garrison and the ships, fountains of water began to spring up around the incoming boats. Grapeshot was like buckshot, you didn't have to aim very well. Every shot splintered or swamped a boat. The new breechloaders were able to fire an eight inch carronade shell every fifteen seconds with a good crew. They were good, but there were a lot of boats coming. On the beach, Ted Garrett and his companions had emerged from the tunnels and taken positions behind the surviving barricades. They worked rapidly to mount mortars and machine guns before the invaders beached. The fire from the ships had almost stopped, and most of it seemed to be aimed at the cannons. Ted looked out on a white wall of boats being rowed as fast as scared crews could move.

At Todville, the hunleys had moved out. They had a mile of bay to the headlands and then another two miles of open ocean to get to the invader fleet. Captain Watson's boat was still on the surface. Twelve men sat on benches cranking the prop. The dive officer sat facing backward in the extreme bow with the ballast pump between his legs and the bow planes levers at each elbow. He would have to bend forward to reach the diving valves that flooded the tanks. Watson sat at the periscope with his feet on the rudder pedals and the torpedo triggers on the walls beside him. Behind him, the fan man slowly cranked the air fan, bringing air down through the front snorkel and forcing it out through the rear pipe. Light was flooding though the open hatch above. When they dived, glass ports in the entrance hatch and sides would let a dim light though. A small lamp hung from the ceiling, unlit until they needed it.

As they rounded the headland, he leaned aside from the periscope and called out, "Fan man, secure the hatch. Prepare to dive to periscope level." As the hatch closed he called out, "Dive to periscope". The dive officer was the only other experienced crew member. He watched a small depth gauge in the wall while he opened the dive valves. Soon they were traveling eight feet below the surface and heading for the invader fleet. Captain Watson knew from experience that sitting at the crank was frustrating because you had nothing to see and no idea what was happening. As a result, he kept up a steady and sometimes irritating chatter. "Our objective is the gun ships. The yellowbellies have got some big bastards of ships that carry huge guns. We can tell which they are because they are fat, waddling bastards with big guns barrels sticking out and only one row of guns. That's what I'm looking for in the periscope. Our job is to try for the third one in line."

They were be unable to communicate with the other boats once they submerged, so the captains had to agree before they set out which gunships each boat would attack. It took less than an hour of cranking to get within range of the fleet. It was like riding down a city street lined with black ships instead of buildings. There had be to well over a hundred ships there, anchored in a about forty feet of water. He figured that the gun ships would be anchored on the shore side of the fleet. When he found them, they were easy to recognize. They were lined up bow to stern well to the shoreward of the main fleet. They were wide brown lumbering cows, each anchored to the seabed with four tight chains. Large gun barrels poked permanently from the starboard side of each one. Two of the them were firing at a slow rate.

"Target in sight. Slow ahead." Damn, it was hard to line up the torpedo. The boat waddled and over corrected on every turn and just would not stay lined up. He had drifted so close to the side of his target that he was afraid the snorkels would be seen. He had one final idea, "Gentlemen, row slow astern." Being landlubbers, it took the crew a second to realize that he meant "Back up." However, they got themselves cranking the other way. As the ship began to move backward, the bow stopped weaving.

As the center of the gun ship passed by his sights, Watson yanked the cord attached to the first torpedo. He could see bubbles in the water ahead but after a minute, nothing happened. He turned to the crew. "It seems to have been a dud, we're going to try again. Forward slow."

This time he waited until he was forty yards from the gunboat. He could see the individual gunners though the gun ports when he launched the second torpedo. He watched the bubble trail as it approached the gunboat. Suddenly he was on the floor, no, the roof of the hunley. The roar had been so load that it was no longer sound, just pressure. As he became aware of his surroundings, he realized that the boat was over more than ninety degrees, but not completely upside down. Water was coming in the snorkel tubes. Slowly the ballast began to right the boat. It came upright and swayed several times before resting. Forward, the dive control officer was unconscious in his seat. Several crank men were slumped in the seats and in two cases, lying over the crank. "Injuries. Who's hurt?"

"My man here seems to have a broken arm, rest of us back here are okay."

He made his way back into his seat and looked out the periscope. "Jesus Christ, we really hit something. Men, the waddler is gone! We must have hit the powder room, 'cause there's nothing left but splinters." While he watched, another waddler took a hit and began to fill with water. It's hard to sink a wooden boat, but it helps when the enemy fills them with too much cast iron to carry.

The inside of the hunley was cramped at best. The dive officer had yet to regain consciousness. He turned in his seat, "You two on the end, we have to get Charley out of his seat. One of you will have to take the position until he comes too." They struggled for several minutes to get charley out of his seat and laid out on the limited floor space. One of the crewmen wiggled into Charley's seat. In the back, several crewman had removed their belts and shoes to make a crude splint for the broken arm. While they worked, sounds continued to filter through the hull. The whoomp of big guns had stopped and was being replaced by the sounds of torpedoes and the cracking of ships timbers. Watson looked over his crew. "I know that we have severe injuries and you're all shook up. But, if you can still row, we have four torpedoes left and a lot of targets."

An anonymous voice came from the back. "No point in going to a party and not dancing. We'll get you there."

The problem was that every damned shot had to be lined up by bruised and aching crank men. He stopped trying to be accurate. Just get too close to miss and send the torpedo. They got shaken at every hit, but nothing like the first one. When all six torpedoes were gone, they steered back toward shore. Knowing his men were exhausted, Watson surfaced a quarter mile from the fleet and opened the hatches. He climbed up to look out of the hatch above him.

The ships seemed to stretch forever. They all seemed to shooting or burning or both. Small, fast paddle boats belching smoke were mixed in with the fleet, firing rockets and machine guns as they passed the larger ships. Several of the invader ships had managed to cut their anchor ropes and get sails set. They moved slowly and majestically along the line of ships looking for targets, their bow and stern guns firing as they lumbered along. All of the waddlers were burning and two were capsized. As he watched, one of the paddleboats exploded.

He forced himself to drop back down into the boat, "The greatest battle the world has ever seen is going on up there. Everyone who can move better get to one of the hatches. You don't want to tell your grandchildren you missed this one!"

He climbed down to let the fan man go up for a look. The crank men started squirming around to get up the rear hatch. One by one all of the men except the still unconscious dive officer got a look. Even the crank man with the broken arm got boosted up for a look. It was like the worlds greatest fireworks show done in slow motion.

Captain Watson resumed his seat under the hatch. "Time to go home. We're out of ammo and almost out of targets. All ahead."

Back at Galveston things had started to heat up about ten minutes before the hunleys opened fire on the first waddler. Garrett was crouched behind a concrete wall holding his Winchester close to his chest. About twenty feet away, a mortar crew was slowly feeding their gun. He peeked over the wall at the invaders who were coming in, in spite of shells splashing around them. A lot of boats were getting hit, but there seemed to an endless number still there. He watched as the first boats hit the sand. The Brazilians screamed something angry sounding and jumped over the sides of their boats. The Texans opened fire and most of the first wave of invaders went down. Some got back up again when their armor stopped the rifle bullets. The Texans learned fast that you had to try for a head shot to kill them. The second wave behind them was already firing from their boats. The fire was intense enough to keep the Texan heads down. Garrett rolled into a prone position, peeking out from the edge of the wall and kept firing. On the beach, the invaders were walking over the bodies of their dead and still coming like army ants. Lots of them. He heard his sergeant yelling, "Pull back, Pull back."

As he got up, he glanced up at the walls to see yellow uniforms attacking the cannon emplacements. He just had time to wonder once how they had scaled the walls and then he was behind an overturned wagon a block from the waterfront. Twenty men were with him. A hundred yellowbellies came up from the beach firing sten guns and rifles. The Texans fired two volleys that took out the front ranks and then retreated another block. There were just too many yellowbellies and too few Texans.

On the hill above, the emperor had signaled the reserves to charge the city and then spurred his horse to join them. As the Texans inside retreated street by street, building by building, slowing down the invaders, fifteen thousand reinforcements ran out onto the plain in front of the city and headed for the open gates. Amazingly, some of the invaders had managed to traverse the city walls and get on the landward walls. The Texans started to take casualties from firing on the walls. Even worse, some of the gates had been closed by fast thinking invaders. They were in the process of storming their own city. One fast thinking Texan squad dropped their mortar to the ground and blew open two gates that the Brazilians had closed and Texans began to pour through. Two of the three mortar men failed to survive the answering shots from the invaders. After that, it was man to man, squad to squad. There was no strategy, just blood. The biggest operational unit was a twenty man squad and, for the next two hours, none of them knew what the other squads were doing unless they were side by side. The emperor led a twenty man mounted squad though the city gates and down the main street. They jumped the overturned wagons and boxes in the streets and ran down invaders with lance, saber, and pistol. With the gates secured, cavalry began to arrive in larger numbers and they finally turned the tide. By mid afternoon, the situation was stable enough for the emperor to set up a headquarters in the city hall and coordinate the counterattacks.

Any Brazilians that came into the open were overwhelmed with the mobility and hitting power of the horsemen. It was easier to bypass armor with a saber thrust to the throat or a pistol shot from ten feet away. The ones in buildings and warehouses had to be dug out one at a time.

A few Brazilians tried to get back to the boats only to find most of them destroyed by Texans and their fleet on fire. They had no where to go and no way to get more ammo or supplies. Certain that they would be executed anyway, pockets of invaders continued to fight hard until an hour before nightfall. When darkness was about to fall, the Texans set fire to the buildings still occupied by invaders and shot them as they left.

It was not an easy victory. The invaders had come with almost fifteen thousand men. At least thirteen thousand had made it to the beach. The first wave of invaders had virtually wiped out the beach defenses before help arrived. The horsemen were effective once they closed in, but they took a lot of hits trying to get close. The Texans had well over two thousand dead and twice that number wounded. Thanks to Winnie Wigwam and Samuel White, most of the wounded would live and even keep their arms and legs.

The biggest single problem was what to do with the three thousand unwanted Brazilian prisoners.

Chapter 49 The Last Meeting

Except for Artimus and Jeremiah, the entire committee was there. Every member sat around the large conference table in the full formal dress, bright Sam Houston waistcoats, white pipe stem pants, ruffled shirts under paisley silk vests. Most wore their medals and carried gold watches in their vests. The women were in long silk dresses and embroidered shawls under carefully coiffed hair and dripping with gold. The mood was festive.

The emperor opened the meeting by slapping his fist on the table. "Ladies and Gentlemen, I welcome you to the last meeting of the Archeology Committee. I know that you are all anxious to get the festivities, so I'll keep this very brief.

"Congratulations, you won. You won bigger and better than almost anyone in history. Thanks to you, Texas survived the invasion and has moved into the industrial age.

"You have put yourself out of business because you were so successful that your work no longer has to be secret. Those of you who are interested are invited to join the new, and public, Progress Monitoring Committee. It will be a public body with the stated purpose of protecting the society from evil science and the real purpose of continuing the work you have done so successfully.

"The last order of business is the envelopes that are at your chairs. You have already received your stock in Winnie wigwam. The envelopes contain stock in the new Imperial Railway, the Steam Works, and the new Imperial shipyard. It is our sincere feeling that no one who has risked what you have for the good of others should ever be allowed to worry about the roof over your head or the state of your cupboards. The Empire of Texas is eternally in your debt.

"Now, the ballroom is full of spouses, girlfriends, music, food, and drink. It's time for a celebration."

The emperor walked the path with the only man allowed to call him "Burt." They strolled though the New Boot Hill, stopping to read an occasional name from a white cross. "It might be a bright new world, but the old Texas never needed a national boot hill. Fighting used to be personal."

"I know, Burt. But we lost over three thousand men. The families are grateful for this place. It gives them a feeling that their loved ones didn't die alone. It's beautiful here on high hill over the sea. I've seen families come here with a picnic basket and spend the afternoon. It seems to make them feel better."

"You know, Wilson, that it's going to get larger, this place. The world is a smaller place now and armies are getting bigger. I just realized that I don't know where the boys who will die in Brazil are going to end up."

"Then you have decided, Sire? We are going to Brazil?"

"There isn't much choice. While we were fighting in Galveston, they hit a dozen small villages and took hundreds of Texans prisoner. We're going to team up with the Yorkers and go after our people."

Wilson sighed, "Well, it will be good to see old friends again."

They had reached the edge of the cemetery overlooking the sea. They looked out from a bright new world into a closer and scarier world outside.

---THE END---

Chapter 50   The Star Of India-For Those Who Wonder

(The Star of India is real ship. She sits in San Diego where she is cared for and sailed by a group talented volunteers. None of whom, unfortunately, appear in this story)

Year Zero, BNE.

If the world weren't going to Hell so fast, it would have been a perfect seashore morning. Warm breeze. Salt smells. The sound of sea gulls in the air.

Phil was walking up the ramp of the world's oldest sailable ship. He and his wife had walked this ramp three nights a week and most weekends for twenty years. They were volunteers on the *Star Of India*. After twenty years, Phil was virtually in charge of the ship.

The *Star of India* was the world's oldest active ship. She began her life on the stocks at Ramsey Shipyard in the Isle of Man in 1863. One of the first iron ships, she bore the name Euterpe, after the Greek goddess of music. She was over two hundred feet long and 1318 tons. She was a full-rigged ship until 1901, when the Alaska Packers Association rigged her down to a barque.

She sailed the Britain to India routes until 1871. Then she began hauling immigrants to New Zealand, sometimes also touching Australia, California and Chile. She made twenty one circumnavigations in this service, some of them lasting up to a year. It was rugged voyaging, with the little iron ship battling through terrific gales, "laboring and rolling in a most distressing manner," according to her log. She ended her active life with twenty five years as the renamed *Star Of India* hauling passengers and cargo from California to Alaska and canned salmon from the Bering Sea To Oakland.

Phil and his wife, Marie, were part of a long line of volunteers who had spent the last fifty years restoring, rebuilding, and eventually sailing the *Star of India*. Thanks to them, the *Star* was in is as good a shape as the day she first sailed from the Isle of Man.

When they got to the main dining room, over a dozen of the other volunteers were already sitting under the brass and glass skylight of the mahogany paneled room. Normally, they would have met in the crews mess, but today was supposed to be special. They, and about sixty others, had been working for six weeks to get the ship ready for its annual sail up the coast. Smells of coffee and hot sugar filled the dining room as Henry, the self appointed cook of the *Star,* had filled the steaming pots and laid out sandwiches and fresh home made donuts on a sideboard. Despite the elegant settings and the comforting smells, the atmosphere was gloomy.

With the news from the east coast, the sailing was now obviously not going to happen. The entire country was in a panic as the plague traveled west.

Phil had no more gotten his coffee and sat one of the long padded benches when someone asked, "What's the news? Anything happening out there?"

Phil answered. "Just more bad news. The damned thing seems unstoppable. The quarantine line is now the Mississippi, but that's a joke. Pockets are everywhere. There's a rumor that Las Vegas is in a bad way and the city officials are covering it up so 'it won't hurt tourism'. Damned stupid. The world is ending. We're all dying and they are worried about hurting tourism."

His best friend, Albert, snorted. "Don't be too harsh on them. We're here and I'm worried about the *Star*. I know it's stupid, but I've spent the last fifteen years of my life keeping her going." His eyes glanced over the brass lighting fixtures and paneled walls that he had helped restore.

Albert was a slender, healthy looking man in his late fifties with grey hair and a wife beside him that proved that couples do get to look alike after thirty years of marriage. His wife leaned forward to look down the table. "Doc, how bad is it going to be?"

Doc Henry had that rugged look shared by most at the table. He also had the expression of a doctor trying to figure out how to tell a patient bad news. He was wringing his hands while he spoke. "Bad. Look, we've been friends for a long time and I'm not going to give anyone any bull. This thing is damned deadly and it's getting worse instead of better. With airplanes, cars, and motor cycles, you can't quarantine anyone these days. Frightened people run and they carry it with them faster than ever before in history.

It took the black death five years to get from China to Britain in the 1330's. It took just ten days for this thing to get from Africa to Boston. We're not even sure that it's going to follow the traditional Rules of Plague."

From the other end of the table, George Solter, the helmsman on the *Star*'s occasional cruises, asked "What in the Hell are these 'Rules of Plague'?"

Doc answered, "All plagues end. The rule is that plagues commit suicide. The better they are, the faster they die out. If a disease kills too fast, there isn't much time for the host to infect someone else. If the thing kills too fast, it runs out of nearby victims and there is no one to spread it. Look at syphilis, in the early days, it killed in days or weeks. It eventually evolved into a disease that killed in twenty years. Aids is a great example. It is a poor, weak disease. It's hard to catch. You have to have repeated sex with a diseased person or inject it right into your veins to catch it. Your body fights it successfully for years. If it was any weaker, you wouldn't die. However, it takes ten to twenty years to kill you, so there's plenty of time to spread it. As a result, it has killed a few hundred million people. Anyway, the rules of plague are pretty much 'The worse it is, this faster it dies out'. This is the worst that we have ever seen."

Albert looked thoughtful. "What you are saying is that if we could keep from catching this for a few months or a year, we might live though it? People, I've got an idea how we might save ourselves and the *Star*, and I'm certain that everyone of you has had the same idea." He smiled as he looked around the table. "We're sitting in a life raft. Come on, most of you must have had the fantasy once or twice. The world goes to Hell and you sail away on the Star to some safe place. Well, this is it. Everyone is dieing because you can't get away from the plague in the modern world. Right? Too many airplanes and cars. Right? Well, what if we were not in the modern world? What if we were someplace without airplanes, without even ships? We hold up for a year or so and wait until this thing follows those plague rules and dies out. Now, don't tell me that you haven't thought about it. Late night fantasies where the world ended and you took off to parts unknown on the *Star*. Well, the world is ending and we're sitting on the life boat. It's a nightmare – or a dream – come true. Te world is ending, but something you daydreamed about can save you."

Phil was smiling wide, "You're right. We must have all thought about it once or twice. The *Star* is ready to sail. With her, we can go anywhere in the world. No fuel or spare parts needed. We can find our Pitcairn and hold up and wait it out."

By now everyone was talking. Phil realized that he had to turn this into a working meeting. He looked around the table, "Gentlemen and ladies! It seems that we are all in agreement. But, we have to do this fast. That stuff is literally coming at jet speed. I suggest that we stock simple and leave on the tide tomorrow night. Now let's figure out what we need to do. Steve, you're the quartermaster. Why don't you get a few people together and figure out what stores we should lay in. Scott, you've done more repair work than anyone else here. Would you get together the rest of the group and figure out what tools and spares we need that we don't have."

Before they broke up into groups, they decided to invite the other seventy five or so volunteers and their children. No mothers-in-law, no friends, neighbors or relatives. They didn't want a panic that would swamp the ship with too many useless passengers. If they ended up on a deserted island as they planned, it might be impossible to feed themselves if too many were aboard.

Then they broke into groups to prepare lists of what they could take and how they could get it in one day. It was handy that no one needed to worry about maxed out credit cards and bad checks. The bills would never come due.

Two members opened up their cell phones and started calling the absent members. They called ten people and asked them each to call others. Within an hour, other people began to show up and join the planning groups. By evening, all the volunteers knew the basics of the plan, and had been warned to keep quiet about it.

The planning was continuing as late arrivals swelled the group. This was a group of bright people used to working together. The newcomers joined the two already working groups or formed small informal gatherings of their own.

In the quartermaster group, Scott was saying, "We don't need to worry about space or capacity. This is a 1200 ton ship. We could carry ten years of supplies for a crew our size, if we had the time to get them loaded."

Marie joined it. "Well, we don't have the time or the supplies. Like Phil said. We need to leave now, on the tide tomorrow. I suggest that we stick with the staples. We get all the flour, sugar, beans, rice, salt, cooking oil, canned meat, coffee, and vitamin pills we can carry." She smirked a little, "We can pay them when we get back."

Another woman added, "Some tea would also be nice, potatoes, apples and cured meats like bacon and ham also travel well."

Scott added, "If there's time, we can load up on canned goods. They last forever, but I agree, but we need to concentrate on the basics first." He looked down at figures he had scratched on his napkin. "I figure that we need a minimum of about sixteen tons of food to feed a hundred people for a year. We have a total of less than a ton of snack food and lunch supplies on board. That's our first goal.

Sixteen tons of protein, carbohydrate, and vitamins."

The woman who earlier mentioned tea and apples sounded worried. "Ok, but how're we going to get sixteen tons of food. Albertson's doesn't carry that much and pretty soon, people are going to start cleaning out the stores."

Andre leaned forward, with a little difficulty as he was a little more pot bellied than most of the crew members. "It's not as much as it sounds like. Continental E&G or L&C Food Distributors could deliver that much in about two or three truckloads. If we can get a list together, we can call them in the next hour or two and get deliveries tomorrow."

In the crews mess, Albert and his wife, Scott and a few others were working on the parts list. Of course, the *Star*, like all ships, had a standard supply list. However, the list was for cruising, not living, and assumed that spare parts, fuel and repairs were going to be available. Scott set the tone. "We'll want to avoid anything that wears out or needs fuel. We may be away for a long time."

Albert's wife started the discussion. "Every boat store around here stocks solar panels for battery recharging. We should pick up every one we can find. They don't wear out, don't need fuel, don't have moving parts and can give us radio and lighting power for years. "

Agricultural tools were added to the list: shovels, hoes, saws, knives, axes, hatchets. They decided on one chain saw, but knew that it would stop when it ran out of fuel, oil, and chains. A few two man buck saws were needed for when it quit.

Norman and Carla spent almost as much time in their gardens as they did on the Star. It was decided that they would head for a farm supply store to pick up all of the vegetable seeds they could carry. Preference would be given to high calorie and high nutrient foods – corn, yams, seed potatoes, and cabbage first, good tasting stuff second.

The ship was already stocked for the annual demonstration sail. The water tanks and auxiliary fuel tanks were full, spare sails in the lockers. The annual sail was only a day long, but part of the fun was stocking up the ship as if it were going on a real voyage. Doc would raid his clinic for all of the medical supplies that he could transport. At his insistence, the Star already had a well equipped infirmary both for tourists and for the annual sail.

By evening, they had done all the planning that they could. By that time most crew members were on board and had helped with the planning. The lists had been made, and tasks assigned. Everyone was talked out and tired. Phil ended the evening. "Go home. All of you. Come back as soon as you can with everything you can carry. You may not get new t-shirts or panties for a year or more, so bring all of your clothes, and the family album. Free your pets and keep everything a secret from your neighbor. The Star is now a life raft and any life raft can be sunk if it carries too many passengers."

"You've probably all seen 'Junk Yard Wars', that TV program where they give teams 8 hours to build anything from a lawn mower to a nuclear reactor with parts from a junk yard. Tomorrow, you will all feel like you are on that program. Any changes, stocking and fitting have to be done by dark. We'll start early and push all day. With luck, we leave on the tide, and live."

By noon the next day, Phil, Scott, and Steve Martina were going over the progress with Captain Fontaine. As quartermaster, Steve was doing his best to keep up with the flow of supplies onto the *Star*. He looked at his clipboard. "Food is the big problem. Continental delivered our order this morning. It was about half of what we need. L&G hasn't shown up. I called the warehouse and I don't think that anyone is working today. The panic may be starting."

Fontain nodded. "Phil, I suggest that you get some of the men who aren't needed here and send them over to L&G. Pick whoever drives the biggest pickups. Send enough help to load what we need in a hurry. I think things are starting to fall apart out there."

He nodded at Martina to continue. Martina flipped through his clipboard. "We are doing better than anyone could expect. It's only noon and we already have most of our stores, food excepted, on board. Some of the crew have been very creative. You know we gave them all blank checks and told them to buy anything they think we would need. Well, Norman and Carla came back driving two large pickups. They got the seeds alright, but they also brought back four pigs, four goats, and a couple of crates of chickens. They filled the rest of the space on the trucks with chicken feed, chicken wire, and animal feed."

Phil smiled. "We didn't think about farming, but I'm glad they did. Anything else we need to know about."

"Well, Bill Tyler turns out be something of a gun nut. He brought smokeless powder, lead, casings, reloading tools and even a couple of crossbows. He also loaded a couple of sealed crates that I think we should leave closed until later. Some of the women didn't like the idea of having guns on board, so I suggest that we keep it quiet until everyone realizes how primitive this is going to get."

"On the sober side, some of the women brought hair dryers and some men brought power tools, and we had to convince both groups to leave them behind. Wherever we go, if 110 volt current is available, we're too close to civilization."

Captain Fontaine stood from behind his desk and gestured to the door. "I think we should continue this discussion while we look at what's happening in the holds." They emerged thought the hatch to the squeal of pigs who did not like being airborne in a cargo net. There were people everywhere and everyone seemed to be in motion. The crew had rigged both the fore and aft cargo booms and were winching things over the side as well as carrying them up the gangplanks. High above the deck two teen aged boys, working with serious expressions, were attaching a radar antenna to the top of the forward mast.

Captain Fontaine pointed at the two young men on the mast. "I thought we were going to avoid using things we couldn't replace."

Phil shrugged. "There is a plan two. If you can't replace it, keep spares. We have two complete spare radars and enough solar cells to make certain that they will work until we get back."

As soon as the pigs disappeared into the hold, the crane swung back out to be loaded with feed sacks. Fontaine, Phil, and Scott split up to help heave sacks. Time was too short today for anyone but the quartermaster to limit himself to supervision.

By evening, they had eighty two adults, fourteen children and all of the supplies on board. They knew that there would not be tugs where they were going, so two of the davits held powerful ski boats that could also double as poorly designed tugs. They also had loaded enough small sailing boats into the cargo deck to provide escape for everyone in the crew. They were in a hurry, but there was plenty of space and the concept of 'Belt AND Suspenders' was a survival philosophy when you are leaving civilization.

In spite of their reservations about depending on civilization, two additional one thousand gallon fuel tanks and four spare generators had been lowered through the hatches and were secure in the hold – and filled. The work was cruder than they were used to doing, but fast. Two extra one thousand gallon water tanks were also in place and filled. The holds smelled of welding, fuel oil, gasoline, and steam.

By late afternoon, the improvised tow boats were easing the *Star* away from the dock and out to sea. As Phil watched the boats strain against the ropes, he glanced at captain Fontaine, "Who's speedboats are those?"

Fontaine grunted, "Hell if I know. If we're right, the owners will never miss them. If we're wrong, we'll bring 'em back someday."

Phil decided not to ask about the ownership of the two longboats, two zodiacs and the skiff in the hold. Scott Fontaine was right. With most of the population soon to die, property titles didn't mean much right now.

As old as she was, *The Star* was one of the last commercial sailing ships and, unlike earlier ships, she didn't need dozens of men climbing around the rigging to handle the sails. Everything was operated from the deck with winches and the big square sails rolled up and down like window shades – big window shades. When she was a commercial hauler, she carried a crew of only 24 and they took a full day to set the sails. The triangular fore and aft sails were set first on a barque. She didn't have much rudder and the small sails helped steer her. Then the big square sails were set one at a time. With over 80 workers on board, they got enough sails set to maintain headway before it got too dark to work. Walking the capstans was a mystical experience for more than one crew member. Out there was a world of jet planes, televisions and miracles. Here on the deck, a man breathed salt air, pulled on ropes, and listened to sound of air filling canvas and of ropes creaking over pulleys, just as men had done for thousands of years.

By full dark, they were on a steady tack moving west, southwest, slowly away from the shore.

Fatigue fought with excitement as some people found soft places to sleep while others stood or sat on the deck and watched the lights of civilization fade into a glow on the horizon. They did not yet realize that the lights were the death dance of their world. Many of the power stations were already unmanned and the lights would soon fade away forever.

On board, the *Star* was lit up like a small liner and covered in the sweet smells of fresh air and salt water. In the clear night, the windows of the cookhouse painted the deck with light as Henry and his newly appointed helpers served up tea, coffee, and chunks of fresh baked bread to the exhausted crew members who stumbled up to the window. Light flowed from the portholes as crew below shifted cargo and possessions to make soft spots to rest on. *The Star of India* had once been a passenger ship, but she ended her active life as a cargo carrier and she only had bunks for about 25 people. The rest would have to sleep on sacks and blankets scattered around the hold.

By one A.M., the ship was dark, the only people still awake were the few diehards still on deck, a worried Captain Fontaine pouring over charts in his cabin, and the deck crew.

Chapter 51 The Star, Outbound

Morning came early on *the Star Of India,* but it did not come with a bang of energy. The entire crew had been driven by nerves, haste, and excitement the day before. Most had spent 16 hours carrying, moving, stacking, and struggling without noticing the fatigue or pain. This was a morning when people crawled out of bed or hammock or off the flower sacks and stumbled up on deck nursing aching joints and pulled muscles. Most just laid on the deck and tried not to moan.

Henry and the cooks were as tired as anyone, but they managed to get scrambled eggs, bacon and home made biscuits onto the window ledges of the cook house. Then they, too, collapsed into grateful lumps of inactivity.

Slowly hunger began to overpower pain and people picked up plates of food to eat while sitting on the deck. One mother began looked more sad than exasperated when she told her young son, "I know you don't like tea, Harry, but it's going to be long time before you see another Coke, so you better get used to it." Her small smile was brave enough to hide her sudden realization of just how far away they were going.

By nine o'clock, a small committee was meeting in the main lounge to pick a destination. There was no point in even raising the rest of the sails until they knew where they were going.

Captain Fontaine spread out world map on the table. They sat in the main dining hall that had been refurbished in the grand dark wood paneled style of the ships heyday. Fontaine was the captain, but was used to following Phil's lead and his position was becoming closer to Admiral. He sat at the head of the long mahogany table. The captain and ten other crew members sat on the matching yellow upholstered benches that flanked the table.

Fontaine gestured at the maps. "I spent the night looking for what we need. We need an island with fresh water, enough land to plant on, and no people. A bay and a deep river would be good, we don't have to have that. Of course, it has to be far enough away from land and normal shipping lanes to assure our privacy, since isolation is the main purpose of this venture.

It turned out be a lot harder than I expected. Everything empty is empty because it's no only uninhabited, but uninhabitable. The only empty islands are bare rock, or poisoned ground or too damned close to Arctic to grow food."

He shook his head tiredly. "Just about everything from Fiji to Tonga is inhabited. The newest glitzy hotel trend is to put resorts on otherwise uninhabited islands. If there's a flat spot to land on a plane on, and sand to walk on, there are people nearby. Even the normally uninhabited spots are often national parks, well visited by tourists."

He pointed to a spot about a thousand miles southwest of India. "Drop into the uninhabited Chagos Archipelago in the Indian Ocean, and you'll see the sign that the customs man will be around to pick up the $5 fee on Monday and, 'Please put your trash in the containers provided.' This world has gotten mighty damned small."

Phil raised a tired hand to scratch the back of his head. "I think there is a place. Actually, Marion, Albert's wife came up with it. She was reading a news account on one of her female oriented web sites. It seems that Pitcairn may be empty, after all these years. A couple of years ago six 'brave' women on Pitcairn accused thirteen men of sexual abuse. Said they were talked into having sex too early and sometimes the men insisted when the women weren't in the mood. The men pointed out that the island was independent and had no age of consent or spousal rape laws. People had always had sex early on the island. Guess there wasn't much else to do. Anyway, England asserted authority on some excuse and arrested thirteen of the twenty one men on the island and put them on trial. AS few of the men went to jail, but ALL of the men left and refused to return to the island. The woman couldn't hack it alone, or didn't want to, so the last person left the island about three years ago. It has buildings, wells, generators, and a few roads, and it's now empty."

Fontaine thought for a second. "It's famous for having no harbor, but we can probably work something out. Lets get everyone together on deck and see if we can get a consensus. Hell, at least it's somewhere to go."

The decision to go to Pitcairn was made quickly once everyone gathered on deck. A few asked why they couldn't go some place closer, like the channel islands and Fontaine pointed out that anything that close to the coast would certainly attract plague carriers in small boats. Since no one had any better ideas, the vote went down in less than an hour. However it took over two hours to turn *The Star Of India* north to pick up the westward trade winds.

On the second day out, they were healed enough to start work on the passenger cabins. Albert Holland drew up plans for enough cabins to accommodate all eighty people on board. Single crew members and some of the teenagers would stay in the existing crews quarters in the bow, and everyone else would have small but comfortable cabins. They planned a comfortable common area for the area between the rows of cabins. Fortunately, one of the scrounging crews had cleaned out a Home Depot before they left, and, even more fortunately, getting to work took their minds off of the problems behind them.

About a week out of San Diego, they met a container ship on a course for Los Angeles. Phil was in the wheelhouse when the radio call came in. "*Star Of India*, this is the container ship Shanghai Lady. Come in Please. Come in." Phil keyed the mike, "*Shanghai Lady*, this is the star, go ahead."

"What the Hell are you doing this far out, I thought you only sailed around the harbor?"

Phil answered, "We decided to extend the training cruise this year. We're taking a little bit longer trip."

"This is the captain of the Shanghai Lady. We aren't getting much we can trust from the radio. Do you have news from the states?"

Phil keyed the mike again. "Yes, we do. And it is all bad. The plague seems to unstoppable. People were panicking by the time we left, and some of our people had to fight their way back to the ship with supplies. I do not suggest that you try to dock."

There captain of the *Shanghai Lady* seemed tired. "Unfortunately, we are under orders to deliver this cargo there and I don't see any alternative to following our orders."

Phil replied, "Think about it. Those orders were given to you by people who are probably dead by now and no one, repeat NO ONE is going to be at Los Angeles to offload cargo or give a damn about delivering it. Save yourselves."

"We've thought about it *Star*, but we don't have unlimited supplies. In a month or so we will have to make landfall."

Phil looked over at the container ship, as big as a mountain compared to the *Star*. "It might take creative thinking and a little scrounging, but I see thousands of containers on your decks. Some of them must hold food or bottled water or something else useful. Raid them! Keep what you can use and dump the rest of the containers overboard. If the owners survive, let THEM come back and look for the stuff. There is nothing but death in Los Angeles."

There was a long pause before the radio came to life again. "You might be right, we've considered staying out to sea. Now that we know how bad things are, we just might do it."

The *Shanghai Lady* was slowing down before she got out of sight.

A week later, the Star was overtaken by a Suezmax sized oil tanker. The giant ship passed silently on the starboard side without noticing the *Star*. Three crew members hung over the rail, obviously dead.

They did not see another ship all the way to Pitcairn.

Chapter 52   Home Away From Home

By the time the *Star Of India* reached Pitcairn, there were very few radio broadcasts to pick up. One after another, commercial radio stations and amateurs had dropped off the air. By landfall, the last commercial stations from South America and New Zealand had stopped broadcasting. They knew that there was no good harbor at Pitcairn, and that the Star would have to ride at anchor in Botany Bay like the *Bounty* had done.

Most of the crew was gathered on deck waiting for Pitcairn to appear on the horizon. GPS had taken the romance out of the crows nest, but human anticipation remained the same. Paul, the first mate, and the captain were in the wheelhouse watching the radar screen as the island appeared on the radar. Suddenly the captain poked the screen and yelled at the top of his lungs, "Shit. Reef the sails!"

Pitcairn was surrounded by small boats. As the *Star* slowed down, Fontaine sent a crewman up the mast for a look. They couldn't see anyone on the island, but the numerous boats told them that other people had had the same idea about getting away. They knew that there was also a small emergency air strip inland might have been used by other escapees.

The ships complement overflowed the main dining salon, the galley, and the crews mess as they debated what to do next. They eventually voted to continue on. There were now too many people on Pitcairn for them to feel safe. The Star continued a hundred miles northeast to Henderson Island. It was larger and flatter than Pitcairn and had a coral lagoon to anchor in. The entire island was six and a half miles long, three and a half miles wide and about one hundred fifty feet high. This was the island that the survivors of the whaling ship in the real Moby Dick story had been stranded on. Due to it's location and the scarcity of good fresh water, the island had been uninhabited since the Polynesian population had died out in the fourteen hundreds.

The entrances to the coral reef lagoon were relatively small and had coral heads in them. However the largest was thirty feet deep and might allow the Star to get in if they were careful. They wanted to get the Star in a protected lagoon near the beach for their long stay.

They hove to and broke out the zodiacs. The Star was a big ship, but it was lightly loaded and might get through the coral reef. The zodiacs did sounding on two passages and found out that the Star had about two feet of clearance from the bottom, if she was careful, more if they waited for high tide. It took the rest of the day to find a safe path through the coral heads in the lagoon.

By the end of the second day, the Star was anchored in the lagoon almost close enough to the beach to walk and the speedboat-tugs were being hoisted back into the davits. After a few days of wandering the beach and enjoying the lack of swaying, the crew got down to serious planning. They decided to plan for a stay of four years. Doc had estimated that the plague, if normal, should burn itself out in a year. They would leave a three year margin for safety. Then they would return to whatever was left of civilization. Surprisingly, no one voiced a desire to simply settle down permanently on Henderson. These were city people who wanted to go back to civilization, if there was one to go back to.

The work was heavy at first, but these people were used to working together. They started by digging wells in the highest part of the island. They eventually got a small but adequate supply of fresh water. One of the engineers on board scouted the island until he found the best combination of hills and low spots to build a rain trap. With some channeling and filling, they reshaped the hillsides to trap rainwater into a small reservoir.

They waited for a water supply before they cleared off a few acres of the scrub forest and planted a garden. The pigs ran wild on the island, only coming home for handouts.

Phil's wife was worried. "Honey, aren't we changing the ecology here forever? We're going to wipe out all of the native birds and we are going to change the island forever."

Phil looked just slightly annoyed, "Yep, but you and I and our friends are much more important than the birds and I have no intention of starving to save them. When we leave this island, there may be one more place in the world that humans can come and live and find food and water. I say, good. Let the birds build their own damned place."

Some people still listened to the radio. The only traffic that they could pick up reliably was to and from Pitcairn. There were about four hundred people there. They had re-started the island's generator and re-occupied the shacks the original inhabitants used. However, the island had never held more than three hundred people. It was crowded and getting hungry.

Pitcairn caused the only unpleasant episode in their stay. About four months after their arrival, the Pitcairn people trusted one too many airplanes. Perhaps they thought that anyone well enough to fly was well enough to land on the island. Unfortunately, the last pilot to arrive on the island died a few days later. The plague had arrived on the island.

Realizing that the people on Pitcairn were well aware of Henderson Island, Captain Fontaine got on the radio. "Calling Pitcairn, Calling Pitcairn. This is the *Star Of India*. We have been moored off of Henderson Island. Henderson is now infected. Everyone on shore is dying. We are headed for Oeno. There is water there and no plague. We will meet you there."

Oeno was a small island close to Pitcairn that the original Pitcairn residents had used for vacations. They had dug a well and put up some huts and rain fed showers. As it was a coral reef island, it had the sandy beaches totally missing on Pitcairn.

Word of Pitcairn's plight got around the ship fast. Several of the crew were gathered on the deck talking among themselves. As Fontaine walked up, someone asked, "What do we do now? They'll kill us all."

Fontaine answered, "I hope that message we sent will fool them into going the other way. If not, we run away or run them off – without getting too close to them. If they do decide to come here, they're only four or five hours away. We can't get under weigh that fast. Has anyone seen Bill?"

Bill was standing at the rail looking out to sea with the expression of a man thinking hard.

"Bill?"

"Yes, Captain."

"Is there anything in those crates you brought that will do us any good here?"

"That's was I've thinking about. The rifles aren't much good because we don't want them to get close enough to be in rifle range. Unfortunately, I was a gun hobbyist and not a survival nut, so I didn't have any rockets or mortars. I did, however, manage to get hold of three world war two 50 caliber machine guns and a 50 caliber bipod rifle. I'm just trying to figure out how to guard fifty miles of coast line with them."

Fontaine thought for a second and said to the group. "We know they are coming from the southeast, if they come. There are only two or three good landing points on this side of the island. We put the machine guns there. Issue rifles to some of the men and give them posts around the rest of the island."

He turned to Bill, "Can we mount one of the 50s on a speedboat?"

Bill thought for a quick second. "The single shot tripod rifle would be easiest. It makes a hell of a noise and a big splash. It has a scope and an effective range of about a mile. They should be able to scare the Hell out of someone without getting too close. Of course, they won't be able to actually hit much. If you want a chance to really stop them, use one of the machine guns."

"Ok, you pick a boat and get some people to help you and a bullhorn. Mount the machine gun. I hope that we don't need to use it, but you have to convince them that you can hit them if you have to. We'll want you outside the reef on patrol in two hours. Use the speedboat with the radio. We'll need to talk."

Phil's wife, Marie, was visibly distraught. "We're talking about shooting innocent people just trying to get away from the plague like us!"

Phil looked and her and said loud enough for everyone to hear. "No we're not! We're stopping people who are carrying the plague from killing us. It's self defense, and we won't kill anyone if they just go away! Their choice! In fact, we don't want to kill them. Dead bodies are dangerous sources of contamination. We want to scare them off."

Marie was still upset. "What if they don't have the disease. That's murder."

Phil was close to the edge of his patience. "They just spent five days living in a small space with a carrier. If they don't have it, it would be a miracle. There are now five billion people dead, and I don't want us to join them!"

Phil turned to the people listing and said, "If anyone else feels like Marie, feel free to drop out, go hide, or join the people on Pitcairn while the rest of us try to keep breathing. Anybody?"

A few of the crew's more liberal members muttered something under their breath, but they were all intelligent people. Everyone wanted the intruders stopped if they came, even if they did not relish joining in the stopping.

Two boats did show up the next day. Two sailboats about thirty foot long appeared at the horizon. They were both contacted by radio and warned off. One didn't heed the warning. Bill took the speedboat to about a half mile from the intruder and put a short burst of three shots into the water near it. That gun did make a big noise.

The intruder got on the radio, "Back off Henderson. You know we can't go to Oeno. You're sentencing my and my family to death."

Fontaine was tempted to say, "You are, sadly, already dead." But instead he replied, "You got a good ship and the whole wide world to wander in. I suggest that you continue on to Ducie Island. It's uninhabited and you are already going in the right direction."

Bill, who had been listening to the conversation on the radio, punctuated the last sentence with a another short burst over the bow.

"That's the last warning. Patrol boat, fire for effect if they do not turn away now."

The intruder changed his tack and began to sail southerly to pass Henderson. Bill tracked the boat for two hours until his path was clear. Then he got on the radio so that the intruder could hear him, "Southern station. Continue to watch the intruder. If he changes course, contact me. If he approaches the island, you are to fire for effect."

The intruder didn't know that the "southern station" was two guys on a hilltop with one rifle. But it sounded impressive enough to make them keep going.

Within a few weeks, everyone on Oeno was dead and Marie shut up. No one ever found out what happened to the boat going to Ducie. Maybe they got lucky. Not much chance, but maybe. They left the 50 on the speedboat and kept it ready for months, but no other boats approached – ever.

After the garden was in and the excitement over, the problem became one of passing time. There is only so much cuddling on a sandy beach that you can do and conversation wears out after a few months in close contact with the same people. Most of the crew continued to live on the Star. She was running in a low power mode as they never could be certain how long their supplies would have to last. Jess, an engineer, had mounted all of the twelve volt solar panels on the deck and wired them to charge the batteries. They had lights for the cabins and power for the radio and radar. Other than that, they powered down. Cooking, for instance, was with wood chips or solar cooker. The water tank was hand pressurized once a day.

There was plenty of room. She had carried up to three hundred passengers and crew when she was an immigrant ship. They built huts on the island for convenience or simply to get away, but the Star had running water and showers. Most preferred to stay on board.

To pass the time, they decided to finish the tasks that they had begun in San Diego. They had been in the end stages of refurbishing the ship again. This time with new materials that should last longer than anything available before. The idea had been to give themselves more time to enjoy the ship and less time in maintenance.

They had most of the material on board before they even thought of leaving. New clear deck coating that should last for years, stainless steel fittings with brass plating, new acrylic paints with a lifetime measured in decades, water proof, mold proof, age proof carpeting for the human areas. It had been expensive, but the Star did well as a tourist attraction and the labor, lots of it, was free.

It also passed the time once the gardens were put in.

They stayed over three years before their patience wore out. There had been no radio broadcasts of any kind for two years. The world seemed to have gone quiet.

Chapter 53   The Trip Home

They left most of the pigs and chickens, harvested the last of their gardens, and left for home. The trip from Pitcairn to California is 4450 miles in a straight line, but the winds and currents dictated a route that looked like a big arc to the south. Going to Pitcairn, they were able to use the trade winds that blow thirty degrees north of the equator. To catch the westerly trades back, they would have to dip below the equator and end up near Peru or Chili before heading north.

When they began their northward cruise about two hundred miles off the coast of South America, they began to pick up some amateur radio traffic. Most of the shouts were on the order of, "Is anyone out there? Everyone here is dead except me!"

They tried to contact most of the incoming, but didn't get much information until they got near the Canal Zone in Panama. There they picked up an English speaking operator who had been listening carefully for months.

"Hello, *Star of India*. You made a good decision to run for it. This was a bad one and it isn't over yet. I read somewhere that the black plague killed over twenty five percent of the population. That was like a mild cold compared to this."

"Canal Zone, this is *Star of India*. Do you know the latest casualty figures."

"Yes, sort of. Look in your atlas. Take the population of any country in there and multiply by .999. That's the approximate casualty count. This thing killed nine hundred and ninety nine out of a thousand people everywhere. We're back to the stone ages here. Last contact I had with home said that there were maybe two hundred thousand people left in the states. They've been burning the cities just to get rid of the corpse smell. It might not be safe to go back anyway. People have gone nuts everywhere. When half the population died, the media started running crazy stories about how this was caused by the governments and medical research gone wild. Pretty soon, the survivors started trashing libraries, doctor's offices, even some hospitals. The medical staff couldn't do anything to help and everyone was convinced that doctors and all the new research had to have caused this."

The man in Panama paused for a bit before continuing. "A few weeks later, the media was gone and seventy five percent of the population was dead. That's when the back to nature nuts started wandering the streets preaching about God's wrath. The survivors in most places began to get very religious. They started burning cities and moving out to the country. The crazy ones thought is was God's punishment for civilization and the smart ones just figured that the farther away you are, the safer you are in a plague. We got off pretty lucky in the Canal Zone. There are about three hundred survivors here. Most of our families were back in the States. We still went through a rough time, but at least we didn't have to watch them die. We've got a small village going and there are no crazies around. We did get a couple of nuts at the fence screaming about our electric lights the other day. They claimed that God would punish us, too, for our arrogance. For a while, it looked like they were going to try to carry out 'Gods will' themselves, but we finally got them to leave. One of the survivors here was a psychologist. He says that when people go though this kind of horrible stress that they can go nuts forever. I guess it varies, though, the people in this village seem okay so far."

"Canal Zone. This is Doctor Donald Henry. Do you have a doctor in the village."

"No we don't. Are you volunteering your services?"

"No, canal zone. I am too far away and have a practice going here. I was looking for information on the plague."

"*Star of India.* I have had contact with a doctor in Baja California. If you are going North, you may be able to raise him. He may not answer, though. Doctors have been killed because they couldn't help when people expected it. Some of the nuts are blaming all the doctors for the plague. I can tell you whatever I have heard by radio. Will that help?"

"Thank you, Canal Zone. Has the plague changed since we left?"

"Not much. It seems to take a little longer to die now. About fifty percent of newborn babies get the plague, but it takes a few months now to run to the end. Most parents don't let it go that long, if you know what I mean. It's a bad death."

"Then the plague is still active? There are new cases?"

"I don't know of any new cases among adults or children for over a year. Maybe everyone who was going to get it did. But newborns still get it, so it must have found some way to survive. One of the last things I heard before the commercial broadcasts went off the air was a doctor saying that they had found more than one variation. The damned thing seems to be like AIDS, it can mutate and still kill."

"Canal Zone. Did you people who survived the plague get it and recover or just not get it?"

"Most of us got a mild flu and recovered in a few days. Some never got caught anything. If you are asking if we can be carriers, we don't know. The newborn death rate might say we are. If I were you, I would keep hiding out as long as possible. I hear that the Channel Islands and Catalina Island are empty and the Falklands are still under a successful quarantine. If I were you, I would head back where I came from or go to one of the empty places."

Both sides were so happy to hear from outsiders, that the conversation went on for well over three hours. People drifted in and out of the wheel house to listen or ask questions. Finally, the people in the Canal Zone apologetically said they had to get off the air for dinner.

This time the meeting was held on deck. The grand dining room could only hold about twenty five people even with standing room only. This meeting concerned everyone.

Phil, Captain Fontaine, and Doc Henderson were seated at a table on the bow end of the main deck. The others, all of them, had gathered on deck. Some brought chairs or cushions, some sat on the deck or rail.

Captain Fontaine opened the meeting. "As you know, we have been in contact with survivors in the Canal Zone of Central America. We have learned much about what has happened and about the plague. First, as to what has happened. Most of you already know. To put it simply and brutally, what we most feared has happened. The world is not decimated, it is destroyed. The death rate was the biggest in history, far greater that what happened to the Pre-Columbian natives of

North America. It is not just that our loved ones have died. Only one person in a thousand has survived. We are a lucky few to have lived. Keep that in mind as we decide what to do. No matter how bad the situation is, we few are very, very lucky to still be breathing."

"Our options to keep breathing are limited. Doc Henderson will explain what choices we have to make."

Fontaine sat down and Doc stood up so everyone could see him. "The news on the current situation with the plague is not good. It seems that most of the survivors did catch the disease. However, there are two ways to be immune. Either your body fights off the virus, or your body is immune to whatever the virus does. In the second case, you have the disease, but it doesn't bother you. It looks like the second case was the most common. That means that at least some or even most of the survivors are also carriers. The world is full of Typhoid Marys. That means that we don't dare land where there are any people who have had the plague and lived through it, because they can probably still kill us. Now, there have to be other safe places to go. We survived at Henderson and the people at Pitcairn would have survived if they had been a little more careful. There have to be naval bases, remote Siberian villages, other islands that have either not been infected or where everyone is dead."

Someone asked in a loud but calm voice, "How can we be safe if the place is full of dead bodies with the virus in them."

Doc answered, "This thing is a plague, not a devil. It only seems supernatural. It's not a movie monster that never dies. It's just tough and deadly.   It's very unlikely that it can survive long without a living host. Viruses are just small DNA strands and they don't do well out in the environment. It is probable that if we found a place where everyone, and I emphasize 'everyone' was dead or gone, we could probably stay there. The Canal Zone people tell us that the Falkland Islands are not infected. At least East Falkland and Pebble Islands are clear. Apparently several ships of the Royal Navy went to the islands early and established a blockade.

The islanders also shut down the main airport within hours of hearing about the outbreak and stationed police at all of the small airports to keep anyone from taking off or landing. There are probably other clear places."

A woman on the rail spoke up, "Why don't we go there? It sounds like a good place."

Doc snorted. "Do you remember how we treated the people who wanted to come to Henderson? The navy blockade is still there. We'll radio the Falklands, but I doubt that they will let us in."

After an hour of discussion, the group agreed that they would look for a clean place to take them in. However, they would also continue up the coast to the California Channel Islands as a probable destination.

The Channel Islands were small, but all had some modern facilities and with their small initial populations, might be unaffected or uninhabited now.

It turned out that the Falklands would consider taking them in. The story about being isolated on Henderson was just enough to get them looked at. The navy had established a quarantine station on Pebble island. A brave, very brave, volunteer would examine them and their log books to determine if they should be admitted.

He would stay on board until a final determination was made.

In actuality, if the volunteer was alive in a month, he would recommend their admission.

The crew of the *Star of India* spent the rest of their days in the Falklands staving off the collapse of technology that isolation guaranteed.

Eventually, it became obvious that the *Star* would never sail again and a few very old men decided to save their life's work for another time. They stripped her of her solar panels, radar, radio and other items needed more at East Falkland than in the future and sailed and towed the *Star* to a dry-dock in Curacao. With the rising of the earth's water level, the dry-dock now sat on its own island, its doors, once fifty feet above sea level, were now less than half as high out of the water. There the Star was left for another day.

Worldwide, the plague continued to find victims on every continent. However, people soon learned that quarantine and privacy were the only safeguards. The survivors did not mix. No one traveled. With populations too small and too traumatized to keep civilization going, the lights began to fade.

However, mankind is a resilient animal. The average human has more curiosity than a monkey and the staying power of a mammalian cockroach. The geneticists tell us that onetime, about seventy five thousand years ago, the human race got down to as few as one thousand breeding age adults.

They survived and became the world of billions that eventually wiped itself out with airplanes, and trains, and cars. In doing so, they proved the most important thing about mankind.

No Step Is the Last While Breath Remains.